WHERE THERE IS DESPAIR, HOPE

A JOURNEY OF LOVE AND HEALING

BY KEVIN B. HULL

ISBN 13: 978-1-935986-96-6

First print edition, November 2015

Published by Liberty Mountain Publishing.

Printed in the U.S.A.

Liberty Mountain Publishing

Lynchburg, VA

www.LibertyMountainPublishing.com

**A DIVISION OF
LIBERTY UNIVERSITY**

To Taylor and Katelyn: When in doubt – Play.

"You can discover more about a person in an hour of play than in a year of conversation." -Plato

ACKNOWLEDGEMENTS

I am deeply indebted to my wife, Wendy, for her patience, encouragement, and insight that proved to be invaluable during the writing of this book; and to Tina R. Hull for her editing expertise and suggestions. To Brittany Meng, for her creative vision, editing proficiency, and encouragement. Finally, to Sarah Funderburke and Arielle Bielicki and all the staff at LU Press for bringing this work from an idea into reality, I offer my sincere thanks.

EPILOGUE

All the characters in this story are fictional; but all are based on real people and events. The stories of play therapy in this story are true but some of the facts of the cases have been changed due to protecting the privacy of those who were involved in the cases. The power of play therapy shared in this story is absolutely true and the main focus of writing this story is to help people understand the power of play therapy and to give understanding to both sides: The view from a therapist's perspective who is a witness to healing through play, and the view from the young person's perspective who leads the play. The character of Dr. Capstone is taken from various professors and mentors that I have been blessed to learn from over the years. Being a therapist who uses play has given me amazing experiences. I count myself fortunate to have learned so much from the young people with whom I work and to them I owe a great spiritual and emotional debt in allowing me to be present during such a sacred process. I will never stop working to bring light and hope to those lost in the dark corners of this world. *Where there is despair...Hope.*

Kevin B. Hull
February 16, 2013
Chapel Hill, North Carolina

THE PRAYER *of*
ST. FRANCIS OF ASSISI

Lord, make me an instrument of your peace.
Where there is hatred, let me sow love;
where there is injury, pardon;
where there is doubt, faith;
where there is despair, hope;
where there is darkness, light;
and where there is sadness, joy.

O Divine Master, grant that I may not so much seek
to be consoled as to console;
to be understood as to understand;
to be loved as to love.
For it is in giving that we receive;
it is in pardoning that we are pardoned;
and it is in dying that we are born to eternal life. Amen

1

FEAR

Pierce Emerson was swinging. He loved to swing and everything about it. He loved to see his feet flung out in front of him, the trees and clouds getting closer as he soared to meet them. He loved the feeling of being able to fly. He especially loved how swinging made you forget stuff. Like forgetting that his mom was in a dirty trailer next to the park with a bunch of scary men and that she didn't come out for a long time. Like forgetting that when she did come out of the trailer she acted strange. One time she didn't know who Pierce was and that scared him. Swinging helped Pierce forget that his mom was sick most of the time and that the sores on her face were getting bigger, and that she didn't talk to him very much anymore. She just sat and stared.

"Mom, hey mom, what are we going to eat?"

Nothing.

"Mom, am I going to school today?"

Nothing.

Today, she told him to stay in the park *no matter what* and not to talk to anyone.

"I'll just be a little while, baby," she said. For the first few hours it wasn't too bad. Other kids played at the park and Pierce joined them, which kept him from thinking about Mom. The kids came and went but Pierce was still there.

Waiting.

Hungry.

Scared.

He kept his eye on the trailer, and when he heard a door slam he hoped it would be Mom coming out. But it wasn't. Just a long-haired man who got into an old car and roared away, dust flying. Pierce got on the swing, gripping the chain as tight as he could. He pushed off and pumped, gradually getting higher and higher. He felt like he could fly. He was flying. Up and away, no more tight tummy and throat. Just the sound of the wind whistling in his ears and the sight of the ground, sky, and trees, coming closer and then moving away.

Mom brought him to the park for the first time a few months ago. Pierce hoped they were going to play together. But Mom said she was going to visit some friends and then went to the dirty trailer.

"What do you do in there?" Pierce asked.

"Now, don't you worry. Just play here at the park and *don't talk to anyone*," Mom responded.

"Can I come?"

"No! You just play and don't worry about me," said Mom. "Don't talk to anyone!"

Pierce nodded, and walked to the swings. He needed a push. An older girl came over to the swings and hopped on the swing next to him.

"Why ain't you swingin'?" she asked.

"Cuz I need a push." Oops, he had violated the rule. He talked to someone. But this girl was a kid and he supposed that talking to kids was okay.

"Are you a baby or something?" said the girl, making a snarly face that made Pierce want to knock her off the swing.

"NO! I ain't no baby! I'm six years old!" he retorted, jumping off the swing and stomped away.

"Hey, Look!" the girl called out.

He turned to watch her, shading his eyes with his hand. "You give yourself a little push, just to get movin' and then you move your legs like this," she said, magically beginning to move as if an invisible grown-up was pushing her. It's called pumpin'!" The girl continued to demonstrate how her legs moved back and forth, stretching out and then tucking underneath the seat of the swing. "You pull at the same time and then you just keep doin' it, and then you go higher and higher. My brother showed me, you wanna try?" Pierce walked hesitantly back to the swing and hopped on. He tried to remember what she said. *Give a little push to get going, then move your legs. It's called pumpin'.* Soon, Pierce was swinging like a pro and felt as though he had discovered one of the hidden secrets of the universe.

His mom's visits to the dirty trailer became more frequent and she seemed to stay longer each time. Today, Pierce noticed that the afternoon shadows were all the way to the tops of the trees. His stomach growled. It even hurt a little. All the children who came to the park that day were long gone. Walking by one of the trash cans he noticed a half-eaten bag of chips. He looked around, and reached for the bag. He devoured the chips and walked to the water fountain and took three big gulps. He stared at the trailer. He looked at the sky and noticed the sun was beginning to set. His heart started beating faster and the nice cold water evaporated in his dry mouth. Something was wrong. *Momma, where are you?* He looked around and a whimper sound came out of his mouth, but there was no one to call to for help. He thought of screaming, but then thought of his mother's angry face, and decided not to. He walked out of the park and towards the trailer. There was a high fence around the trailer, with straggly weeds growing up from the base of the fence. A dragonfly buzzed Pierce's head and he jumped. He became very still and listened. He could hear music and muffled voices coming from inside. Suddenly, the voices got very loud and Pierce ducked down behind some of the weeds. He heard yelling. His heart pounded very hard inside his chest. *Momma, are you okay?*

Pierce jumped when the door of the trailer flew open and a man with a red cap and wild eyes bolted out of the door, stumbled, and fell on the ground and rolled towards Pierce. Before Pierce could say anything the man got up and ran towards a car, cursing as he started the car and slammed it into reverse amid a cloud of dust. Pierce looked back to the trailer and saw smoke coming out of the door and some of the windows. People began to pour out of the door of the trailer, stumbling and yelling. Suddenly he saw his mother appear at the door, and for a brief moment their eyes met.

"Momma!" he screamed and grabbed the fence.

"Pierce, run!" his mother screamed while gripping the side of the trailer. "I'll come and get you! Run to the park!"

Pierce began to cry but jumped up and ran to the park. He heard screams and shouts behind him. He looked back to see his mother had fallen and was trying to get up but got knocked down by someone running past her. Pierce turned to run back to her when all of a sudden the trailer exploded, sending a ball of flames high into the air. The roof split open like a tin can. The force of the blast knocked Pierce onto his back. Flames shot out from underneath the trailer like tongues, licking up everything close to it. He felt the heat from the explosion and watched as his mother and everyone near her were consumed, their bodies burning and arms flailing like possessed scarecrows. Pierce would always remember the scene every Halloween when he saw a scarecrow. He screamed as loud as he could but no sound seemed to come out. Debris began to fall around him, and he was almost hit by the kitchen sink. Pierce ran to a large concrete pipe that sat on a rise of ground, the "tunnel" that the kids played in and ducked inside. He watched and hoped that Mom would get up. But she didn't. He could see her charred body lying awkwardly twisted with her arms reaching to the sky. Two more explosions ripped the trailer apart, leaving nothing but a black, smoldering piece of twisted metal and when the smoke cleared the bodies were gone. A putrid stench filled the air and Pierce's head felt strange. He vomited. Off in the distance he heard sirens. His vision blurred and the last thing Pierce felt before falling asleep was the gritty, unfinished cement on his cheek.

· ·

Cade Dalton sat in the back of the classroom watching graduate students arrive for their first play therapy class. He thought back to his first day with Dr. Capstone and smiled. It was thirteen years ago when he met the man who would become his mentor, and the man Cade would replace as lead play therapist at Boyd Home. Boyd Home, or Boyd as it was often called, was a hundred year old residential foster home for orphaned and abandoned children. Set on hundreds of acres and funded through a generous endowment, Boyd had grown from a single building in the form of a run-down mansion and a barn to a multi-dimensional facility complete with several cottages, gymnasium, administrative offices, and a school. Dr. Cap, as he was affectionately known by students, was the lead play therapist for over forty years. A champion of play therapy, Dr. Cap was responsible for instituting a play therapy curriculum at the University and had made Boyd a nationally recognized center for play therapy training. Cade often felt overwhelmed with such large shoes to fill and often sought Dr. Cap's guidance. Thankfully, Dr. Cap had agreed to remain at Boyd in a limited capacity, especially during the transition when Cade took over as director. Cade felt good to be back in a classroom and heard the room hush as Dr. Cap entered.

"Greetings, students," he said as he put his leather bag on the desk. "Welcome to your introductory class in play therapy, I am Dr.

Capstone. It is a great honor for me to be teaching all that I know and continue to learn about play therapy." He smiled and looked at each student, then adjusted his glasses and walked around to the front of the desk. Leaning back on the desk, he took a worn piece of paper from one of the books on the desk and gently unfolded it. Cade sat up and leaned forward; he felt the hair rise on the back of his neck. Dr. Cap began to read softly and reverently; his voice mesmerizing:

Lord, make me an instrument of your peace.
Where there is hatred, let me sow love;
where there is injury, pardon;
where there is doubt, faith;
where there is despair, hope;
where there is darkness, light;
and where there is sadness, joy.

O Divine Master, grant that I may not so much seek
to be consoled as to console;
to be understood as to understand;
to be loved as to love.
For it is in giving that we receive;
it is in pardoning that we are pardoned;
and it is in dying that we are born to eternal life. Amen

When he finished, Dr. Cap paused, and then read the prayer again. Following the second reading, he kept his eyes on the paper, studying it as if he was going to read it again. Instead, he took a chair next to the desk and moved it closer to the students. He then sat, staring at the class. The students stared back. No one spoke for almost a minute.

"I have read this today because it is something that is very meaningful to my heart," Dr. Capstone began. "This class is part one of the last series of therapy classes you will have in this program. Many of you have already begun your dissertation work and have moved into the world of actually *doing* therapy beyond your practicum and internships. You have studied hard, absorbed much, and I know you have already impacted those with whom you are working. However, those who have spent time with me - and most of you have -" he smiled at each student, "know that one of the key elements that I emphasize is the *relationship* with those you work with. Empirical studies of the effectiveness of psychotherapy emphasize repeatedly the importance of the client feeling a connection with the therapist - that it is in the relationship between client and therapist that brings the impetus of change."

He paused, and those close to the front of the room could see tears gathering around the corners of his eyes. Cade thought back to the very first class he had with Dr. Cap and remembered that much of it had been spent discussing what therapy *really* entailed; he recalled how passionate Dr. Cap was in emphasizing the relationship between therapist and client.

"You see," he said softly, "there was a time when I thought that theory and technique was the essence of the work...that if a child, adolescent, adult, couple, or family really wanted to change that I would simply lay the tools at their feet and they could either change, or stay where they were." He paused and took a sip of water. "But then I met someone..."

Cade looked around the room. All the attention was riveted on Dr. Capstone.

"This prayer," began Dr. Cap, "was given to me by a nun who worked at the orphanage where I completed my internship at the end of my graduate training. It marked a turning point in my life that shaped my focus in how I did therapy and led to my belief that relationship is the most important part of the therapeutic process. When I got to the orphanage I was a bit brash, and very full of myself. Like many graduate students my idea of the internship was to get it out of the way and collect as much data as I could for my dissertation and move on."

Cade was all too familiar with what Dr. Cap was talking about. Graduate students, eager to complete their degree requirements, take what is offered to them in the form of internship opportunities: old community mental health centers, underfunded inpatient psychiatric hospitals, ill-run institutions designed to help children in the foster care system, and so on. The goal is simple: Come up with a fairly benign dissertation topic, use the people or children available as subjects at the site who are desperate for any form of therapeutic care, and get out as quickly as you can in order to graduate with your degree. With the graduate student soon-to-be-psychologist's departure, there will be another short-lived, "Mary Poppins" character readily available to replace him or her and repeat the cycle again.

Dr. Cap continued. "The orphanage was old, underfunded, and smelled like Swiss cheese - Swiss cheese that was starting to turn!" He laughed and shook his head. "At first, I thought about just getting back in my car and telling my clinical supervisor this whole thing was a big mistake." The students laughed. "The truth was, the place intimidated me. Because I wasn't really into making a difference, it was hard to get going. I spent the first few weeks barely interacting with anyone – I pretended to set up a therapy room and tried to look busy, but in truth, I was simply avoiding the actual work I was there to do and building a psychological and emotional wall to keep myself safe." He took a sip of water and went on. "The nuns at the orphanage were nice, actually too nice if you want to know the truth." Dr. Cap chuckled, "Their round, angelic faces and optimistic spirits started to annoy me. You could tell they *really* loved the children; they *really* wanted to play with them and teach them. It made me feel guilty, honestly I felt like an imposter. I was scared, I didn't know what I was doing, and the nuns were really expecting me to make a difference. One nun in particular,

Sister Angelique, was always coming by see if I needed anything and bothering me."

Cade nodded, remembering his own insecurities when he arrived at the Boyd Home for his internship. He found it ironic that after so much training he could feel so helpless, and Cade was very grateful that Dr. Capstone's early experiences led to him create a solid training experience so that novice therapists, like Cade, would feel supported and could grow and learn while the recipients of the therapy received quality care.

"Sister Angelique was what I later came to think of as a Jedi warrior" chuckled Dr. Cap. "Wise, calm under pressure, and extremely insightful, she had a knack for wizardry. She shared with me early on that she had been studying the theories of attachment and therapeutic approaches involving play with children who had been abandoned. Since there had never been a dependable delivery of psychological services, she had taken it upon herself, through self-study on her own time and efforts, to help the children who suffered emotional and psychological neglect. It was incredible!" Dr. Cap paused and held out his hands, "This round little woman knew just as much as I did, if not more, and knew how to apply the knowledge to actually help these kids. Needless to say, I was intimidated and humiliated all at the same time." He took off his glasses and cleaned them with a handkerchief.

"Here I was," he said softly, "acting a part but not being authentic. And here she was, as genuine as could be, hoping to engage me in dialogue and eager to hear the insights that I could offer her, while observing me in my work so that she could learn and grow. Little did she know that I had little more to offer her than a few labels, a whiff of a theoretical construct, and very little in the area of an *actual* therapeutic skill set. I felt like a fraud and very uncomfortable in her presence. I began to avoid her like someone with a very contagious disease, but she sensed something in me and would not leave me alone, popping up here and there and scaring me half to death." The students laughed and Cade smiled.

....

Ronald Capstone walked to the corner of the field and picked up the ball that had been thrown past him for the fiftieth time. It was hot and he was getting annoyed.

"Get the ball, slowpoke!" yelled the boy behind him. "C'mon, we ain't got all day!" he said, laughing.

Ron took a deep breath and turned around. He flashed a fake smile and flung the ball towards the boy. The ball made a "pop" as it hit the glove and the boy stared at the ball for moment.

"Are you mad?" the boy asked.

"Nope, I'm fine, just enjoyin' throwin' the ball with you," Ron lied. He was frustrated. He should be inside gathering data for his dissertation, not chasing baseballs thrown by a kid that couldn't hit the broad side of a barn. But kids like Curtis didn't want to be inside. Curtis wanted to be outside - running, throwing, and kicking. It was their fourth session together. The worst part of it was that Curtis really liked him, and despite Ron's feelings of annoyance, he actually liked Curtis too. The nuns shared with Ron that Curtis's behavior improved greatly since they began meeting. While Ron was glad to hear the news, he was baffled. In the last three sessions with Curtis all he had done was thrown and kicked balls with Curtis. It was the only thing that got Curtis talking. Could it be that simple?

Curtis threw the ball back to Ron and he noticed Sister Angelique sitting on a bench near the field. She nodded and waved to him. They were supposed to talk after his session with Curtis. Ron noticed a feeling of initial unease, although he felt like their last conversation was very helpful. He told Curtis it was time for them to stop and walked Curtis back to his cottage. Ron then joined Sister Angelique on the bench.

"Good day Ron," she said smiling. "So good to see you and Curtis interacting so well together. I hear he is really coming along."

"Yes, Sister, he is really doing well, thank you," Ron said.

"Tell me," she said, "how are things with the other children?"

"Well, I took your advice, and I'm spending more time in activities with them instead of just talking with them," Ron responded. "But like I told you in our last conversation I wasn't trained very much in working with kids. No one was. It's sort of a new thing, I guess."

"No need to defend yourself, Ron," Sister Angelique said, patting him on the knee. "Remember, we are all here to learn something and after all, isn't that what life is about?"

At the time, Ron wanted to tell her no, that isn't what life is all about. He had been in school for the last seven years and needed to get his dissertation completed so he could move on to bigger and better things. He didn't say this, of course. After all, this place was kind of growing on him. Sister Angelique had turned out to be wise and she had finally confronted Ron about him not really wanting to be there. He couldn't lie to her.

"You're right, Sister," he said, after she had confronted him. "Honestly I wasn't happy about coming here and now that I'm here I find myself really wanting to help these kids, but gosh, I don't know where to start."

"Look, we are just happy to have someone to work with the kids at all. But there is something about you, you know. Something that draws the kids to you. Something in your presence that creates a feeling of safety. I feel it, and I'm not just saying this to make you feel good. Lord knows I wouldn't do that!"

Ron laughed. "That's for sure."

"Here." She handed him a book. "I've been reading this and studying for some time."

"*Play Therapy* by Virginia Axline." He turned it over. "I've never heard of it."

"It's fairly new. I ordered it from the University. One day, when the intern counselor didn't show up, I sat with a young girl and we played with a doll house that had just been donated. I was very tired and so I just sat on the floor with her and I was shocked to see how she played out various scenes from things that happened to her. I didn't know what to say or do so I just sat there. I saw such a change in her that I had her come to my office every day that week."

"Had you ever seen play therapy done before?" Ron asked.

"No. But listen, this particular girl had severe behavior problems, as well as nightmares. Would you believe that all that ended a few days after she played?"

"I have heard of that happening," said Ron. "Once a guest lecturer came and addressed my advanced therapy class. Our professor sort of made fun of the guy after he left, reminding us that the approach lacked scientific integrity." Ron laughed. "I remember thinking that it sounded really interesting and would probably work since kids naturally play."

"Well, after I saw how the girl changed so much, I went to the University and spoke to a child psychologist and he recommended the book by Virginia Axline. I read it two times over as soon as I got it. I was relieved because before that I felt helpless to really connect with the children and help them."

Ron was silent, feeling slightly stunned by her story. He thanked Sister Angelique for the book. He opened the front cover and saw a folded piece of notebook paper. "What is this?" he asked, picking it up.

"Oh that," replied Sister Angelique. "This is something that was given to me many years ago and has always brought me a sense of peace and purpose when I didn't know what direction to go in." She took the paper from Ron and held it up. "It's the prayer of St. Francis." She read it to him and Ron listened, riveted. He took it from her and read it again. Something stirred within him, deeply touched. He felt his soul light up. He had found a purpose.

• •

Pierce was awakened by a man's voice and felt someone tugging on his legs. He lifted his head and noticed it was dark outside, the darkness punctuated by flashing lights of red, yellow, and blue which gave off a psychotic energy. He jerked away from the man to run, but someone grabbed his ankles. He thought of his mother and wanted to cry out for her, but then the memory of her burned body slammed into his conscious mind. "*Don't talk to anyone!*" The man was trying to talk to him.

"What's your name son?" the man said repeatedly.

"*Don't talk to anyone!*"

"C'mon son, help us out. What's your name? How did you get here? Who brought you?"

Pierce did not respond. The picture of his mother's charred body created a black hole that sucked his ability to speak completely out of his body. He stared blankly at the men. They shook their heads.

"Can you move out of this pipe or do you want me to drag you?" said the man holding Pierce's ankles.

Pierce pushed backwards with his arms and wiggled his legs and the man let go as Pierce inched towards him. Pierce slid out of the pipe and looked around. He could still smell the bad smell in the air.

"Well at least we know he ain't retarded," the man said. "C'mon son, let's go over here. There's more people that want to talk to you."

Pierce slowly walked with the man. His feet felt very heavy. His whole body felt like it was made of rusty bolts and joints. He wanted to cry, but Pierce shoved the tears back down. His head began to feel funny again and he stumbled. The last thing he felt before passing out was the man next to him grabbing his arm. It hurt.

Darkness.

• •

Cade walked with Dr. Cap to his office following the lecture. There was not a dry eye in the class after the reading of the prayer and the story of how it found its way to Dr. Cap. Each time Cade heard the story it touched him deeply. The original copy of the prayer from Sister Angelique was under the glass on Dr. Cap's desk, and the worn copy of *Play Therapy* sat on the bookshelf nearby. Nearly forty-five years had passed since that day. Dr. Capstone stayed on at the orphanage another four years after graduating but it was closed due to a lack of funding. For the next forty years he would labor at the Boyd Home, building it into a nationally recognized center for play therapy. Due to Dr. Cap's efforts, play therapy became a state-wide practice for all children in foster care. For the last twenty years Dr. Cap taught at the University, and created a clinically supervised practicum and internship program in which play therapy was taught to new generations of practitioners. Sister Angelique died about fifteen years ago. When the orphanage closed she went back to her native Puerto Rico and ministered in an orphanage there until her death. Dr. Cap stayed in touch with her until the end of her life.

Dr. Cap's office was the last one at the end of a long corridor and offered a commanding view of the courtyard. Dr. Cap motioned for Cade to sit.

"Well, my young successor, whaddya think?" smiled Dr. Cap.

Cade shook his head. "Even though I know how the story goes, I never get tired of hearing it."

He reached for a wooden box sitting on the corner of Dr. Cap's desk. It was a game of Tic-Tac-Toe with marbles inside the wooden box and a grid on top on which the game was played. The hand-carved game was a gift from Sister Angelique and had been the very first toy he used in connecting with the children at the orphanage. He loved to challenge his graduate students to a game of Tic-Tac-Toe, surprising them in the middle of a serious conversation by simply asking "Blue or White?" Taken off guard (Cade had been no different), students would slowly agree to play, soon finding themselves after five or six games enjoying themselves immensely and completely forgetting about the solemn conversation they were engaged in minutes before. Dr. Cap used this as a demonstration of how play could help shift the brain from a defensive mindset to one that was more open and light. "More people need to play Tic-Tac-Toe in this world," he often said.

"Bah!" Dr. Cap said, waving his hand. "They just feel sorry for an old man." He winked at Cade and moved a big stack of papers from his desk to the floor.

"Blue or white?" asked Cade, pouring the marbles from the Tic-Tac-Toe game into his hand.

"I'll take blue," said Dr. Cap. "Now, tell me about your new cases."

"Nothing much to report," Cade said as he blocked Dr. Cap. "But there is one new kid that came a few days ago. I haven't seen him yet but I'm supposed to meet him. Staff says he's quite a handful."

"Cat's Game. Reset. So what's the story on him?" Dr. Cap asked, picking up his marbles.

"Mother died a few years ago in a meth house explosion. Never knew his father. Supposedly the kid saw the whole thing when his mom blew up. The report I got said that he's bounced around in the foster care system and that he didn't speak for a year after the incident."

"Hmmm." Dr. Cap hesitated briefly and then plopped down a marble. "Gotcha both ways, hotshot."

"Dang it!" Cade exclaimed. "You get me talking and then I don't pay attention!"

"Works every time, my man." Dr. Cap leaned back in his chair and looked out the window. "What brought him to Boyd?"

"Well, apparently the system tried to put him with foster families because he was so young at the time, but he kept running away and was a major behavioral problem at school. Likes to set fires. The families were afraid he would burn the house down. The case worker said that Boyd was the last stop and that a judge ordered him to come to us. I think he just turned nine."

"Oh boy," he said, smiling at Cade. "This one's gonna either take you down or be your shining star, but either way I have a feeling this kid's going to change your life."

"Yeah," said Cade, putting the marbles in the box and standing up. "I've got the same feeling."

"But I can't think of a better therapist to work with him," Dr. Cap said as he winked at Cade. "You've done a masterful job in the last four years and all I hear are good things."

"Thank you, sir." Cade felt relief flood him. "You'll probably be seeing a lot of me with this one."

"No problem," said Dr. Cap as Cade headed towards the door. "You know where to find me."

2
QUIET

The playroom where Cade conducted play therapy was the same one that Dr. Cap used for nearly twenty years. The playroom building served many functions over the years at Boyd. It was originally a chapel but was used as a dining hall for many years. A new dining hall was erected as the number of children grew, and the building sat empty until Dr. Cap converted it into his play therapy room. The size of the room offered wonderful opportunities for play. There was a large sandbox in one corner, dollhouses and stuffed animals in another. An arts and crafts table was in the corner opposite the sandbox complete with easels, paints, and clay. The high ceiling was a bonus for launching toy rockets and throwing balls high into the air and in one section model airplanes, paper clouds and paper dragons of many different colors were hung with fishing line. Bookcases filled with all sorts of toys lined the walls. A large colored carpet surrounded by several bean bag chairs filled the middle of the room. It was a paradise of sorts, for young people and play therapists.

The large bay windows allowed natural light to pour in from both sides of the building. As Cade entered the room each morning, streams of sunlight danced across the space, giving it an enchanted glow. Cade felt a sense of reverence each time he entered the room. The room held a sense of sacredness, and it felt as though it was alive. Today, as Cade looked about the room, his thoughts were consumed with meeting the new boy, Pierce. He sat down at his desk that sat in the far corner of the room and pulled out three folders which contained the details of the last three years of the life of Pierce Emerson. Cade started to open the first one, but then he hesitated. Sarah, Pierce's caseworker had told him a lot of information already, and the folders were heavy. While having background information was helpful, sometimes Cade found it got in the way of building a relationship a child. Sarah told Cade that Pierce spoke to no one and was withdrawn. In the two years she had known him, she had only heard about ten words. He exhibited extremely violent behavior at times, and had been hospitalized for hurting others as well as himself. It appeared that his intelligence was quite high, but due to his behavior, no formal testing could be done. At times, caregivers reported that he seemed almost animal-like, eating with his hands and unable to hold a pencil. He was constantly reading and writing stories. It seemed to be his only source of comfort. When Cade asked about what type of books he read, Sarah told him that they tended to be sci-fi and fantasy. "Angels, demons, dragons, medieval soldiers, that type of thing," she replied. "And stuff that kids his age shouldn't even be able to comprehend, but that's what he likes and it keeps him calm." Cade asked about what he wrote. "The same type of stories that he reads – fantasy sci-fi type stuff. Actually, the ones I've read are really good." Cade was relieved to know there was something that interested the boy.

There was a knock at the door. It was Pierce's case worker and behind her, with an angry, disinterested look on his face, stood Pierce.

"Hi Sarah," Cade said, holding the door open. "C'mon in, guys."

"Dr. Cade, this is Pierce, and Pierce, this is Dr. Cade."

"Hi Pierce, I'm Dr. Cade. I'm glad you're here." Cade said, dropping to one knee. "Welcome to the playroom. Please feel free to look around, okay?"

Pierce made no eye contact and did not respond. He walked slowly past Cade and looked around the room.

"Well, I'll leave you two alone to get acquainted," Sarah said, stepping back from the doorway. "Pierce, I'll be back in a little while to take you over to meet your teachers, okay?"

Pierce said nothing. He was staring out of one of the windows. He looked very small in the large room.

· ·

Another strange place, more strange people. Wood floors, pieced together like a puzzle. Strange smells. This room is big. Too many toys, too much stuff. What do you do with TOYS? What are they for? How can I get out of here? Better not run. They try to catch me. They always catch me. Last stop on the train said the judge. He was not nice. None of the court people are nice. Men in suits. They all looked like clowns, pushing around carts of papers and carrying briefcases. Mother's dead everyone kept saying. Mother's dead. Mother was a meth-head. A head of meth. Meth-Head Mom. I watched her die. She will come for me at the park. Body melting, body burning. Scarecrows at Halloween. More burning, always burning. I don't have to talk. *Don't talk to anyone!* I will run. They will see. I'll be gone soon. I see the window. Big tree outside. We had a tree once. Me and mom. Outside the trailer. Sitting under the tree. A picnic mom said, *pick-nick, pick-nick.* Mom talked *a lot* that day. Lots of stories. The sun was so warm, the breeze felt so good. Mom's long hair blowing in the wind.

· ·

Cade watched Pierce as he stared out the window. He walked around the room until he was about five feet from Pierce and sat down in one of the bean bag chairs and looked out the window too. Pierce did not move a muscle. Cade tried to see what Pierce saw. The big oak's leaves moved gently with the breeze. A squirrel jumped to a branch and sat munching an acorn. A blue jay lighted for a moment and then flew away. He looked at Pierce's face and saw the thousand yard stare. It was the look of someone transported by a memory to a faraway place. Cade felt a jolt of sadness at the thought of what this small boy had experienced over the past few years.

"You are looking out the window," Cade said softly. "The window is big. I see a squirrel eating a nut, there's a blue jay...I wonder where he's off to. That tree must be almost a hundred years old."

Pierce's eyes shifted slightly when Cade spoke, but he said nothing.

"Sometimes it's hard to come to a new place," Cade continued. "Remember that this is a safe place and you are free to explore when you are ready. I'm just going to sit right here."

Pierce's body moved slightly when Cade spoke, but he stayed silent.

....

The *man* wants me to talk. I don't want to talk. I will *not* talk! *Don't talk to anyone!* The *man* is sitting. The tree is nice and big. I wonder what it would be like to live in the tree, like the squirrel or the blue jay. I want to be a squirrel or a blue jay. I want to look around the room but that man is going to watch me. I know it. They all do. This is awful. I hate new places. My mom died. I watched her die. I have no one in this world. I am alone.

....

Cade glanced at the clock on the wall. Forty minutes had passed since he first sat in the middle of the room parallel to Pierce. Pierce had moved very little. He stood awkwardly, staring out the window. It seemed as though he might walk around the room at any moment, but an invisible force held him to the spot. Cade could see the battle raging inside the boy. Over the years he met with many children ravaged by the effects of trauma, and he knew that one of the main effects was the child shutting down when he or she encountered new people and places. Pierce appeared as though he was more than shut down – he was paralyzed. Cade waited.

"If a child won't communicate or respond in any way," Dr. Capstone had said in a lecture, "even better. Run with it, go with it, and just let what is going to happen, happen. Play will fill in where the words are absent. Just be, don't force things, and let your presence be one of unconditional acceptance and patience."

Dr. Capstone stressed the importance of never thinking that a young person was unreachable.

"I think it is an absolute tragedy when a therapist breaks off sessions with a child because the child won't verbally communicate. We must build the space, meet them where they are, and help their brains shift over to a place of peace and safety. This may take two months, or it may take a year; be patient and do not rush. The child chooses the speed at which healing will take place."

Cade thought for a moment about Pierce's past. His story was similar to many of the resident's experiences who lived at Boyd Home and with whom Cade worked: no father, drug addicted mother. Pierce had been removed from his mother soon after his second birthday and put in foster care due to a lack of eligible family members with whom he could be placed. He was moved around to three different foster homes because of "oppositional defiant behavior," and by four and a half was reunited with his mother. At age five, a report from Pierce's kindergarten teacher resulted in an investigation and Pierce was removed from his mother's care for six months due to "neglect and unfit living conditions." He was placed in foster care again but reunited with his mother just before his sixth birthday. By this time, his mother was deep into meth addiction. A few months later, Pierce witnessed her death. More foster care. Cade counted at least seven different placements in three years, not to mention all the mandatory counseling, which was not successful. Cade knew why, and it was the very reason he believed that he could help Pierce.

• •

The *man* is sitting. He was talking to me. Now he is quiet. He is a Counselor-Man. I have met many Counselor-People before. Mom said they are *bad* and not to talk to them. *Don't talk to anyone!* They want to *brain-wash* me. This room is quiet. I like quiet. The sun feels good. I like how it looks when it comes through the window. I see a lot of stuff in here. I like the sandbox. I saw it when I came in. It's big. I see a castle too. I like castles. Mom said we could live in a castle someday. When you live in a castle you can shut the big door and no one can hurt you. The castle has a red door. I like the red door. Maybe I'll move a little closer to the castle. I want to touch the sand. It's white and looks soft. But I don't know if I should. I hope the Counselor-Man stays where he is.

....

Cade, lost in his thoughts about Pierce, glanced over to where the boy was standing and was stunned to see that Pierce had moved. Careful to not startle him, Cade slowly turned. Pierce was standing by the sandbox, staring at it. Cade did not say a word, and something told him to stay put. He could again see a war raging inside Pierce: to touch the sand or not touch the sand. He knew that children were naturally drawn to the sandbox - after all, who isn't? Even grown adults cannot resist the urge to dig in the sand and build things at the beach, and this sandbox was indoors. Eight feet by eight feet of pure white sand, and it was big enough to climb into if the child so desired. After a few minutes Pierce bent down, staring at the sand. Cade saw his hand hovering over the sand for a moment and then Pierce pulled it back. Then he reached out again, and once again pulled back. This went on for about five minutes. Finally, Cade decided to speak.

"I see you found the sandbox, Pierce."

Pierce flinched but said nothing. Cade could see his eyes looking in Cade's general direction, but not directly at him.

"Have you ever seen a sandbox inside a room? Most people haven't. It's okay if you want to touch it, or you can just look. The sand is clean. It's been washed and actually comes in bags. Feel free to keep looking around. I'm just going to sit here, don't mind me."

30

Cade waited. He knew that it was important for Pierce to be familiar to the sound of Cade's voice, but at the same time he didn't want to overwhelm him with a lot of talking. He sat back in the beanbag chair and looked out the window.

....

Counselor-Man talked to me. I knew he would. At least he didn't say much. The sand is white and smooth. I think I see a rock in there. The rock looks smooth, like those rocks that come from the river at that one foster place that Mrs. Frances said I was not to touch. But I did. I took one. I wonder where that rock is. I want to touch the rock in the sandbox. But I can't. *I won't!* I could run out of here. Miss Sarah is probably waiting outside. She would catch me or call the police. They always call the Police. Mom said Police are bad. *Don't talk to Police!* I like this room. There is a lot to see. Miss Sarah said I'll be coming here a lot. Counselor-Man is looking out the window. He isn't like the others, bombing me with words. *Words, words, words!* Too many words! He is quiet. I like quiet. I am going to touch the sand. I want to. No, I am *not* going to touch the sand. Counselor-Man said I can touch the sand if I want. He said it's clean. I want to put the castle in the sandbox. Mom said we could live in a castle someday. I am going to live in a castle someday. It will be big, made of gray stone, with a red door just like that one over there.

....

Cade shifted in his bean bag chair so that he could watch Pierce. He noticed that Pierce was interested in the large castle on the shelf by the sandbox. He wasn't surprised. Children, particularly survivors of abuse and neglect, were drawn to the castle. Pierce walked slowly around the corner of the sandbox and approached the castle. Cade took special note of the careful way that Pierce moved. Each step was like that of a ballerina. His movements were cautious yet graceful, purposeful yet guarded. It was evident that Pierce had been damaged and he worked hard to keep himself safe, especially in new environments. While his eyes rarely focused on the face of another human being, they missed nothing when it came to noting the detail of objects. Cade could see his eyes examining the castle. Each tiny rivet and block, every contour and curve, nothing was missed. After an hour and twenty minutes Pierce had yet to touch anything in the room, but Cade felt encouraged that Pierce unlocked himself enough to move around the room.

"Hey Pierce," Cade said softly.

Pierce became rigid again, his eyes moved in Cade's general direction.

"We are going to have to stop in about ten minutes, okay? Miss Shaw will be here soon to walk you back to your dorm and you and I will see each other tomorrow, right here, in the same place. Okay?" Pierce said nothing. Cade noticed that his body did not flinch or stiffen when Cade spoke to him.

Progress.

••

I'm closer to the castle. I notice a box of soldiers and weapons next to the castle. I remember I had a Soldier-Man when I was five. His armor was blue and red. Mom got him at a garage sale. He had a blue sword and a red shield. There is a soldier in the box that looks like him. I named him Slane because there is a castle in Ireland named Slane castle and U2 did a concert there and mom had the DVD. I like the name Slane. I played with him and he made me feel strong. I wonder what happened to him. All my toys are gone. The red tractor with the real rubber tires and smelled like real rubber tires. My Gameboy. My Soldier-Man. Gone. I liked to play with him. I didn't have to see what was happening. My Mom died. She had such pretty hair. She burned. I played and nothing mattered and I was safe. *Safe.* Safe went away from me. Safe in quiet. It's quiet here. The soldiers are old looking. I think there is a soldier in the box that is just like Slane. How did Slane get here?

Counselor-Man talked again. I was waiting for him to tell me what to do. I was waiting for him to try to make to talk but he didn't. He said I'm coming here tomorrow. I want to come here. I want to see if Slane is in that box. I think it's him. Counselor-Man seems like he's nice but I'm not sure. I will wait and see. Mom said counselors will try to brainwash me and to not talk to them. *Don't talk to anybody!* But he didn't talk or try to get me to talk. Maybe he'll just sit and let me explore. He's kind of boring actually. I think I'll be okay here. *Don't talk to him!* No, I won't talk to him, but I'll come here and I'll see what's in that box and what the sand is like. I will, I might.

••••••••••••••••••••••••••••••••••••••

Non-directive play therapy, as we have said before, may be described as an opportunity that is offered to the child to experience growth under the most favorable conditions. Since play is his natural medium for self-expression, the child is given the opportunity to play out his accumulated feelings of tension, frustration, insecurity, aggression, fear, bewilderment, confusion. By playing out these feelings he gets them out in the open, faces them, learns to control them, or abandons them. When he has achieved emotional realization, he begins to realize the power within himself to be an individual in his own right, to think for himself, to make his own decisions, to become psychologically more mature, and, by doing so, to realize selfhood.

– Virginia Axline, *Play Therapy* (p. 27).

3
THE SAND

Cade watched Alexander, an eight year old boy, play excitedly in the sandbox. "Then, this guy climbs up here, see?" said the boy, moving a green, plastic army man and setting it on top of a small hill of sand.

"I wonder what will happen next," said Cade.

"Well, then the bad guy jumps down and takes the army guy cuz the army guy didn't see him and ya wanna know what?" asked Alexander excitedly.

"What?" Cade said, inquisitively.

"Well, the bad guy here," said the boy, breathing heavily and picking up a plastic figure sporting a blue cape, "grabs the army guy and throws him into the prison here." Alexander lifted the green army man and put him into a prison made of Lincoln Logs. "But ya wanna know what?"

"What?"

"Well, the army man wants to go to prison because that's where his Dad is, and then he can free him! And the bad guy doesn't even know it, cuz he's so dumb!" said Alexander triumphantly, putting his hands up in a victorious gesture and flinging sand all around them.

"Oh I see," said Cade, ignoring the shower of sand, "so it's the dad that's in prison..."

"Yes!" exclaimed Alexander. "Remember I said he was in there?"

"I didn't know it was his Dad, but now I do!" said Cade, matching Alexander's excitement.

"And ya wanna know what?" asked Alexander, reaching for a small plastic barrel.

"No, what?" Cade responded, sincerely eager to know what would happen next.

"Well, Alexander…I mean, the *Army man*! Gosh, I said my name," Alexander paused and blinked several times with a faraway look. "Anyway" he said quietly and then built up the volume in his voice. "The *Army man* hid some dynamite." Alexander held up the small plastic barrel. "And now, his Dad and him are going to use it to bust out!"

"Wow, what a great plan!" said Cade, and he and Alexander locked eyes and shared the same look of joy and satisfaction.

"It is almost time for us to stop, buddy" said Cade. "But we can leave everything just like it is and I'm going to take a picture of this so we don't forget what happened and we can pick up here next time, okay?"

"Oh man…" said Alexander a bit crestfallen. "That went by superfast, ya know?"

"I know, but remember, you'll be back again soon, okay?"

"Okay…hey ya wanna know what?" said Alexander eagerly, not even waiting for Cade to respond. "Next time we can see how they escape and blow everything up and put the bad guy into prison!"

"Hey, that will be something to see, wouldn't it?" said Cade, leading Alexander to a sink where they both washed their hands.

Alexander hummed softly to himself and splashed the water on his hands. Cade observed his contentedness with tenderness and handed him a paper towel.

"Okay buddy, gotta get you back to your cottage so you don't miss game time."

"Oh yeah," said Alexander, wide eyed, as if he just realized he had just spent an hour playing and forgot everything about his life outside of the therapy room.

"I think we are doing dodgeball today in the gym. I'm really good at that!" he said flinging his arms pretending to throw a ball as hard as he could.

Cade stepped aside to miss the windmill of Alexander's arms.

"Watch out there," he said with a smile, "Don't want to hurt yourself before you even get there!"

"Oh man!" said Alexander, half-whining. "I'm the best player out there, you don't even *know*!" He swept his arms in front of him in a majestic gesture, reminding Cade of the Lion in the *Wizard of OZ* during the *"What do they got that I ain't got? - COURAGE!"* speech.

"Of course you are, my man!" said Cade opening the door and flipping off the light. Alexander followed him and they walked towards the cottages.

"Hey, ya wanna know what...?" Alexander jabbered all the way back to the cottage.

He talked about the lights, the door, the grass, a dried, crusty worm on the sidewalk (which he tried to pick up but Cade discouraged him from doing so). The boy who was once so locked up that he did not speak for days, was now openly sharing, eager to experience the world.

....

Cade looked at the clock. *Twenty minutes.* He smoothed the sand and straightened the toys on the shelves that flanked both ends of the sandbox. It was the same routine that he did before every play session: to present a pristine playroom that is open for exploring, creating, and imagining. Apprehension. *Why? It's got to be just right.* More smoothing. *I think we made a connection. I hope we made a connection. Alexander was emotionally paralyzed too. Look at him now.* Relief. He stepped back and surveyed the playroom. *He might want the dinosaurs.* He arranged the dinosaurs in neat rows. Cade scanned the far side of the room. *He might want to color or paint.* He arranged the paints in straight row and made a rainbow bouquet of markers that sprouted from a round tin container. Cade walked back to his desk and sat in his chair. *Ten minutes.* He looked back over the playroom and smiled. *Freedom.* There it was. It washed over him. *That's what kids feel when they are here. Complete freedom. Free from the discouraging words and disapproving looks of adults. Free to say what they want. Free to create and then destroy what they have created if they want to. Free to feel. Free to think. Free to grow.* "Isn't it interesting," Dr. Cap remarked in class one day, "the times you really grew and learned on the path to adulthood were during times when you were free to explore."

A knock at the door jolted him from his thoughts. It was Pierce and Miss Shaw. Cade opened the door and welcomed Pierce inside.

Pierce glanced up at Cade for a brief instant and then walked straight to the sand box and the shelf of toys.

"Feel free to look around, Pierce, I'm glad you're back. I'm just going to sit here and if you need anything just let me know."

•••

I am back. Here is the room. There is Counselor-Man. I hear him. He is sitting down. There is the sandbox. There is the box of toys. I get to explore. The sun is shining. There is the big tree. Everything is as I remember it. There is the quiet. I like quiet. Sandbox. Box of toys. Sun shining. Quiet. The sand is smooth. I wonder who smoothed out the sand. I like the patterns and lines in it. I like to look at things like that. The wind smooths out the desert sand. This is like the desert. I want to put the castle in the desert. I want to get it out but I don't know if I should. What if Counselor-Man gets mad? He doesn't seem like he would but you never know. *Don't trust adults!* Mom said. Mom died. She burned. Halloween is coming and the scarecrows remind me of her and the people trying to get away. Her arms reached towards the sky. Mom burned…I still see it.

•••

Cade followed Pierce to the sandbox. *No hesitation! The kid wants to be here!* But as easily as Pierce entered, he now seemed stuck again. Frozen in place. He stood staring at the sand, then at the castle, then back to the sand again. *Relax. There is no rush.* Cade waited, watching every movement. *Be patient!* A poorly timed comment or pushing the process along by being too eager would impede the process. He debated on whether to get up and get the castle down for Pierce, or if he should wait it out, letting Pierce battle the anxiety within himself until his will finally won out. He vividly remembered Dr. Cap discussing these very moments in Cade's training.

"This battle is an important part of a child's early visits to the playroom," Dr. Cap told Cade. "The child is used to environments where they are not in control. Being in a new place and given free reign creates anxiety. You know, like when you suddenly have a lot of choices you didn't have before. Part of you likes this, but part of you is a bit overwhelmed. When the child's will wins out in the battle against the anxiety of having the freedom to explore a new place and be in control, it sets the stage for future growth and establishes the playroom as a sanctuary of healing."

"You are looking at the sand and the castle," Cade said to Pierce, speaking slowly and softly. "You are wondering if it's okay to touch the sand and mess it up, and if it's okay to take the castle down. You are in a new place and you don't want to make a mistake because that would feel bad."

Pierce said nothing, but he moved towards the castle. After a minute or so, he reached out and ran his hand along the top of a turret, feeling the intentions of the outline with his index finger.

"You touched it," Cade continued. "You know that it's okay now. You are feeling the castle."

Pierce continued to touch the castle and soon had both hands feeling the walls and roundedness of the rock base on which the turret was built. Finally, his hands rested on the red door. He stepped back, not taking his eyes off the castle. He bent down and looked at the sand.

"The sand is smooth," Cade said. "It is clear and clean. The sand is waiting for you. You are not sure if you are ready to touch it. When you are ready, it is there."

Pierce sat very still. He leaned forward. It was as if he was examining every grain of sand. Cade glanced at the clock. Twenty minutes had passed.

• •

I wanted to touch the castle and I did touch the castle! It is big. It is just like a real castle. It has bricks and the tower has windows in it. I like the castle. I want to put the castle in the sand. I will, I might! Counselor-Man talked. But he didn't tell me what to do. I *am* brave. I want to touch the sand. Counselor-Man said, *It is waiting for me. When I am ready.* I like how smooth it is. *Smooth!* I feel very happy now. I don't want to leave this room. I don't want to go back to school or my cottage. I like it here. I hope I have a lot longer time today. The sand is sparkly from the sun. Like diamonds. Millions of diamonds. *Millions. Billions.*

• •

Cade looked intently at Pierce, searching for some sign that he was content. There was none. His facial expression had not changed at all. His body, which appeared relaxed when he touched the castle, was again stiff and he sat like a rock staring at the sand. *Patience!* In times like this, he let his mind drift to conversations with Dr. Capstone. He remembered a rainy afternoon when he and Dr. Cap were reviewing a video recording of Cade's sessions with a young girl.

"See, right there," began Dr. Cap, "you are suggesting she play with the dollhouse instead of just commenting that she saw the dollhouse."

Cade threw up his hands. "Obviously she *wants* to play with it! What's wrong with me encouraging her to do so?"

"That's not the point. Remember, the whole goal is to encourage the development of her self, her being, who she is going to be. At this stage in her life, she has been abandoned and rejected. The natural part of her that is supposed to explore and play has been severely damaged. So, if she never has the experience of freedom to explore and express herself through play, that part of her will never develop. She will more than likely grow into someone who does not like herself and have difficulty making major life decisions."

"So I should just mention that I notice that she sees the dollhouse and that it is there, or mention that she is looking at it, right?"

"Yes. Exactly. Don't push it, let her explore and let the battle between her will and anxiety play out. This is very important. Your job is to *just be*: there is no time here. Forget time!" Dr. Capstone grabbed Cade's shoulder. "I know that it's not natural, but that is your quest!"

Cade smiled as he thought of Dr. Cap's passion and his skills. He felt a deep sense of love for this man who dedicated his life to the service of children trapped in the foster care system. Cade felt his stomach squirm. Apprehension. He focused his attention back to the small boy in front of him. *Would Pierce allow himself to touch the sand?*

....

The sand here is like the sand I remember at the playground. I liked how it felt in my hand and how it was cold when I buried my hands in it. I found a red car in the sand. Someone forgot it. The doors opened. I took it home but it got lost when we had to move. In the middle of the night. We moved a lot. In the middle of the night. We always lived with people. Mom's friends. Mom took me to the park. There was that trailer next to the park. I stayed in the park all day until dark time. I remember lying in the sand and wishing I could fall into it and that there would be another world waiting for me. A world with no bad people. A world with no drugs. The first Counselor-Lady I saw told me my mom was a drug *addick* and did bad things. She said my mom was gone, as if I didn't know *that!* I watched my mom die. I watched my mom burn. I hated that Counselor-Lady and broke a crystal paperweight because I knocked if off her desk. It felt good to watch it shatter. I pretended like it was an accident but I think she knew that I did it on purpose. *On purpose!* She told my foster-mom that I had *Oppensational-Defiant* disorder. Or something like that. That Counselor-Lady didn't really like me from the beginning. None of them did. I'm scared of Counselor-People. Mom said they try to change you. *Don't talk to them!* I figured out I could just break Counselor-People's stuff and they would ship me off to somewhere else. This sand looks like I could just fall into it and vanish to a new place. This is what the desert looks like. I want to go to the desert because there are no people there. Only lizards with spiky backs and snakes.

Counselor-Man is sitting in the bean bag chair. He lets me do what I want here. I'm glad. If I touch the sand it will mess it up. I wonder if that's okay. I think it would be okay. I can smooth it back out; I'm good at smoothing it. I might write my name in it. I will, I might. I wonder if the sand is cold. I will touch it.

· ·

He's touching the sand! Pierce turned and looked at Cade for a second before doing so, making sure it was okay.

"It is sometimes scary to try something new in a new place. The sand is to be explored. It's fun to explore when you know that it's okay," Cade reassured Pierce.

If only I could be inside his head. Cade could see the struggle going on within the boy. Pierce sat for at least fifteen minutes staring at the sand, seemingly lost in thoughts. *What could he be looking at? What does he see?* The thought of Dr. Cap's admonition to be patient again came to Cade's mind. To allow the child to acclimate to the playroom in their own way and at their own speed. Now, finally, Pierce was feeling the sand. After a few minutes, Pierce reached out with his right hand, gently placing his palm on the surface. It appeared as though Pierce was experiencing a powerful memory through the contact with the sand.

"You are feeling the sand," Cade remarked. Pierce turned slowly and looked at him. It was the first time the two made sustained eye contact. Cade smiled at Pierce and Pierce quickly looked away. Without warning Pierce shoved both hands into the sand and he spread his hands all around, running them back and forth as if he was painting and his hands were large brushes. Cade got up from the bean bag chair and walked slowly towards the sandbox. Pierce noticed him approaching and paused momentarily with his head shifted towards Cade, then resumed moving his hands in the sand. Cade sat down cross-legged a few feet from Pierce.

"The sand feels good," Cade said, watching Pierce.

"Good," Pierce whispered.

"You are happy, playing in the sand."

Pierce nodded. He began to hum softly. Cade sat and watched him. Pierce reached farther and farther into the sandbox, pushing the sand with his hands until he was stretched out over the sand. He glanced back at Cade.

"You want to know if you can climb in the sandbox," Cade said, continuing to talk in a slow, soft voice. "You can explore the sand however you wish."

Pierce hesitated for a moment and then carefully lifted one leg over the edge of the sandbox. He looked back at Cade.

"You are climbing in now. It's fun to explore new things."

Pierce balanced on his hands and one knee and gently pulled his other leg into the sandbox. His facial expression did not change. He began to hum again, this time more loudly. Cade tried to make out the tune but was unable to do so. Pierce spread his hands wide in the sand, and moved his arms in a flowing sweeping motion.

"It feels good to feel the sand. See the way your hands make shapes in the sand. You are happy feeling the sand."

Pierce continued to hum and spread the sand, and then he stretched his arms out as far as they would go and laid his body down in the sand. He turned his head and rested the side of his face on the sand, facing Cade.

"You are lying down in the sand. It feels good to lie down in the sand."

Pierce became very still and closed his eyes. He began to hum softly and tucked his hands underneath his upper torso. His humming became louder. Unexpectedly, he rotated his lower torso until he was lying on his side with his legs tucked up and curled himself into a ball, with the side of his head resting in the sand. His eyes were closed. His humming gradually turned into a whimper and then a wailing cry. Cade watched him, stunned, and said nothing. *What should I do?* Cade had not witnessed a reaction like this before. The look of anguish on Pierce's face told Cade that this young boy was experiencing an intense memory. The sound of Pierce's cry ripped through Cade. *I need to do something, to help in some way.* Helplessness. Cade felt a huge lump in his throat. He ached to give comfort to this boy who had seen so much.

....

I'm touching the sand! It feels good, just like I thought it would. It feels smooth, just like I thought it would. I'm touching it with both hands, it feels like water. Cool, clean water. I could swim in it. I will I might. Counselor-Man talks to me but not much. He doesn't ask me any questions. If he doesn't ask me anything then there is nothing for me to tell him. *Don't tell him anything!* He tells me the sand is for exploring and I am exploring. When I move my hands, the sand ripples like waves. Then I smooth it out. Rough. Smooth. Rough. Smooth. Over and over again. I want to get in it. I want to feel my whole body in the sand. I want to lay in it. Counselor-Man says it's okay, he says I can explore the sand any way that I want to. The sand feels like the sand at the park, I remember laying in it watching my mom die. My mom burned up. I could have saved her if I got her out of there. I could have saved her if I didn't let her go in the trailer. If I lay down in the sand and close my eyes I can go back and save her. I am going to lie down in the sand. I am stretching out. It feels good to stretch out; it is like lying on a bed of water. The sand feels cool; it makes my whole body feel cool, like I'm in the ocean. I put my head down on the sand. I can feel it on the side of my face. It's scratchy just like that day I watched my mom die. My mom burned. I watched her burn. I see her running out of the trailer and then I see the explosion. For a split second, she hangs in space, I reach out to her. *I can save her!* If I could run over there…but I was there and she told me to run away, I remember now. She said she would come to the park. I was doing what she told me to do *Run!* and I went where she told me to *Go!* and I did it *Good Boy.* There was no way I could save her. I couldn't save her, no one could save her. It's not my fault, it's over and it's not my fault. I couldn't have saved her, there wasn't time and I did what she told me to do *Good Boy. Good Boy.*

....

Pierce lay in the fetal position, moaning and groaning with a grimaced look on his face for about ten minutes. Cade watched him, trying to put himself in Pierce's mind, trying to see what he might be seeing. *He is reliving something and it must have been awful. I feel so helpless. But Pierce is exploring the sand. He broke through huge barriers today. I have created the ideal environment and I'm going to just be present and affirm his behavior. I only wish that I could give comfort to this little boy who has seen so much.*

"Actually," Dr. Cap would tell Cade when he talked with him about Pierce, "that's exactly what you did."

44

4
THE CASTLE

"I swear he just curled up in a ball and started moaning and moving around. He had the most awful look on his face."

"What did you do?" asked Dr. Capstone.

"I just sat quietly and watched him."

"How did the session end?"

"He came out of it, you know, he just kind of sat up blinking. To me, he seemed relieved. I told him it was time to stop and he got out of the sand box. He actually told me goodbye when his case worker came and got him."

Dr. Cap nodded and smiled.

"I've never seen anything like that. It really surprised me. Have you ever had an experience like that?"

"Yes. But, remember, I've been doing this for a long time."

"Well of course," Cade said. "I remember you telling us some pretty amazing stories in class."

"Oh, yes, there have been many. One interesting case came to mind while you were sharing about Pierce. There was a girl I worked with at the orphanage. She, like Pierce, had been traumatized to the point where she would not talk. I haven't thought about her for some time." Dr. Cap leaned back in his chair and swiveled to face the large bay window that looked out into the courtyard.

"This work provides us with some unexpected miracles," he said, taking a sip of water. "Her name was Abigail, and of all the kids I worked with, she made me a witness to the miracle of forgiveness. All I knew about her when she was referred to me was that she had been sexually abused from the age of about two or three until just a few months before she came to the orphanage. As you know, this was not uncommon experience for children who ended up at the orphanage."

Cade nodded. He had worked with several children in his short career who had been sexually abused and had been privileged enough to have a hand in their healing.

"The nuns had gotten Abigail the necessary medical attention and she was physically cleared to attend school and participate in activities. The only problem was that she would not talk, and that's where I came in. She was severely emotionally delayed, and would often have temper tantrums, yet she was very bright. Perhaps the smartest kid I ever worked with," he laughed.

"She played so many tricks on me that I began to be afraid of her! But I noticed that she played tricks because she trusted me and it was always in a fun way."

"What was the best trick she ever pulled?" Cade was completely curious, imagining how he would handle such a child.

"Well, I had installed a small fish tank in the corner of the playroom and most of the children liked to look at the fish. I had one or two, just guppies, you know, pretty hardy fish, and I had hoped they would have babies. Now, at this stage of my work with Abigail, she was still not talking and it had been probably three or four months that I had been seeing her. Because of the nature of doing therapy at the orphanage, I was free to see the kids two or three times per week, or more, if need be. Sort of like what you have at the Children's Home. It turned out that play therapy was perfect because she was so emotionally stunted that she was immediately drawn to the toys for toddlers, which, ironically, was around the time that her abuse began. As you know, children often choose toys that represent their emotional age, which allows the child to be free to regress through their play and go to the stage in which healing needs to occur."

"So what did she do?"

"Well, let me tell you, she was brilliant. I mean, what she pulled was absolutely Houdini-like. Down the hall from the playroom were a bunch of offices where the nuns did paperwork, and there was a nurse's office as well. Outside in the hall in between the nurse's office and the other offices was a water cooler; all of the nuns and the children alike loved to grab a paper cup and get some water as they passed through towards the main dining hall. Abigail and I had finished our session and I walked her down the hall from the playroom towards the dining hall. I walked her to the dining hall and watched her join her classmates in line for the food, and I remember one of the nuns came up to talk with me as I stood there. Just then, a blood-curdling scream filled the great hall and echoed into the dining hall, and everyone collectively *gasped* and then went silent, and turned, as did I, to see who screamed. I then saw Sister Jolene on her knees by the water cooler, a cup of water on the floor, and two other nuns trying to help her to her feet. Honestly, I thought she had slipped and that the other nuns were helping."

"So what was it?" asked Cade, imagining every part as Dr. Capstone was telling it.

"I ran over to Sister Jolene and she was out of breath and the other nuns explained that she had fainted, but that one of them (Sister Bethanie, I think was her name) happened to be walking by and had caught her just in time. I tried to get Sister Jolene to talk to me, but she simply could not. All she could do was point at the water cooler. Her eyes bugged out as if she had seen something completely horrible. I followed the end of her shaking white hand and there, swimming as happy as could be, in the water cooler, was one of my guppies!"

47

"No way!" Cade exclaimed. "How in the world did she do that?"

"I never found out – none of us did. She was never punished because no one could prove anything and she didn't talk, so nothing happened to her. Of course, some of the nuns wanted to punish her anyway, but I intervened and reassured them that somehow it would be *useful for the therapy process* or some such baloney, and they bought it, but to this day I can't tell you how she managed it. Getting the fish out of the tank without me noticing is one thing; but getting it into the cooler, I mean, the tank must weigh a good twenty pounds even half full…it is simply astounding."

Cade sat back in his chair, grinning. He loved hearing stories of children tricking adults. He had done his share of tomfoolery, but this trick was simply masterful.

"And," Dr. Capstone said. "She had to have done it between the time we left the playroom before I took her to lunch; otherwise, someone would have noticed the fish in there, it was so obvious." Dr. Capstone sighed. "I have thought about that event for many hours trying to figure it out."

"What about her and the forgiveness stuff?"

"Oh yes, I almost forgot." Dr. Capstone cleared his throat. "Well, the play therapy sessions were amazing. I could have written a book, or many books, just about the journey that took Abigail from a shut-down, broken girl, to a strong, opinionated young lady. I did manage to get an article about her therapy process published, some years later. As I said earlier, she was initially drawn to the toys for younger children, which is common for young people who have endured experiences similar to hers – it was as if she became a baby before my eyes once she entered the playroom. I remember she took to the dolls that were in the playroom. She really loved the dolls! One aspect of her play that was quite remarkable and one that allowed me to know that she was healing, was how she went from simply touching the dolls and handling them like things or objects, to actually building relationship with the dolls – holding them, rocking them…displaying a nurturing quality. She would coo to them, and make sounds as if she was talking, but it was very soft and I couldn't make out any words."

Dr. Capstone shared the growth of Abigail and how she evolved in her play, moving from holding the dolls and pretending to be a mother to creating a family with the dolls and using a dollhouse, which represented shelter and safety, to using a car for transportation of the doll family, which represented the freedom to come and go. She interacted more and more with Dr. Cap – gradually motioning for him to hold a doll while she put shoes on it, or pointing to him to show her how something worked on the dollhouse. Over time, Abigail's demeanor softened, not just in the playroom, but everywhere she went. The nuns said she started smiling, helping others, and engaging in group play with the other children. The tantrums lessened as well.

Abigail played frequently with a doll that Dr. Cap came to realize represented her. She played out scenes of abuse that was her way of showing Dr. Cap what had happened to her. It (she) was slapped, thrown, and left alone and locked away; then every so often one of the male dolls would arrive and Abigail would simulate sexual acts with the doll, bouncing them up and down on top of it (her). She would grunt and make guttural sounds during this play. Her eyes would glaze over in a faraway stare while her hands whisked the characters through the play sequences. During these intense scenes, Dr. Capstone said nothing. He did not interpret, judge, seek to soothe, or make any attempt to either stop or join what was happening; instead, he stood firm in one of the most important tenets of child-centered play therapy: That the child will dictate what is played with, how it is played with, and for how long.

Cade nodded as he listened to Dr. Capstone. "I remember a child that did much the same thing, only with puppets. It was remarkable to see the transformation in the child as he actually became the object of the puppet and the child's inner self developed through the play process."

"Yes," said Dr. Cap. "Transformation is the perfect word. She also began to show me characteristics of various family members through her play. Her doll character was the one doing the cooking and I guess cleaning…it was hard to tell from her play but I assume it was cleaning or doing some sort of organization. The adult doll characters obviously were either drunk or using drugs or both – they were lying around a lot of the time. Then there were other characters that came by now and then, but they did not live with the family…these were the ones that performed the sexual acts. Abigail's character was clearly in a victim role at this point – staying hidden, working in the background, and hiding and caring for the younger children and animals. Then one day, an amazing thing happened."

"What was that?" asked Cade, waiting while Dr. Capstone took a sip of water.

"Well, she took a gun from the collection of military toys – tanks, Army men, and other assorted military themed play items. She brought the gun that was originally designed for a G.I. Joe character, and put it under her doll's pillow. I was surprised and excited. I knew that a dramatic addition to a child's play scenarios like a gun meant somethin' was about to happen."

"What in the world did she do with the gun?" Cade asked, thinking back to the many children with whom he had worked that had used guns in their play. "I bet she was going to waste somebody," he said with a chuckle.

Dr. Cap smiled. "Her play changed from that moment on. She didn't use the gun right away and I kept waiting for her to use it, to give her that feeling of power over the abuser. But she didn't so I waited. Her play became more intentional. Even though the gun was not used, it seemed like it represented some sort of power source that enable her to stand up for herself. Her doll character wasn't afraid, or didn't seem to be; the doll no longer hid or cowered. The doll stood up to the adults who tried to hit her and even shoved them back; no longer did the strange male dolls come into her room to freely have their way with her. Instead, the doll fought them off and turned them away. In fact, these characters never showed up anymore in her play. All that was left were the dolls that represented her immediate caretakers: A father figure, a mother figure and perhaps a grandparent of some sort. A surprising development at this stage was that she became more verbal. While she was not actually using words, she was mimicking conversation through sounds that came from her throat and even intoned these with inflection, making her voice go up or down depending what was going on with the characters she was playing with. It was as if she was just about to talk," said Dr. Cap, "like right before a moth bursts from the cocoon there is the struggle and then *Boom!* – out it comes. I'll admit that it was very difficult to be patient during this stage."

"As you're talking," said Cade, "I'm thinking of Pierce and how it's been hard to be patient with him sometimes because I see him growing and healing so much and I want to push him along."

Dr. Capstone nodded in agreement. "Patience is one of the greatest attributes of the play therapist."

"So what happened next?"

"Well, the next few sessions that led up to this monumental event were incredibly powerful and I've thought about them many times over the years," resumed Dr. Capstone. "As I said earlier, Abigail's character's play became more intentional and powerful. She took on a dominant role and was no longer passive and timid. One day during her session, she lined everyone up, including the characters that had perpetrated the sexual abuse, and this time, the gun was in her doll's hand. I remember her breathing heavily during this sequence of play and her body and hands were a flurry of activity as she set up the characters. Once she had them lined up, she moved her doll in front of the characters and pointed the gun at them. She did not make a sound at this point – she only held the gun out and pointed it at each character, walking the doll slowly in front of the characters who sat before her. I remember watching her and nearly forgetting to breathe; I noticed that her face was red but she was purposeful and intentional in her actions."

Dr. Capstone got up from his chair and stood at the large bay window that overlooked the courtyard. It seemed as though he was gathering strength to finish the story. Cade watched him take something from the window sill. It was a small black plastic gun. He handed it to Cade.

"This is the gun. This is the one thing that I took from the playroom when I stopped seeing children individually a few years ago."

Cade took the gun. He turned it over and over in his hands. It was worn from years of use and it had a large nick in the handle. He imagined all the children that had used the gun in their play over the years. He handed it back to Dr. Capstone who sat back down and leaned back in his chair.

"So here she is," he began, taking the gun and turning it over in his hand, "moving the doll in front of the other characters, pointing the gun at them. 'They must be very scared,' I said softly, tracking her behavior and letting her know that I was with her and noticing what she was doing. She paused for an instant and then nodded, making a slight sound that sounded just like the words 'very scared.' She moved the doll closer to the characters with the gun pointed directly in the character's faces, and she moved the gun vigorously lunging it at them. At first I thought she was shooting them, but she made no sound so I was pretty sure I knew what was going on. 'She is telling them that they can no longer hurt her and that she won't let them,' I said softly. She nodded and again uttered sounds in a soft tone that could have been 'You won't hurt me and I won't let you,' but I wasn't sure about that. What happened next is the miraculous part of this story..." Dr. Capstone paused and looked out the window again, watching doves bathe in the birdbath in the courtyard.

"Abigail then suddenly made her doll throw the gun aside, and I watched it slide on the floor towards the sandbox. She moved her doll over to the character on the far left and slowly bent her doll's head forward, so that the head of her doll touched the head of the doll in front of it; and as she did this, she made the sound of three or four words, but I didn't know what they were. She looked at me after she made the sound, and I realized that she wanted me to speak the words, but I was lost. Again she made the sounds, as she moved her doll's head towards the first character and made them touch foreheads. This time the cadence of the sound of the words she wanted to say were more pronounced – *bum-ba-bum bum* but I couldn't figure it out. Inside I was panicking because it was obviously a huge moment and for the first time in this play sequence that she had begun almost a year ago she was inviting me to join and put a voice to the words and I didn't want to mess it up.

"She looked at me again with a look that said *Can't you get this?* and I could see she was getting frustrated...her face was red and her eyes told me that something was about to be released; the pressure from whatever it was had created very unpleasant emotions inside of her. *Bum-ba-bum-bum*, there it was again, four syllables, three words, at least I knew that! *But what in the world could it be?* I asked myself in my mind. This went on for an agonizing minute, and suddenly I said 'Write it out!' to Abigail, and she wildly looked around, as if needing to find something to write with and something to write on; her behavior was such that if she did not find something in the next few seconds her body would actually fly apart. She flung herself over to the sandbox in a lurching manner on her hands and knees, and grabbed a plastic wand from a box of sandbox toys and using the wand, carefully wrote something in the sand. She then threw the wand down and pointed at the sandbox with emphasis, bobbing her pointing hand up and down as if to say *Get over here and read this!* and I got up from the floor and crawled on my hands and knees towards the sandbox, while Abigail resumed her position in front of the lineup of dolls, firmly clutching her doll in her hands. I neared the sandbox feeling flustered and with trepidation. *What if I can't read what she's written? What if I get it wrong again and she loses faith in me? Don't mess this up, Ronald! C'mon get with it!* I peered cautiously into the sandbox and immediately I was relieved. I could make out her letters. Somehow, somewhere in the hell of her early life she had either attended enough school to learn to write…or perhaps, she had simply taught herself, who knows?

"My eyes scrambled to find the first word – 'I' I whispered to myself. Then, to the next word – 'F-o-r-g-i-v-e' *Forgive? What in the world…?* But I remembered my mission, my mind picturing her determined face and demonstrative pointing at the sand on which she had written. The last word came automatically: 'Y-o-u.' I looked at Abigail, who had no doubt heard me as I whispered the words to myself. She still sat poised with her doll a few inches from the first character and waited. 'I forgive you,' I said, and immediately she bowed her doll's head to the head of the doll before her. And then, she said as plain and clear is if she had been speaking every day that I had known her, '*I FORGIVE YOU; I FORGIVE YOU; I FORGIVE YOU*'…and on down the line she went – putting the forehead of her doll to each doll that was before her and saying the words 'I forgive you' to each figure."

Cade felt all the hair along the back of his neck and arms stand fully erect. His brain swirled as he tried to comprehend all that Dr. Capstone had told him; imagining the scene, and what that must have been like to have witnessed such an event.

"What did you do after that?" he asked, his mind still reeling.

"Well," Dr. Capstone began, "I was so stunned that I stared at her without saying anything, and then my clinical training kicked in and I quickly relaxed my body and tried to refocus myself. You know, I have often imagined what it was like for Anne Sullivan who worked with Helen Keller, or Oliver Sacks and others like him, when they realized the exact *moment* of transformation for the person they were working with; that very second in time where their hard work and patience *clicked* along with the healing or insight of the individual – almost like watching a rainbow form before your very eyes. I had witnessed my moment, something that defied explanation, and even telling it now both exhausts and exhilarates me at the same time." Dr. Capstone paused, looking out into the courtyard. Cade saw tears rolling down Dr. Capstone's cheeks; and he was surprised to feel hot tears of his own.

"I saw," he said reverently, "in Abigail's eyes that had tears in them, a grace and beauty that translated for me just the degree to which she had healed. It's interesting to me that while I witnessed this event, I find it very difficult to put it into words…then and now. All I can say is that from that day on she spoke – to the nuns, to her peers, to me. It was as if she had never been silent, and I never asked her about being silent. I believe that she was so stunted and wounded that before that moment, speaking was impossible."

"How long did you work with her?" Cade asked, his brain and body feeling buzzed from the story.

"Abigail and I worked together right up until the day she left the orphanage. The state found a distant aunt who lived in North Carolina who, when she was contacted, jumped at the chance to adopt her. Abigail was about sixteen when she left."

"Did she continue to grow?"

"Her growth was phenomenal! As she healed, she not only talked, but she gained the ability to be creative in the form of art, music, writing…and arguing," Dr. Capstone said smiling.

"Arguing?"

"Oh yes, this girl turned into a spitfire and it was marvelous to see. I rejoiced when I would hear of her getting into a scrap with one of the nuns or fighting for her independence. The nuns soon realized that I was no good to consult on disciplinary considerations in regards to Abigail – everything she did that the nuns interpreted as rebellious I saw as magnificent and necessary. I've told you before that many adults see a child's rebellion as a bad thing; oh, how I disagree! You remember from my lectures how I abhor the diagnoses, the labels of *Oppositional Defiant Disorder* and *Conduct Disorder* that the modern psychological establishment seeks to slap on nearly every child in the foster care system..." Dr. Capstone took a deep breath and continued, his voice much softer. "If I had been abused, abandoned, and never been able to trust most adults in this life, doesn't it make sense to fight them? Doesn't it make me *normal* for wanting to run, to fight, to get away? She's the one I think of when I read the *Prayer of St. Francis* and the line, 'Where there is despair, hope.'"

Cade nodded, remembering the kids he had seen who had been in many scrapes, fights, and attempts (some successful) at running away from anything and everyone. He thought of Pierce and all that he had seen and how he, like Abigail, was completely non-verbal.

"I have to ask," Cade smiled, "Did she ever confess to putting the fish in the water cooler tank?"

"I only asked her about it once after she began speaking," Dr. Capstone said, leaning back in his chair, stretching his arms and yawning. "It was a couple of years later and we were leaving the therapy room and I noticed her watching the fish, who did happen to have babies, by the way."

"What happened when you asked her?"

"I said, 'Abigail, I have to know, did you put that fish in the water cooler?' She simply stood up and looked at me and smiled, her eyes twinkling, and she gracefully put her finger to her lips: *Shhhhh.* And then, with all the mysteriousness of a Greek siren, she walked out of the playroom and down the hall. It was classic Abigail, and I wonder now why I expected anything different."

●●

Cade watched Pierce playing with the castle in the sandbox. Since the emotional release a week before, Pierce's behavior in the playroom had changed. He was bold and intentional. He was talking, although only in a whispered tone. His demeanor towards Cade was different also. He no longer regarded Cade as an enemy or in a standoffish manner. *He has included me in his play. He trusts me to be here and gradually his defenses are coming down.* Today, Pierce assembled soldiers taken from the box of toys next to the castle and placed them around the castle. He made a barrier around the castle with the sand. There was one soldier in particular that held Pierce's interest. The soldier, battered and worn from years of play, wore a stern, determined face. This soldier was slightly bigger than the rest and, though scuffed in some places, had a quality and character that set it apart. Cade had no idea how old the toy was. He only knew that it was there when he began using the playroom under Dr. Capstone's direction. *What could Dr. Cap tell me about this soldier?* Pierce's play was very organized and methodical. He took great care in making sure the castle was level and he set the soldiers around the castle exactly six inches apart. After assembling the soldiers, Pierce paused and sat completely still. He stared at the castle and waited. *Play paused again. What is he thinking?*

●●

I am playing with the castle! I got it down all by myself. The soldier is Slane! I knew it was him. He looks just like the one that I had. He is strong and powerful. I want to be like him. The castle is just like I think a castle should be. It has strong walls and towers and the red door goes up and down. There is a catapult and machines in the towers that launch weapons. It is perfect. I want to come here every day.

Counselor-Man, his name is Cade, said that I can come here three days a week and I'm gonna. Miss Sarah said I could too. I like it here. I am free. The castle is ready and I have set it right there. I have built a small wall around it. It will work for now but eventually it will need more protection. Slane is a great warrior but his life was very hard, especially in the beginning. Just like me. Slane never knows what danger there will be or what adventure awaits him. Just like me. I will tell the story of Slane and his adventures. This giant sandbox will be Slane's world and I will join him in his quests. It's almost time to go but I'll be back tomorrow. I will see you tomorrow, Slane!

5
THE QUEST

Slane began his life as everyone does – a helpless, squalling baby. He was born to a gypsy woman, said to be a sorceress who came from a faraway kingdom. She was considered less than, a nothing. She had no family and was a wanderer. She was so unimportant that no one even knew her name. Despite this unfortunate beginning, Slane was fortunate enough to have royal blood coursing through him. Slane's grandfather, Roland, had been a great warrior king and was a hero to the people. He had helped liberate the surrounding land and protected it from enemies. Under Roland's rule and protection, the townspeople experienced a long period of peace and the Cities of Light prospered.

During one of Roland's conquests, a band of bandits that he and his men were chasing hid themselves in a village. An old woman approached Roland and asked that the village be spared. If not, the woman (who happened to be a witch) threatened to cast a spell on the King. She said that his wife would die in childbirth and that his firstborn would be completely opposite from him in every way. Whereas Roland was brave, his son would be a coward. Where Roland sought to do good, his son would strive to do evil. While Roland fought for the rights of innocent and good people and sought to protect them, his son would partner with evil men and destroy the innocent and good. Roland scoffed at the old woman and rode on. And because the bandits refused to surrender, Roland and his men burned the village, killing most of the bandits. The rest fled and Roland and his men continued onward, purging the land of those that sought to do evil.

Years passed, and despite his best efforts to forget the old woman's curse, Roland could not shake the image of her standing before him. Her withered finger pointing at him the recitation of the fateful words haunted his dreams. His wife died giving birth to their son, Sean. Roland clung to the hope that this was a mere coincidence, but to his horror he found it was not. As Sean grew, Roland could see darkness in his eyes. He was harsh to others even as a small boy, and created chaos in every situation. Roland disciplined him consistently, even harshly, but the darkness would not leave him. To Roland's horror, the old woman's prophecy had come to pass. Each time Roland tried to talk to his son, the boy rebuffed him and Roland felt as though he was talking to a "soulless being." By the age of thirteen, the boy had been brought before the council several times, and the members voted to banish him, at Roland's urging. Roland's heart was broken as he knew the only thing to do was to let Sean go. Roland attempted to talk to Sean on the day of his banishment. He wanted to bear his heart and let his son know how difficult this was for a father, and that no words could express how terrible Roland felt.

Sean stared at Roland with cold, steely eyes. "Are you finished?" he asked, in a flinty tone.

"Son, please know how much I love you."

Sean said nothing. He faced his father and the council, and then looked at the villagers.

"As I have been cursed, so now you will forever feel my pain. As long as I have breath, I will wreak havoc upon you and your children." With that said, Sean turned and walked down the road that led to the vast wilderness just beyond the kingdom. Roland would never see his son alive again.

This wayward son became Slane's father, a bad man of the darkest kind who had been banished from the village because he was a thief and a coward and did evil wherever he went. Sean formed a group of bandits made up from various miscreants from the surrounding villages. Angry that he had been banished, Sean vowed never to stop trying to destroy the Cities of Light. And so it was that Slane entered the world without knowing his mother, and with a father who was branded a criminal and banished from society.

One night, Roland was awoken out of a deep sleep and was told by one of his soldiers that a gypsy woman had come to the gate of the village and claimed to be pregnant with the child of Sean, Roland's grandchild. She was seeking asylum and stated that she had no family and nowhere to go. After much questioning, Roland's council of elders determined that she indeed was carrying Sean's child. The council decided to give her asylum out of respect for the fact that the baby was Roland's grandchild. Soon the time came and the baby was born. Roland announced he would name the child Slane after Roland's great-grandfather. Slane's mother said that she would nurse the child but then would return to the land of her people, the gypsies. She said that it was too dangerous for her to live in the kingdom because Sean would surely find her and kill her. She said she loved Slane enough to leave so her child could be safe. Roland refused to allow her to leave and said that he would protect her as he would his own daughter. However, one night after Slane had been nursed to a good health she slipped away and was never seen again. Roland was distraught and demanded that she be found, but it was to no avail. Roland released the news that Slane's mother had died, to protect her from Sean and ensure that he would not go looking for her. Sure enough, news spread to Sean that he had a son and that the mother had died, and that his father had custody of his son. Sean decided to take his son as he did not want Roland to raise him. Sean mounted a fierce attack on Roland's kingdom, and both men were killed in a bloody battle that claimed many lives and destroyed part of the castle.

Following the battle, the Cities of Light mourned the death of Roland. There was a question of what to do about Slane the orphan. Some of the council members believed that Slane also carried the curse. They said that Slane was filled with "bad blood" and should be put to death to be sure that the curse was indeed ended. Others believed that Slane could be raised to become a great leader like his grandfather Roland. After all, they argued, he carried Roland's blood as much as his father's blood. The debate raged on for many weeks. Finally, in order to settle the matter, the oldest member of the council, the "Wise Woman" was called upon to make the decision. She was the supreme judge of when the council found themselves deadlocked on an issue. She was very old, although her exact age was unknown. Some said she was over two hundred years old; some said she was an "angel spirit" that had been in the Cities of Light since ancient times. She said that to kill the boy would be cruel, and evil would come from such a deed, for there was warrior blood in him. Yet, to allow him to live among the people would be disastrous because he carried "both bloods" and would always struggle between being who his father wanted him to be and who he was born to be. The old woman said that he must be banished to a faraway land, the Dead Lands, a place so desolate that people died before they got there. The only things that lived there were the Black Wolves, a band of mutated wolves that were terrible; their breath alone had the power to kill a grown man. If the boy lived, it would truly be a miracle and his struggle for life would create in him the ability to become a warrior; if he could not find this inner strength he would surely die. If Slane the Warrior lived, he would return and rule as a warrior king after his grandfather Roland. This was the prophecy that the Wise Woman told the council and all those loyal to Roland.

And so it was determined that Slane would be taken to the Dead

Lands. A band of warriors were selected, along with the woman who was his caregiver since birth. The Wise Woman gave them detailed instructions. They would carry Slane across the Great Desert and over the Great Sea to the Dead Lands. She told them to take him to the Great Tree in the middle of the Great Pit in the very center of the Dead Lands. There they would leave him, wrapped only in a blanket with a jug of water and one loaf of bread.

A large group of villagers gathered the next morning in a steady pouring rain to see the band off. The men were somber and many of the women sobbed. A gray feeling of uneasiness permeated the crowd. This feeling, born at the time of Roland's death, now reached a fevered pitch in the residents of the Cities of Light as they all wondered who would lead them. Many believed sending the boy out to fend for himself was foolishness. He could be their leader, they said. We could train him, they said. But what was decided was decided. There would be no going against the Wise Woman or the council. The group set off into the dreary morning haze, and with a single wave from the last warrior in the line, they disappeared into the mist.

••

Cade sat on the floor near the corner of the sandbox and watched Pierce arrange the soldiers. At the beginning of the session, Pierce placed the castle on the far side of the sandbox and buried Slane underneath it. *I wonder why he did that?*

"You have buried the soldier under the castle," Cade remarked, tracking Pierce's behavior.

Pierce said nothing. He then slowly walked around the room gathering toys. He chose a plastic baby wrapped in a blanket from the Barbie Doll section, horses, and a tent from the Army toy box, and some string from the arts and crafts section. He also took the queen piece from an old chess set. He built a few structures in the sandbox using Lincoln Logs and placed various Weeble Wobbles in a circle around the soldiers. Pierce placed the queen in front of all the other characters, apparently as some sort of authority figure. He spoke occasionally during the play, but only in inaudible whispers. He then placed the baby on one of the horses and attached it with string. It appeared as though the soldiers and the baby were going somewhere.

"It looks like they are going on a journey," said Cade.

Pierce paused for a moment and glanced in Cade's direction but said nothing. He began to move the caravan across the sand.

....

I, Pierce, have made Slane's story and I will tell it. Slane is small right now, and nearly helpless. No one knows if he will survive, but I know that he will. Just like I have survived. Slane's father, mother, and grandfather died. My father and grandparents are all dead. My mother died. She burned. I have no one and Slane has no one. But someone is watching out for him. Me! I will make sure that he is okay. I know exactly what is going to happen to him and I will make the story happen. It is going to be a long tale. It will be a saga.

6

ALL ALONE

The girl, a fourteen year old with dyed black hair, stared at Cade with eyes that could have bored holes into solid steel. She was not happy to be in the therapy room and Cade knew it. He was working hard to appear unintimidated. But he was. The girl's story unfortunately was one that was quite common: Broken home, drug abusing parents, foster care, oppositional defiant disorder, Boyd Home, and as a last resort, counseling. Cade knew he possessed the clinical skill to help her – it was just a matter of weathering the blustery act that usually accompanied angry adolescents. Usually, this "act" lasted thirty minutes at the most, and then the resistant teen would eventually let the walls down. Little by little tidbits of personal information would be revealed, then thoughts and emotions. Once trust was established, the therapeutic relationship formed which led to growth and healing. *Just be patient and accept her as she is.*

The girl, named Victoria, leaned sloppily across the couch in the office, and tugged at the hood strings of her black hoodie. She liked black, which was evidenced by her shoes, jeans, and the paint on her fingernails. She had been in the office for eighteen grueling minutes and had yet to speak. She had, however, sighed, grunted in an annoyed tone, and looked around the room; then focused on the hood strings again, rolling and unrolling them at least a hundred times. Cade waited.

He had already gone through his "Welcome to Counseling" speech, complete with an explanation about confidentiality, and the history of the counseling program at Boyd Home and how he came to work there. He reassured Victoria that there was no agenda and no expectations. She said nothing. She glared at him. *Wow, she is really angry. Her anger is like a boiling cauldron. This girl has been really hurt.*

"So, tell me about your previous experience with counseling?" he asked.

No response. Smoldering stare.

At least she looked at me.

He waited. Still no response. He noticed her eyes fell back to the hood strings where her fingers still busily rolled the cords.

He gazed out the window and then checked the clock. He shoved the thought of time out of his mind. He made sure he checked the clock without her noticing. She hadn't and then Cade rechecked Victoria's body language. Still languishing across the couch, she had tucked one leg underneath her and then laid her head down on the large pillow at the end of the couch. She glanced at him and then quickly looked away.

"Have you been to see a counselor before?" Cade asked.

She sighed deeply. *A response!* Her sighing was at least some sort of reaction and it came after one of his questions. Perhaps he could get a verbal response if he proceeded wisely. She looked around the room. Cade followed her eyes. She spent some time looking at the toys on the shelves.

"I used to have one of those dolls."

Bingo!

Cade turned to look. "Which one?"

"The one in the pink. It cries and you give it the bottle and it stops."

"I wonder how it feels for you to see it again," Cade replied. He turned back and looked at Victoria.

"I was about six when I had it." Her voice trailed off.

Don't say anything. Let the room do it's work.

"You let kids play in here?"

"Yep. They can play with any of the toys in any way they want to."

Her eyes continued to scan the room. "I like the big windows."

"I rarely have to turn on the lights thanks to those windows," said Cade.

Her eyes rested on the artwork in the corner of the room.

"You let kids draw in here?" she asked.

"Yep, they are allowed to draw anything they want."

Now we're getting somewhere.

Suddenly Victoria sat up. She reached for a drawing tablet and pencil that Cade had strategically placed on the end table near the end of the couch. She twirled the pencil once and began drawing but quickly ripped the first page away from the tablet, crumpling the paper. She began drawing again but this time was more cautious, gently guiding the pencil with her right hand and steadying the tablet with her left, her eyes intensely focused on what she was doing. *I wonder what she will draw.*

"I know that you have my file," began Victoria. "I won't sit here and pretend to engage in this dance and tell you stuff that I know that you already know. I know how this works."

Thank you! Perfect! Hearing an angry, broken teen speak for the first time was like watching a birth; everything is new but it's a little scary at the same time. True to form, she was vying for control right from the start. He expected nothing less. *You're right. I know everything about you, Victoria. I know about your screwed up childhood and how you were abandoned by every birth relative on the planet. I know you like to fight and that you've been physically violent in every placement the system has put you in. I know you like to cut, and I know where you like to cut. I also know about your very high IQ. The only positive thing the file mentioned was that you had a natural talent for drawing. You're wounded. You're scared. But you are not going to show it. Not today, anyway.*

"So here's the deal," she said without looking up from her drawing. "I had crappy parents who did drugs and I went to live with relatives, who also did drugs. I left there and went to like a jillion foster homes and now I'm here at this stupid place. I don't need therapy and I'm not going to talk and I don't want to come back and see you. Oh, and yes, I've been to therapy before and it's stupid and it sucks, you people are all *wacko*."

"Okay," Cade responded.

Victoria slammed her pencil down and looked him in the eye for the first time.

"Okay?" she retorted, "What's THAT supposed to mean?"

"I heard you, and I'm glad you told me. I appreciate your honesty and I think that's a great place to start. I have read some of your file, but not all of it. I don't like to do that. But what I was looking for when I skimmed it was to find out what you like to do for fun, hobbies, you know? Stuff like that. Then I realize that they don't put the positive stuff like that in there, which bugs me. One day I'm going to start a file and chart system with only positive things like what ice cream someone likes or what happened on their best day ever."

Victoria looked down and said nothing. She kept drawing and now had both legs tucked underneath her. He remembered one of his professors encouraging him to pretend to be the client and to take on the client's body positions as a way to better understand him or her. He thought she looked like a wounded animal – trying to be as small as possible yet protecting herself from a possible attack. She had put the hood on, making her eyes invisible to him while still drawing.

She looks like a Benedictine monk. Cade smiled. "Look, I know that you don't want to be here, and that's okay. You don't even have to talk to me, either."

"How stupid is that?" Victoria snapped, sitting upright, looking him in the eye and whipping the hood off. The pencil in her right hand and drawing tablet in her left. "I mean, how can anything happen if I don't talk to you?"

"You don't have to talk to communicate," Cade said calmly. *I thought you weren't going to talk to me, remember?* "What I mean is that I am here to simply allow you to be in a safe place and if you *need* to talk and if you *want* to talk then you can; if not, I want you to know that I respect your silence. Many of the young people who come to see me have difficulty putting thoughts into words and I use all sorts of ways to communicate with them that doesn't involve talking back and forth."

"Like what?"

"Like play."

"Play?" She scoffed.

"I'll show you," said Cade, leaning forward. "What are you doing right now?"

"I'm drawing, duh!" Victoria snorted.

"Okay, and why are you drawing?"

"Because I like to." She paused. "Because it makes me feel good."

"Yes!" Cade said with exuberance. "You are relaxed and your spirit feels free, right?"

"I – I guess so," replied Victoria. "When I was a kid, we were too poor for toys but there was always paper and pencils laying around."

"Why did you start drawing?"

Victoria was quiet for a while. "One day when things were really bad, I just drew a picture of a beach that I wished I could go to. I literally threw myself into that drawing and worked and worked and suddenly the palm trees looked real. I was about four, I think. To make a little bit of money when I was in first grade, I charged classmates a dime to draw their portrait. For some reason, I was good at faces. It made the bad stuff go away."

It's been your coping mechanism all these years and probably saved your life. "Is this how you play?" asked Cade.

"Play?" Victoria smirked, her eyebrows shooting up to her blunt-cut bangs. "Sure, I guess." She paused as if rolling the word around in her mind, then smiled for real. "Yeah, I guess you could say that I'm playing when I draw."

Cade smiled. "And by the way, you're not thinking how terrible it is to be in here right now."

Victoria's smile vanished and she pretended to ignore him again. They sat in silence for the next few minutes. She sketched furiously while Cade stared out the window.

Finally Cade broke the silence.

"We only have few minutes left, Victoria," Cade said. "I want to thank you for coming and I appreciate you talking with me. Is there anything that you want to say before we stop?"

Victoria simply shook her head "no" and put a few finishing touches on the drawing. She held it out to study it one last time and then put the tablet face down on the couch and set the pencil next to it. She picked up the crumpled paper that was sitting beside her and put it in the front pocket of the hoodie; her left sleeve slid up as she put the paper in her pocket. Cade saw the scars and fresh cuts on her wrist; deep, savage slices that were a testament to her pain. She quickly pushed the sleeve back down and stood, looking out the window. *There is strength inside her. She looks like a warrior!* She glanced over at him, and for another brief moment, he saw in her eyes every bit of the pain and terror that she had experienced as well as the embedded rage that she carried with her wherever she went. *She's testing me. She wants to trust me but isn't so sure.* He did not look away, only held her gaze and waited. He smiled slightly and she looked away. *Your walls are coming down. A few bricks at a time.*

"Okay, let's go," Cade said, motioning her towards the door.

"Bye," Victoria said softly, walking towards the door.

"Goodbye Victoria. I'll see you next time," Cade said. He walked her to the waiting area where her case worker was waiting, and then headed back to the therapy room. He opened the door and thought about the exchanges, both verbal and non-verbal that he and Victoria had shared. Her body language was so closed off, angry, and defensive.

Fight or flight. It makes perfect sense.

Following the advice from Dr. Capstone, he laid on the couch like Victoria. He tucked himself into a ball, with his legs drawn underneath his body. He looked around the room, seeing it as she had, and imagined all the thoughts and feelings that probably coursed through her. He imagined having to fight from day one and ending up completely alone at age fourteen. He sat up, and felt something next to his leg. It was the tablet she had been drawing on. He turned it over, and sucked in a quick breath. There before him, was a pencil sketched portrait of himself that was so accurate it almost looked as though someone had traced a photograph. He sat stunned for several minutes on the couch unable to move. Underneath Cade's picture, written in heavy, dark Gothic lettering was one word: Faith.

....

"Do we really have to take him all the way, like the old lady said?" asked the soldier, spitting into the fire.

"The 'old lady' is the Wise Woman, Garrison, and you'd better show some respect. She can probably hear you right now," his companion glared.

The other soldiers murmured their agreement.

"Oh come on, we could die doing this you know. I've heard the wolves can kill you with their breath."

"Aye, and you'll probably be the first one to go!"

There was laughter all around and the clanking of tin cups.

"Well, I say we leave him as soon as we hit the Dead Lands. We'll tell her we did our best but the journey got too hard. Look how marshy this land is already – our horses will probably be dead in a week."

"I wish Roland was here so he could throw you in that swamp over there," remarked a large soldier named Stephen, standing up and approaching the man. "I'm actually thinking of doing it myself!"

"I'd like to see you try it, Stephen, come on then!" The soldier stood, threw down his cup, and put up his fists. "I think I need a little exercise, come to think of it."

"Aaaargh!" Stephen rushed forward and grabbed Garrison by the waist, hoisting him off his feet and then slammed him to the ground. Several soldiers intervened and pulled them apart.

The chief guard, Mikan, stepped forward towards both of the men. "Enough! It's bad enough we lost Roland, and that we must risk our lives to go to this God-forsaken land with this – this *thing*! Now, must we all kill ourselves before we even get to the Dead Lands? We are completing this quest, gentlemen, and even if we die in so doing, we *will* complete this quest! Now, either you're with us or against us, Garrison! Which is it?"

Garrison stared at the ground sheepishly. "I'm with you; I'm with all of you. Forgive my fear; I forgot the heart of my leader."

"Aye, you're forgiven," replied Mikan.

"Men?"

"Forgiven!" cried the soldiers.

"There you have it then, we be on our way. It's at least three days hard ride to reach the edge of the Dead Lands. The sooner we get there, the sooner we complete our quest. Move out!"

And so the band gathered their belongings and continued their journey towards the Dead Lands. The next three days were difficult. A cold rain pounded the caravan, which made their way muddy and bogged down the horses. The acrid stench of the Dead Lands reached their nostrils and the nostrils of the horses. It seared their eyes, making it nearly impossible to see. Everyone covered their noses and eyes, but the burning sensation became nearly unbearable. Slane cried continuously, and the woman assigned to care for him nearly fainted from the fatigue of trying to comfort him in the poisonous air. Mikan did his best to rally them and they pushed on another few miles. Ahead was the Great

Pit in the middle of the Dead Lands. They could hardly breathe and a few turned back; two horses had collapsed and the others that were left were frothing at the mouth, gasping for breath. Mikan finally told the members of the group to turn back; he and two other soldiers would go by foot the rest of the way. Taking Slane in his arms, he and the others began walking. They soon discovered that they could go no further. Their lungs were on fire, their eyes too seared from the gassy fumes. The great tree was at least two miles away and Mikan knew they would never make it. He looked one last time at Slane, who was just one month past his first birthday. The small boy appeared nearly dead. His crying had long ceased, his eyes bugged out of his skull with a faraway stare.

Using a jagged piece of rock, Mikan made a small dugout and laid Slane in it. He placed the water and the bread next to him. After a quick prayer, he and the other two soldiers turned to follow their comrades. They vowed to never tell anyone that they didn't make it to the tree. After all, Mikan said, there was no way Slane would survive even a few more hours in this hell. They didn't need to worry about keeping quiet, however. As the soldiers rushed to get back to the others, two wolves bore down on them before they reached their party and slaughtered them. The others waited only a short time before deciding that the three were lost forever. And they were right. Slane, who had lived in the care of strangers following the death of his mother, father, and grandfather, was now completely alone.

• •

Cade watched Pierce move the toy figures around the sandbox. Every now and then he could hear him speak out loud as he played forcefully with the soldiers. His actions were vigorous. *He's feeling intense emotions.*

"The soldiers have to take the baby somewhere," Cade said, giving Pierce reassurance that he was present.

Pierce did not acknowledge Cade's presence. This was Pierce's seventh session and he made eye contact with Cade at the beginning and end of the sessions but had yet to speak to him. Cade was getting reports from the staff around Boyd that Pierce was coming out of his shell. Although he did not speak to anyone other than Sarah, his caseworker, (and only did so in a whisper) he was engaging in group activities such as sitting at the table with his cottage mates for meals. His teacher remarked that he was doing his work and seemed more comfortable in the classroom. Cade shared with her that in another month a clinical psychologist was scheduled to conduct psychological testing with Pierce. He assured her that she would be informed of the results.

Pierce groaned loudly as he placed the small, plastic baby in a small hole in the sand. There were only three soldiers with the baby. Pierce had tossed the other members of the group out of the sandbox. Pierce moved the three soldiers away from the baby and then took two plastic dogs which attacked the soldiers, apparently killing them. Pierce threw the figures to the far corner of the sandbox. He returned to the baby and sat staring at it for nearly five minutes. *What does he see? The baby must be a representation of him.* Cade could see that the baby was now alone. The group had abandoned him for some reason. Pierce wore a pained, grieving look upon his face and Cade could see that the hair on his forehead was wet with sweat. The session was as intense as the day Pierce laid in the sand and cried.

....

Slane is alone. I am alone. I am left in the care of strangers after the death of my mother. She burned. She got all burned up. I have seen aloneness. It is the blackest of midnights, and it is the scariest terror one can imagine. Alone is like death and it can eat you like a cancer. I have felt alone most of my life. Even when my mom was with me she was always with someone else. I felt alone even when she was sitting right next to me. She loved Meth. More than me, so I was alone. I tried to get close to her, but she was like the wind. Like a shadow, she would appear and then vanish. She was like three or four different people. Why wasn't

I good enough for her? Just like Slane, people think I'm cursed. Slane became a burden, I am burden. I will write the story of Slane and in so doing I will write the story of me. It seems like Slane has no chance. I felt like I had no chance. I've been in the Dead Lands before, and it's really bad. Slane needs help. I need help.

7
RESCUED

Peter the Great Fox smelled something. It floated on the wind and caught his nostrils for only a brief moment. But it was something. He lifted his head. Every facet of his sense of smell was activated. The smell was gone. But just as he started to put his head down on his paws, he smelled it again. His hind legs readied themselves to stand. He waited. There it was again. He stood and took a step out of the mouth of his cave, his home for the last five years. The smell was coming from the Great Pit. Peter saw the fog rising from the boiling cauldron of slime. *At least today the stench isn't so bad.* Probably the reason he could detect the new smell in the first place. He scanned the skies for Cassius but did not see him. The odor came to him again, this time a bit stronger. He pointed his head towards the direction of the smell and strained his eyes as he looked over the landscape but saw nothing out of the ordinary. *Where was Cassius?* He searched the sky again but saw no sign of the Great Eagle. He decided to venture down towards the pit and follow the smell. There were no wolves about today. They had recently killed and would not be hunting for some time.

Peter ambled down the trail that led from the mouth of the cave. Carved by years of weathering and erosion, the trail was tricky to navigate. Peter's nimble feet had no trouble finding just the right places to step. He grinned when he thought of the clumsy and oversized wolves that often started up the trail to investigate his cave but turned back when the path became too treacherous. Wolves had power, but the foxes had agility and cunning. He paused for a moment to check the wind. The smell was getting stronger as he followed it. Peter was careful as he left the head of the trail and turned towards the Great Pit. While the wind gave him the assurance that the wolves had feasted on some type of flesh, Peter's instinct of carefulness heightened when he traversed these grounds. He looked again to the sky for Cassius but he was not there. Peter knew part of the reason that he moved so deftly around the wolves was because Cassius was a perfect scouting companion. He hoped Cassius showed up soon. It would be nice to have the help of his best friend, his eye in the sky.

Suddenly, Peter was startled by a rush of wind and commotion behind him and he whirled, teeth barred, ready to tear into a wolf. It was Cassius. Peter's feathered friend cackled with laughter at the sight of Peter's startled look and fur sticking out all over.

"That's not funny!" roared Peter, his heart nearly jumping out of his chest.

"Oh man, you should have seen yourself!" Cassius said, still laughing and trying to catch his breath. "I've been watching you for over five minutes, deciding what would be the best way to scare the fur off you and I did it!"

"For your information, I'm tracking something and I could have used your help half an hour ago!" exclaimed Peter, still perturbed, but starting to relax. "Bug on a Wart Hog! Sometimes you can scare me half to death!"

"Calm yourself, my red fuzzy friend. Life is bad enough here in this God-forsaken wilderness. The least we can do is laugh now and then."

"I wish I had your sense of humor, trust me. But someone has to keep a level head around here, otherwise we'd be Wolf food before sunset," Peter said, looking around again to make sure nothing was sneaking up on them.

"So what's this thing you've been tracking?" Cassius asked.

"I can't say for sure – it's a new smell though. Something I've never detected before." Peter raised his head and waited for the wind. There it was. He took a few more steps. "C'mon Flaps, follow me. We'll talk as we track."

Peter asked Cassius if he had seen anything strange that morning.

"Funny you should ask. I saw the remains of a wolf kill and I can't say for sure, but it looked like human parts."

"What?" Peter asked incredulously. "There haven't been humans here in years, at least not since we came."

"I know. I didn't go in for a closer look just in case wolves were lurking around, but from my aerial vantage point I'm pretty sure that's what I saw."

The scent was very strong now. Peter picked up his pace. Cassius took to the sky and noticed something in the distance. He turned back and hovered above Peter.

"There's something odd about a quarter-mile ahead," he called, looking down at Peter. "Just stay on the same course and you'll come to it. I'm going to take a look." With a flap of his wings, Cassius was gone.

Peter picked up his pace and tracked Cassius in the sky. He was sprinting now. He saw Cassius hovering over something and then landed. *What could it be?*

He arrived where Cassius had landed and burst through the spiny bushes that dotted the landscape on the edge of the Great Pit.

"Look!" cried Cassius, "It's a human baby!"

Peter did a double take. "That's im – im – possible?" He stammered. But Cassius was right. There before him was a human baby, dirty, but alive, arms stretching out towards the sky.

"How the Wolves didn't find him I'll never know," gasped Peter, approaching the baby cautiously.

"They made a kill of the humans that left the baby, so they probably didn't even bother to look."

"Cassius," Peter began slowly, "You don't suppose this is the 'quest' that we were told about when we were banished here, do you? The one that we were told would lead us out of here?"

Cassius, astonished, stared at Peter. "This could be it! Hey, look, there's some sort of paper wrapped around the bread. See what it says."

Peter moved closer to the bag and the baby reached out and touched his snout. He instinctively started to pull away but waited. The baby's hand rested there for nearly a minute. Peter sensed that the child was very weak. He nosed open the bag and found the paper that Cassius mentioned.

"To Whomever Finds This Child: His name is Slane. He has been banished from the Cities of Light. His Grandfather was a great warrior and leader. His mother was a sorceress gypsy with no family. His father was a dark man and drawn to evil. Slane was born under a great curse and therefore he has been placed here in order for the curse to be broken."

Peter looked at Cassius and whispered, "It is our quest! It has been revealed to us."

"I – I can't believe it. We are saved," said Cassius, quickly wrapping the blanket around Slane with his beak. "Come, quickly. We must get to the cave before the Wolves see or smell us."

Peter tossed the water and bread in the blanket and took the blanket in his mouth. He lifted Slane and as he did so one of the corners let loose, causing Slane to slip, nearly dumping him on the ground. Slane let out a cry.

"Careful!" Cassius exclaimed.

"I've got him!" Peter shot back. "It just slipped. There, now I've got it."

Peter and Cassius set out on the path back to the cave. Slane's cry was reduced to a whimper and now had stopped altogether. While he didn't want to scare the boy, Peter was relieved to hear Slane cry and to know that a good amount of life still stirred within him. The kid was tough. Toughness would be his only ticket out of the Dead Lands.

Cassius took to the sky to scout ahead and Peter settled in at an even trot, careful not to drop his precious cargo. They arrived at the cave without incident but Cassius told Peter that a band of Wolves had found the site where Slane had been left and would no doubt follow the scent to the cave. They both would need to take great care in keeping Slane safe until he would be old enough to fight. While the Wolves had never been able to reach the mouth of the cave because of the treacherous path, Peter knew that if they became desperate enough for human blood they might find a way. *Can't think about that now, we've got to keep this little guy alive.*

....

Slane has been rescued! The Fox and the Eagle are taking care of him. The Wolves are going to try and kill him but his friends will keep him safe. The Eagle can fly and the Fox is the smartest animal alive. I really like this mountain that is here in the playroom. It has a perfect cave. I wish I had a mountain with a cave where I could live. I would stay on my mountain and never come down. No one would know that I was there. If they did try to come on my mountain I would make a rock slide and kill them. I would make people think the mountain was haunted so they would stay away. Mountains are safe just like castles are safe. I am safe here. Slane is safe and he will grow. The Fox and Eagle will care for him and he will get really strong. He will learn to fight and hunt. Slane will be smart but no one knows it yet. I am smart but nobody knows it. I like it that way. Slane is safe in the cave. I am safe in here. I don't like to leave this place. Cade lets me do what I want and doesn't ask me questions. I don't like questions.

....

Pierce held a stuffed eagle high above his head. He turned and turned, circling his body and holding the eagle in his hand, his arms outstretched. Finally, the eagle dove down and landed right behind a stuffed fox that Pierce had gotten out of the bin of stuffed animals earlier that day. Pierce threw the fox in the air as if it had been startled. *Pierce is smiling! I'm so happy for him!* Pierce mumbled as the fox and eagle faced each other. Clearly, the two were talking but Cade could not make out what they were saying. Pierce moved them along in the sand, stopping every now and then to fly the eagle above the fox. The eagle landed a short distance from the fox in the sand where Pierce had placed the baby wrapped in a blanket. The fox soon joined the eagle and more dialogue took place. Cade saw Pierce put the baby in the fox's mouth. *Is the fox going to eat the baby? No, he is carrying the baby.* Pierce stopped the action every so often to fly the eagle around the area above the fox and the baby as if it was a lookout scout. Finally, he took the fox, eagle, and the baby to a mountain that he had moved out of the corner of the playroom and placed near the sandbox. Built out of chicken wire and paper machete, the mountain was part of some long-forgotten play that had never been thrown out. It had a small cave in the middle of it where Pierce placed the toys. Pierce then sat motionless on the floor, staring at the cave. *I wonder what he's thinking when he just sits and stares like that.*

8
GROWING PAINS

Slane continued to grow. At twelve years of age, he was as capable of surviving in the wild as a seasoned warrior. Peter and Cassius kept Slane safe and healthy, fed him, and taught him the art of survival. He tracked and killed prey deftly and became nearly invisible when danger approached. Peter taught him that stealth was more valuable than power. Cassius taught him to use his imagination to see from above and shift his perspective. Peter taught him to use his mind; Cassius taught him to use his might. Both came to love Slane and he loved them. Every night around the light of their fire, Peter and Cassius told Slane stories. They told Slane of the great lands that lay outside of the Dead Lands, and told him stories of great warriors from past ages. A strong desire grew in Slane to leave the Dead Lands and travel to the Cities of Light and become the leader of the people who lived there. Peter and Cassius began to notice a restlessness in Slane. He was venturing farther and farther from the cave and returning from hunts with bigger game. In the past few months Slane had fought and killed two Wolves. The skull of one of the beasts, huge and foreboding, hung on the wall of the cave. It's gaping, dead eye sockets and dagger-like fangs made Peter uncomfortable, but he knew that it was important for Slane to display his trophy. Slane was very proud of his kills; he repeated the stories of his exploits to Peter and Cassius each evening around the fire. His inner desire to explore and conquer was nearing unquenchable and he often quarreled with Peter and Cassius when they tried to warn him that he was not invincible. Their warnings did no good. It seemed as though Slane mastered a new skill with each month that passed. Peter and Cassius knew that he was destined to be a warrior.

Peter and Cassius decided that it was time to tell Slane their story and how they came to live in the Dead Lands. Slane was smart and since he was five years old had been asking questions like, "Why are there no other Eagles or Foxes that live here?" He surmised that his two friends were not living in the Dead Lands by choice, but neither Peter nor Cassius could decide the right time to tell him.

"We've got to tell him now," Peter said to Cassius after Slane left the cave to go on another hunt.

"I don't know if he's ready," cautioned Cassius. "If we tell him too soon he'll be ready to leave immediately and start the journey back to his homeland."

"And what's wrong with that?"

"At twelve years old? Just getting out of the Dead Lands will be challenging enough, not to mention what must be conquered once we reach the kingdom of his fathers."

"But, if we wait too long," said Peter, "he'll leave us anyway and we can't have him going off and getting himself killed." Peter walked to the edge of the cave and watched Slane saunter down the path. "The boy is wise and skilled beyond his years – I think he is ready."

Cassius sighed. "Oh, I guess you're right. Part of me just wants to shield him from what lies ahead, but I know that would probably only hurt him in the long run."

"I want to shield him also, Cassius. I have grown to love the boy and I see myself staying by his side for as long as he will have me."

"As do I, my friend. As do I."

And so they decided that they would tell Slane the story of how they came to live in the Dead Lands that evening.

"I'll let you do the talking," Cassius said, bowing his head.

"I'm way ahead of you, my feathered brother," replied Peter with a determined look.

"Is it one I've heard before?" asked Slane, excitedly. He was always ready for a new story. The fire crackled happily and the light created dancing shadows all around the cave.

"No, I'm afraid not," said Cassius. "And before we tell you this one, Slane, we want you to promise that after you hear it you will do exactly as we tell you. Understand?"

Slane looked into the eyes of his companions. They were serious. "Yes, I understand," he said reverently.

"Long ago, Cassius and I were human – as human as you are."

Slane's eyes widened. He tried to imagine his friends with a head and legs and arms. He shook his head.

Peter went on. "Yes, I know that it's hard to imagine, but it's true. We were turned into animals by a spell in order to escape execution."

"But how…why?!" exclaimed Slane. "Why would someone do that?"

"My boy, you have much to learn about the evil that lurks in this world," Cassius chuckled. "Go on Peter."

"Before we came to the Dead Lands we lived in a thriving kingdom called Kerrahn. It was the outermost city of the kingdom known as the Cities of Light. Kerrahn was ruled by a great man named Tiberius, who was very wealthy, wise, and kind. He adopted Cassius and I, our parents having died in a great fire when we were babies. He had no children of his own and decreed that we would be heirs to his fortune and rule the kingdom after his death. We were appointed princes, and given the best academic and military training. Tiberius favored us, but his wife the queen never accepted us as her adopted sons."

"Why?" asked Slane.

"We don't know," Cassius replied. "Perhaps it was because she was so bitter over not having any children of her own."

"Regardless," Peter continued. "We were given all the privileges of sons by Tiberius. Our days were spent in play, learning, and adventure. It was a glorious time, full of wonder and excitement. We wanted for nothing and travelled to all sorts of amazing places and saw many wonderful things. We were schooled by the finest professors, taught to hunt by the finest huntsmen, and shown how to display the grace and duty of princes by the finest dignitaries in the land. We were adored by the people in the kingdom and everywhere we went people welcomed us with open arms. We attended banquets, participated in sporting events, and were involved in important meetings with heads of state from around the kingdom."

"We were respected and honored everywhere we went," Cassius added, his eyes wistful.

"So how did things end up like this?" Slane asked, picking at his teeth with a piece of bone.

"Well," Peter went on, "as life seems to go, my boy, things that go up must come down. And that rang true for us. Tiberius suddenly became sick and died."

"Oh no!" Slane cried.

"Yes," Cassius interjected. "We were heartbroken."

"Beyond words," Peter said solemnly. "We believe that the queen's jealousy mounted as we became older and she longed for the power and money that the ruling position offered. We believe that she orchestrated his death."

"But how?" Slane asked, imagining the feeling of the great loss Peter and Cassius felt.

"Probably poisoned him," Cassius replied, "And paid off the doctors and other officials to not say anything."

"Regardless," Peter continued, "She was out for blood – our blood. As soon as Tiberius was in the ground she illegally ordered his will changed and framed us for his murder."

"But how?" Slane cried. "You were the rightful heirs!"

"True," Cassius said, "But the law stated that if it was found that the heir murdered the king, he was to be put to death and the throne passed to the next heir. In our case, since we both were being blamed for his death, everything – his crown and fortune – passed to the queen."

Slane threw the piece of bone into the fire. "It's not fair!" he yelled. His face felt hot. He staked around the fire and then sat back down.

"What happened next? Slane asked.

Peter looked down at his paws. "It was terrible," he said quietly. Slane looked at him and saw tears swimming in his magnificent eyes.

"We were dragged before the court," said Cassius. "She hired rich and powerful lawyers to destroy our reputation and threatened anyone who spoke out on our behalf. One by one those that we thought were our friends betrayed us and forgot us. We tried to reason with the queen. We begged her to remember our love for Tiberius; we assured her that we would care for her and provide anything that she wanted. But she would hear none of it. Her jealousy turned into black fury. We were stripped of all our possessions and rank and banished to the dungeon."

"The dungeon!" Slane exclaimed.

"Yes," said Peter. "A fate almost worse than death. In fact, we prayed for death in those days following our imprisonment. On the third day we were told we would be hung."

"Hung!" cried Slane, a chill raced down his spine as he thought of his friends having to die for a crime they didn't commit.

"Yes," said Cassius. "Death by hanging."

Peter went on. "On the evening of the day we received our sentence, the queen appeared in the dungeon. She told us she never loved us and hated her husband for adopting us. She told us we would be hung at noon the next day."

"What did you say to her?" asked Slane.

"I told her I would rather be hung and have my conscience clear than to live another minute in a kingdom where she was the ruler!" Cassius said, flapping his wings.

"What did she do?" Slane asked.

"She sneered at us and left the dungeon," Peter responded. "And we cried and felt great despair."

"How awful!" Slane exclaimed. "Did you try to escape?"

"We tried, trust me," replied Cassius. "But the queen posted extra guards that watched our every movement and our cell was searched twice each day. We were allowed no visitors which prevented us from getting any tools or supplies."

Peter went on. "It was a terrible feeling to know that in the morning we would die at the hands of a lying, evil woman. But our luck was about to change. That night we were awakened by one of the guards who said the queen had allowed a priest to visit us. The guard let the priest into our cell and we lit a small candle. The guard said we only had ten minutes to meet with the priest. As soon as the guard left the priest pulled back his hood and we both jumped back with surprise. This was no priest – it was a woman!"

Slane's eyes widened with amazement and he felt the hair stand up on the back of his neck. "Amazing!" He leaned forward. "Who was she?"

Cassius laughed. "Slow down, my boy, let Peter finish."

"Sorry. Go ahead, Peter."

"Well, she was beautiful with long dark hair and piercing black eyes. I recognized her instantly. Her name was Reborah and we had met some years earlier."

"How?" Slane asked incredulously.

"Well, one day while on a ride in the woods I heard screams and saw a woman cornered by a bear. I killed the bear with an arrow shot from my bow and saved her. She thanked me and told me her name was Reborah and that she had nowhere to go. As we walked, she told me her story. She said she had been banished from the kingdom. I never found out why, but she seemed very sad. She cried as she told me that because of her beauty, men found her irresistible and women hated her. She had been shunned by regular society and because she had the ability to tell the future and to give life to inanimate objects – for example, turn a mushroom into a toad – she was labeled a witch and banished from the kingdom. She had no family because they had all died in the great plague. She lived with an old woman at the edge of town who cared for her and taught her the ways of the Ancient."

"The Ancient?" Slane asked. His brow wrinkled.

"The Maker and Sustainer of all life," Cassius replied.

"Oh yeah, I've heard you guys mention Him before – like when we found the small pond of water underground until the rain came."

"Precisely," said Cassius. "Go on Peter."

"Well, the old woman was very kind and told her of a prophecy. Reborah said that the prophecy told of a Warrior King that would come and rule the Cities of Light after a very bad time. Reborah came to love the old woman, but she suddenly died, and Reborah was once again alone in the world. I knew of a village of gypsy folk many miles from the kingdom where I thought she would be safe so I took her there. I wished we could have spoken more but at this point in her story, we had reached the gypsy camp and I left her in their care. After that, I lost track of her."

"So, how did she find you in the dungeon?"

Peter continued, "When word of our predicament reached her, she wanted to repay my kindness for saving her that day. So, a band of her fellow gypsies traveled to the castle and she disguised herself as a priest. She told us that she could get us out of there."

"We both laughed at that one," Cassius said.

"Yes we did," replied Peter, who stood and stretched. "But she did not laugh. She said that our future had been revealed to her in a dream;

we would be called upon to complete a valiant quest by protecting someone, someone very special. She said that she could turn us into animals and that we would live in the animal world until the Quest was completed, and then we would turn back into our human forms. 'The Quest will find you and come to you,' she said. We heard the guards moving so we told her we had no choice but to believe her. She gave us each a small concoction of herbs and mushroom stems and told us to eat it in the morning as soon as we awoke. She said that I would become a fox, surefooted and smarter than any animal in the forest. She told Cassius that he would become an eagle, a hunter and protector of the skies. Together, we could outsmart and overpower any enemy that we encountered. As soon as she said this, she put the hood back over her head and the guard came and said it was time for the priest to leave."

"What would've happened if they caught her?" Slane asked, thinking of his two friends huddled in the dungeon and being helped by this beautiful woman.

"Her death would probably have been worse than ours," Cassius said as he stretched his wings.

Peter walked to the front of the cave and sniffed the air and then came and lay back down. Slane threw a few more sticks on the fire. Peter resumed the story.

"Neither of us slept anymore that night. At daybreak, we each ate the mixture that Reborah prepared for us."

"Did you feel anything happening then?" asked Slane, hanging on Peter's every word.

"No, in fact, I felt incredible despair and thought that this was all a bunch of hocus pocus," replied Cassius. "And it tasted terrible."

"I felt hopeless," said Peter. "But when you are facing death, you'll try anything in order to get out of it. The next morning we were taken to the gallows where a large crowd had gathered. The Queen wasn't there, of course. She was a coward. Our charges were read and we were ordered to step forward. At that moment I saw looks of surprise on the faces of those in the crowd and suddenly I noticed my body felt different. I glanced down and saw paws instead of hands and red fur covering my arms. I could see a snout in front of my eyes, and suddenly my senses were overwhelmingly keen. And I felt smart, really smart! like I could see things before they were going to happen. All my senses increased tenfold. As I glanced to my left, I saw Cassius sprout brown feathers with a beak, piercing eyes, and talons. With one quick flap, he was ten feet in the air, and then twenty. He called to me and told me to run, but I was already gone. I whipped through the crowd, headed for the outskirts of town."

"Whoa! That must have been a great sight!" roared Slane, rolling on his back. "I would love to have been there! What happened then?"

"It was remarkable and to this day I still can't put into words what if felt like to go from human to eagle," said Cassius. "One minute I'm stuck to the ground thinking I'm about to die, and the next, I'm flying as high as I want! And I instantly knew what to do. We knew we had to get out of there quickly and sure enough, the queen sent every able-bodied person to find us and kill us. But like Reborah said, working together made us a powerful team."

"Our skills matched perfectly," said Peter. "Cassius, with his excellent vision and flying ability could scout out the land ahead. And with my instinct and nimble feet, we quickly put several miles between us and our pursuers. We knew that the queen would send word throughout all the lands about us so our only place of refuge was the Dead Lands, where no humans dared to come. With our combined skills, we could easily survive against the Wolves. So, we came here."

"And found me," Slane said quietly.

"You came to us," Cassius reminded him.

"You are the Quest," said Peter, standing and staring deep into Slane's eyes. "And Reborah was your mother."

"Dr. Dalton?" a woman's voice called to Cade as he crossed the lawn to the Boyd Home administration building. He turned to see Mrs. Anderson, one of the elementary assistant principals. She was running and nearly out of breath.

"Yes, Mrs. Anderson, what can I help you with?"

"Well, I'm afraid I don't have good news about Pierce today."

Cade frowned. "Oh no, what happened?"

"Well," she said, trying to catch her breath, "He got into a tussle with another boy and beat him up pretty badly."

"What!?"

"Yes, I know. He had been doing so well. He'd always been sort of stand-offish towards other children, but today he just snapped."

"What did the other boy do?" Cade asked, defensively. "I mean, how did it start?" He was suddenly aware of his protective instinct towards Pierce.

"Well, you remember how I told you that Pierce is constantly writing stories?"

"Yes, he loves to read and write."

"Well, some of the other children have been teasing him. You know how children can be."

"Certainly, and I know that Pierce can appear to be a bit odd, especially to peers. But we're all weird in some way, don't you think?"

Mrs. Anderson ignored him. "Well, Joshua, one of Pierce's classmates, asked him what the story was about and, of course, Pierce didn't respond. He still doesn't talk to anyone. Scott, another boy grabbed the paper and began running with it and reading it aloud, and that's when Pierce went into action."

"What did Pierce do?"

"Well, by the time I got there he had bloodied Scott's face and punched another boy who tried to intervene. He told all the children that he would kill them one by one when they went to sleep and he would not rest until they were all dead. I'm not sure what scared them more – seeing him react violently or hearing his voice for the first time. Either way, the staff came and put Pierce in the detention room where he's been curled up ever since. He's not speaking to anyone, just like before. We thought you should know. Here's the story he was writing that Scott took from him."

"Thank you, Mrs. Anderson. If you could let the staff know that I'll be just a few minutes. I want to read this before I come to see him."

"Fine. If you ask me, I think all this fantasy stuff he's writing is part of the problem." Mrs. Anderson stalked off in a huff. Cade started to respond and then thought better of it.

Cade took the pages and walked to a bench and sat. He opened the papers and began to read. The story was about a warrior named Slane. *The baby. The fox, the eagle. The cave in the mountain. The Wolves. He's playing out the story! He's working through his issues through play and this is his story! He's healing! I can't believe I'm reading this. It all makes sense now! He's not talking to me, but yet he's saying so much through the play.* Cade re-read several parts of the story. The writing was extraordinary for a boy who was not yet ten. He couldn't wait to tell Dr. Capstone about this. *Dr. Cap is going to flip!*

Cade stood and made his way towards the school building that housed the detention room. It was a place Cade was all too familiar with. He hated it when one of "his kids" had to be disciplined for acting out. But it was also to be expected as it was part of the process of healing and growth. Thankfully, most of the staff at Boyd understood, but it took a long time and a great deal of training from Dr. Cap when he was the lead therapist, and now this responsibility fell to Cade. Cade also had to remind cottage staff and teachers that when a child who had suffered abuse and neglect acted out, it was the result of their new self emerging, a way of shedding the old self. The process could be ugly and uneven. Cade remembered Dr. Cap reminding students and staff of the general cognitive and emotional upheaval of all children, even those from stable, two-parent homes.

"Why should we be surprised when a child who has suffered abuse and neglect, like those who come to Boyd, act out, lose their temper, hit a peer or staff, etcetera?" Dr. Cap said in a staff training. "If the healing process is progressing correctly and a new 'self' is being put together while the old self is being shed, then there will be some tumultuous moments. Not that we should condone destructive acts by the child towards themselves or others, but we should approach them in a non-reactive, neutral manner. This lets them know that the relationship we have built with them is still intact and cannot be lost. The emphasis is placed on the behavior being undesirable, not the child. This gives the child the insight and energy to learn to control their emotions and behavior. The child who learns that love is conditional becomes a divided and broken self – it is the children who know that love cannot be lost who will explore, heal, grow, and conquer the world around them."

The detention room was not a torture chamber or a place of shaming. It was a safe, secluded place where an out-of-control child could be placed so that he or she could calm down and think. It had soft colors and chairs and a couch made of a soft, rubbery material. Cade approached the room and saw Pierce through the large glass windows that framed the room. The staff said that Pierce had calmed down once he entered the room but had been curled up on the couch and hadn't said anything. Cade thanked them for treating him with respect and entered the room. He quietly walked over to the couch and sat cross legged on the floor. He said nothing for a few minutes. Then he spoke softly.

"Hi Pierce. It's me, Cade. I know about what happened and I came as soon as I found out."

Pierce made no sound or movement.

"I want you to know that nothing will change about you coming to see me and you will be able to use the playroom just as before. You don't have to tell me anything about what happened until you are ready. It sounds like you got upset when someone took your private stuff. That's normal, and you must've felt scared and angry."

Pierce continued to sit in a ball on the couch with his arms covering his head. Cade wondered what he was thinking and if anything he was saying was reaching him. He thought back to Pierce's story. He felt comforted that Pierce was aware that his reactivity was due to the intense trauma and abandonment that he had suffered.

"I want you to know that I've got your story and that it's safe. Don't worry."

Pierce shifted in his seat and Cade saw an eyeball peeking at him through crossed arms. Cade summoned every ounce of kindness and empathy he had and focused on Pierce's eye.

"I'm with you in this. You are not alone."

Pierce's eye held Cade's gaze for a moment, then went back into hiding.

"One thing I need to know is that you aren't going to try to hurt anyone. You said some things that were very threatening and while I don't think you mean to carry them out, I need to be able to tell the staff that you're okay to be around the other kids. Do you understand?"

A muffled sound escaped from Pierce. "Yes," he said.

•••

I hate those kids. They took my story of Slane. They were making fun of it. I hope they all fall in a giant hole. I hope something terrible happens to them. The staff people keep trying to talk to me. They are so *stupid!* I am much smarter than they are. I hate them too. Can't they see I want to be *alone!?* They will probably put me in a dungeon. I hope they do. I probably won't get to go to Cade's room anymore. They will punish me. And it will be harsh. I have no family. Just like Slane. I am not going to move. I don't want to go to the Cottage. I don't want to go anywhere. I hate everything about this place. Except for the playroom. I hate it that my mom died. She *burned.* I saw her burn. I hate drugs. They stole my mom. Those people made her into someone she wasn't. My mom wasn't bad. Slane's mom wasn't bad, but people thought she was. People thought my mom was bad, but she wasn't. I wish I could escape this place. I *could* escape this place. I will go to a Mountain and live there forever. It will be *my* Mountain where no one else can come. I don't belong here. I don't belong anywhere. I don't fit. Slane didn't fit and he went away. Peter and Cassius found him. Cade found me. Cade lets me be me. He accepts me. I get to go to a different world in the playroom. I feel good when I play. I feel good when I get to tell the story of Slane. I will write Slane's story. I think Cade is good. Like Peter and Cassius are good.

Someone is coming. They opened the door. *I will not talk!* They are sitting on the floor. The only person who would do that is Cade. It *is* Cade. He's not mad at me. He said I will still get to go to the playroom! He wants to know if I will hurt anyone. I *want* to hurt those kids. They are the Wolves to me. I will find ways to outsmart them. I will not hurt them directly but I will outsmart them and let them hurt themselves. I will tell Cade that I won't hurt them.

·······································

Cade nearly jumped when he heard Pierce's small and pitiful "yes." It was the first verbal response that Pierce had ever given him. He fully expected the boy to stay in the ball all night and not speak.

"Do you want to go to the playroom for a while before you go back to the cottage, Pierce?" Cade asked quietly.

Pierce nodded his head "yes" and instantly stood up. He made no eye contact with Cade or the staff and followed Cade out of the room. Cade and Pierce stayed silent all the way to the playroom.

·······································

Slane stood at the mouth of the cave and looked out at the Dead

Lands. It was early morning and Peter and Cassius were still sleeping. He felt as though he barely slept. He pondered the story that Peter told the night before. His head felt thick and jumbled. He felt angry. At who or what he had no idea. He needed to walk. He slung his quiver of arrows over his shoulder and grabbed his bow. He set out on the path that led up to the cave; the cool morning air felt good on his body.

The details of last night's story churned in his mind. He imagined his mother, so beautiful and alone in the world. A deep painful ache throbbed in his heart. This was a new feeling and one that confused him. He had never met his mother or spoken with her. Yet, the sudden longing for her was like a hurricane that seemed like it would rip apart the very threads of his soul. What of his father? Peter and Cassius knew that part of the story also but when he asked about his father they said they would talk about him another time. He hated it when they did that! After all, he was twelve! He could hunt. He could kill things three times his size. He could handle whatever they had to tell him. It annoyed him when they acted like…well, *parents*.

He came to the bottom of the trail and turned towards the Great Pit. He hoped to find an animal for breakfast. His thoughts drifted back to Peter and Cassius being human. *What did they look like? Were they handsome?* They said they were princes and loved by everyone. The most bizarre part of the story was the fact that Peter and Cassius would one day be human again. How could that be? And how did his mother know about him? He felt his head start to swim again. He looked up at the sky to get his bearings. The sun had inched further up the horizon and he could feel its warmth on his face.

A slight rustle in the bushes pulled Slane out of his thoughts. He crouched low and peered into the brush. He saw a pheasant cornered amongst the tangled branches. An easy kill. He instinctively reached to pull an arrow out of his quiver when something stopped him: There was a look of terror in the pheasant's eyes, but Slane realized that it wasn't because of him. He looked deep into the eye of the pheasant and saw a dark shadow moving in the eye's reflection. It was something coming up behind Slane and he immediately laid himself flat on the ground. The dark shadow flew over him and crashed into the bushes where the pheasant was hiding. A Wolf! The pheasant screamed and flapped violently, which startled the Wolf who was so focused on Slane that it had not noticed the large bird. Slane pushed off the ground, whirling to face the beast, while at the same time whipping an arrow from the quiver to the bow with lightning speed.

The beast turned to face Slane, its red eyes glinted with the pulse of an ancient evil. Drips of yellow saliva hung on exposed fangs. Slane smelled the stench of the beast and felt the heat of its breath, even from eight feet away. He pulled his bow as taut as he could and aimed the tip of the arrow between the beast's eyes. "Now you are mine," he whispered. Suddenly, something slammed into his side and took his breath away. The last thing he saw was the arrow flying up into the air as his head smashed into the ground. A rush of wet warmth filled his side where he had been hit and he looked up to see the snarling fangs of a second Wolf. He had not seen it approaching and now it had him. Pain from the wound in his side crashed into his consciousness and he screamed while at the same time slamming his fist into the throat of the Wolf that stood above him. The blow stunned the Wolf long enough for Slane to roll out from underneath it, but just as he did the first Wolf leaped in and clamped its jaws deep into Slane's thigh. Slane screamed again and coiled his body away from the Wolf, reaching out to grab a rock and slamming it into the beast's head. The Wolf yelped and released its grip on Slane's leg, taking a chunk of flesh with it. Slane stood and faced both Wolves, shouting at the top of his lungs. He reached down and grabbed a stick, waving it in the faces of the two beasts, who inched closer and closer to him. He could feel the blood pouring from his wounds, and his head pounded. *I'm so dizzy.* He kept the stick pointed at the Wolves but his hands shook. *I think I'm going to die!*

Suddenly, out of the corner of his eye he saw a brown streak diving out of the sky. Cassius crashed into both Wolves with a force that knocked Slane backwards. He heard a sickening scream from both Wolves that pierced his ears and for an instant, Slane thought that Cassius was caught in their vicious jaws. Cassius thrust his claws at their heads and then the great bird leaped forward with a thrust of his wings, pulling his feet upward as he did so. Slane heard a ripping sound as the flesh of the Wolves' faces were torn off by the powerful talons. He saw the Wolves' faces dripping with blood, with eyeballs hanging by optic nerves. Cassius flung the bloodied mess and circled once more, his eyes glowing yellow as he zeroed in on his prey. Instead of aiming for the heads of the beasts, he instead tore into the backs of the Wolves, digging into their spines. More flesh, more fur, more blood. The Wolves howled in pain and rolled on the ground, then got up and ran. Stumbling blindly, they headed towards the Great Pit.

"Slane!" Peter cried, running towards him.

Slane's vision dimmed. "Oh Peter, forgive me! I didn't see them, I-I…"

"Don't talk, lie down. We've got to get you back to the cave, but first I have to stop this bleeding. Here, hold this against your side."

Slane reached over and held a piece of animal hide with his left hand. Peter tied it using his teeth and paws.

Cassius swooped down and dropped a flask of water next to Slane. Slane looked up.

"Cassius, my brother! I-I didn't see them, I'm so sorry!"

"Drink!" called Cassius. "I'm going to get raven weed; then I'll help you get to the cave!" And with a powerful flap, he was gone.

"Here, hold this as tight as you can," Peter said, clenching twine beneath his paws. "Press down firmly."

Slane pushed on the wound on his thigh. Drenched in pain, he leaned over and threw up.

"Drink as much of that water as you can, my boy. Drink!"

"I-I feel so weak," Slane said as he reached for the flask.

"Drink. Don't talk. Drink."

Cassius returned with the raven weed. Slane saw the blood stains on his claws, feet, and legs.

Slane wept. He felt ashamed for being so careless, yet so hopelessly relieved to be loved. In such barren wilderness where he had been left to die, two comrades who sacrificed their lives to protect him had come to help him.

"No time for tears, boy. Come, we must get you up the trail."

Peter and Cassius lifted Slane onto his feet and helped him hobble over to a makeshift sled that Slane had made to pull large amounts of supplies up the trail to the cave. He never dreamed that the contraption he built would play a role in saving his life. Cassius and Peter dragged the sled up the trail. Slane felt every rock and bump and nearly lost consciousness twice by the time the trio reached the mouth of the cave.

"I feel so cold," Slane told them.

"He's lost a lot of blood, Cassius."

"I'm more worried about infection spreading than that. Here, get him by the fire, Peter, and I'll get some more wood."

"We're going to need more raven-weed and meat."

"I'm on my way," said Cassius, dropping two logs on the fire. He paused to look at Slane, who was pale and weak. "Don't worry, my boy. We'll have you up and around in no time."

Slane gave him a feeble smile. He wasn't so sure. *Everything is going dark.*

•••

Upon arriving at the playroom, Pierce immediately moved the mountain next to the sandbox. He grabbed the soldier action figure and the eagle and fox. Cade knew from reading Pierce's story that the soldier was Slane, the eagle was Cassius, and the fox's name was Peter.

He placed the fox and the eagle in the cave and walked the soldier down to the sandbox. Every so often Pierce made Slane pause, as if the toy was thinking deeply. Pierce took two plastic hideous looking beasts that were part of a monster set and hid them in the sand behind the Slane. Suddenly, he took the beasts out of the sand and violently attacked the soldier. Slane tried to fight but the beasts were too powerful. *They've got the soldier cornered. What's going to happen?* Pierce jumped up and grabbed Cassius and slammed it into the beasts. *His play is violent today.* Cade found himself wincing at the intensity. Grunting and growling noises could be heard as Pierce played out the struggle. Pierce flung the beasts into the far corner of the sandbox. *The eagle saved the soldier. This is really intense! Slane the solider is wounded. The fox is helping him now. He's playing out the feelings from today. Attacked, hurt, and broken. But someone is helping him. Is that me?*

• •

Slane is wounded! The Wolves got him. Cassius fought them off – he was amazing! There was a lot of blood and Slane is hurting very much. His wounds are very deep and he may die. Cassius and Peter will take care of him but it is very serious. I was attacked too. Just like Slane. I don't want to go face those people but I know that I have to. I like playing. I like this story. I wish I could sit inside and write stories all day. Some people do. I don't want to go back to my cottage. I wish I could stay here. Someday I'll live somewhere where I can do whatever I want and be free. Someday.

9
ENLIGHTENMENT

"This is amazing," Dr. Capstone said as he read Pierce's story. He rubbed his chin as he re-read part of the story. "It's so detailed…names, places, and the background information."

"I was stunned when I read it. I knew you'd like it," said Cade, looking out the window at the courtyard below.

"It is remarkable how he picks up on emotions and paints dialogue, yet he appears so shut down in real life." Dr. Cap turned another page.

"This is the written account of all that he's been playing out. As I read it, it was like I was getting all the blanks filled in. It explains the soldier, the stuffed animals, the castle, everything. His cottage parents told me that after his sessions he goes to his room and writes furiously."

Dr. Capstone set the papers down and looked out the window. "This was the story that the other children were teasing him about?"

"Yes. Apparently they grabbed it and ran around reading it aloud. That's what set Pierce off. The kid definitely knows how to fight, that's for sure."

"I don't blame him," said Dr. Capstone. "I can see how this story represents his journey from a great pit of loss and rejection to finding himself. It's very private and intimate. You say that he's started talking to you?"

"Yes. Since the fight he's responded to questions and makes a bit more eye contact with me now. I think he trusts me."

"He most certainly does. Good job, Cade. You've built a foundation and created a wonderful opening for him to continue to grow and heal. Nicely done."

"Thank you, sir," said Cade smiling. "The only problem I have now is dealing with his teacher and some of the staff."

"What do you mean?"

"Well, you know how this goes. A kid who is actually healing and growing has an outburst and the staff forget that when a kid is developing a new self, he may not have the emotional or cognitive resources to handle new situations and emotions."

"Very true. I've battled that problem my whole career and it's one that I talked about a lot in class. Do you know what to do?"

"Well," Cade said, clearing his throat, "I guess it means I have to provide re-education for the staff."

"Yes, and please don't blame them. It's a natural part of our makeup to reject or avoid those human beings that we perceive as unpredictable and unable to control themselves. This is why much of society rejects young people. They scare the crap out of adults!"

Cade laughed and Dr. Cap went on.

"You are the one person who knows where Pierce is and what he needs. You are his advocate and voice to this outer world where people tend to see him as an object. You see him as a person, and not just a person, but a growing self that is pretty fragile right now. Just like a baby that needs special care – that's the state he's in right now. Your role is to educate those around him so that their caring, nurturing instinct will kick in, instead of a predatory, rejecting instinct."

Cade was quiet, letting Dr. Cap's words sink in. He thought of the metaphor of Pierce's new emerging self being like a newborn infant. Fragile. Small. Unknowing. He thought of the many children with whom he worked in the past in the same predicament. He thought of all the children out in the world who never got a chance to heal and grow – the ones whose selves hung suspended in space and time. *These are the kids who stay in survival mode their whole lives, and many go on to perpetuate the cycle of abuse and violence.*

"Do you think this will be a setback for Pierce, getting into the fight and all?" asked Cade, pulling himself out of his thoughts.

"It could." Dr. Cap turned in his chair to face Cade. "There's always the possibility of that. But from what you told me about the session that happened before you took him back to his cottage, it seems as though the playroom is his safe place, and as long as he can keep going there I think he will continue to progress."

"Anything you think I should do that I'm not doing?"

"See if you can join the play."

"Really? But isn't there a danger that I'll be forcing myself into his world?" *I don't want to lose Pierce's trust! He's making so much progress.*

"I don't think so. You'll be waiting until he invites you anyway. He trusts you and I think it may help him to attempt to verbalize who the characters are and sort of introduce them to you. In fact, I think he wants to but doesn't know how."

"What makes you think that?"

"Just a hunch," said Dr. Cap with a wink. "You know, that wise old sage type stuff. Just a hunch, that's all."

Cade spent the rest of the evening thinking about Dr. Capstone's advice. *I trust him completely and I know he'd never advise something that would potentially jeopardize my relationship with a kid.*

• •

Slane's wounds were healing. He felt stronger. Peter and Cassius proved to be good caretakers. Peter saw to the changing and dressing of the wounds while Cassius took charge of catching food and finding rare herbs that helped speed Slane's recovery. Because Slane could not move and there was not much else to do, Peter and Cassius told Slane stories – stories of their youth, exploits, and the dreams they had when they were Slane's age. Slane was full of questions about his mother and the story he heard before the attack. He also wanted to know about his father and other family members.

"What do you know of my father and grandfather?" Slane asked his comrades one morning after breakfast.

Peter and Cassius looked at each other.

"Well," Peter began as he stared out at the mouth of the cave, "Your father was drawn to evil, while your grandfather was drawn to good."

"So they were, like, opposites?"

"Let me tell you the story, Slane," Peter began. He looked at Cassius. "Here is what we know." Peter told Slane everything, from how great and beloved Roland was to how Sean was determined to destroy him and the Cities of Light. He told Slane about the great battle and the death of the two men. Slane listened intently. When Peter finished he was silent for several minutes then he spoke.

"Did you two know Roland?"

"We knew of him," Cassius answered. "We never met him, but we hoped to. We heard great stories of him from Tiberius."

"He died around the time that our trouble with the Queen began," Peter added.

"Who reigned after Roland?" asked Slane.

"Well," said Cassius, "The Queen took over all of the kingdom eventually."

"What?" exclaimed Slane.

"We know this from a tattered pamphlet that Cassius found in some of the belongings left behind by a group of outcasts," said Peter.

"He's right," said Cassius. "It was some sort of decree that all the Cities of Light were under her rule. That's all we know."

"Who were the outcasts?" asked Slane. "Do you think they were part of my father's men? I wonder if they were looking for me."

"It appears they were," said Cassius, ruffling his feathers. "I saw their fire in the distance on one of my night flights and went to get a closer look. I hid in the bushes near them. I heard them talking about your father, and it seemed as though they were his comrades."

Slane looked up at the ceiling of the cave. "What did they say?"

"They were looking for you," said Cassius. "Apparently they heard the story of how the Wise Woman ordered you to be banished and came here looking for you. I think they thought you were killed because they found the remains of the soldiers that had been eaten by the Wolves."

"So they went away?" Slane looked worried.

"I watched them pack up and move on and I haven't seen anyone since. That was years ago, about a month after we found you."

"Cassius made regular searches for outsiders for nearly four straight years after that," said Peter. "But we never saw any other travelers or suspicious characters. That's the good thing about living in a place like this. No one will come to bother you."

It was quiet for a few minutes until Slane broke the silence. "How can a father be good and a son be bad?"

"The same way that something that can help you can also hurt you if used in the wrong way," replied Peter.

Slane looked puzzled.

"We all carry within us the power to do good and to do evil, Slane. That's why even the vilest being may do something good at some point in their lifetime."

"Where does evil come from?" asked Slane, after thinking for a moment.

"Evil has always been here," replied Cassius. "Like Peter said, each person makes choices. And we all have the capacity to choose to do evil or good."

"But what makes a person choose either evil or good? What's the *thing* that makes that happen?"

Peter stood and stretched and then yawned. Slane watched his mouth widen and noticed the rows of perfect white razor-sharp teeth. "There is the matter of the spirit, the will, and life's circumstances. For some, there is a *bent*, a *yearning* to travel away from goodness and the virtuous path. Perhaps they seek excitement. Perhaps they feel more alive to be going *against* those that have attempted to guide them. Whatever it is, people must come to terms with that part of themselves and decide what course their lives will take. The spirit, that deep part that is in all living things and comes from the Creator of all life, can be nurtured towards or away from a good path. Life circumstances, things that happen to us that no one can control, also play a part in determining how a person will behave."

"I guess I'm worried," Slane said, lifting himself up on an elbow. "I mean, if my grandfather and mother were good, and my father was bad, what will I be? Is it true that I have both bloods in me, and if so, what can I do about it?"

"That's what Peter is trying to tell you, Slane," said Cassius, who was good at breaking down Peter's heady philosophies into understandable thoughts. "You have proven yourself to be honorable, loyal, and a devoted friend."

"Yeah, but I also get mad at you guys and was ready to leave you when I got the idea into my head!" Slane interrupted. "In that moment, I didn't give a hoot about either of you, despite the fact that I owe my life to you." Slane bent down and put his head in his hands and began to sob. His body heaved. Peter and Cassius looked at each other.

Cassius smiled and leaned toward Slane, placing a wing over his head and back. "There, there, my boy. Let it out, yes, that's a good one."

Slane continued to sob.

Peter and Cassius said nothing.

When Slane's sobs subsided, Cassius continued. "You have shown that the good inside you is greater than whatever evil may lurk there.

When you left the cave angry that morning it was your immaturity and selfishness getting the better of you, which is far different than a pattern of behavior."

"What are you afraid of, Slane?" Peter asked.

Slane wiped his nose with his sleeve and took a deep breath.

"I'm afraid…I'm afraid that I'm going to turn evil like my dad and when I do, there won't be any coming back."

....

Slane has good and bad in him. I have good and bad in me. He is worried; I am worried. Sometimes when kids mess with me I want to kill them and punish their souls forever. I want them punished beyond death. I want them to hurt forever. Sometimes when I see a kid that's sad and has been hurt like me I want to sprout wings like Cassius and swoop down and save them. Taking them away to a safe happy place. That's the good in me. Slane is a afraid that the evil will win, that there will be no coming back. I feel the same way. Like mom, she couldn't come back from the bad people, from the bad drugs. Not even for me. Not even when I needed her. What if that happens to me? I feel so alone. I see Cade. He lets me play and he tells the story of what is going on as I play. I want him to play with me. He could be in charge of Cassius and Peter. Then I could be Slane. I could be Slane the whole time, all the time. I think I will ask him.

....

Pierce sat in the sandbox with his knees pulled up and put his head down. He looked like a human hedgehog. This session was spent with whispered dialogue between the stuffed fox and eagle and the soldier. It appeared that the soldier was still wounded and unable to move and was being cared for by the animals. Cade verbally tracked some of Pierce's behaviors in the play and noticed that just as Dr. Cap has suspected, Pierce seemed increasingly comfortable with Cade's monologue of his play. Pierce and Cade both sat in silence. *I need to get into the play like Dr. Cap said, but how?* Cade waited for some sort of movement, a sign that something else was going to happen. He looked out the window and watched the branches of the big oak sway with the wind, losing himself in thought. After a few minutes his mind returned to the present and he looked over at Pierce. He was surprised to see Cade staring directly at him. Pierce swallowed.

"I really like the story," Cade said.

Pierce continued to stare at Cade. Cade smiled warmly.

"What's the name of the eagle?" asked Cade.

"Cassius," said Pierce.

"And the fox?"

"Peter."

"I see. Cassius and Peter," said Cade, keeping his voice low and even. "They are protectors and take care of the soldier."

Pierce nodded.

"Slane is the name of the soldier, right?"

"Yes."

"You seemed excited to see him when you first came here."

"I had a soldier just like him when I was young. He looks exactly the same."

"You wrote about Slane in your story that I read."

Pierce nodded.

Cade sat and said nothing. He looked at the clock. Five minutes left. He expected that the session would end this way like it had so many times, with Cade walking Pierce back to his cottage in silence. Then he heard Pierce's distinct voice.

"Mr. Cade?"

"Yes, Pierce."

"Next time will you play with me? Like you could be one of the animals and I could be Slane."

"I would love to, Pierce," Cade said, his heart pounding. "You'll just have to tell me the story and tell me what to do and I'll do it."

"Okay, I can do that," Pierce said as he stood and brushed the sand from his jeans.

"You know, you are a very good writer," Cade said as they walked to the door.

"I know."

10
RELATIONSHIP

When Cade arrived at the playroom the next morning, he found a sealed brown envelope that had been slipped under the door. It contained the results of Pierce's psychological testing. Cade set it on the desk and walked over and opened the blinds, allowing streams of sunlight to dance on the floor and walls. Cade felt the energy of the light pulsing through him. He was curious to see what the testing revealed. Dr. Gilbert, the clinical psychologist who conducted the testing was someone that Cade respected very much. She was good with kids and built a relationship with them prior to doing the testing. Since many of the young people Cade worked with had suffered significant trauma, it was important for the child to feel safe and as relaxed as possible to yield the best results.

Cade took a breath and opened the envelope. He pulled out a stapled document of about twenty-five pages. The opening page contained a brief letter from Dr. Gilbert: *Thank you for the opportunity to administer the tests to Pierce...* the last few sentences of the paragraph caught Cade's eye and he re-read them over a few times.

I have never seen an IQ this high nor have I ever encountered a child with such a dichotomous nature. On the one hand, it appears as though Pierce is shut down, and the various autistic traits that were flagged support this. On the other hand, it appears as though there are fountains of creativity that have been locked away. Certainly the play therapy with the emphasis on resolving trauma will be most helpful. Please keep me updated on Pierce's progress as I have never encountered such an amazing child.

Yours,

Dr. Gilbert

Cade turned the page. He began with the IQ section and was stunned at the numbers he saw. He shook his head as he imagined Pierce trying to navigate the world with a mind that operated at such a high level. There was no indication of processing problems or attention deficit problems, in fact, there was an indication that Pierce took in such a great amount of information that at times it was probably too difficult to process so much. There was a section where Pierce was instructed to complete several drawings such as a person, a family, a tree, and a house. The drawings appeared as though a preschooler had drawn them. The people had strangely shaped heads with no facial features and appeared to float above the ground. They also lacked clearly distinguishable limbs. For example, one appeared to be a blob for a body and head and only had one arm. The trees looked like sticks with strands of string for branches. Each trunk had a large hole drawn in a heavy black circle. The house looked especially ominous with large windows but no door. It appeared to stare out at Cade with two big empty eye sockets and seemed as though it wanted to scream but had no mouth with which to release it. The house floated above the bottom of the paper, tethered to nothing. It baffled Cade to see images so devoid of creativity; yet Pierce's writing sprang to life with huge amounts of detail. *Gosh – based on these drawings it looks like he's been severely traumatized and abandoned. No wonder he has a hard time understanding others.*

Reading further, Cade found the section where Dr. Gilbert highlighted several traits of autism in Pierce's profile. She did not make a formal diagnosis due to the significant amounts of trauma that needed to be resolved, as the trauma clouded the picture of what was clearly going on. Cade agreed. *Time will tell. Resolve the trauma issues first, and then see what else is there.* Cade scanned down to Pierce's answers from the Sentence Completion section.

My best memory is: "Getting ice cream with my mom."

My best friend's name is: "Myself."

I hate it when: "People look at me."

The safest place: "Is the place where I get to play."

My mom: "Got burned up."

My dad: "Is dead."

I'm afraid of: "Being evil."

I wish: "I never had to go to school again."

People: "Are not as smart as me."

Cade smiled. *The safest place...the place I get to play.* Cade thumbed through the rest of the psychological report. It ended with the recommendations for therapy: *Play therapy should continue to resolve the trauma issues.* The prognosis for Pierce was positive should the therapy continue. Cade put the report down and looked out the window.

What will become of you, Slane? Will you carry Pierce to where he needs to go?

···

Slane was feeling better and could walk without assistance. Just about the time he thought he was going crazy from having to rest, his body rewarded him with strength and vigor that matched his mind's youthful exuberance. Cassius and Peter were the best of nurses, but they were just as ready for him to be able to get up and move. Everyone had a case of the stir-crazies. One day after finishing his meal, Slane thought it would be funny to throw some of his leftover scraps at Cassius who was taking his afternoon nap. Cassius was tucked and fluffed with his big white head laid back behind his wing, and Slane waited until could see the one visible big yellow eye close tightly. He took a small piece of bone in his left hand and tossed it, landing it perfectly on the broad brown back of the sleeping bird. Cassius jolted awake, pulling his head from its resting place and staring wide eyed around him. Slane muffled his laughter and quickly looked down, pretending to be drawing in the sand. Again Cassius found his sleeping position and Slane whipped another bone fragment. *Bonk!* It landed perfectly on the back of the winged giant and again Cassius fluffed and flew awake, ready to tear into an intruder. This time Slane could not hold in his laughter and looked up to see a deadly stare and a huge talon resting on his knee.

"Tell me, young blood," began Cassius. "Are you interested in walking again?"

Slane felt the razor sharp talon dig ever so slightly into the flesh surrounding his kneecap. He looked up at Cassius with an impish grin but Cassius was as hard as a rock, never changing his expression. He finally released his grip on Slane's knee.

"Let's have no more of that. I would hate to have to rip you to shreds to teach you a lesson about respecting the sanctuary of sleep of your elders," Cassius said while he walked back to his perch.

Slane sulked. "Nobody has any fun around here," he said, but no one was listening. He looked over at Peter who was sleeping in the corner. He was lying on his back with his tongue lolling out. Every now and then his front paws would twitch. Slane thought about trying to toss a pebble into Peter's half open mouth, but then decided not to. More lectures from the Brothers Grimm, no doubt. He was annoyed with the both of them. He was ready to move and get out of this cave!

Slane's physical strength returned at a steady pace, but his emotional and mental recovery took longer. He experienced terrible nightmares and flashbacks about the wolf attacks. But there was more, much more. Visions of two men fighting to the death often appeared in his dreams. The faces were blurred, but Slane knew that it was his grandfather and father: Roland and Sean, good versus evil. The two faced each other and looked like two snarling animals as they circled, waiting for the right moment to move in and strike. They did not notice Slane sitting off to the side, but he could hear what they were saying. They were talking about him.

"You will *not* have the boy!" Roland bellowed, slashing his sword towards Slane's father.

"You are weak, old man!" cried Sean, blocking the blow and swiping at Roland's legs with his heavy blade.

"The boy must be protected from you, lest you corrupt him with your destructive ways!" Roland lunged and the edge of his sword sliced into Sean's arm. Blood ran freely. Slane stood up and cried out. "Father!" Neither man turned to look at him.

Sean, surprised at the old man's deftness, looked at the wound and then back to Roland. He laughed mockingly.

"Oh the Great Roland has struck me! Oh my, I think I shall die now. Let the world know that I am going to die!" Sean yelled, dancing a little jig. Slane covered his eyes. Suddenly, Sean screamed and ran at Roland with his sword moving at lightning speed, cutting through the air with a *swoosh* sound followed by a hissing *zzzzzz* at each stroke. Slane peeked through his fingers just in time to see Sean slam his elbow like a battering ram into Roland, who fell back and the old great warrior went down. Roland covered his eyes with his hand to shield them from the sun.

"So you have me now, and what will you do?" Roland asked, his breathing hard and uneven. "What does killing me get you? Do you think you will find Slane and own him? Do you believe that you could make him love you? Look at you! Strong but without honor; skillful with a sword, but with a mind that lacks depth or truth."

Sean stepped forward. "Silence, old man. Accept your death with honor. Now is the time for you to die." Slane watched in horror as Sean lifted his blade and thrust downward towards Roland's neck with frightening speed. Just as Slane was about to cry out, he awoke.

He never saw the actual deaths in his dream. He always woke up right at that moment. The visions always had the battle theme, but sometimes Roland bested Sean and was in the position to kill him. Sometimes the battles seemed to last for hours until finally one of the two prevailed. Either way, Slane experienced the visions nearly every night and was bothered by them for a few hours after he awoke. Cassius and Peter witnessed Slane's violent dreams and asked him what they were about. Slane had not told them yet about the theme of his father and grandfather in the dreams, he simply said they were about the wolf attack and that was that. This explanation made sense to the pair and they did not inquire further. Slane thought he would eventually tell Peter and Cassius the truth, but for now he wanted to mull it over. What did the dreams mean? *Is this the good and evil fighting within me?* Peter had once shared with him to pay attention to dreams. "That's how the light finds us when we are in the midst of a great darkness." If this was light leading Slane somewhere, he did not want to follow it.

Last night, the dream was bloodier and more violent. The grunts from both men and the sound of ripping flesh echoed in Slane's ears as he remembered the detail of the dream. Limbs were chopped off and grew back again, and then were chopped off again. Blood flowed from wounds and gathered on the ground, creating shiny pools of glistening gore. Slane remembered his blood that poured out of his leg from the wolf attack and shivered.

"What's on your mind, ole chap?" Peter asked, up from his nap and scratching behind his ear. "Looks like you're doing some heavy-duty thinking."

Slane knew there was no way that he could fool Peter. In a way it made Slane feel good that someone was watching, that someone knew.

"Actually, there's something I need to talk to you about."

Peter shifted his position and turned directly towards Slane. His blue eyes were full of wisdom and love. Slane felt a sense of peace come over him.

"What is it, Slane?"

"Well, I've been having these dreams, actually visions, I guess. They are very real, like so real I can smell stuff and the images stay with me all day."

"Vivid."

"Yeah, like that." Slane sat up and tucked his knees to his chest.

"When did you start having them?" Peter asked.

"About a month ago, I think. It was around the time that I started walking again and us talking about getting out of the Dead Lands. It was around then."

"Whom and what do you see in your visions? Describe them to me."

Slane glanced up and met Peter's gaze. "My grandfather and father. They are always fighting. To the death. One of them always dies. I wake up before I actually see one of them killed, but I know it's going to happen." Slane shivered and looked down. "It's really bloody with lots of detail, like flesh tearing and tendons hanging out. You told me to pay attention to my dreams. You said that they would lead me towards some kind of wisdom, but I really don't know what this is about. I mostly feel really freaked out."

Peter stood and walked to the front of the cave. He sniffed the air and turned back towards Slane. He sat.

"You're not a child anymore, Slane," Peter began. He took a deep breath and looked deep into Slane's eyes. "Soon we will be leaving this place. You are nearly recovered and together, you and Cassius and I, we will face the obstacles that stand in our way and get you back to your homeland. It is our quest, the quest we were born to complete. We will restore you to the throne of your grandfather."

Slane's only response was a confused expression.

"I know, I know, but what about your dreams," Peter quickly responded. "Remember when you told Cassius and I about how you were afraid of having both an evil side and a good side?"

Slane nodded.

"Remember how we told you that all men possess such dual traits, and that despite your father's bent for evil that he too came from good?"

"Yes, I remember that."

"Yes. Well, wisdom is cultivated through insight, but that takes some time. Much like the soil is readied before the crop can sprout, our internal mind and spirit must be ready to take our insight and observations before they can be born into wisdom."

"I don't understand."

"Your dreams are proof that your spirit and mind are trying to make sense of all that you know."

"But these dreams are horrible!"

"Yes, that is for sure. Think about your worst fear regarding your father. What is it?"

"That I will be overcome by the desire to hurt people and do evil things and that there really is a curse and that I have no control over it!" Slane burst into a sob and placed his head down between his knees. Peter stood and nudged his body against Slane.

"Yes, but what character, what figure stands as proof that your fear won't happen, or at least will block it from happening?"

"Roland, my grandfather."

"Yes!" Peter shifted his position and stood in front of Slane. "There, you see? Your worst fear emerges and then it is struck down by other facts that you know. This is the great battle and it is made manifest in your dreams where you are trying to work this out."

"I want the dreams to stop!" Slane wiped his nose on his sleeve and then stared at the shiny trail of snot. It reminded him of a slug's trail of slime that shimmered in the early morning sun.

"Who do you want to win?"

"What?"

"Which one do you want to win, your father or grandfather?"

"I don't know," Slane responded with a worried look on his face.

"I think that your dreams will end when you figure out which one you really want to live."

Slane stared at Peter and said nothing.

"C'mon, let's go for a walk. We need some air," said Peter as he stood and headed for the mouth of the cave. Slane followed him.

They stood at the mouth of the cave and Slane felt a surge of energy as the sun hit him full on. The two of them waited a moment for their eyes to adjust to the brightness.

"I'm stronger now," Slane said as the two walked down the path on the side of the mountain.

"Yes, you are."

"I think I'm ready for us to get out of here."

"I know that you are," Peter said as he nimbly stepped over a rotten branch that had fallen from an old pine.

"So what are we waiting for?"

"Good question."

Slane felt annoyed. He hated how Peter could kept him at arm's length with his Mr. Wise Man answers. He kicked a rock. "Okay, so *when* are we leaving? A week, a month, a year?" Slane's voice ended in a frenetic whine. He felt foolish as he heard his voice trail off and echo in the nearby canyon.

Peter paused as if allowing the feeling of foolishness to sink in. "We must plan this very carefully, Slane. We'll need food and water and we'll need to stay hidden from the roving packs of wolves. It will be no small thing to escape from the Dead Lands."

Slane did indeed feel foolish. "I didn't think of all that."

"Tell you what, tonight around the fire you, Cassius, and I will talk about our plan and what we need to do. How's that?"

Slane nodded his head. "Okay. And I think once we get out of here those dreams will stop. At least I hope so."

"So do I," said Peter as he nudged his body against Slane's hip. Slane draped his arm over Peter's thick auburn fur and felt a great sense of hope. *It's really happening! We are going to be leaving the Dead Lands!*

· ·

"The soldier is hurt. Slane got hurt by a wolf." Pierce looked up at him. Cade sat at the edge of the sandbox watching Pierce with the soldier, the fox, and the eagle nearby.

"But he's getting better, isn't he? Getting his strength back and moving around?"

Pierce nodded.

"That's good. It feels good to feel better and be able to move around," Cade said as he searched for the right words to reflect Pierce's play.

Pierce looked down at the soldier.

"Slane's friends are Peter and Cassius," said Cade. "They are loyal and brave."

"Peter and Slane have been talking," said Cade.

Pierce nodded. He looked shyly at Cade.

"It's time for them to leave the Dead Lands," he said softly. "Slane is stronger and now they are talking about finally getting out of this place."

"They are finally leaving," Cade said, matching the softness of Pierce's reply. *He responded to me! A breakthrough!*

"It will be hard for them," said Cade.

"Yeah, it will be really hard." Pierce sighed and looked out the window at the big oak. "Everything is hard in this place."

The two sat still for a few minutes.

"I want you to be Cassius the Eagle," Pierce said.

"Okay, I will be Cassius the Eagle," Cade replied. "You'll have to tell me what I need to make him do."

"I will. Next time I come here they will be leaving the Dead Lands and I'll need your help to fly Cassius around overhead looking for danger."

"Okay," Cade said, looking down at Pierce. "I know from reading your story that Cassius is wise and very serious."

"Well, Peter is the serious one but Cassius is a fierce fighter."

"Okay. I will remember that."

"Cassius goofs around sometimes, but not too much," Pierce said, pushing some sand around with his shoe into a tiny pile. I'll let you read more of the story and you'll know what to say and do with him."

"Sounds good to me."

The two sat still. Pierce broke the silence.

"Hey, Dr. Cade?"

"Yes, Pierce?"

"Thanks for not ever asking me questions. I hate questions."

"You're welcome and don't worry, I hate questions too."

11
EXODUS BY MOONLIGHT

Slane stared at the moon. It was nearly full. Approaching clouds would soon blot it out. Peter said he could smell rain coming and it would probably rain all night and into the morning. The moon seemed to stare back at Slane as if he was supposed to ask it a question. Slane imagined the thousands of years in which the moon had watched over the earth. He thought of all the people since the beginning of time, from all walks of life, staring up at the great white orb seeking some sort of solace or answers just like Slane did now. The thought both comforted and haunted him. The light of a full moon had brought him comfort from the time he was little. And hope. Just like now. The swirling clouds reached around the moon and covered it. It shone for a few more moments and lit up the clouds, sending out rays of moonlight through the clouds. Slane marveled at how beautiful this desolate land could be. It would be the last time he witnessed this picturesque enigma. Off in the distance he could see lightning flashing across a huge thunderhead. He smiled. Peter's weather predicting ability was still perfect.

"Are you going to stare at the sky all night, or are you going to help me?" Peter's gruff voice yanked Slane back into reality.

"Sorry, Peter," Slane said, feeling foolish. "It's just so beautiful. I was just taking one last look."

"Yes, it is an incredible sight," said Peter after he put down the pack that he was holding in his mouth and joined Pierce. "Now that we're leaving, I'm so ready to go that I have forgotten my own advice to stop and notice the beauty around us."

"You're right about the rain," said Slane as lightning ripped again through a distant thunderhead.

"Ah yes, I think that will actually help us but it won't make walking easy. You sure you're up to it?"

"I can do it, don't worry," Slane said without hesitation. He was more than eager to test his body.

"Glad to hear it," Peter said, nodding his head. "As we near the center of the Dead Lands the rain will have turned the ash into a thick muck. But it will keep the wolves away and that's what we need. If we can make a good start tonight we can put a good deal of distance between us and them. Have you seen Cassius?"

"No, he left about an hour ago to go scout." The moonlight broke through for a moment.

"He'll be back soon," Peter reassured Slane. "I'm glad the storms are holding off and the moon is giving so much light. Here, help me with the pack Slane. As smart as I am I still can't figure out a way to tie leather with these paws."

They both laughed. As Slane tied the ends of the pack together with rawhide he heard the hissing of wind and a rustle of wings and turned to see Cassius land just a short distance from himself and Peter.

"Whew, you know I'm sort of going to miss flying into this old cave," Cassius said as he gave his wings a shake and settled them into place. "So what are you guys up to?"

"Just getting the last of our supplies packed up," replied Peter. "We're ready to go. What did you find on your scouting trip?"

"Good news, comrades," Cassius said as he took a hop towards them. His eyes were exceptionally bright in the firelight. "The largest pack of wolves appears to be heading towards the outer border of the

Dead Lands. That's probably because this is the birthing season for the hogs that live in the Border Lands and they can get some easy meals."

"What about the other smaller packs?" Peter asked anxiously.

"Well, the good news for us is that both are camped fairly near to each other."

"Isn't that a bad thing?" asked Slane. "I mean, if they're closer together then that means they could easily band together and pursue us."

"No," said Peter. "It will be easier to lure them away from our route."

"Exactly," said Cassius.

Slane looked bewildered.

"Remember the plan?" asked Peter.

"Oh! Is this where Cassius is going to start a fire or something?"

"Yes!" Peter said, slightly perturbed. "Don't you pay attention when we tell you important things?"

"Yeah, I was sort of paying attention but I figured you guys would let me know what I need to know as we go along."

Cassius stepped forward and stared deeply into Slane's eyes. "You should know, young man, that our chances of getting out of this place without any encounters with the Wolves are slim to none. There are only three of us, and only one can fly. You have to pay attention to every detail and I mean *every* detail. There will be times when the three of us will have to separate and you'll have to make decisions on your own. Do you understand?"

Slane swallowed and nodded. He felt foolish. He was very much still a boy, despite his physical abilities. Cassius was right. There was likely to be encounters with the Wolves before the three of them finally got out of the Dead Lands. Even without the Wolves, escaping the Dead Lands was no easy task. The lack of water, food, and falling into muck pits were just a few of the obstacles.

"I won't let you down, I promise," he said meekly.

"We didn't spend over twelve years here to not make it out alive.

Our chances are slim but I like our chances," Peter said giving Slane a forgiving look.

The three friends sat and reviewed the plan for the first part of their journey. Cassius would fly northwest and start a fire. For days he had been stockpiling wood in that direction. The two smaller packs of Wolves would be drawn to the fire, thinking that it meant an easy meal of human flesh. Once there, the rains would come and the Wolves would likely seek shelter to wait out the storm. They hated rain as the ashy ground of the Dead Lands thickened so quickly when combined with water that it made tracking prey or walking nearly impossible. With the packs of Wolves out of the way, Peter and Slane would make their way to a hidden underground cave that Peter and Cassius had covered with brush over the past three months. There they would wait until nightfall when they would set out again. They would only travel at night and use their supplies as sparingly as possible. Cassius would scout from the skies for food and water during the day while Peter and Slane rested.

As their meeting came to an end, Slane noticed his heartbeat increase. He glanced around the cave that had been his home for as long as he could remember. Images of reality and memory swirled into one surreal vision. Cassius, carrying a small bundle of supplies for the fire, hopped to the edge of the cave and looked back.

"See you soon, my friends," he said, and with a great flap he was gone.

"Grab the pack, Slane," said Peter. "Let's go."

....

"Dr. Dalton?"

Cade turned to see Mrs. Hammonds, one of Pierce's teachers at Boyd rushing to catch up with him.

"Hi, Mrs. Hammonds," he said politely. "What do you need?" It was her first year teaching at Boyd. Cade had heard that she took the job thinking that the pace at Boyd might be slower than in a traditional educational setting. She was older and probably nearing retirement, and he had first met her during a seminar that he conducted for new teachers. She had confronted him regarding his stance on not punishing the behavior of children like Pierce, who might act out due to a trigger in the environment that reminds them of something or someone from their past.

"Our goal is to teach new behaviors and ways of thinking and to help the child understand why they do what they do," Cade said near the end of the seminar. "Punishment falls short of this goal – the consequences we implement are designed to create learning, not shame." Mrs. Hammond's hand immediately shot up. For the next few minutes she challenged him on the issue. So far she had not been a problem with the kids he counseled, but he was worried when he saw that Pierce was in one of her classes.

"I just wanted to say what a wonderful job you are doing with Pierce," she began, huffing from expending the energy to catch up with him.

"Thank you, Mrs. Hammonds." *Here it comes,* thought Cade.

"Well, you know how I have *several* children with special needs, and God knows I do my best with *all* of them," she gushed. "I mean, it seems they keep giving me the ones who are more difficult, but that's neither here nor there is it? I don't want to bore you with how difficult my job has become."

Please don't. We all have difficult jobs. She was one of these teachers that thought the teaching profession was *so* difficult and that no one else in the world knew what it was like to work *so* hard. At a staff meeting a few months back she took five minutes explaining how she actually had to grade papers at home sometimes. *Imagine!* Cade thought of the nights he worked on reports and treatment summaries well past midnight.

"What exactly is the problem with Pierce?"

"Well, Pierce seems to be extra difficult lately and I was wondering if he is going through something?"

At least she's checking in with me. It felt like she was tattling on Pierce.

"What is he doing that makes him *extra* difficult?" Cade asked, working hard to keep his voice calm as he felt his blood pressure rising.

"Well, it's his...well, you know, *issues*."

Cade hated it when people talked about the kids he worked with like this. They used the word *issues* as if it was some sort of communicative disease. The truth was that kids like Pierce made adults feel stupid and utterly ill-equipped.

"Yes, as Pierce's therapist I am well aware that he suffers from post-traumatic stress, abandonment, unresolved grief, and falls somewhere on the autism spectrum. Are those the *issues* that you meant?"

Mrs. Hammonds stared at Cade, blinking nervously. "I see I may have upset you," she said with a fake smile.

"I'm not upset, Mrs. Hammonds," Cade lied. "I just really want to know what's going on so I can help you help Pierce in your classroom."

Her demeanor instantly changed. Her words were no longer dripping with false sweetness. "He is disruptive and he is threatening to the other children," she said curtly.

"You still haven't told me what has happened. What did Pierce do?"

"The other children are afraid of him. They steer clear of him. He makes noises sometimes and I think he does it to try and scare them. And he's always writing."

"Other children's reactions to Pierce are out of our control. You still haven't told me what the real problem is. You said he threatened the other children. What did he do?"

Mrs. Hammonds said nothing. Her eyes did not waver from his gaze.

"Well," she finally said. "I just think the school setting here at Boyd isn't the best fit for him. I think he needs to attend a different school."

"And let me guess," Cade said in a biting tone. "You're going to do everything in your power to make that happen, aren't you?"

"Dr. Dalton, I don't like that you're insinuating that I am going to sabotage this boy's success!" she retorted, taking a step back and looking around to see if anyone was listening. "Perhaps we should set up a meeting with the Dean about this situation. Good day, sir!"

"I already know you're going to set up the meeting, Mrs. Hammonds," he called out as she turned to scurry away from him. He raised his voice. "You know, just because a kid is a little different isn't a reason to throw him away!"

Cade turned away and felt the anger boiling inside him. *Why can't she see him like I do?* How could he put into words the transformation that he had witnessed in Pierce in the past few months? He kicked a rock that lay on the sidewalk sending it bouncing three times before it veered off and found rest under a gardenia bush. He thought of how Dr. Capstone told him that one of his greatest challenges in his career was working around the teachers and administrators who simply didn't see the children in the same way. "How could they?" Dr. Cap said with arms outstretched. "The play therapist not only forms a deep relationship with the child but, much like a surgeon, is transported to layers and depths of the child that most adults could not comprehend." Dr. Capstone had told him that the hardest thing to balance was objectivity when talking with the teachers and administrators and to help them see the child as not just a bundle of behaviors and symptoms, but as a living, growing being that was in various stages of development.

"They just don't understand," Dr. Cap told Cade one day as they sat in the playroom. "A kid who has just played out his abandonment from his parents or some other traumatic event is going to have a lot of thoughts and feelings stirred up. Then he goes back to the classroom or dorm and some kid says or does the wrong thing and BAM! Out comes the aggression! Unfortunately, the staff has a hard time seeing the situation from anything other than a behavioral perspective and in a way, we can't blame them. They have to keep the other kids safe and keep order. But you and I will always defend our kids to the administration, teachers, and the general public. We have to. There's no other way."

Cade wished it wasn't so but it was. He knew there would be a meeting with the Dean. That was a sure bet. Pierce represented a child that she couldn't change and so she saw herself as failing with him, therefore he must be moved. He imagined her waddling to his office right now. Pierce was odd there was no denying it. He knew that Pierce had trouble interacting with other children. That was the part of him that put him on the autism spectrum. Pierce had also suffered a great deal and was still healing. Couldn't she see that? A figure outside the playroom snapped him out of his thoughts. It was Victoria. His next session; he had almost forgotten.

"I guess I just hate everybody," Victoria said, pulling back her brown hair into a ponytail.

Cade was quiet. He was still decompressing from his run-in with Hammonds the Hun. He looked out the window. A blue jay landed on the branch closest to the window and seemed to stare at Cade. "Why are you inside on a day like this?" he seemed to mock. Cade turned his gaze towards Victoria.

"What's the problem?" he asked.

"Oh, it's over some stupid thing I drew," Victoria began. "There was this girl, Samantha, remember I told you about her? Well, she thinks she is the best at everything and so one day when I was sketching I drew her holding up a sign that said 'I'm The Best at Being an Idiot,' and I never ever meant for it to get out but Taylor saw it and then told some people...so yeah."

"So you got in trouble?"

"Of course. It became this huge deal and Ms. Griffin got all the high school girls together for a 'bonding' experience. It sucked. It was a scene right out of the movie 'Mean Girls.' I am so ready to get out of this place."

"Not much longer, huh?"

"As soon as school is done I'm outta here."

"Your college stuff is all cleared?"

"Yep, I got the notification last week," Victoria said in a matter of fact tone and pulling a manila envelope from behind her back and handing it to Cade.

He looked at the certificate of acceptance. "You must be proud."

"Well, DUH."

Cade laughed. Victoria smiled.

"I knew your art could be your ticket to take you places. You just had to believe in yourself."

"Okay, there you go with your therapist stuff! Gosh, why do you people always have to go into 'state the obvious' mode?"

Cade said nothing and stared at her.

"Wow, okay, I was a bit harsh there wasn't I?"

"Were you?" He smiled.

"Stop it!" She smiled as she pounded the pillow next to her.

Cade's sessions with Victoria were intense, but her growth was immense. Angry, sullen, and with a hard shell, she was like a boil that needed a surgical needle right in the exact spot to let the poison out. When the poison came out it was ugly. She cut herself numerous times and got in several fights. While she continued to struggle with accepting past events, she had done well in school and had become more confident in her drawing. Her biggest struggles were in getting along with others and accepting herself.

"Savannah College of Art and Design, here you come!" Cade exclaimed as he stretched his arms over his head.

"I know," Victoria said sheepishly. "I can't believe that I got a full scholarship."

"Last session we were talking about the possibility of you getting the scholarship and you said that it would freak you out if you actually got accepted."

"Yeah, I mean, that's a lot of pressure."

"How so?"

"Well, I come from people that don't amount to much, remember? I don't know any successful people…oh my gosh!" Victoria blushed and covered her face in her hands. "I mean, *you* are successful but I mean like people that have real jobs, wow! Okay, I really can't talk today!"

"So, it seems that we really need to focus on your social skills before you get out here," Cade said laughing.

"Are you mad?" she said, looking at him through her fingers.

"No, silly. I think you meant that you don't know anyone personally who finished high school, went to college, and then began a career at something. I don't count because you haven't known me your whole life. Am I close?"

"Yes! That's what I meant." Victoria let out a sigh and looked relieved. She paused for a moment, as if forming her thoughts slowly. "It's weird that I have a talent and that it could take me places, that's all. For so long I saw myself, because of where I come from, as not supposed to amount to anything." She glanced up and met Cade's eyes. "So it's still hard to accept."

Cade knew exactly what she meant. For people who grew up in middle class to upper middle class homes, high expectations came with the territory and the idea of moving upward and outward into the world seemed to be coded into the DNA. For those who live in poverty, upward mobility is neither taught nor expected, and those who try may be cut down or rejected by their family of origin. As he and Victoria sifted through her experiences and worked through the trauma, her anger towards herself melted away and her art become vibrant and alive. As she began to love herself, she began to see options for her future. But she still struggled with self-doubt.

"One day at a time," Cade said reassuringly. "We can't go backward or forward one second. Remember how we worked on dealing with the thoughts and emotions of this very second, letting them come and go like water through a hose?"

Victoria nodded.

"You'll battle insecurity for perhaps the rest of your life. Fear is a constant companion and it's part of the human experience. It's what gets us out of bed in the morning and creates great energy for learning, loving, and growth."

They sat silent for a while, taking in the afternoon sunlight as it filled the room and watching the birds and squirrels on the big oak.

Cade broke the silence. "I have something for you," he said as he got up. He went to the shelf behind his desk and picked up something wrapped in brown paper. "I hope you like it," he said as he handed it to Victoria.

She unwrapped the item carefully and drew a breath as the paper fell onto the floor. "Wow," she said softly. "It's beautiful. I can't believe how it turned out."

The gift was a sculpture that Victoria had made during one of her sessions that Cade took and got fired at a local pottery store. Cade used her love of art as a main part of their work together and she was as gifted at sculpting as she was at drawing. She sculpted out various memories and experiences. Sometimes she would create figures that represented family members or people that had hurt her and then she would destroy them. One day during a session, she talked about her mother abusing her and how no one in the family came to help her. She created about seven figures and mashed them into a ball. As she and Cade talked about her feelings she crafted a stunning figure of a young woman that arose out of the crushed clay. Victoria talked about her future that day and said for the first time that she could see herself going to college and becoming a successful artist. She told Cade that she wanted to talk with the guidance counselor at Boyd about possible art school scholarships. She wanted to use art to help kids like herself deal with the hardships of foster care life.

"I remember the day I painted this," Victoria said, turning the sculpture. The afternoon sun caught the deep red and black that formed the base. Blue, purple, and lavender sprang from the female figure's hair and face. "I wanted to represent my favorite colors that came out of the darkness and the damage. This is how I see myself now," Victoria said. "Where did you get it fired?"

"There's a shop downtown where you can paint your own pottery and they gave me a name of a lady who has a kiln. I want you to have it and never forget all that we have worked on."

She smiled. "You should know that you're good at what you do. When I first came here I thought you were kind of a weirdo with all of your toys and stuff in this place, but I realized that you really want to help people like me," Victoria said looking around the room. "I'm going to miss this part of Boyd."

"Thank you, Victoria. Best wishes," Cade said as he stood and walked her to the door. He closed it behind him. For the rest of the evening he smiled with the glow of a satisfaction that was hard to put into words. It was one thing to help a young child, but to help an adolescent who had been through hell and then to have her compliment him was a very rare thing.

12
TESTED BEYOND LIMITS

"Cassius has to divert the Wolves," Pierce said forcefully. Cade was surprised to hear his voice be so direct and clear. "He is going to make a fire and draw them from Slane and Peter. It is the only way they are going to get out. Here, I wrote the next part. You can read it but don't let anyone see it. After you read it lock it up in the file cabinet where you told me you have the other parts of the story."

"Okay, I will. There is one other person who read the beginning."

Pierce looked worried. "Who was it?"

"Don't worry, he's a man that I trust and love as much as my own father. In fact, he is like my father."

Pierce still looked wary.

"His name is Dr. Capstone and he is my mentor and he trained me to do what I do. He's like my Obi wan Kenobi, you know the guy from *Star Wars* who trains the Jedi's?"

Pierce nodded, relaxing a bit.

"But I haven't told him anymore about it. Pierce, he thought it was one of the best stories he's ever read."

Pierce's eyebrows shot up. "Really?"

"Yes. But if you don't want me to talk about it with him – and trust me, he's the only person with whom I would share it – I won't say anything more about it to him. It's your call."

Pierce was silent for a moment. Then he spoke.

"Okay, he sounds alright. But if I tell you there's something you can't share you have to listen to me, okay?"

"I give you my word," Cade said, kneeling down and looking him in the eye. Pierce caught his gaze for a moment and then looked away.

"Okay," Pierce said almost in a whisper.

Cade took the tattered papers and began to read. *Wow. He's amazing.* Not only had he written the story, but now he was directing the action just like a movie director. Cade was nervous about joining Pierce in his play. More than any other kid with whom he had worked, he did not want to mess this up. Dr. Cap's reassuring words echoed in his head: *Just be. When the invitation is made, the child will tell you exactly what to do or not do.* Dr. Cap's words rang true. Pierce was giving Cade explicit instructions.

Pierce pushed the paper machete mountain against the sandbox. He took Slane and Peter and a small leather pouch that he attached to Slane's back. He dug some holes in the sand and placed some of the black plastic dogs in them. "You'll be over there with Cassius," he said, pointing to the far end of the sand box. "This scene is pretty much going to be Peter and Slane trying to reach the rendezvous point. I'll give you the signal when Cassius needs to join us."

Cade nodded. He picked up Cassius and imagined what it would be like to be the Great Eagle. He watched Pierce make the final preparations in the sandbox and scanned some of the pages that Pierce gave him. Similar to the previous chapters, it was written in Pierce's childlike scrawl but the detail and descript language was on an adult's level. Cade sat on the floor at the edge of the sandbox and positioned Cassius on a small rise of sand. He took some small Lincoln Log pieces and put them in a small circle that resembled a fire pit and waited. Pierce worked frantically for a few minutes more and then suddenly stopped. He picked up Slane and Peter and positioned them at the mouth of the cave at the top of the mountain.

A long low roll of thunder rose in the distance as Slane and Peter began their descent down the trail towards the bottom of the mountain. A slight shift in the wind caught Slane's attention. Instinctively, he looked at Peter's nose and saw it quiver.

"We should have enough time to get to the old forest, judging from where Cassius said the Wolves are packed together," Peter said, sniffing the air. "Then once he gets the fire going we can move faster towards our meeting place. Keep your weapons ready at all times, Slane."

Slane nodded. He tapped his bow and nudged his quiver (filled with over two hundred arrows) with his left hand and touched the hilt of his knife with his right. He was ready. The warrior in him savored this quest. He longed to test himself against the elements and the Wolves and whatever else stood before them, but he kept this to himself. He was tired of the lectures from his friends about how young and inexperienced he was. He had learned much from his near death experience from the Wolf attack and had spent a lot of time thinking of how foolish he had been. He would never let it happen again.

Slane and Peter walked carefully down the trail making sure to avoid anything that might cause a noise. Peter's eyes scanned the brush and the distant trees. There was no small talk between them as they left the safety of the mountain trail and moved down into the flatland. As they left the clearly defined path of the trail, there was more scrub and brush to navigate. Slane followed Peter's lead as he nimbly moved between and over obstacles. Peter had taught Slane the art of moving without being seen or heard and to anticipate each footstep before it was taken.

They traveled for a little over an hour. The wind picked up and Peter smelled the rain that would soon cover the Dead Lands. He instinctively picked up his pace. His eyes scanned the horizon looking for the fire. He wondered what was taking Cassius so long and then reminded himself to not worry. His friend had proven himself more than capable over the years and he refocused back on the path in front of him. He glanced back at Slane and was pleased to see him keeping up. Peter and Slane approached a large fallen tree surrounded by a pile of jutting rocks. Peter instructed Slane to hide behind the trunk of the tree and he climbed to the top of the rock pile. He scanned the horizon but saw nothing.

"See anything?" Slane called up to Peter.

"No, not yet. I don't think we should move until we see that fire. And don't drink any more water, we don't know how much longer we may have to wait."

Slane nodded and put the water skin back in the pack.

Slane noticed the moon was continually shrouded by clouds now. He was glad to rest but found himself unable to think about anything other than Cassius and the fire. What was taking him so long? He thought of life once they got out of the Dead Lands and the journey back to his homeland. His homeland. It sounded good to him and focusing on that helped push the fear of what may lay ahead out of his mind. He imagined a kingdom, complete with knights and lush green lands. And horses. He had dreamed of riding a horse since he was a small boy, like the knights in so many of the stories that Peter and Cassius told him.

"I see the fire!" Peter called down to him. "There, on the horizon! Pack up Slane, we must hurry!"

Slane jumped up and rolled the pack quickly and slung it around to his back. Peter came down from the top of the rocks in a flash.

"Follow me!" he called to Slane.

Slane felt the razor sharp tips of the scrub bushes that grew in this part of the Dead Lands slash against his skin. He instinctively tried to steer away from them but that only pushed him into more razors on the other side. He pushed away the pain by focusing on the white tip of Peter's tail that flashed every time Peter made a turn or jumped over a fallen tree. A huge rain drop hit Slane right between the eyes and he looked up just in time to see a bolt of lightning rip across the sky. Soon the rain was falling at a steady pace. The air became choked with the ash and Slane's eyes filled with tears. He blinked repeatedly to clear them.

Peter and Slane pressed on. They could hear the howls of the packs of Wolves in the distance. The fire had worked perfectly as the Wolves were lured to it and away from Peter and Slane's course. Peter was relieved that Cassius was okay and that the first part of the plan had worked. He felt a surge of energy. "About two more miles!" Peter yelled back to Slane. The sky was thick with lightning and the rain pounded the ashy ground relentlessly creating a thick muck. Slane now found it hard to keep up with Peter. His feet stuck in the mud and his legs felt like they weighed a hundred pounds each. He looked for the white tip of the tail but it got farther away with every stride.

"Peter!" he yelled, feeling his left foot sink deep into muck. "Slow down!" He pulled out his left foot and felt his right foot sink nearly as deep. He fell forward and his hands went into the slime up to his forearms. Peter was gone. A sense of dread and panic overcame him.

"PETER! HELP ME!" he screamed. As he lifted his hands he fell sideways as he tried to get his footing. Once again it was an awkward dance of left foot right foot and before he knew it he was completely turned around. He looked up but saw nothing but black rain pouring down on him. He turned to the left and then to the right, fully conscious of his feet sinking deeper into the black muck but he could see nothing. He finally broke his feet free and stomped forward blindly, waving his hands hoping to touch something.

"PETER!" Slane yelled again, but he heard nothing. He was alone. *Don't panic! Stay calm and think! I am not dying or in immediate danger; I am simply separated from Peter.* The most important thing for him to do now would be to find some sort of shelter and get his bearings. He closed his eyes and did his best to gain a sense of direction. His brain pointed him to the right and he opened his eyes and began to walk methodically in that direction. He focused on each step, not letting his feet sink too far into the muck. The sense of panic and dread from feeling lost continued to surface but he pushed them away and concentrated on moving forward. The lightning showed flashes of his surroundings and he could see a large rock a few hundred yards away. Slane made it to the rock and was pleased to find that the ground around it was stable. He felt his way around the rock and found a small cave just large enough to protect him from the rain. Using his bow he swept along the back of the cave just in case a critter of some sort had the same idea he did but he found nothing. He sat down and instantly felt relief. Leaning back against the back of the cave a new feeling replaced the sense of dread. Exhaustion hit him like a heavy cloak and his eyes began to close. He fought it off knowing that if he slept he was putting himself in danger. He slapped his face and pinched his arms and the cloak lifted, but then it floated back down again. He focused his eyes out into the blackness, but he saw nothing.

The rain pounded him. Lightning lit up the sky followed by deafening thunder. Trying to find his way now would put him in more danger, especially if he fell into one of the muck pits without anyone to pull him out. *My only hope is to wait out the storm.* He reached out along the opposite side of the cave and found a large, thorny bush growing. Using his knife he cut as many branches as he could and piled them in front of the cave, creating a makeshift door and barrier to anything that might try to enter. He took the pack off his back and cradled it in his arms, but he kept his bow and quiver slung around his left arm and put his sword in his right hand. Then he laid his head against the back of the cave and let sleep overtake him. *I pray they find me.*

....

Pierce suddenly became still. Cade watched and waited. He could see that Slane was alone and Pierce created a makeshift shelter where he laid the soldier. Pierce's play had been frantic as he moved Slane all over the sandbox. With grunts and groans, Pierce held Slane's feet in each hand and made each step a gargantuan effort to pull them out. Peter was nowhere to be seen. Cade remembered from the story that a great storm was passing over the Dead Lands and that the rain would make the land muddy and difficult to traverse. Peter and Slane had become separated. *He's playing out the scenes of his life. Alone and fending for himself.*

"Fly Cassius to the cave," Pierce said to Cade. "Over by where Peter is," he pointed.

Cade helped the stuffed bird flutter and flap from his resting place and made him soar over the sand box. He lowered Cassius towards the opening of the cave where Peter the Fox rested and swooped in and placed him at the entrance of the cave.

"Good. Now sit over there and watch."

Cade said nothing and did as he was told. Pierce bent over Slane and examined him in the makeshift shelter. Pierce rocked back and forth and his lips moved slightly but Cade couldn't hear what he was saying. Pierce made a moaning sound and moved Slane back and forth. He made crashing noises that sounded like thunder. He made *whooshing* noises that sounded like rain and wind. Suddenly he came over to where Peter the Fox and Cassius the Eagle were sitting.

••

"What do you mean you lost him?!" Cassius yelled. "Why didn't you check and see if he was following you?" He gave his feathers another shake, more out of aggravation than the need to dry them.

"I thought he was behind me. Forgive me Cassius! I was sure he could keep up!" Peter yelled as a clap of thunder and bolt of lightning occurred simultaneously.

"You knew this ground would turn to muck! I knew you would go too fast! You knew that he is still not at full strength!" Cassius shouted. He had never been this angry at Peter and so afraid for Slane. He felt a growing pit of dread in his stomach. Finding Slane in this storm would be difficult if not impossible.

"We've got to go find him or the Wolves will!" Cassius yelled. "Are you up to it?"

"Yes! Peter replied, feeling a surge of adrenaline at the thought of Slane lost in the storm. "I will go back the way that I came – you fly overhead and see what you can see."

Cassius nodded. "I'll call out every so often! Let's go!"

··

Slane was awakened by a flash of lighting and crash of thunder that was so loud he thought his eardrums would explode. He jumped to his feet and wondered how long he had been asleep. He peered out into the storm and saw nothing but black. The rain, driven by the wind felt like tiny needles hitting his face. He ducked back into the cave. *I've got to think!* He knew that Cassius and Peter would come looking for him once they realized that he was missing. It would do no good to stay here, but he risked becoming more lost if he chose the wrong direction in which to walk. And there was the matter of the muck. And also running into a Wolf. Fighting off a Wolf in this soup would be nearly impossible. He needed to be able to walk without getting stuck. He looked at the thorny brush and suddenly an idea struck him. "I know!" he exclaimed. "I'll tie branches to my shoes which will spread out my weight and keep me from sinking!

Using the brief bursts of light from the lightning to see what he was doing, Slane quickly cut some of the thicker branches and used the rest of the leather strapping that was in the pack. He spread out the branches and laced them together with the leather straps and then tied them over his shoes. *Not the greatest, but they'll have to do.* He threw aside the remaining brush and took a step out of the cave. Then another. Then another. He walked straight to where he was when he realized Peter had left him. He instinctively turned right and began to march. He readied his bow with an arrow and plodded forward. The shoes worked well and balanced his weight so that he hardly sunk into the muck at all. The lightning flashes helped him see occasional glimpses of the way ahead. The thought that he might be heading in the wrong direction continued to surface but he brushed it aside. He was doing the right thing. Being out in the open gave him a better chance at being found than hiding in the cave. Besides, Peter and Cassius told him that Wolves hated rain and rarely ventured out in storms for fear of falling into one of the muck pits. He kept his bow ready just in case.

· ·

"See anything?" Peter hollered up at Cassius.

"No! Not yet! Are you sure this is the way you came?" Cassius yelled back, hovering above Peter's head and trying to ignore the pelting raindrops that soaked his feathers and made him feel like he weighed a thousand pounds.

"Yes, just keep moving! He can't be too far!"

"I'm going to go ahead and then come back. I'll only be a few minutes!" Cassius called and flapped into the darkness. Peter yelled something but he couldn't make it out. He could feel his energy depleting rapidly from hovering and flying in short spurts. With a few strong flaps he pushed forward and used every ounce of his exceptional vision to scan the landscape. The lightning flashed every ten seconds giving him a perfect snapshot of the ground below. He released his cry for as loud and long as he could hoping it would reach Slane. The mix of the roar of the pouring rain and thunder, as well as the splatter from the rain hitting the ground reduced the ability of Cassius's cry to travel very far but he kept his distinct call going. *Where could you be, Slane?* After a few minutes he decided to turn back but something in him, perhaps wishful thinking spurred him to keep going. *Just a bit further!* A brief flash of lightning lit up the landscape. There! Up ahead something was moving. Cassius lowered his altitude and slowed his flight. Another flash showed a figure. He released another cry and prayed for another lightning flash. Just then a bolt ripped through the darkness and Cassius saw that it was Slane.

"Cassius! Cassius!"

The great Eagle heard Slane calling for him. He swooped down and landed right next to the soggy boy moving clumsily but purposefully through the muck.

"Slane, I'm here!" yelled Cassius.

"Oh Cassius, my friend!" cried Slane, throwing his arms around the giant bird and released a torrent of tears.

"There, there," said Cassius, releasing himself from Slane's hug. "Listen! We've got to get back to Peter. You were going the wrong way but our paths intersected perfectly."

"Which way?" yelled Slane, gathering himself.

"This way! Follow me! And keep that bow ready!" Cassius urged. Cassius half-hopped half-fluttered in front of Slane so that he wouldn't lose him again. Every twenty seconds he let out a cry and kept his eyes peeled for Peter. There was less lightning now but the rain had not let up. Cassius' perfect sense of direction kept them on track. Off in the distance he heard Peter's howl. He answered. The howl got closer. A flash of lightning revealed Peter about twenty yards away.

"Cassius! Slane!" Peter called, breaking into a run.

"Peter!" Slane shouted, trying to run but unable to because of his oversized shoes.

Another brilliant flash of lightning lit up everything around them and out of the corner of his eye Slane saw two red eyes and the form of a Wolf breaking into a run to overtake Peter.

"Peter!" Slane cried, "Get down!" Peter instinctively crouched and Slane released an arrow and readied another in less than a second. A horrible howl coupled with a growl filled the air. Slane waited for another flash of lightning and when it did he saw the Wolf writhing on the ground. He released another arrow and the trio heard a high-pitched whimper and then silence.

"Great shot, Slane!" yelled Peter. "Hurry, we must get back to the cave! There will be more coming!"

"Go!" yelled Cassius.

The trio made their way through the muck and driving rain and finally reached the cave where they originally planned to meet before Slane got lost. Much like the cave they lived in since Slane was a baby, it was located along the side of a hill. Cassius had been gathering brush and sticks over the past three months to hide the entrance. Slane collapsed near the back of the cave. "Hey! Don't fall out yet! I need your help!" Peter called. "Help me push these logs."

Slane untied the branches attached to his shoes and tossed them next to his pack. With the last remaining strength in his body he and Peter rolled two large logs in front of the entrance. Peter arranged the piles of brush and then collapsed next to Slane and Cassius. "Get some sleep comrades, I'll keep watch. No fire tonight, too dangerous. We'll eat in the morning. Tomorrow night we move out again."

••

"Okay, Cassius and Peter have to look for Slane. Make Cassius fly over Peter," said Pierce.

"Okay," Cade said. "Let's go, Peter we must find Slane!" he exclaimed. He looked at Pierce and saw him smile.

"Let's go!" said Pierce.

Cade and Pierce worked together and Pierce told him what to do. Pierce played out the parts of Slane and Peter. Cade threw himself into the part of Cassius and found a voice for the Great Eagle which delighted Pierce.

"Keep doing that voice for him!" exclaimed Pierce, smiling.

"I'm going to fly ahead and look for him!" Cade said, flapping Cassius's wings.

"Not too far! You'll get lost too!" Pierce said, moving Peter up and down on the sand.

Cade spent a few minutes flying Cassius over the sand and occasionally made the sound of an eagle screeching.

Pierce followed behind with Peter. He moved in front of Cade with Slane and placed him in between two plastic rocks.

"I see him!" Cade exclaimed, making Cassius swoop low and landed the eagle next to Slane.

"Slane! Peter!" Pierce yelled, moving the figures closer to each other. Suddenly he grabbed one of the black plastic dogs and moved it behind Peter. "Get down, Peter!" he yelled, moving Slane forward. "Whish!" he cried, imitating the sound of an arrow shot from Slane's bow. "He's hit!"

"Slane, be careful!" Cade shouted, lifting Cassius into the air.

"Whish!" said Pierce, "Got him!" He rolled the black plastic dog onto its back on the sand.

"We must hurry back to the cave!" Cade said, lifting Cassius up and down to simulate the flapping of his wings.

"Let's go!" Pierce exclaimed, moving Peter and Slane towards the cave.

"We're finally here, we made it!" Cade said as he slid Cassius into the opening and towards the back of the cave.

"I'm glad to be out of the rain," Pierce said as he put Slane and Peter next to Cassius.

"Here, let's block up the entrance." Cade handed Pierce some Lego pieces and they boarded up the opening of the cave.

Once they were done, they stepped back to admire the trio safe in their hiding spot.

"Safe and sound," Cade said, brushing sand off of his hands into the sandbox.

"Yep," Pierce said, going to the sink to wash his hands. Cade joined him.

"It's not easy getting out of the Dead Lands," Cade said as he held the door open for Pierce. They began to walk towards Pierce's cottage.

"Slane has his friends and together they will make it. But it will be hard," Pierce said. He looked up at Cade and smiled. "It'll be really hard."

•••

Cade looked around the newly furnished waiting room of Dean Michael Wortman. It looked like a room one would find at an Ivy League school. The dark wood paneling on the walls and floor did not seem to fit at a place like Boyd. Bronze sculptures were displayed on polished oak end tables. The leather couch Cade sat on looked almost white compared to the dark walls and floor. Dean Wortman's giant desk, also made of oak, was visible through the cracked door of his office. Paintings of the English countryside in lavish frames graced the walls. Rumor had it that Dean Wortman had spent nearly five thousand of his own money to renovate the office. Cade sighed, unimpressed and annoyed that he had to be here.

Michael D. Wortman was related to one of the wealthy members of the Board of Directors. His previous places of employment included being a CEO of a large company somewhere in the Northeast. He boasted a Ph.D. in business and had been on the faculty at a prestigious business academy. When the previous dean retired, a man whom both Cade and Dr. Capstone had liked very much, Dean Wortman was hired. He said in his acceptance speech that while this was part of his semi-retirement, his position at Boyd would be to not only oversee the academics but also to raise the "public's awareness of Boyd, and institute fundraising to help raise the quality of education and living status of the residents." Cade remembered that after this utterance the room erupted in applause, but he and Dr. Capstone had exchanged worried glances. True to his word, the money poured in. Dean Wortman was a "who's who" in the community and lived among the wealthy. New buildings replaced old ones, grounds were improved, and new teachers were hired. Weekly staff meetings included an emphasis on the "academic

145

rigor" of Boyd and updates on the various banquets and fundraising events that were on the horizon. Dean Wortman was always in a suit or, at the very least, a dress shirt and neatly pressed slacks.

Cade made it a point to avoid the administrative offices of Boyd and did very little mingling with those high in command. He followed the advice of Dr. Capstone very carefully: "Lay low, do your job, and the less they see you the less likely they are to interfere with your sphere of the world." When forced to interact with members of the administration, Cade represented the counseling branch of Boyd professionally and due to the fact that the young people with whom he worked usually improved, the administration saw him as a valuable asset. The legacy of Dr. Capstone helped boost Cade's credibility and he alluded to that legacy when promoting the counseling program during meetings with the administration. Dean Wortman was always cordial to Cade but Cade felt an air of condescension from him. Fifteen years Cade's senior probably had something to do with it, as well as jokes about Cade's "professional" attire. Cade made no apology for his wearing of jeans on most days, and even shorts if he was taking a kid fishing or hiking. Once, during a staffing when Cade was discussing play therapy and how it had helped transform a difficult child, Dean Wortman remarked, "How interesting that you still get to play with children's toys!"

"Dr. Dalton? Dean Wortman is ready for you now. This way, please."

Dean Wortman's secretary guided him towards a conference room and Cade took his seat at a large table. Mrs. Hammonds was already present and sat across from Cade. She smiled curtly but did not say hello. Cade returned her smile wryly and then opened the folder that contained the details of Pierce's therapy. Dean Wortman entered the room and shut the door behind him.

"Mrs. Hammonds, Dr. Dalton, thanks for coming. It has been brought to my attention that one of our residents, a Mr. Pierce Emerson, is whom we will be discussing today and I hope that we can come to a resolution.

Dr. Dalton, do you mind if Mrs. Hammonds starts things off?"

Cade nodded. "That's fine with me."

Mrs. Hammonds began with her "concerns" about Pierce and the difficulties that he caused in her classroom. She talked about his social awkwardness and problems with "appearing odd" to the other children. "You know, he has no friends. Not one child wants to sit with him at lunch."

Cade watched Dean Wortman while she was speaking. He sat with a serious look on his face with both hands clasped together and his forefingers forming a triangle. Every now and then the triangle poked his lower lip. Mrs. Hammonds went on about Pierce's tendency towards dark writing and how he became violent when he was confronted about taking another student's pencil. Cade groaned inwardly. She was doing her best to paint him as some psycho lunatic who might kill all the residents while they slept. He reminded himself to stay calm and to channel his frustration to formulating a response to her ridiculous claims. After several minutes Mrs. Hammonds finished.

"What is your recommendation, Mrs. Hammonds?" Dean Wortman asked.

"Well, I think the best thing for this child is to be moved to a special school where they work with children such as Pierce. I feel as though he is putting other children in danger and that the isolation from his peers may instigate violence of some sort. I think him living here at Boyd isn't the best fit for this young man."

"For the young man, or for you?"

"Excuse me?" Mrs. Hammonds eyes flashed at Cade.

"That's enough, Dr. Dalton," Dean Wortman said raising his hand. "Let's keep this civil. I can tell you both care very much about what you do but remember that we won't get anywhere with you both throwing barbs at each other."

Cade nodded. Mrs. Hammonds glared at him.

"Mrs. Hammonds, you have many years of experience teaching children," Dean Wortman began. "No doubt you have encountered some difficult students over the years. What concerns you the most about Mr. Emerson?"

"Well, I just see how odd he is and how difficult it is for him to socialize. Sometimes it appears to me that he doesn't have empathy. It scares me – he scares me, to be honest."

"I see." Dean Wortman leaned back in his chair. "Thank you Mrs. Hammonds. Dr. Dalton, you have the floor."

"Call me Cade, please, and thank you for this opportunity to add my input and professional clinical opinion."

"Go ahead, Cade."

Cade cleared his throat. "Sir, there is no doubt that Pierce has had some adjustment issues upon coming to Boyd, but I believe that there is an explanation for his issues and I also believe that from a clinical standpoint, Boyd is the best place for him. I also believe he is healing and growing. This young man suffered acute trauma in witnessing the death of his mother and secondary trauma from years of emotional and psychological neglect and abandonment. Recent testing shows that he is still suffering to some extent from this trauma. The testing also showed an incredibly high IQ as well as several traits of autism, in addition to being gifted in science and mathematics."

Cade paused and looked at Mrs. Hammonds and Dean Wortman. He thought he saw a glimmer of empathy from both of them. He went on.

"I am meeting with Pierce nearly every day for play therapy. His growth is immense and he is working through emotional issues such as fear, sadness, and anger. The writing that Mrs. Hammonds alluded to is an allegory to his healing and is not only amazing for a kid his age, but also gives us a window into his soul that shows us how he is growing."

Cade discussed the facts of Pierce's background and facets of his play in therapy. He talked about the social and emotional struggles of individuals on the autism spectrum and how many appear to lack empathy but simply struggle to show it. He showed reports from Pierce's cottage parents that documented his improvement over the past year. He also made the point that Pierce's disturbances in the classroom this year were in reaction to being provoked by the other children and then he looked right at Mrs. Hammonds.

"I also believe that Pierce is bored and is distracted in the classroom because he is not being challenged."

"Well! Are you saying that I'm not a good teacher?" Mrs. Hammonds fumed, raising off her chair a little. "How dare you!"

"Enough!" Dean Wortman raised his voice and held up his hands.

"Sir, let me clarify, please," said Cade, looking at Dean Wortman. "I am not criticizing Mrs. Hammond's ability to teach. I am simply saying that she may not be the best teacher for Pierce given his immense capacity for learning and intelligence."

"Dean Wortman, I take great offense at this man saying I'm not equipped to teach and I won't sit here and be insulted!" She grabbed her things and began to leave.

"Mrs. Hammonds, please sit down," said Dean Wortman calmly. "Dr. Dalton – er Cade, is not implying anything against you personally."

Mrs. Hammonds plunked down in her chair and looked like an angry child who had just had her candy taken away.

Dean Wortman sighed. "While I think that Mr. Emerson has his issues, it appears that he is under excellent care for his autistic and emotional issues. I believe that it is in Mr. Emerson's best interest that he remain at Boyd."

Mrs. Hammonds let out a sigh and Cade felt a surge of gratitude towards Dean Wortman.

"From all that we have here, I am going to talk to the education team about moving Pierce up a grade, or at the very least, make sure that he is taking higher math and sciences. However, I want to make sure that his therapy continues at the same pace."

"It will, Dean Wortman, I can assure you of that. Thank you, sir."

"Good. Will you be willing to meet with the new teachers that Pierce will have so they will have a better understanding of him?"

"Of course, I'd be happy to," said Cade, gathering his papers and putting them back in the folder.

"Thank you both for coming and please let me know if there is anything else I can do." The dean rose and held the door open. Cade looked at Mrs. Hammonds but she wouldn't look at him. She left the room quickly without a word to Dean Wortman. Cade nodded to the Dean as he exited and made a sharp right to the side entrance that led to the dorms and his office. He felt a great sense of accomplishment by fighting for one of his kids. He couldn't wait to share this experience with Dr. Capstone, who had told Cade of many battles with administration to keep a child at Boyd. For now, Pierce's course of healing was preserved. Cade breathed a heavy sigh of relief.

13
OPEN SEASON

Slane munched on a raw potato, virtually the only vegetable that grew in the Dead Lands. It was sometime in the morning and the rain had stopped. The sky was dull and gray. A dank and sickening smell filled the air. Slane's legs throbbed with a constant ache. A thick crust of black mud gripped his legs up to his thighs. He touched part of it and it broke off. Cassius was gone. He was out scouting, checking the route for their journey that would resume that evening under the cover of darkness. Peter lay next to Slane and dozed with his eyes half open. Slane watched Peter's tummy go up and down with each breath. The experience of last night reminded him of the loyalty of his friends. He stood to stretch his legs. Peter's head popped up as he felt Slane stir.

"Just stretchin' my legs," Slane said, patting Peter's head.

Peter laid his head back down and did not respond. Slane walked to the front of the cave and peered out. A misty fog enveloped the region. Slane could see mountains in the distance; perhaps one of them was their mountain that they had just left. The stench began to burn his nostrils. He stepped back into the cave. He was not used to the stench of the Dead Lands. Most of his life had been spent in the cave and up in the mountainous regions. This part of this God-forsaken world was unknown to him. Off in the distance he heard the cry of an Eagle and he looked out. It was Cassius. He watched him circle and then drop like a stone. He was in the cave two seconds later. He carried a small animal in his mouth.

"Got lucky this morning!" he said, excitedly. "No moldy vegetables for me – I shall have meat!" He ripped the head from the creature while holding the body with his claws and then dug into the body with his beak.

"What is it?" asked Slane, feeling hunger begin to surge through him. He imagined half a hog roasting on a spit over the fire in their old cave.

"Don't know, don't care," replied Cassius, his mouth half full of fur and bloody meat. They heard Peter stir behind them.

"Did you bring me anything?" Peter asked sleepily, giving his body a shake.

"Not yet, my friend, but I'm going back out soon. I had to eat something," Cassius replied.

"No worries," Peter said. He looked very tired to Slane. "Got any potatoes in the bag, Slane?"

"Sure," Slane said, pouring out several potatoes. Peter sniffed them and then picked one up and began to eat it.

"What did you find out on your scouting trip Cassius?"

"Good news, comrades. I only saw two packs of Wolves within a five mile radius."

"How big were the packs?" Peter asked, picking up another potato.

"Twenty to twenty-five, give or take. The big packs must have stayed in the highlands after last night's storm." Cassius ripped another flap of flesh from the rodent and tossed the carcass aside. "We need to bury that later," he said looking at Slane.

Slane nodded. "So what's the plan for tonight?" he asked, munching another potato. "And when can we make a fire?" He imagined a stew of meat and potatoes.

Peter spoke, "We will leave under complete darkness. There will probably be more rain tonight but I don't expect it to be like last night."

"More rain?" Slane groaned.

"Actually, it's going to help us," said Cassius, wiping his beak against a rock.

"We need darkness. It's easier to move at night and we have to put distance between us and the Wolves. Remember, Slane: There are only three of us. A small pack of twenty would be too much for us. Even with your expert bow skills."

"I could take 'em," he said smiling.

Peter ignored him. "We'll walk until morning and hopefully we will make it to the Pine Forests. There's water there and better cover. We'll rest there and head out in the afternoon. It will be at least a week until we reach the upper pass that will eventually take us over the mountains and out of the Dead Lands."

"Can we make a fire there?" Slane asked.

"Perhaps," said Cassius. "We just have to make sure we're out of danger before we get too comfortable."

"He's right, Slane," Peter said as he stood and peered out of the mouth of the cave. "Better to be cautious and hungry than fat, happy...-and dead." He turned and looked at Slane. "This will be the greatest challenge any of us have faced. When you are hungry, tired, and feel like you cannot go any further, remember that very few living beings have ever gotten out of this wretched place alive. But we will, and we will do it by being careful and conservative."

Slane watched an ant drag a piece of grass across the floor of the cave. It struggled to get over a few pebbles but eventually cleared the obstacle. When he was a small boy, Peter taught him about all the animals and told him that the ant, while small, was actually the strongest of all living creatures because it was able to pick things up many times its size. Slane thought of the three of them getting out of the Dead Lands. He wished they were ants.

The day passed without incident. Cassius went out and brought back another small rodent for Peter who ate it in two gulps. Cassius slept while Peter and Slane kept watch and then they switched. By early evening each was rested, fed, and ready to move out. Slane packed and re-packed their supplies. He checked and rechecked his weapons. He felt restless. His body felt slimy and gritty at the same time. He imagined a blue-green lagoon filled with warm water. He dove in and felt the water cleanse him, the grit and slime melted away and he emerged clean and refreshed. He climbed out and sat on one of the smooth flat rocks that surrounded the lagoon. He imagined a girl with long dark hair and eyes like his own sitting with him. He would tell her of his exploits in the Dead Lands. He would tell her of how, long ago, he killed the great Wolves and how he and his two friends escaped the grip of a Land so barren and terrible that words could not describe it. She told him he was so brave and rubbed his arm, pulling him close to her. Searing pain brought him out of the fantasy and he saw that a large black horsefly had attached itself to his leg and was happily sucking his blood. Slane let out a yelp and whacked the insect with the end of one of his arrows. The stunned insect lay on the ground until Slane mashed it with a rock. Blood and yellow guts flew in all directions. *Vile insect! Vile wretched place!*

He thought back to his vision. He had never seen a girl except in his imagination which sprang from the stories that Cassius and Peter told him of their youth. He found himself thinking of women often and yearning for their company. How could this be? To yearn for something that he had not even seen? It was a mystery. He felt the urge to talk to his comrades about this. Cassius was out on one last reconnaissance mission before nightfall. Peter lay on his side watching the front of the cave. He caught Slane looking at him.

"What's on your mind?" Peter asked, lifting his head.

"Nothing," Slane responded. "Well, actually, there is something," he said, feeling his face grow hot. "Many times in your stories, you and Cassius have told me about the girls you have loved. I have been thinking a lot about girls lately and I don't know why."

Peter stood and sat next to Slane and looked out at the mouth of the cave. The light was starting to dim. "What does it feel like?"

"It feels weird," said Slane. "Like sometimes I could run for days or that I'm going to jump out of my skin. I find myself imagining being with one of these girl-things and talking with her and walking with her. Tell me again of what one looks like and acts like. You said they were just like me but they have curvy bodies and long hair and they smell good."

Peter laughed. "Well, kid, you should know that this is completely normal, okay? You're not weird or bad or broken. I remember being your age and feeling all that energy." He gave his fur a shake, licked his paw, and continued. "Girls are like us in many ways – I mean, they are human and have bodies. Faces, arms, legs, you know. But that's about where it ends. Women, girls, have great wisdom and are powerful creatures. The honest and true love of a woman can take an average man and make him an extraordinary man."

"But how?"

"Well, that's a mystery. I can't really put it into words, but I think it's about how humans find a balance in each other."

"What do you mean?"

"Men are designed to hunt, defend, build, and face challenges. Women give us a reason to do these things, because we naturally want to provide for them and protect them. Women too are designed to face challenges, and they will hunt for and defend their children. A woman has great wisdom and problem solving abilities. When she feels protected, it is natural for her to love and give, and share her wisdom and spiritual knowledge. When a man feels honored and respected, he will stop at nothing to give the woman all she desires. She inspires the man to face the challenges of life and he feels as though he has a purpose. You are becoming a man and so you are beginning to yearn for the companionship that a woman will bring you."

"What do you do with a girl, I mean, woman?"

"Well, you talk, spend time together, work together, play together. It takes a man and woman for a child to be born, so you raise children together. Basically, you build a life. You both help each other to be the very best that each of you can be."

Slane silently contemplated Peter's words. "What if I don't want to be with a woman?"

"What do you mean?"

"Well, I kinda like doing my own things, you know, like getting up when I want to and stuff like that. It sounds like you're kinda tied down. Do I have to be with, um…what's the word? *marry*, a woman?"

Peter paused for a minute. "No, you don't have to. But you don't have to make that decision now. Just take each day and see where it leads you. Okay?"

Slane nodded. He felt better, but he still felt an ache deep in his heart.

"Ah, there's Cassius," Peter exclaimed. Get the pack ready; we'll be moving out in just a few minutes."

•••

"So Dean Wortman was on our side, huh?" Dr. Cap leaned forward in his chair. "Well, good for him and good for you, Cade. It's a big deal to have the Dean believe in you."

Cade took a swallow of his Coke. "I wasn't sure which way it would go, especially with old Hammonds painting a picture of Pierce as a mass-murderer in training. I gave everything in that meeting to protect that kid and keep him here. Can you imagine if they'd shipped him away somewhere?"

Dr. Cap nodded. "There have always been those at Boyd who want to help kids, but they only want the ones that are easy and well adjusted. It's ridiculous. This place was founded on the principles of helping all children regardless of their mental or emotional state. I battled for my kids too when I was in your position. And now it's those kids who are now adults that the Board members want to come back and speak at the fundraisers. Kind of funny, now that I think about it."

They were sitting on Dr. Cap's porch enjoying the evening breeze.

"I remember one time during an open house they told me to keep 'my kids' in the therapy room," said Dr. Cap chuckling to himself.

"What happened?" Cade asked.

"Well, this particular open house was specifically staged for a group of well-to-do folks from one of the local churches who gave quite a bit of money and the Board was hoping to get this group to put a large sum of money towards a new administration building. The children were warned to be on their best behavior and it was a miserable weekend that involved cleaning and scrubbing and cleaning some more. Some of the Board members got a bright idea that all the 'troubled' children, which were the ones I worked with, should stay with me and that I should keep them out of sight for the entire afternoon. 'Keep them at the back of the campus in the therapy room,' they said."

"What did you tell them?"

"What could I tell them? Children with emotional and mental problems have always been seen as second rate so no amount of cajoling from me could get any of those business men to change their minds, but I was really mad about it. So I suggested they let me take the truck and we could go to the lake for the day and go canoeing. Of course, that would cost money and more staff so that was promptly thrown out the window. 'Just keep them occupied and out of sight,' I was told."

"How many were there?"

"Oh man, in those days? Probably about twenty-five to thirty.

And these were some hum-dingers I'm tellin' you. Most were abused, sexually, physically, and emotionally, and in those days there was hardly any care like they have now. Now you have a staff of people that can specialize with each child. Of course you get the tough ones, but it's more than just yourself. There were anger issues, suicidal kids, you name it. The boys would fight and scrap at the drop of a hat and the girls were as mean as snakes. But they loved me and I loved them and we had a certain respect for each other. It was this experience that made me work toward getting Boyd to be connected with the University so that I could get some help."

"So what happened next?"

"The afternoon actually went pretty well for about an hour. I got them corralled in the therapy room and in those days there was a big lot behind it for them to go outside and run around. If the visiting slowpokes would have gone through the tour like normal people, we would have never had a problem. But the Board had to drag them through each cottage and have tea and crumpets like we were some country club. Some of my kids wanted to see what was going on at the cottages and I didn't blame them. One boy started a rumor that all the other kids were going to get presents from the 'rich folks' and that some of them were going to be adopted on the spot. The kids got restless. A few of the boys started to fight in the back lot. We had a lot of rain that month and there was this area behind the lot that got muddy with about two feet of standing water and those boys went right in. By the time I got back there, three or four were stripped down to their underwear wrestling in the mud and about ten others had jumped into the mud for fun. I screamed for them to stop but to no avail and eventually I got pulled down into the slop."

"What a mess!" Cade exclaimed, laughing as he envisioned the scene.

"Oh, that's not even the best part," Dr. Cap said as he tilted back in his chair. "Once I was covered in mud, I was steaming mad and I was determined to get the boys that were fighting back inside. But I couldn't move because my shoes were stuck down in the mud."

"What did you do?" Cade asked.

"I did what I had to do! Left my shoes in the mud and chased those boys. By now they were running across the grass and screaming to high heaven. I jumped out of the mud and started chasing them and when they saw me coming and they tore off across the campus, right past the chapel and just as they came to the front of their cottage, guess who emerged?" Dr. Cap laughed and slapped his leg.

"The visitors!" Cade bellowed, doubled over as he envisioned the scene.

"The visitors, the Board members, the staff. Here's these four or five boys in their underwear, so muddy you couldn't tell if they were naked or not. Some of the kids from the cottage yelled out, 'They's nekkid!' and started laughing and hooting and hollering. Then I came running up and I've got mud from my waist to my ankles. By now all the other kids I had been supposed to watch came runnin' up behind me too and we're all standing there, looking like vagabonds, completely speechless. I'll never forget one of those stuck up Christian women looking at us with such a look of horror on her face!"

"What did you do?"

"Well, I was still angry over my kids being treated like a bunch of Frankensteins so I gathered myself and walked right up to each of the visitors and began shaking their hands and introducing myself. 'Hello there,' I said, sticking my muddy hand into theirs, 'I'm Dr. Capstone, so pleased ya'll could come! Let me know if you have any questions about the therapy program!'" Dr. Capstone laughed again, Cade had tears running down his face. "The Board members turned around and stomped off and the staff grabbed the boys and sent them to the showers."

"Did the visitors end up giving any money?"

"Well, no one spoke to me for about a week, and everyone thought that there was no way Boyd would get a check from this group. But then, miracle of miracles, a big fat check came in. I was a hero after that! One of the women wrote in a letter along with the check that she felt sorry for the poor man with mud all over him and she put in extra so they could hire more staff to help with the psychological well-being of the children. Isn't that something?"

"That's a great story," Cade said, wiping his eyes. "I really needed that one today. Is that muddy spot where the turtle pond was?"

"Yes, it was! Good memory!"

"You showed it to me when I first started here, and I've been meaning to put in another pond one of these days," Cade said as he finished his Coke.

"Yep, that's where it was," said Dr. Cap. "About two years after that I was clearing the grass and muck out of there for the turtle pond and guess what I found?"

"What?"

"My shoes!" and both men doubled over with laughter again.

••

Cassius, Peter, and Slane made their way over a slight rise and lay flat on the ground. They had been travelling for two weeks without incident under the cover of darkness. But now they were faced with a grim obstacle. The waning moon revealed a pack of Wolves directly in their path. Some were sleeping; some were sitting up licking their paws as if they had just returned from a kill. Slane counted at least five large males, a few females, and several pups. The pack was sprawled across a dense canyon with high walls. Slane, Cassius, and Peter were about a mile from the next camping point and daylight would soon come. To try and go around would leave the trio exposed when daylight came, and besides, they had been traveling all night and were exhausted.

"What are we going to do?" Slane whispered to Cassius and Peter.

"They are directly in our path," Cassius hissed. "And morning is coming quickly." Slane and Cassius looked at Peter.

Peter's eyes narrowed and he spoke without taking his eyes off the slumbering pack. "Cassius, you will swoop down and grab one of the small cubs to create a disturbance. That will draw the females. The males will become alert and sit up but won't react. Slane, that will be your cue to start firing your arrows. Kill as many of the males as you can as quickly as you can but leave one badly wounded. This will trigger the others to flee as they won't be able to see where the attack is coming from or what it is. I will stay hidden here with Slane and protect him should they figure out where we are."

Cassius and Slane nodded. Slane quickly laid out his arrows and slid one into position. His pulse quickened. His senses sharpened. It was time to kill.

"Cassius," Peter said calmly, "when you're ready." Then he looked at Slane.

Cassius paused, and then quickly picked out the cub that would serve as the bait. With a jump and flap of his wings, he was off. Slane held his breath as he watched the Great Eagle reach a diving height and then plummeted like a dark missile through the air. Slane turned his attention to the group of males. He pulled back on his bow and waited. A high pitched scream split the silence as Cassius dug his talons into the small helpless cub and lifted it off the ground. The males simultaneously lifted their heads and Slane could see five large shapes against the horizon which was now beginning to brighten with a dull light. He released his arrow and immediately loaded another. The first head slumped as the next arrow slammed into the cranium of the second. Slane's aim was impeccable. Slane released his third arrow and noticed that the third and fourth Wolf heads slumped together.

The arrow found its mark just as the Wolf behind number three moved to get up and the arrow pierced both of their eye sockets killing them instantly. The fifth and final male, weighing at least two hundred and fifty pounds, leaped over his dead comrades and bounded towards the females chasing the Eagle holding one of his dear cubs just above their outstretched jaws. He judged his leap towards the Eagle perfectly when out of the darkness a searing pain from Slane's arrow shattered his right shoulder, dropping him immediately to the ground. He howled in pain, writhing on the ground. The Wolf got up and in a hobbling run left the females and headed in the opposite direction. As soon as Cassius saw the fifth male fall, he crushed the skull of the cub and dropped it. The females, seeing the dead cub and hearing the howls of the leader of their pack, turned to follow him. The remaining cubs scampered after their mothers. Slane readied another arrow but quickly realized that he didn't need it.

"Let's go!" Peter exclaimed, jumping from his hiding place. Cassius was already leading the way by air, scanning the landscape for danger. Slane grabbed the pack and slung his bow over his shoulder. He kept the arrow in his hand just in case and slid down the ridge, feeling the sand filling his shoes as he went. Peter looked like a red flash and Slane ran as hard as he could once he reached the bottom of the ridge to catch up to him.

The trio made their way to a large rock embankment and found a cave. Slane and Peter gathered brush and wood to block the entrance. Slane lit a torch to check the back of the cave for potentially dangerous creatures. The morning sun broke full over the horizon. Cassius set off to scout for Wolves and find food. Slane thought he noticed green trees off in the distance. Peter told him that they were moving towards the outer edges of the Dead Lands and that for the first time in his life Slane would see green trees, grass, and rivers. Peter said the water in the rivers was blue like the sky. Slane had seen a green plant on a hike once when he was about seven. Peter and Cassius doubted his story but came nonetheless to the place where he said it was. Sure enough, a tiny green sprout had pushed forth out of the volcanic muck, no doubt from a leftover seed that had lain dormant from another lifetime. Slane remembered that Peter and Cassius bent down and cried when they saw it.

"It's a promise," Peter said, admiring the tiny tree.

"What kind of promise?" Slane asked.

"It's a promise from the Ancient," said Cassius. "You're too young to understand yet, but soon you will."

"What does the promise say?" asked Slane, annoyed at being told he was too young to understand anything. "I wanna know!"

"The Ancient has whispered to us yet again, my young soldier. And He wants you to know this by showing this to you," Peter said softly.

"Kinda looks like a weed, huh?" Slane said laughing.

Cassius turned to face him. Slane saw the pupils in his eyes dilate like a thousand telescopes. Slane's stomach sank. He was being funny in a serious moment. Obviously, from the look on his comrades face, a very serious moment.

"Do you know how improbable it is for us to see this?" Cassius asked.

"Do you have any idea how impossible it is for anything living to grow here?" Peter said, stepping forward. "This is a miracle, boy! A message. It is here so that we do not give up hope. It is a guidepost that says 'Keep living, keep going, don't give up, I am with you'. This tells us that our quest is still before us and we must stay the course."

"This is the promise from the Ancient," Cassius began softly.

'Though the fig tree does not bud and there are no grapes on the vines, though the olive crop fails and the fields produce no food, though there are no sheep in the pen, and no cattle in the stalls, I am here and you can trust Me.'

"What does it mean?" Slane asked.

"It means," Cassius began, "That even in this awful place we are being watched and cared for. It also means that what may appear as banishment is part of a bigger plan that will lead us to greater blessings in our lives than we ever thought. That is our hope and this little green sprout is a reminder of that."

"Remember Slane," said Peter, "You will face very dark times in your life but there is a pulse, a heartbeat, out there." Peter looked up at the sky. "A heartbeat that keeps everything in balance. Trust it, believe it, and live your life without fear."

The three were silent for a while. Slane saw the green draining from the leaves of the tiny tree and it began to droop. Within minutes, it was a brown stalk. Slane plucked it from the black, tarry sand and most of the remaining leaves, brown and crinkly, dropped off. Slane carried it to the cave and laid it next to his bed. He kept it there until the day they left to begin their journey out of the Dead Lands. From that day on, Slane looked for signs just like Peter and Cassius had told him to, and he found them. Food always appeared when they needed it. Their water source never ran dry. While there were lean times and although life was difficult, they always had what they needed to sustain their lives. He was amazed as they left the Dead Lands that there was always food, water, and a cave waiting for them.

"Help me with this log, Slane," Peter called to him. Slane picked up one end and slid it towards the opening of the cave. Peter pulled two large tumbleweeds on top of it. "Is the back of this cave clear?"

"Yes, nothing but a few roaches and spiders way in the back."

"Any Wolf tracks?"

"No, but I found some tracks that I didn't recognize. Come and see."

Slane showed Peter the tracks. They were slender and pointed.

"What is it?" Slane asked, pointing his torch towards the ground.

"Deer tracks!" Peter said excitedly. "Just as I thought! This means we are nearing the pass over the Great River. We've got a ways to go yet, but we are close my boy, close!" Peter nudged Slane's leg with his shoulder.

Slane smiled. Peter's excitement was infectious. He felt a surge of energy at his companion's reaction.

"Is that the river that divides the Dead Lands from the rest of the world?"

"Yes, it forms a natural barrier. This time of year the river is lower and there is a shallow area that forms where we will pass. We will reach it just in time. It is a very dangerous river to cross any time of the year, but this is our best chance. Once we cross, you will see a whole different world, Slane. Still one with danger, but one of beauty and amazing creatures."

"Can we build a fire? Look, there's even a hole in this cave."

Peter looked up and shook his head. "Nope, it's too risky."

"But there aren't any Wolves around! Oh how I miss cooked food! Please?" Slane pleaded.

"We've come too far to be foolish, my son. Our freedom is coming closer with each step. do you want to risk all that we have sacrificed for some cooked food? Is your life or mine, or the life of Cassius worth more than an onion?"

Slane felt foolish and shook his head. Peter had a way of putting things into perspective.

"Keep your head about you. Don't allow your physical or emotional yearnings to cloud your reason. Stay sharp. One day you can eat all that your heart desires but for now we must stay hidden. Now ready your bed and get some rest. I'll take the first watch."

Slane said nothing and got his bed ready. He knew Peter was right. He shoved the thought of cooked food aside. He heard Cassius's wings as he landed just outside the opening to the cave. Slane turned to see Cassius hop over the makeshift blockade carrying two small vermin. He tossed one to Peter and began to rip the flesh from the other. Slane reached in the pack and felt around for a potato. He took it out and began to munch on it.

"What's wrong with him," Cassius asked Peter, as they both turned to look at Slane.

"Just tired and hungry and sick of this place like us," Peter replied.

Slane said nothing and took another bite of the potato.

"Hey kid," Cassius said as he hopped across the floor of the cave. "Tell ole Cassius all about it. What's eatin' ya?"

"Well, for one thing you have rat guts hanging from your beak," Slane said, looking annoyed.

"Well, you smell like a dead rat that's been baking in the sun for a week," Cassius shot back.

"At least my guts stay on the inside!" exclaimed Slane, feeling even more irritated.

"'Til I rip your gut open with these here claws and eat 'em while you watch me," Cassius said, lifting his spread claws and reaching for Slane's stomach.

"Hey!" Slane jumped up and threw his half eaten potato at Cassius. It hit him in the chest causing him to fall backwards. He squawked and opened his wings as wide as they would go, charging at Slane. Slane retreated backwards and tripped over a rock which sent him flying backwards. He landed on the ground with a thud. He sat for a moment and then crash! Slane disappeared from view! Cassius, in mid-charge, stopped suddenly and looked at Peter.

"Slane!" Peter yelled, rushing to the gaping hole. Cassius joined him and they looked down.

"Slane?" Cassius shouted. "Are you okay?"

They heard the sound of rushing water and noticed a blue-green glow coming from the hole.

"I'm okay!" Slane yelled.

Both Peter and Cassius sighed in relief. Cassius felt foolish for getting so angry at Slane, but that kid could really ruffle his feathers sometimes.

"C'mon down guys! It's an underground river! All the water we need!"

Peter and Cassius looked at each other. "Let's go!" Cassius said as he jumped through the hole and lighted on a rock. "Look!" Cassius said, "It's like a stairway, Peter!"

Peter looked down the hole and saw that the collapse left a pile of rock and boulders that resembled a staircase. He gingerly descended to the river's edge and looked around. They were surrounded by waves of blue and green light coming from the roof and along the sides of the cave. Each tiny light pulsed, creating a rippling effect across the top of the water, which cascaded gently by. The water was crystal clear and rushed by like a thousand diamonds.

"What are those?" Peter asked, looking up at the lights.

"Conctoca Spirals," said Cassius. "Tiny mushrooms filled with mold that glows when kept from sunlight. Millions of caves have them but rarely does anyone see them because light kills them instantly."

"Hey you two, time to get wet!" Slane yelled as he rushed up to Cassius and Peter and splashed them. Peter turned and chased him. Slane let out a whoop and dove under the surface. Peter dog paddled a short distance and then turned back. Cassius dunked his whole body under the water repeatedly and spread his wings as far as they would go. All three let the cool clear water wash over their tired dirty bodies.

"I have forgotten the last time I took a bath," Peter gasped as he came up from putting his head under the water.

"I haven't seen water like this since we were banished," Cassius said.

"Where does the river come from?" Slane asked, leaning his head back and dunking his hair in the water.

All three turned their heads towards the water source. They noticed that the water was coming from around a bend. Peter walked towards the bend and almost disappeared from view. Soon his head popped around the corner.

"Come quick! You have to see this!" he shouted.

Slane and Cassius hurried to meet him and both gasped in

amazement. The cave opened and appeared at least a mile wide and half a mile tall. The twinkling lights of the Concocta Spirals created a dazzling array of blue and green light and the river reflected the light and magnified it. Slane followed the river as far as his eyes would let him and he saw a cascading waterfall. It appeared that the river went on for many miles.

"It's the great river, that's for sure," said Cassius, staring up at the ceiling.

"No doubt," said Peter. "I believe that if we follow it, it will take us to the border."

"And no Wolves," Slane said. "I'm up for that!" he exclaimed as he cupped his hands in the water and threw it into the air.

"Not so fast," Peter cautioned. The water feels good now but we don't know if there enough bank for hiking further along. This could be the only open space and we don't know how narrow it may get up ahead."

"So we'll swim it," Slane answered eagerly.

"I don't think you understand, Slane," Cassius replied. "Not only would I not be able to swim, but if the cave narrows and we are forced into the water for long periods of time that would drain our energy and create all kinds of problems."

"Not to mention finding food. We don't know how long we would be underground," Peter added.

"I could do it," Slane said confidently. Peter and Cassius stared at him.

"I can!" Slane exclaimed, irritated by their condescending looks. "Look, there is light here. And it stretches as far as we can see. If there is bank here, then there will be bank up ahead. You mentioned food. Well, all I have eaten is potatoes for weeks and there are enough in the bag to feed me for two weeks more. Besides, I bet there's fish in these pools. It's cool, there's water, and it's no different than being up above with the intense heat, Wolves, and whatever else that threatens our survival."

Peter noticed Slane's voice deepen and his face took on the appearance of a man much older and seasoned. *The Warrior King is speaking now.*

"I know that it would be difficult down here," Slane continued. "But Cassius, you could make it. There's obviously room to fly and you're doing a lot of hopping around up there anyway. Yes, this is unknown down here, but isn't everything unknown? We didn't know those Wolves would be in our path but we dealt with it. You believe in the Ancient as do I, and that there is provident force guiding us. Didn't the Ancient lead us to this? Wouldn't we be foolish if we did not accept this great challenge?"

Peter and Cassius looked at each other. They knew he was right. Slane was no longer a boy. Neither argued with him.

"Let's go get our stuff then," Peter said, motioning to Slane with the turn of his head.

"Really?" Slane said surprised and excited. "You guys are going to listen to me? So we're really going to follow the river?"

"Why would we doubt you?" Cassius began. "You spoke just now like our king not our comrade. We will follow you, anywhere," Cassius said, bowing low and sweeping his wing in front of him.

"Worship him later," Peter interrupted, "we better get up there and get our things before the Wolves find out where we are." He nimbly went up the rocky staircase and disappeared. Slane and Cassius followed. Their cave was undisturbed. Belongings were quickly packed and the trio made their way back down but not before they boarded up the entrance to the cave with sticks, brush, and logs. Slane dragged a pile of sticks and brush over to the hole in the floor of the cave and pulled it over the opening as they descended to the river.

"I think that's a good place to camp over there," Peter pointed with his nose where the bank stretched towards the back of the cave.

"It looks fairly dry," said Cassius, picking up Slane's bow in his beak and hopping towards the area.

Slane realized in all the excitement that none of them had slept.

Suddenly, fatigue gripped him. The gentle sound of the river, glowing lights, and the coolness of the cave caused a dreamy sensation, and he stumbled as he prepared his bed.

"Sleep well, comrades," Peter said. "We'll get some rest and move out when we awake." For the first time since they had begun their trek, no one had to keep watch.

•••

14

FROM DARKNESS INTO LIGHT

"I want the blinds closed," Pierce instructed Cade. "Make it dark."

"Okay," Cade responded, getting up to close the blinds. The lights were already off. It seemed a crime to use them with the natural light from the big windows.

"How's that?" Cade asked, looking around the room.

"That one, over there." Pierce pointed towards the door at the front of the room.

Cade went to the door that led into the playroom and pulled the shade that hung at the top of it.

"Over there." Pierce pointed towards the back door.

"I'll have to get paper for that one," Pierce said, walking towards the back of the room. He took a piece of black construction paper and taped it over the small square window at the top of the door.

"Good?" He turned and looked at Pierce.

Pierce scanned the room. He nodded and began to work in the sand. He dug a trench from one end of the sandbox to the other. Then he cut strips of blue paper that fit into the trench. *This must be the river that I read about.* Pierce had not brought him any stories lately, so he was unsure as to what was going to happen next. After Pierce got all the paper in the trench he began to cover the river with various objects such as Lincoln Logs, and plastic lids. It appeared as though the river was underground. Pierce took Slane, Cassius, and Peter and laid them on their side under a large lid that he propped up with a stick. As far as Cade could tell, the trio had found an underground river that would guide them out of the Dead Lands.

"Looks like they are going underground now," Cade said, sitting on the edge of the sandbox.

"Yep," Pierce responded as he smoothed the sand with a plastic ruler.

"When we left off yesterday, they were in the cave after the great battle with the Wolves," Cade commented.

Pierce nodded.

"I wonder how they found the underground river."

"I wrote it up last night but I forgot to bring it," Pierce said quietly.

"Huh. Well, I guess you'll let me know what I need to know and when I need to know it," Cade responded.

Pierce continued to smooth the sand with the ruler. Cade waited, not knowing if Pierce would respond. As their therapeutic bond deepened, Pierce engaged in more conversation. But Cade had learned to not expect conversation with Pierce, nor did he pressure him with questions or lead him.

"They got into the cave and they were getting ready to rest. There was an argument between Cassius and Slane. Slane fell backwards and the floor of the cave gave way. He crashed through and ended up underground where there is a river. They can see because of the special moss and mushrooms that grow down there. Slane made a speech and told Cassius and Peter that the best chance they have is to follow the river. Cassius and Peter now see him as a leader and warrior, not just a boy."

"They are seeing him as a leader now," Cade responded. It was the most that Pierce had ever spoken to him. He remained calm, waiting to see what Pierce would say next.

"Even though he is still young, he is smart and can do more than just kill Wolves. He is a leader and a king," Pierce responded.

"Young people are smart and strong and can do great things," Cade said.

"But a lot of people think kids are just stupid and selfish. But they are not," Pierce said, putting the ruler down and smoothing the sand with his hand.

"You think people think you are stupid but you're not," said Cade.

"No I'm not!" yelled Pierce standing in the sand with his fists clenched. He took in huge breaths of air, causing his chest to heave up and down. He stared at Cade with passion swimming in his dark eyes.

"You're smart!" yelled Cade, jumping up with his arms held high.

"Yes I am!" yelled Pierce, putting his arms up in the air and stretching as high as he could.

"You're strong!" Cade yelled.

"Yes I am!" Pierce responded.

"Like Slane!" shouted Cade. "You feel like Slane!"

"Yes I do! I am Slane!" Pierce yelled once more and then collapsed into the sand. He lay on his side and watched Cassius, Peter, and Slane lying on their side under the shelter. He was so still Cade thought he might be sleeping but Pierce's eyes were open, watching Slane sleeping. Cade breathed a prayer of thanks for this beautiful exchange with Pierce, and he felt a great sense of gratitude that Pierce was healing and growing.

•••

"He's forming an identity, which is very important," Dr. Cap said. "Through the safety of the play room he has distanced himself from the trauma which has allowed him to get on his developmental path again."

Cade was sitting in Dr. Cap's living room after he finished up at Boyd.

"It's incredible to witness," Cade said, getting up to look out the window.

"The healing of a soul and mind – to witness the growth of a human is a pure miracle, and you are in a sacred place, my friend. I'm almost jealous. Oh, how I miss the playroom!"

Cade laughed. "Some days I'd like to switch places with *you*," he said grinning.

"No, you really wouldn't."

"That's true. Especially when I think of a kid like Pierce. I never know what's going to happen in our sessions."

"His identification with Slane is very telling," Dr. Cap said, leaning back in his chair.

"What do you think about that?" Cade asked.

"Slane is a warrior with a broken family. He is misplaced but fighting to find himself and reestablish himself in his rightful place as a king. All sorts of forces fight against him, but with the help of his friends he knows he can get there. This kid's a fighter and in my experience the fighter's usually come out okay."

Cade nodded. "You're right, I think Pierce sees himself in much the same way. He's a survivor but he's clearly showing that he does not see himself as a victim. Instead, he identifies with the warrior and intends to take his place in this world as someone who is going to do great things. Just like Slane."

"Yep, just like Slane," Dr. Capstone acknowledged.

"How is school going for him?" Dr. Capstone asked.

"Better. We moved him up a grade in math and science, and he's joined the chess club."

"I bet he's good at that."

"Incredible. I only played him a few times, but the kid knows his way around the chess board."

"Is there a particular piece that he likes?" Dr. Cap asked.

"The Rook. The Castle. Remember the old chess set you found at the garage sale that was missing some pieces?"

"Yes! The pieces were huge and I figured that kids would use them in the sandbox somehow."

"Right. Well, Pierce found the Rook from that set on his second visit to the playroom. He went to it every day and carried it around. He spent a lot of time examining the intricate castle design, as if he was memorizing every brick. Now, he sets it in the corner of the sandbox the whole time he is playing out the Slane scenarios."

"Very interesting," Dr. Cap said rubbing his chin.

"I'm wondering if the castle from the chess set is the castle that he sees Slane living in someday," Cade said, as he stood to leave.

Dr. Cap rose with him. "In children's play, castles represent a fortress of safety for those who feel emotionally vulnerable. It also represents a form of the self. It appears from what you've told me that Slane and Pierce are developing together and the castle represents some kind of end point. Keep the play going, Cade. Enjoy this journey, my friend. This one's special."

Cade gave his mentor a large bear hug. "I will, and I'll keep you posted."

••

Dr. Cade said since I like to write I should keep a journal. He said that it's a good way to get out my thoughts and feelings. I don't know about that. I've never done it before. Well, here it goes. Slane is a warrior and not just a boy. He is strong. He is going to lead Cassius and Peter. He is brave. The underground river will give them water and lead them out of the Dead Lands. I wonder what creatures are down here. Slane can't think about that now. He must keep leading and keep going. He is smarter than what people think. I am smarter than what people think. I am in this place that I don't like. But I have a safe place and a safe person who believes in me. Cade is good. I can trust him. I like him. He reads my story and likes it. I was right to let him be in my story and play the part of Cassius. I liked it when he got me to yell the other day about how strong I am. I want to do that again. *This seems okay. I think I'll keep going.*

The playroom is still my favorite place. I am never sad in the playroom or when I am writing my story. I get to go there almost every day. After I'm there, it makes me feel like I can do anything. At night

I write my story. I keep it secret. Cade is the only person who sees it. When I get to my room at night, I write using my flashlight. We are not supposed to but I've learned how to hide under my bed and write there. I make lumps in the bed to make it look like I'm in the bed. I pull the quilt all the way to the floor and I am underneath the bed but no one knows it. My roommate Jeffrey is fat and snores real loud. I doubt a hurricane would wake him. He seems oblivious to what I do. I like that. His parents were bad people and he was taken from them and put here. I heard him crying once after we went to bed. I wanted to tell him about my mom but I felt frozen, like I couldn't move. His crying made me think of my mom and I saw everything again…the explosion, the fire, her burning body with her hands reaching for the sky. I couldn't move even though part of me wanted to talk to Jeffrey. I know he wanted to talk to me but I pretended to be asleep. I couldn't talk to him because I was thinking of my mom. I realized that I had not thought of her in a long time. It hurt all over again. But then something happened.

When I did think of her again, even though I remembered those awful things and I could see them in my mind, I noticed that they did not make me paralyzed. Before I would be paralyzed when I thought of the explosion and seeing her burn in my mind. But this time I thought of Slane and how he doesn't have a mother or a father just like me. I thought of how he has seen awful things and almost died when the Wolves attacked him. I thought of how he has to be strong and rely on his friends. I have to be strong in life without a mom or dad too. But I have Cade and I think I can rely on him.

That night I fell asleep and did not have any bad dreams. I got up the next morning and went to all my classes and not once did I feel angry or like I was going to hit anybody. It's like I can remember what happened like I saw them on the news and they don't make my head hurt. I had a good day at school, and ever since they moved me up I have had good days. I like my new classes with the older kids. They leave me alone. I can do the math easily and I know more than the teacher but I'm not going to say anything. Sometimes the kids whisper that they think I'm weird and they think that I don't hear them but I do. I smile on the inside because I like other people thinking that I'm weird; when they think you're weird they leave you alone. English and history class is where I pretend to be taking notes but I work on my story. Cade mentioned one day that he didn't know how I could write so much in such a short amount of time and I think he knows that I do some writing during my classes. But he doesn't say anything. But I think he knows. I think he knows that I know that he knows. *Hey, I kind of like this journaling stuff!*

Cade is smart. He knows how to juggle. A few days after I met him he juggled three tennis balls. Then he juggled a soccer ball, a tennis ball, and a stuffed dog. Then he juggled the stuffed dog, a stapler, and a tape dispenser. He dropped the tape dispenser and the roll of tape flew out and rolled across the floor. Cade laughed. He did not get mad or yell. All of my mom's boyfriends yelled a lot. They got mad real quick. Cade is not like that. I didn't know that there were men like Cade in the world. Mr. Sims, my math teacher seems to be the same as Cade. He has never yelled or got mad at me or anyone else in the class. I used to think all men were mad and dangerous. I was afraid of them. But not now. Slane's dad was bad and he had bad men with him, but Slane's grandfather was very good. Peter and Cassius are good and they are men. They had bad things done to them by the Evil Queen. I have a feeling her curse will haunt them for a long time.

Cade can do other things too. He made ten shots in a row in the Nerf Hoop one day. He said he does it all the time when no one is in the room with him. He said he practices juggling when he is alone. He said juggling helps him think when he is writing his books. He has had a few books published. He is a writer, counselor, and he told me he sometimes teaches at the University. He also plays the piano and grows all kinds of plants and little trees. One day I saw him throw a football with another kid and he threw it really far. How can someone do all those things? I want to be a writer so I don't have to talk to people. I have read about authors who write and send out their manuscripts through the mail and make their money through writing. I have always felt like I wanted to be alone. Cade helped me understand that some people just don't like talking to others. They are called introverts. That's what I am. He said as I grow I'll learn how to talk to people better, but that I'll probably always be most comfortable by myself. He said that the most important thing is that I like myself and just let me be who I am. That made me feel really good that day. I can just be me. He probably thinks that I'm not listening because I don't say anything back when he talks to me like that, but I listen and I like hearing him talk. I know that he is trying to help me understand myself and I do feel better. I know that I'm not a mistake and I can do great things in life. I want to be a writer and I will be a writer. *And I'm writing right now!*

I do think of my mother sometimes. I have learned to think of her when she was fun and think of our good times, not just when she burned. I learned that from Slane. He was really sad one day because he was thinking about not having his mother and Peter helped him to think of her as strong and beautiful. Peter told Slane that he was a part of her even though she was gone. Peter told Slane that the best way to honor his mother was to make good choices and fight his way back and claim the throne that was rightly his. I remember good times with my mom. She liked to walk and she would take me on walks when I was younger. We used to find pretty rocks and trinkets, she called them…pieces of broken glass and plastic key chain parts. She was good at finding things. Once, she found a gold bracelet that was so shiny it almost blinded me in the sun. We pretended to be wealthy people and she talked in an English accent and that made me laugh so hard. When she found the bracelet I remember her admiring it and the sun was behind her. She looked like an angel standing there, her hair bright and shining and her smiling so big. She was happy then. I remember there was no man to get in the way and I don't think she was using drugs then. We played during the day and she was working at night, I remember staying with her friend, Aunt Janine. She was nice too. She let me stay up later than I was supposed to and watch TV with her. I think she was very lonely.

Another day I remember with my mom was when we got free tickets to the State Fair. She and I laughed all day and ate hot dogs and cotton candy. We rode all the big rides that I was allowed to go on and I won a huge stuffed dog for her at the ring toss booth. She hugged me so tight. She named the dog Jerry. It was the happiest day. A few months later she was actually with a guy named Jerry who had a dog named Jerry and that dog ripped up the stuffed dog. I remember I cried really hard because it was the only thing that I had ever actually earned to give to my mom. I remember wanting to kill the Jerry's right then and there. My mom told me to stop crying because Jerry the Man might get angry if I woke him up. I wanted to tell her that I was going to kill him in his sleep because I thought that then she might realize that she didn't need any more men because she had me but I didn't because she was crying because I was crying. A few months later Jerry the Man got arrested for some reason and we got stuck with Jerry the Dog, who turned out to be nice when Jerry the Man wasn't around. I sort of came to like Jerry the Dog. One day I was outside with him and he chased a cat across the street and never came back. Like everything else – he went away. What makes it hard with my mom is all the good stuff is followed up by bad stuff. Then the bad floods out the good and I'm sad again, and when I'm sad I always remember her dying and what I saw. Someday I will ask Cade about how I can just keep the good memories. I think he will know how. *There. I think I'll stop for now. Wow, I can't believe how much I wrote just now.*

•••

Slane awoke to Peter's wet, cold nose nudging him under his chin. Peter's yellow eyes glowed mysteriously from the light of the Concocta Spirals.

"Time to get moving, Slane," Peter said.

"Where's Cassius?" Slane said, sleepily wiping his eyes. He heard the river and felt the dampness of the cave.

"He's over there, catching fish."

"What?" Slane stood up.

"Yes. Not only did your instinct about the river leading us out of the Dead Lands prove to be correct, but it's also full of fish."

"No more potatoes?" Slane exclaimed.

"No more potatoes!"

"Cassius!"

Cassius turned with a fish in his beak. Slane laughed and ran toward him, almost slipping on the pile of fish next to Cassius.

"Hey, you're up! Look at all these fish!" Cassius tossed his last catch on the pile.

"Great, but how are we going to eat them?" Slane asked.

"What do you mean?" Peter said, ripping into one of the fish with his razor sharp teeth while holding the fish in his paws.

"Yeah, what do you mean?" Cassius asked incredulously.

"We have to cook them, right? I mean, you know, a fire and everything?"

Peter and Cassius laughed. "He thinks," Peter said doubled over with laughter and pieces of fish came flying out of his mouth, "that we are going to cook for him!"

Cassius roared and fell back on the ground with his feet in the air.

"Very funny," said Slane, picking up a fish and wondering where to take his first bite.

"Go for the belly," Peter said, feeling compassion for Slane. "Go ahead, don't be shy."

Slane suddenly realized that he was hungry. He opened his mouth and brought the fish closer; the smell of it hit his nostrils. He felt the roughness of the scales scrape over his tongue and he clamped down and tore into the meat. A juicy sensation filled his mouth. He felt the roughness of the scales. But then, a rich flavor touched his tongue. He wanted more. *This isn't so bad!* Slane realized that if he scraped the fish first to remove the scales, the process was much more pleasant. Peter and Cassius had neglected to tell him that part. After putting away three more fish, he sat back and looked at Peter and Cassius.

"Not bad, not bad at all," he said as he leaned on the pack and patted his stomach.

"Welcome to the carnivore club kid," Cassius said. "You're one of us now."

After breakfast, the trio gathered their belongings and began to follow the river. It was easy going and their spirits were high. Slane was grateful to be out of the pounding sun and dusty conditions of the land above. The cave, while damp and musty, had no Wolves and no other enemies that threatened their safety. The crushed, smooth pebbles made walking very easy. Slane liked the crunching sound made by his feet and thought it sounded like a thousand soldiers marching in unison. The cave was vast enough for Cassius to fly at short intervals. The glow from the Spirals continued to light the way, pulsing and covering the ground in a bluish green blanket that made Slane feel safe. For the first time since they began the exodus from the Dead Lands, they could talk while they walked and Slane could walk next to Peter instead of following along behind him. The river made a series of twists and turns and at times Peter and Slane had to make their way around small boulders and rocks that lined the edges of the river. Slane realized quickly that he had no idea what time of day it was. He asked Peter about this and Peter quickly told him that it was mid-afternoon, explaining that animals maintain an internal clock more so than humans, and despite living in utter darkness, animals always know the position of the sun.

It felt as though they were making incredible time. Slane felt energized, probably from not having to spend so much energy being on high alert for Wolves, falling into a chasm in the darkness, or getting lost in a rainstorm. He could talk at will without whispering, and Peter, usually very serious when they traveled, made jokes.

"How many humans does it take to build a bridge?" he asked Slane.

"I don't know," Slane said, confused.

"None," Peter replied. "They will tire of it soon enough and decide to just stay put."

Peter followed up with another question. "How many foxes does it take to build a bridge?"

"One thousand?"

"One. He will be so smart that he will get all the other animals to do it for him."

Slane wished he was as smart as Peter. He tried to tell a joke but it always came out wrong.

"How many fish does it take to build a boat?" Slane asked, sounding as witty as he could.

"Fish don't need a boat," Peter said as soon as the question was out of Slane's mouth. And that was how it usually went.

Cassius told them that the river followed a northwesterly course, which was the exact direction they needed to go. The roof of the cave, at least fifty feet high when they began, seemed to be even higher after nearly a whole day of hiking underground. Cassius told Slane he believed this cave was centuries old judging by the cave's massive dimensions and the density of the Concocta Spirals. A young cave, Cassius explained, would be much more shallow and less hollowed out. Since rivers ebb and flow throughout the seasons, there would be times when, during times of great rain for instance, that the river would swell and crash through the cave. This activity would make the bottom of the river deeper by hollowing out the cave. Over the course of hundreds of years, a cave with a river running through it would gradually dig deeper into the earth eventually creating the cavernous effect they were witnessing.

After nearly ten hours of hiking, they all agreed it was time to rest. They found a wide embankment that stretched several hundred feet and where many fish gathered in a shallow pool. Cassius found them so plentiful that he merely sat near the water's edge and picked them out with one foot and slung them over to Peter and Slane. Slane, no longer leery of eating raw fish greedily devoured them nearly as quickly as Cassius tossed them out. Peter bathed in a shallow stream and then joined Slane, creating his own pile of flopping fish that would soon be nothing but bones. After eating, Peter lay with his head on his paws and Cassius preened his feathers while perched on a piece of driftwood. Slane lay on his back with his head against Peter staring at the pulsing vibrating light of the Spirals high above.

"Where did the Spirals come from?"

"From the Ancient," Cassius said without hesitation, pulling at a tail feather with his beak. "He made them."

"But I mean, how did they get here, in this forsaken place?"

"Remember the little green tree you found?" Peter asked.

"Yes, but –"

"Same thing," Peter lifted his head as he spoke. "The Ancient designed a world that would give all living things everything they needed to survive. The Spirals give light in very dark places. The Ancient designed it that way."

Cassius gave his feathers a thorough shake. "Remember, Slane, creation is designed to change and adapt as the world changes. Creation is always evolving and adapting. Just like that little green sprout you found, the Spirals remind us that even here, there is the promise of the Ancient's presence in all places. Even in one that we think is forsaken."

"I remember these words from my teachers," Peter said.

The burning sand will become a pool, the thirsty ground bubbling springs. In the haunts where Wolves once lay, grass and reeds and papyrus will grow. The Ancient will guide you always; he will satisfy your needs in a sun-scorched land, you will be like a well-watered garden, like a spring whose waters never fail."

Slane loved hearing his friends quote from the books of their childhoods. He pondered the words and realized that all their needs had been met. He felt a surge of hope which energized him.

"Did you guys ever see Spirals in your other life? You know, before you came to the Dead Lands?"

"Only once," Cassius replied. "Peter, remember the old cave where we used to let the horses drink?"

Peter nodded.

"I once followed the stream into the cave and went quite far back and suddenly when I turned a corner I saw the ceiling light up with Concocta Spirals. It was an amazing sight."

The three were silent for a while. Slane broke the silence.

"Is the Queen dead?

Peter and Cassius looked at each other.

"We don't know," said Peter.

"The Dead Lands have been our only life these many years," Cassius replied. "We have no knowledge of the happenings of our old world."

"What if she is still alive? Will we have to kill her?"

Peter and Cassius looked at each other again.

"Well, we might as well tell him!" Cassius said, holding out his wings.

Peter looked down at his paws and then at Slane.

"Slane, on our quest to get back to the land in which you will be restored as King, we will have to pass through the land from which Cassius and I came. The Queen may be dead by now, but probably not. Regardless, we will pass through undetected. There are only three of us and we do not know who is in power, nor is it of any concern to us."

"But don't you want revenge if she is still alive?" Slane asked incredulously. "The Queen ruined your lives!"

"Revenge is a waste of time," Cassius began. "Our quest is to get you back to your land. Seeking revenge would be selfish and take us off our course."

"I don't understand that. I mean, I appreciate you both wanting to help me, but if it was me I would want to make that evil woman pay for what she did to you."

"The wise do not seek revenge," Peter said as he stood, causing Slane to sit up. He turned and looked directly into Slane's eyes. "It is the way of the Ancient. Cassius and I determined when we found you that we would trust the quest. If we are supposed to go back to our land after we fulfill our duties to you, we believe it will be revealed to us. But we will not seek revenge against those who have wronged us, and we want to teach you to do the same. The wise warrior who will become King must learn this important lesson."

Slane watched the swirling ripples from the water's current that reflected the dancing light of the Spirals. He felt confused. He knew that Peter and Cassius were right, but he felt a great desire to kill the Queen. His friends had given up their freedom for him, living as animals in this awful place in the hopes that returning him to his land would somehow give them their lives back. But what life would they have when and if they got back? And how much had been lost already? Love, careers, homes, families whom they loved and cherished – things that Slane could not understand, yet he felt the emptiness at times in his own bosom. It made him angry that these two friends – more than friends, fathers actually – were men who were good and just had been so wrongly accused and mistreated. He felt a fire within him.

"What is this fire I feel inside me?" he asked Cassius.

"It is the Warrior-Fire," Cassius explained. "It is the urge to destroy and fight, to make right that which you think is wrong in the world."

"You will always have the wise king battling the warrior inside you,"

Peter added. "To be successful you need to know which one to summon and which one to quell. It is no small task."

So that's why I feel so much tension! I wonder if we'll even get out of the Dead Lands much less me become a King. Slane kept his thoughts to himself. They finished their meal and prepared for sleep. Slane wished they could make a fire. He missed sleepily watching the glowing embers as Peter and Cassius told him tales and legends from their land. He also missed the warmth. Travelling underground was easier without the heat and the Wolves, but it was damp and cold. Peter and Cassius had fur and feathers but Slane only had Wolf hide blankets which by morning would be damp, and there was no way to dry them. Instinctively Peter lay down next to Slane to help him stay warm. Red fuzzy fur never felt so good.

"Hey, Peter?"

"Yes, Slane?"

"You mentioned that it was the way of the Ancient to not seek revenge."

"That's right."

"But how do you know?"

"What do you mean?"

"Well, did he tell you that?"

"Sort of."

"How? Did he actually speak to you?"

"Not exactly," Peter said, shifting his position. "His words are written in a book."

"What kind of book and where is it?" Slane asked.

"The last one that I knew of was back in our homeland. It was very old. There used to be many books but over time they were lost or destroyed. People that actually talked to the Ancient wrote His words over thousands of years and dedicated people made copies of His sayings. Cassius and I were in classes to study the book and we had to memorize much of it."

"Was it the Ancient's actual words?" Slane asked, imagining a book that was centuries old and the people that actually talked with Him.

"Yes. When it wasn't His words it was the Ancient inspiring the words to be written."

Slane knew what Peter meant. He had heard the Ancient speak. He remembered a morning when he was very small playing at the mouth of the cave. A cool wind surrounded him amidst the crushing heat and he remembered hearing the words, "I Am Here." There were other times when he heard phrases that were whispered on the wisps of the wind. He shifted closer to Peter.

"You said the book was taken away by the Queen, right?"

"Yes," Peter replied. "Right after the King died."

"Tell me the story again!" Slane said excitedly.

"As you wish," Peter replied. Slane smiled. That's what Peter always said right before a good story.

· ·

The classroom was a large room with dark wood paneling and a high beamed ceiling. Stained glass windows with intricate zig-zagging patterns and colors allowed dazzling rays of light to dance across the floor. Professor Mazor, with his long beard and spectacles, entered the room in a hurried and perturbed manner. The students thought nothing of it. He always entered the room in this way, with a tornado of dust and papers swirling about him. As was his usual custom, he picked up a piece of chalk to write the opening assignment on the chalkboard and Peter noticed that his hand was shaking. Something was wrong. Very wrong. He was the instructor for The Study of Ancient Writings since the founding of the school and no one knew how old he was. Peter and Cassius joked that he was one of the original writers of the sacred text. The work in the class was quite tedious, but Professor Mazor's passion for the subject and his keen way of making the archaic script applicable to everyday life created an air of interest in most of the students. It was Peter's favorite class and Professor Mazor was his favorite professor. Cassius alone knew of Peter's desire to be a professor someday in a classroom much like this one.

Professor Mazor put the piece of chalk down and rummaged through a stack of papers on the desk. He looked up at the students. He looked down again and pretended to look for something. Peter and Cassius glanced at each other. Students murmured amongst themselves. Finally, the distracted professor plopped in the chair next to the desk and stared out at the class. He held up his hand and the class fell silent.

"My students," he began, "I am afraid I have some grim news."

No one spoke. Professor Mazor looked down at the floor.

He continued. "I will never teach this class again. No one will."

A gasp rose throughout the room.

"I'm afraid that your education as you know it is over."

Peter raised his hand.

"Yes?" the professor said weakly.

"Professor Mazor, how can this be? This class is the foundation of the school!"

The whole class erupted in questions and bewilderment. Professor Mazor finally put his hands up. The students became quiet again.

"My students, there is much going on that you are unaware of and that I am forbidden to discuss. All I can tell you is that I was told this morning I will no longer be teaching this class, I was forced to surrender all the copies of the Ancient texts and my notes regarding it late last evening."

"By whom?" Cassius yelled out.

"Yes!" Other students shouted. "By whom?"

Professor Mazor again put up his hands and looked cautiously at the door. "By the order of the Queen," he whispered. He slowly walked to the door and looked out the oblong window. Then he turned to the students. "I'm likely to be fired anyway and perhaps imprisoned so I may as well tell you." He looked directly at Peter and Cassius. "You are not safe." He addressed the rest of the class. "For those who have family in other towns, I suggest you go to them, quickly."

The class sat in stunned silence, sharing anxious looks with each other. The professor wept as he told them of how as soon as the death of the King was announced, the authorities came to his home and ransacked his office at the school, taking anything that appeared to be a part of the Ancient texts. Peter always saw Dr. Mazor as a strong, confident man but he was clearly shaken. This was serious. "The tide has turned," he said quietly as he wiped his eyes. "The evil is upon us and those who follow the Ancient will be sought out and destroyed."

Just then there was a loud bang on the door and three armed guards entered brandishing swords. One of them carried a scroll and bellowed, "By the order of the Queen, you are under arrest for treason and attempting to spread lies about the queen! Arrest him!"

The students jumped from their desks and several girls shrieked with terror. Peter jumped up to save Professor Mazor but the professor stared right at Peter and shook his head. "I will go willingly!" the professor shouted. "Don't touch me!" he said as he pulled his arm from the guard's hand. "Goodbye students," he said solemnly. "Pray to the Ancient for deliverance from this madness." The guards took him away. The next few days passed like a bad dream. Teachers, priests, and those who served in the churches were rounded up and arrested. The school was closed. It seemed as though the world had gone mad, just like Professor Mazor said. There were speedy trials conducted by malicious attorneys appointed by the Queen. Professor Mazor and many others were banished to the labor camps the Queen had created in the northern region of the kingdom. Many of the court staff that Peter and Cassius knew since their childhood had disappeared, and all copies of the Ancient texts were ordered to be burned. All the houses were searched and those found concealing copies were sent to the labor camps. Peter never got to say goodbye to Professor Mazor. He still thought about him and wondered what happened to him.

Peter and his friends were heartsick over the loss of the scrolls. It grieved their hearts for the loss of words of the Ancient but also the loss of their cultural heritage. One day while talking with Cassius, they remembered that Dr. Mazor showed them a hidden place in a storage closet in his classroom. Beneath the floorboards Dr. Mazor dug out a small compartment and sealed it. It was there where he kept his "most precious possession," a complete record of the Ancient text and writings.

"It was as if he knew this was going to happen," Peter remarked to Cassius. "Let's go and see if it is there, and if it is, we will take it and keep it safe."

Cassius agreed. One night they broke into the school building and found what they were looking for. Under the cover of darkness, the two friends hid the scrolls inside a watertight barrel and buried it in the cemetery behind a large tree.

"We must vow to return here someday and take the scrolls out of this land where they will be safe," Peter said to Cassius. "Will you make this vow with me?"

"I will," Cassius said solemnly.

"I don't know what is ahead of us, my brother, but I pray that I endure it with you."

"I will not leave your side, Peter. You have my word."

The two embraced and quickly left the cemetery, making sure they had not been seen. In just a matter of weeks, everything in their world changed. They could not have known that in just a few days they would be heading for the Dead Lands which would be their home for the next twelve years.

15
THE MONSTERS WITHIN

Pierce was looking for something. He rifled through a few of the boxes filled with toys on the shelf. Cade said nothing and watched him. The day before Pierce had been removed from a classroom for disruptive behavior. Two days before that he was placed on restriction for getting into a physical altercation with a fellow resident in his cottage. *It's been a rough week for him.* Cade wanted to ask him about the incidents but knew from experience that Pierce probably wouldn't discuss it. *Let him play it out. He'll show me. He's growing. He's healing. He trusts people, other than just me now.* The therapeutic bond was working; Pierce was reaching out to other adults as a result of the bond he shared with Cade. He conversed with fellow students. *He doesn't say much, but at least he's saying something.* He no longer appeared to be a shutdown angry boy. He was an adolescent and was taking some risks in the trust department. Cade had conducted enough therapy to know that growth was usually followed by setbacks, and this week's bumps did not bother Cade. *I worry more about the staff's reactions than what's going on inside Pierce.*

"Found it!"

Cade turned. "Whatcha got? Ah, an octopus."

Pierce smiled triumphantly and held up a purple rubber octopus. He set it aside and began to work in the sandbox. Cade watched, trusting the process of play and resisting the urge to lead the discussion about Pierce's struggles.

"You're digging a large hole there," he said as Pierce scooped a large pile of sand with a shovel.

"Yep. I'm making something."

"It looks big."

"Yep, something's going to happen."

"Oh, I see," Cade replied. He noticed that Pierce hadn't brought in any writing this week.

"You'll be Cassius just like always, but you're gonna have to make him fight."

"Like when he helped save Slane from the Wolves?"

"Yes, just like that."

"Yes, he used his claws."

"They are actually called talons, not claws," Pierce said softly as he put the finishing touches on the large hollowed out space in the sandbox. He placed the octopus in the hole and covered it with a large piece of black cardboard. He grabbed Peter, Cassius, and Slane and placed them next to the long trench he made in the sand that represented the underground river.

"Sometimes bad things are waiting for us and we don't even know it," Pierce said, staring at his creation. "People have no idea when they wake up in the morning what bad things are waiting for them."

"You are feeling like bad things happen to people."

"All the time. Bad things happen all the time."

"Like what bad things?"

Pierce held a faraway gaze and stared at the big oak outside the window.

"Like car accidents, murder, kids get kidnapped. Stuff like that."

"People getting killed and taken away," Cade said as he also watched the big tree sway in the afternoon breeze.

"You can try and be ready for bad stuff but it doesn't matter. It will happen whether you're ready or not," Pierce said as he turned and looked at Cade. His eyes were big, beautiful, and sad. Cade thought he saw tears brimming at the bottom. He held Pierce's gaze.

"You are feeling like something bad is coming?"

"Maybe, maybe not."

"I see."

Cade noticed the lengthened shadows outside. Fall was coming. The days were shorter. Suddenly, he remembered something. No wonder Pierce had a tough week. Sunday of the previous week marked the anniversary of his mother's death. Last year Pierce was completely out of control during this week. His play had been violent with themes of destruction, death, and wounding. If a few behavioral issues were the extent of Pierce revisiting the death of his mother, then much progress had indeed been made. Cade found comfort in this but was frustrated with himself. *I should have remembered. I will tell the staff immediately after our session.*

"Well," Pierce said, breaking up Cade's thoughts. "Let's get started."

∙∙∙

"Is it morning already?" Slane moaned as Peter poked him with his paw.

"Time to move lazybones or I'll lick you," Peter said putting his snout next to Slane's face.

"Yuck! Okay, okay I'm getting up!" Slane rolled over and sat up, rubbing his eyes.

"Get the pack ready, Cassius has some fish for you."

After a quick breakfast, the trio set out. After nearly a week of travelling underground, each member had become accustomed to the conditions. Slane was used to the damp environment, although his fingers and toes stayed wrinkly nearly all the time. Peter's feet no longer ached after a day of walking on the pebbles that lined the underground river. Cassius had become quite good at flying in the blue-green gloom and avoiding obstacles that hung from the roof of the cave.

"How much longer do you think we have to go?" Slane asked.

"'Til we're out," Cassius said, swooping low and tapping Slane's head with his wing.

"Funny, Cassius! I'm serious! Shouldn't we find a way to go above ground and check our location?"

"He does have a point, Cassius," Peter responded. "Maybe we should look for a passageway up above to see where we are."

"Trust the river, my friends," Cassius said, landing in front of them. Besides, we haven't seen any light from the outside world at all. We don't have any tools to break through the rock so it's pointless. We are still heading northwest and that is the direction we need to go."

Peter and Slane looked at one another and nodded in agreement. Cassius was right. Besides, they would lose valuable time and risk potential injury should they dig out. And what if they dug out? What dangers awaited them at the surface? They would trust the river. Peter estimated they had travelled nearly a ten miles underground without any threats. Cassius knew they were heading in the right direction. He believed that in the next few days they would come close to the surface again and the border of the Dead Lands. Slane hoped so. He was getting tired of constant darkness with only the blue-green glow from the Spirals. *I need sunlight. I'm not feeling very good without it. I feel despair at times, but it doesn't make sense; we're out of danger and we have plenty of food.* Peter told him that this was normal.

"You can get rid of despair by focusing on the next step before you. Be grateful for each step in that moment," Peter said.

Peter was right. It helped keep the despair away.

Three more days of hiking brought them to a wide lake where the river pooled and swirled in large circular arcs. It was the largest lake the trio had encountered. Peter noticed that the Spirals did not grow over this lake and he wondered why. Cassius believed it was because the dome was so large. Slane did not care. He unfolded the pack and flopped on the ground. His knees and feet ached and his stomach was getting tired of fish. He imagined a large fire with a slab of meat grilling over it while potatoes roasted in the coals. The vision roused his appetite and he was keenly aware of his empty stomach.

"Can we start a fire?" Slane asked, knowing that the answer would be "no" but feeling an urge to start a ruckus.

"NO!" Cassius exclaimed.

"Why did you even answer him?" Peter responded. "He's trying to get at you. Now look, you ruffled your feathers, old boy."

"Yes, old boy," Slane grinned widely, "Now you have ruffled feathers."

Cassius was annoyed. "I'm going to catch some fish for us – I'll be back." He hopped once and took to the air and landed near the water's edge.

"Why do you want to irritate him?" Peter asked with a scolding glance.

"Because it's so fun!" Slane replied.

After a few minutes there was a rustling of feathers behind them. They were surprised to see Cassius, fishless, looking perplexed.

"We have problem," he said, picking up a rock with his foot and tossing it aside.

"And what is that?" asked Peter.

"There are no fish."

"What?" asked Slane, feeling the ache in his stomach getting bigger.

"You heard me correctly," Cassius replied. "I went all along the edge and over the middle. It's harder to see without the Spirals but there's nothing here. The water is really black and it may be because the lake is very deep. But it's strange. We may have to keep moving or go back a ways to find food."

Peter walked over to the edge of the lake and Slane followed. Cassius was right. The edge looked different than that of any shore they had previously encountered. Maybe it was because it was deep, but Slane felt something was amiss.

"The water does look different," Slane said, peering into the blackness.

He wondered how deep it was. He reached down and tossed a rock. The rock made a splash and Slane watched the ripples race across the water.

Peter lowered his head to the water and took several strong sniffs. "It smells different, almost oily," he said, dabbing the surface with his paw.

Slane threw a few more rocks. It helped take his mind off his hunger. He found some fairly large smooth ones and tried to skip them farther and farther. Peter and Cassius were discussing whether or not to go further up the river or go back to find food. A rock that Slane threw skipped seven times near the middle of the lake and disappeared. Just as he was about to throw another, he noticed bubbles coming up around where the stone went under. He paused. More bubbles. He tossed a rock out to the center of the bubbles. Suddenly there was a large swirl of water and he thought he saw something break the surface, but it was hard to tell without the light from the Spirals.

"Hey guys?" Slane called, his voice cracking. "I think there's something out there."

Peter and Cassius ignored him. Cassius wanted to keep moving and see what was ahead while Peter was sure there were fish at the spot they passed two hours ago. Both were tired and Peter was just about to tell Cassius to do what he wanted when he noticed the water moving at his feet. He thought he saw an eel moving towards Cassius but why would an eel have eyes on the bottom of its belly?

"There's something out there!" Slane screamed, running towards Cassius and pushing him forward just as the creature reached for him. Slane fell to the ground and rolled to the right, out of the reach of whatever it was. He leapt to his feet and ran towards their gear, scrambling to get his bow.

"It's an Octopus!" Peter screamed.

Slane turned. *What in the world is an Octopus!* Four more things that looked like arms with eyeballs on the bottom of them came out of the water and reached for them. Cassius took to the air after Slane pushed him.

"Get back!" Cassius urged Peter.

Slane grabbed his bow and quickly shot four arrows, hitting each of the arms which recoiled and quickly went back into the water. Peter ran over to Slane and Cassius landed next to them. All three were breathing hard.

"Everybody alright?" Cassius asked.

"Good shooting, Slane," Peter said. "That was an Octopus, Slane. Sorry we forgot to tell you earlier but I never thought we would encounter one in this part of the world."

Slane laughed. "Well, from what I saw it's some sort of sea creature. But it doesn't seem that dangerous, does it?"

"We don't know how big it is," Cassius replied. "It could have a hundred arms. That was just one."

"That's right," said Peter looking up. "We didn't see the body. I'm wondering if that's why there are no Spirals above us. I think we should get our gear and move forward. Slane, keep your bow ready."

In a flash, the trio was on its way. They approached the far end of the lake and saw that there was a waterfall that led to the large oily pool. Cassius flew ahead to see if there was a path next to the waterfall they could take. He disappeared in the cavern above the waterfall. Peter and Slane continued to cast nervous glances at the middle of the black water.

"I think we're going to make it out of here okay," Slane said.

At that moment, they both heard a roar and turned to see a wall of water coming towards them. Instinctively, they turned their backs to it and were soaked as it crashed around them. Dashing the water from their eyes, they glanced back to see a huge black creature with yellow eyes. A hundred arms came at Peter and Slane! A large mouth with a razor sharp beak opened and closed rapidly, making a distinct clicking sound. Slane and Peter stood frozen, gaping at the monster. Slane felt a terror rip through his soul that he had not experienced, even in the fiercest battle with the Wolves when he was almost killed. Despair overcame him. *We are going to die.* It was too big, too evil, too overpowering. And there was only the three of them.

Peter snapped Slane out of his trance by grapping Slane's arm with his teeth and giving him a tug. "Run!" yelled Peter who was off in a flash. The pain from Peter's razor sharp teeth breathed fire through Slane's body. Slane followed him and broke into a full run holding his bow. The quiver of arrows and the pack strapped to his back bouncing violently. They headed for the cascading water where Cassius had gone and where the Concocta Spirals were shining brilliantly. The creature must not venture there. Slane did not turn around but he could hear the clicking of the creature's beak and every now and then he thought he saw a tentacle coming closer to him from the side. Peter reached the rocks next to the waterfall and ascended to the top of the pile and turned around. Slane was still a hundred yards away and the Octopus was fully out of the water lurching forward in a rambling, stumbling gait on the coils of the limbs. It reached for Slane with its tentacles but Peter realized that the creature didn't know how to grab Slane because it had never encountered the moving legs of a human. It couldn't grab him from behind. It was forced to move the tentacles in from the side. While this bought Slane some time, Peter realized that Slane wasn't going to make it to the rocks. He threw his head back and released a piercing howl for Cassius. It was time to engage. Peter leaped off the rocks and felt his paws dig into the soft pebbles. He ran straight for Slane as if he knew what was going to happen next.

Slane felt his breath begin to hitch and his legs begin to waver. *I – I can't keep running!* Suddenly, he felt something poke him from the side and a large rubbery object grabbed him around his waist. It tightened. He could no longer feel the ground and his legs flailed violently. Slane instinctively dropped his bow and grabbed the fat rubbery arm that grasped his stomach and pulled to try and release it. *It's no use!* The arm was as strong as the trunks of the gnarled old pines that grew on the rocky crags of the Dead Lands. He pounded it with his fists and with all his might. He dug his nails into the rubbery flesh but to no avail. He felt himself being lifted into the air. *It's going to kill me!* He pushed the thought aside. *Be the Warrior. Focus!* "There is always a way out of every situation," Peter and Cassius had told him during an afternoon of training. He must find a way out of this. Out of nowhere, he saw a flash of red and heard a ferocious growl. Peter had latched onto the tentacle just a few feet from Slane. He could see bluish-purple liquid oozing from where Peter's teeth dug into the flesh. *My knife! In the pack!*

He reached his right arm back as far as it would go and dug into his pack. Rummaging around blindly, he found the knife that was buried at the bottom. *An arrow!* He grabbed the knife tightly in his right hand and pulled an arrow from the quiver pressed against his back with his left. He raised his left arm above his head and, reaching across his body, plunged the arrow into the flesh of the arm close to where Peter was still latched on. He then drove in the knife, next to the arrow repeatedly. The creature emitted a high pitched scream and Slane felt the grip of the arm release. Slane slipped downward and he and Peter hit the ground with a thud. The creature was stunned, as it had probably never been attacked before. While it paused to examine its damaged tentacle, Peter and Slane ran to the rock pile. Slane held tight to the knife and reached back and grabbed another arrow. He wished he had remembered to grab his bow but there was no telling where that was now. The creature, suddenly realized its missing prey, began moving towards them at a rapid pace.

It's coming!" yelled Peter as he stretched into a full sprint.

A piercing shriek from above startled them. Cassius was in dive position and heading straight for the Octopus. Slane turned just in time to see Cassius pull out of the dive. In less than a second he extended his razor sharp claws and plunged them both into one of the eyes of the great beast. Cassius slashed his talons upward, finishing things off with the giant rear claw that sliced a hole three feet in diameter and from which a yellow pus like substance began to flow. The creature screamed in pain, its cries reverberating off the walls of the cave, and stopped in its pursuit, flailing tentacles at Cassius. Cassius was gone in a flash, rising upward towards the roof of the cave and then quickly going into a dive to start his attack on the other eye. Peter and Slane stopped in their tracks and turned back to help their comrade. But Cassius needed no help. The air was his kingdom and he claimed it like no other bird of prey. Cassius shot like a streak from the top of the cave and tore into the other eye of the Octopus. All of the tentacles flailed about wildly, trying to hit Cassius. He gracefully flew out of reach and circled well above the arms of the monster.

"Slane, get your bow!" yelled Peter. "But be careful!"

Slane saw his bow lying fifty yards away and began to run towards it, his eyes on the Octopus and the massive arms that were now swinging hard enough to kill anything they touched. The creature was in pain and was trying to get back to the water. Slane scooped up his bow and felt a surge of adrenaline. *We did it! The three of us did it again!* The creature, still flailing the tentacles aimlessly was now back in the water and moving towards the deepest part of the lake. Cassius landed next to Peter. Slane joined them, checking his bow to make sure it was working properly. He was glad to see that it was. The three of them watched the Octopus slip beneath the surface of the black, oily water. Every now and then a large air bubble burst upon the surface, and Slane thought he could hear the creature's cry of pain as the bubble burst in the air.

"Glad you showed up, old chap!" Peter said to Cassius.

"Just in time I see," Cassius said, cleaning his feathers.

"Will it die?" Slane asked.

"I don't think so," replied Peter. "But it's definitely never going to see again."

"Fine by me," Slane said, putting his bow on his shoulder. "I'm going to have nightmares about that face for the rest of my life."

"Let's get to those rocks quickly, just in case it decides to come back," Peter said moving forward. "Cassius, tell us what's ahead. And please tell me there's food."

As they ran, Cassius filled them in on what he discovered.

"There's good news and bad news," he said, hopping from rock to rock as they made their way to the top of the waterfall.

"Good news first, please," said Peter.

"Well, there is food and there is light. The Concocta Spirals extend as far as I could see. I found several pools just up ahead that have fish in them."

"Excellent," Slane replied, suddenly remembering how hungry he was.

"And the bad news?" asked Peter.

"The cave narrows," replied Cassius. "And I'm not sure how close we are to the surface or if we can dig out. I'm afraid we may be trapped down here."

Slane felt like someone punched him in the gut. *Some plan, Slane!* They made their way to the plateau above the waterfall but with each step Slane felt like they were going deeper into their tomb. Hot tears formed in the corners of his eyes. He did not want Peter or Cassius to see him upset. After all, warriors don't cry! Kings can't show weakness! Suddenly, despite the presence of his two comrades who were the closest thing to parents he would ever know, he felt very alone.

The first order after surviving the attack of the Octopus was to eat. Peter, whom Slane had never seen panic, helped Cassius build a mound of fish and they all sat down and feasted on what felt like the best meal of their lives. Slane noticed that he felt better with food in his stomach. Peter broke the silence.

"That is grim news, Cassius. How far do you think you flew before the narrowing of the cave?"

"Probably three or four miles. I could still follow the river, but at the narrowest part I could barely squeeze through. I didn't attempt to go any further."

"Any cracks of light at all?"

"None."

"Slane, any thoughts?" Peter asked.

Slane paused before answering. He had already been thinking about what to do. Food warmed his blood and he felt confident again. *We made the best choice we could have about this cave with what we knew at the time.*

"Here's how I see it," Slane began. "We've got two choices. One would be to backtrack and waste weeks of progress. Besides, going back to the surface means certain run-ins with Wolves and whatever else lives near the borders of the Dead Lands. There's no guarantee of water or food up there, either. Our second choice is to push forward and see where the river takes us. Even if things get narrow, I think we will find a place to dig through. It might mean slow going, but unless there are more monsters like the Octopus that live down here, I think it's a better route. Besides, Cassius says we're still heading in the right direction and based on his estimates, the border is close.

"Nicely done, Slane. I agree with you," Peter said without hesitation.

"As do I," echoed Cassius.

I am ready! We are together, and together we can conquer anything. We will make it! "We are strong!" shouted Slane, filled with hope and listening to his voice bounce off the walls of the cave.

"We are strong!" shouted Cassius holding his wings opened wide.

"We are strong and we will conquer!" shouted Peter, throwing back his head and releasing a triumphant howl.

And there, under the greenish glow of the Concocta Spirals, hope was restored. Slane, Peter, and Cassius slept peacefully.

•••

The session was the most chaotic that Cade had participated in. Sand flew as Pierce moved the Octopus all over the sand box chasing

Slane and picking up the toy soldier and the fox. Cade wasn't sure what was going to happen, but he waited for Pierce's signal to be the voice and persona of Cassius. *He's allowing me to improvise with Cassius. He trusts me!* Cade knew the character of Cassius inside and out and he knew that when there was a battle, Cassius could do some damage. As Pierce grew in his emotional maturity and development, he was much more verbal. He talked almost non-stop during the sessions when there was a great deal of action, which made it easy for Cade to know what was going on. He said very little during the sessions in which Slane, Peter, and Cassius were resting or trudging through the Dead Lands. Pierce no longer provided Cade with a script. The two had found a rhythm. The damaged young boy had found a voice. His stage was the playroom; his audience was Cade and the universe of imagination that reigned there. Every session held magic and Cade found himself intrigued by this young man, wondering what would happen next.

At the end of the session, Pierce went to the shelf and grabbed a drum. He pounded out a rhythm and marched around the room. *Bum-bum-pa-bum! Bum-bum-pa-bum!*

"I am strong!" he shouted as he banged the drum.

"You are strong!" Cade shouted.

"We are strong! Pierce shouted, looking at Cade. His eyes blazed brightly and his chest puffed confidently.

"We are strong!" Cade repeated, marching next to Pierce.

Look at him go! I love this kid! It was awe-inspiring to see this previously mute and defiant boy bursting with life. For the first year of meeting with Cade, Pierce would immediately fall silent as soon as they stepped outside the playroom. Now, their conversations continued until they reached Pierce's cottage. They usually talked about the story of Slane or about what Pierce would be doing that evening. Cade noticed that if they encountered another person on their walk, Pierce stopped talking until the person was out of earshot.

But at least he's talking. The teachers and staff reported that Pierce still did not engage in conversation with peers or staff, but they noticed that he was much more relaxed and was doing much better with transitions and unexpected change. It had been awhile since Pierce had a meltdown and broke something or hit a staff member. Cade monitored Pierce's progress closely and worked hard to be an advocate for him in the classrooms and around Boyd by teaching the staff about how Pierce's brain interpreted his environment. It was Cade's desire to teach the staff as much as he could about Pierce. He taught the staff about autism and trauma so they would see Pierce in a new way. Cade explained that while Pierce needed firm boundaries, he also required that the staff be understanding.

He did this for all the young people with whom he worked, but there was something different about Pierce. Because of the acute trauma and the overlay of the autism spectrum, Cade felt an extra urge to create as many opportunities for Pierce's healing and growth as possible. But there was more. Perhaps it was because Pierce brought Cade in direct confrontation of his limits and fallibility as a play therapist. *It was the first time in my work that I felt truly helpless.* Despite Cade's training, he had to surrender to Pierce. There wasn't a skill he had that would make Pierce open up. He had to wait. Pierce was in control.

16
PRESSING ON

I am Pierce. I am strong. Slane, Peter, and Cassius are still trying to get out of the Dead Lands. Slane has led them underground and that is the best route for them to take. The Octopus was scary but it was no match for the three of them. They worked together and beat that Bad Thing. I've been thinking about how scary it is for Slane, Peter, and Cassius to leave the Dead Lands. Life is scary sometimes. My life has been scary. Watching my Mom die was very scary. Living here at Boyd Home is scary sometimes. Going to my classes can be scary. I never know if people are going to laugh at me or call me names. I used to be scared of some of the teachers but not anymore. I used to be scared of the other kids laughing at me but not anymore. I am strong!

I don't like talking to people but I'm realizing that not all people are mean or bad. Most of my teachers are kind. But no one is as kind as Cade. He understands me. He knows how I feel. He knows how I think. When he looks into my eyes I can tell that he knows what it's like to be me. He is the only person other than my mom that I have ever trusted, but I'm starting to see that other adults are able to be trusted too – but you have to get to know them. I like the older kids at my dorm but not kids my own age. They annoy me. One day they are nice to me and the next day they are not. One boy named Brian calls me "weird" almost every day. Two girls that are friends with him laugh and whisper that I'm going to be a psychopath murderer when I grow up. It scares me sometimes because I have thought of killing them. I think everyone thinks about killing people that are mean to them, but it doesn't mean that they are going to do it. They don't realize that they murder my soul every day by talking like that. I have never done anything bad to them. I have never done anything bad to anyone until they did something bad to me. People don't realize that I don't want to bother anyone. I just want to go to my classes and get back to my room where I can write.

I am writing every day and my story is getting really big. I have found what I love and it is writing. I will be a writer. My mom told me that I would be a writer someday. When I write no one thinks I'm weird because a story can have anything in it. As big as your imagination is, that's how big a story can be. When I write, I can be anything. I can be a champion, an evil king, or a ninja. I can go anywhere in the world. I can fly if I want to. I have a voice when I write. Even though I don't like talking to people in real life, I can say a lot when I write. I'm confident when I write. I am bold when I write. Acting out my story with Cade is the best part of my day. Someday I might tell him that. I think about him a lot, especially before I go to sleep. I wonder where he lives. Does he have a wife or a girlfriend? Does he play with other kids like he plays with me? He is funny. Today he talked in a different voice when we walked back to the dorms. He pretended to be an old man who was afraid of worms that crawl up on the sidewalk and shrivel up and die. "Watch out for the worms, watch out for the killer worms!" he yelled, pretending to walk with a cane all hunched over. I was laughing so hard. I want to be funny like that someday.

One good thing about being here is that I get to read a lot. Other than Cade's room, the library is my favorite place. I have found a lot of good books. One book I read was "Watership Down" by Richard Adams. It is a great story about rabbits that are working hard to stay alive as they travel to make a new home for themselves. A band of larger, bad rabbits try to kill them. I grabbed the book because I thought it was about ships. But soon I was reading about this group of rabbits running for their lives and facing death. They had to be brave. Just like Slane, Peter, and Cassius. The rabbits have their own language and each one has a special job to do. This book made me feel good because it made me feel stronger as I face all sorts of bad things in this life.

Another book that I read was "To Kill a Mockingbird" by Harper Lee. This book was about how mean people can be and how they can do cruel things. There was a father in this book named Atticus Finch. He was very nice to his kids. I have thought a lot about Atticus Finch. I have never known a father but I have dreamed of one. When I read the book, I realized that Atticus Finch was the father I have dreamed of my whole life. He was patient and kind and let his kids figure things out, but he still protected them. Until I came to Boyd I couldn't imagine a man being gentle and kind to children. I thought that all men were rough and sort of like bigger versions of mean kids. I remember one guy that my mom lived with called Butch who never got off the couch. Ever. I don't even remember him going to the bathroom. My mom had to bring him his food and beer and he yelled at everyone from that couch. Once I didn't do what he said and he tried to swipe at me with his big hairy arm but I was too quick. He didn't get up or anything; he just cussed at me. I stared at him wondering if he was one of those people whose skin grew into the couch and that he couldn't move if he wanted to. I think Atticus Finch would have thrown Butch through the sliding glass door. "To Kill a Mockingbird" was about how people judge others just because of their skin color. It made me think of how other kids judge me just because they think I'm different. It makes me sad to think how mean people are to each other. We are really just skin and bones and hair. Why do people think someone is better than someone else? I wish people were nicer. Until I met Cade and some of the other staff, I thought nice people were only in books. Mom used to tell me to never trust anyone but her because people would try to hurt me, but I'm realizing that there are nice adults in the world. But you have to check them out first.

It's funny that since I've been playing in the playroom, I can remember stuff from when I was little. One person I've been thinking about is my Grammie. Grammie was nice. She was my mother's mother who was very sick when I met her. When I was about four, my mom worked for a while at a convenience store to try and get away from relying on men to care for her. We got to Grammie's house at night and I remember that it was a very old house and that she was on the couch listening to the radio and covered up with a quilt. My mom said that they didn't get along but that she needed someone who was family to watch me so she swallowed her pride and we went there. Grammie was dying of cancer. She said that there was nothing the doctors could do and that she had less than a year to live. She seemed excited to see me and since I didn't go to school yet we spent a lot of time together. She never told me why she and my mom didn't get along and I didn't care. I just knew I liked her house because there was food and no men.

Grammie liked to read. She had a roomful of books. She also liked music. She listened to old music, the kind that isn't on the radio anymore. Her music made me feel safe. She liked the Bible and read it every day. She asked me if I had ever read the Bible. I said no. She read many stories from the Bible to me. She told me about Jesus and his friends. She said that Jesus was a man but was God too. She said He came to die so that people could be reunited to God. She taught me to pray. I asked her why sometimes God didn't answer prayers like when I asked her why my dad didn't show up after I prayed that he would. She said it didn't work that way. She said that people have "free will" and that the only way a person can change is through their heart. If they open their heart to God then they will change. She said people blame God for bad things and say it's Him when good things happen. Grammie said that most things that happen in world are related to what she called "cause and effect." Good decisions bring good results and bad decisions bring bad results. She said that God wasn't an emergency switch people can pull whenever they get in trouble. She said that this explains why God sending Jesus to earth was such a big deal. "Would you give your own child for someone else?" she asked me. I couldn't imagine that since I never had a kid. But I know I wouldn't want to give my dog or my best toy for someone I didn't know.

Grammie called God the "Ancient." She called Him that because her neighbors who were Native Americans taught her about God and that's what they called Him. She read to me from the "old books" in the Bible, like Isaiah, Job, and Zachariah. I liked the sound of the language and how Grammie read the words so slow – like each word was so special. She said that the Ancient knew everything and even though there was bad stuff in the world, it was people that messed things up. My mom's life and her friend's lives were pretty messed up, so I believed Grammie. When Grammie had a good day, we would walk outside and she would tell me the names of the flowers and birds. Her yard seemed like a garden, but she kept saying how awful it looked compared to when she was healthy. I had never seen so many colorful flowers. Red, purple, blue all dazzled before my eyes. She let me smell the roses and they smelled so sweet! I didn't know that a flower could smell like that. I remember feeling the petals and thinking that it was the softest thing I had ever felt. Grammie showed me in the Bible how the Ancient took care of the flowers and the birds.

She showed me ten different kinds of birds that lived around her house. Grammie always kept a big pair of binoculars next to a big window where she liked to sit. One day when we took a walk, we saw a hawk that was sitting in a tree right outside the window. His feathers were so pretty and I remember his fierce eyes looking right at me. He looked to me like he could see right through me. She showed me little barn owls that were right out in the open but people didn't see them because they didn't look for them. Grammie taught me to keep my eyes open and I would always see things that were hidden from most people. She said that most people couldn't see the beauty that was around them because they had been blinded. I never want to be blind. My mom worked long hours. Sometimes Grammie was too weak to get out of bed. But I knew how to pour cereal and milk and warm up chicken noodle soup for her. She would read to me from her bed. I would lie under her big quilt and she would read until she fell asleep. Then I would go downstairs and try to read some of her books. The main ones I looked at were the ones that had pictures to go along with the stories. One book I remember had a green cover and was about birds. It was a big book and I loved to look at the pictures with bright colors and the different shapes of all the birds. Each picture had a description underneath it and I wanted to know what it said. Reading was like figuring out a secret code and I wanted to know every word. Words were like magic to me. I figured out the code and I wanted more. One day I discovered the dictionary a few shelves up from the bird book. There were more words than I could imagine. The dictionary told me how to say the word and where it came from. I was fascinated. I carried it around with me wherever I went. I even read it when we ate meals. Grammie let me. One day mom had a fit when she saw me sitting at the table reading it. Grammie told her to calm down. I was a genius Grammie said. I liked hearing that. Genius was the next word that I looked up. It is still one of my favorites.

I remember the day Grammie died. It was a bright sunny day. That morning, she was different and there was a strange kind of smell in the house. I can't describe it. It was just different. It was a weird smell, not like I had smelled before. My mom stayed home that day because she had been up all night with Grammie. Grammie stayed on the couch and I read to her from the bird book while mom went to take a nap. Grammie slept a lot that day but around lunchtime she woke up and looked at me for a long time. She touched my hand and her hand felt really hot. She touched my face and my hair. Her voice was weak and I had to lean in to hear her. I remember that her breath smelled really bad. She pulled me close and I will never forget what she told me. She said I was chosen and that the Ancient's hand was on me. She said that I must never forget that I am special and because I am special, people may have a hard time understanding me. She told me to never forget the plants, trees, and birds that we saw together and to remember that there is beauty in the world despite all of the bad stuff. She said that I am smart and to never believe anything different, even if I don't do well in school. She told me that she would be going to live with the Ancient and not to worry about her. Then she went to sleep for about an hour. I didn't know what to do so I sat in her big chair with the binoculars and tried to see and name as many birds as I could. Suddenly I heard her breathing really heavy and I ran and got my mom. It sounded like she was choking. Mom and I sat with Grammie for a few minutes and then suddenly she became quiet. Mom said she was gone. I remember how little she looked after she died. I touched her hand and it was so cold. I'll never forget that feeling of cold. I'll never forget how my heart hurt knowing that she was gone and that I wouldn't be able to talk with her ever again. I ran to my room and shut the door. I remember not wanting my mother to touch me or talk to me. I wanted to be alone that day. I wanted to be alone forever.

I'm learning through playing out the story of Slane that everyone has sadness but people express sadness in different ways. My mom was probably sad that Grammie died, but she never showed it or talked about it. We lived in Grammie's house for about a week and then mom said she met someone new and that we were moving in with him. I felt sick when she told me. Things were so good at Grammie's house. It was the first actual house I ever lived in. I told her I wasn't leaving and that she could go. I would be fine and she could check on me now and then and bring me food and stuff. I tied myself to the bed and mom had to get a knife to cut me loose. I remember looking into her eyes and hating the part of her that needed men. Why couldn't it be just us? I hated all those men! I wanted my mom all to myself. My mom dragged me out of the house and put me in the car. I tried to kick out the windows but they were too strong. It was the only time in my life that I remember crying. I didn't talk to my mom for a week after that and I thought about killing the man we moved in with. Soon, it was just like before. Mom lost her job because she couldn't get out of bed and we had nothing to eat. It was around then that I got picked up by social services and not long after, she blew up in the trailer.

Slane thinks about his father sometimes. His father was bad. He never knew him and it makes him angry sometimes. I get angry that I never knew my dad. I hear kids talking about their dads and what jerks they are. At least they got to know what kind of jerks they were. At least they knew them long enough to call them jerks. Sometimes I wonder if my dad is out there somewhere. I wonder if he thinks about me. If he's still alive, he must think of me. What if he doesn't? Why do I care about this? It makes me so mad! He's gone, Pierce. Gone! Stop thinking about him! Shut him out! He's a loser and a scumbag! Leave him! Get him out of your mind! Slane has to carry on and so do you! You have good things in your life, just like Slane. You don't need a dad! I know you get sad and feel lonely sometimes, but you are strong now. Your future is bright. You have Cade and your story is better for what you have gone through! Don't give that idiot five more seconds of your precious time! He had a choice and he chose to let you go. That means he's selfish and him being in your life would only cause more problems than you already have. But I still miss him. Why?

What is sadness? Where does it come from? What about happiness?

What about feelings? Why do I have to feel? Feelings are so confusing to me and people think I'm stupid because I don't jump up and down and get all smiley. I feel happy but my face doesn't get the message. I feel sad but that doesn't mean I have to cry all over everyone or throw things at people. I know that when I write or play out my story I feel happy but I don't know what to do with the feeling of being happy. It just doesn't transfer to the rest of my body. Sometimes I think there is something wrong with me but Cade always tells me that I am me and there is no other me and I am the way I am and that is okay. I guess he is right. He says everyone feels confused by emotions at times but some people don't know how to show it and that is okay. He says I'm not even close to being who I am going to be when I'm an adult and to just have fun and enjoy being the age I am right now. Anger is what I understand the most because I felt that a lot when I was a little kid. Now that I think about it, I haven't been angry in a long time. Other kids bug me, but I've noticed that I don't lash out like I used to or spend hours thinking about how I might destroy them. Peter and Cassius have taught me lessons about not seeking revenge and instead focusing energy towards good things. No one taught me that. My characters in my play taught me. Wow. I just realized that and I think it's pretty cool. Maybe one day I'll tell Cade. He probably knows because he read it in my story. I think he's smarter than what he lets other people see.

•••

The path along the river was noticeably steeper and more difficult to follow. Rocks and boulders littered the way and slowed their progress. Slane had trouble with his footing and even Peter stumbled now and then. Fatigue set in faster, tempers became shorter, and Cassius in particular felt out of his element having lost the ability to fly under such conditions. He hopped from rock to rock but complained that his feet hurt. The river continued to flow past them but there were fewer pools with only a few fish in each. The elevation made it harder to find flat ground where they could make camp and sleep. It had been months since they began the journey underground and their nerves were wearing thin. Slane's thoughts had a common thread: *What if there is no exit?* The Spirals were glowing as bright as when they began and they saw no sign of light from the outside world. Despite this, Cassius was able to tell when it was day or night and made sure that they kept their natural rhythmic cycles. All three were tired, wet, and Slane was losing heart. Slane felt the urge to talk to Peter. When they finally found a flat spot to make a camp, Cassius went to find some fish and Slane flopped down next to Peter.

"How long before we get out of here?" Slane asked, tossing the pack a few feet away.

Peter stared at him. "Are you worried? Where is the warrior that led us into this?"

Slane looked down. "Aren't you worried, Peter?"

"Slane, I can't tell the future. But I know that we're following the river and it is leading us out of the Dead Lands."

"But do you have a feeling that we're going to be okay?"

"We have steadily been going up – have you noticed?"

Slane shook his head. He hadn't noticed.

"Look behind you."

Slane looked and swallowed hard. He saw a winding path that stretched down below from where they were sitting as far as his eyes could see. He suddenly felt foolish. He focused so intently on the rocks, sharp pebbles, and boulders that he missed the fact that they were climbing up at an alarming rate.

"I think we are inside a mountain."

"A mountain?"

"Yes, Slane, and not just any mountain. I believe it's The Guardian, the peak of a sprawling mountain range that creates a border around most of the Dead Lands."

"You told me stories about it when I was younger!" Slane responded, feeling a surge of hope. "The people that brought me came to the edge of the mountain range where the land was flat. You said that we could not leave the Dead Lands that way because there are not enough resources even though it may appear to be an easier route."

"That's right."

"And you said that going over the mountain range would be our best bet to get out, but to your knowledge no one had ever survived crossing the range because of the terrain and lack of food and water."

"Correct."

"But we're in the Guardian?"

"I believe so. There was a legend that the river pours from the top of the mountain. I didn't believe that it could be, but so far it seems that it's true. I have to believe that we're climbing up through The Guardian. Do you feel how cold it's getting?"

"Yes."

"And it's a bit harder to breathe?"

"Yes."

"That's a sign. I think we're going to eventually find a break through to the outer world. Don't lose heart, my boy. Your instinct to lead us to follow the river is going to be the very best decision you've made thus far in your young life."

Peter looked up at the ceiling and the sides of the cave. "To think we are inside the Guardian," he mused to himself.

"What are you two blabbering about?" said Cassius, tossing three large fish in their direction. Slane grabbed the biggest and began to munch.

"Peter thinks we're inside the Guardian," Slane said with his mouth full. Bits of fish fell out as he talked. "What do you think, Cassius?"

Cassius hopped towards them and leaned his back against a rock. Slane noticed blood on his feet but couldn't tell if it was from the fish or having to hop on the rocks.

Cassius tore into his fish, ripping a long strip of flesh from the end of the gill to the tail. He flipped it up in the air and swallowed it whole.

"Well, I'm afraid Peter's right," he said, flipping the fish over and repeated the process. Slane watched the lump move down his throat. "We have been steadily climbing upward for a week now and I estimate we're making about a mile each day. We have to be getting close to the top of this thing soon. I expect that the Spirals should thin out as we get to the top and closer to some openings. My only fear is what we find when we break out. Probably snow, and there won't be an easy way down, I promise you that."

Slane was quiet as he imagined popping out of the mountain and standing at the top of world only to see a drop of several thousand feet.

"The Guardian is no happy place," Cassius continued. "There are many legends surrounding it. It got the name because it and the surrounding mountain range literally divide one world from the other. On a clear day it was visible from our Kingdom. I remember one day my friends and I were talking about climbing it. An old man with one arm overheard us and told how he and a band of hunters camped at the base looking for the giant elk that roamed the snowy side of the mountain."

"What did he say?" asked Slane.

"The snow was heavy, the wind was terrible, and to make matters worse there was an avalanche. All perished but he and three others," Cassius replied in a solemn tone. "His arm had to be amputated as a result of the avalanche. He said that the other three were killed by Wolves in the middle of the night at their base camp – didn't even hear them coming. He was spared only because he was up in a tree because he refused to sleep on the ground. He barely got off the mountain without dying and would have perished if some gypsies hadn't found him. He told us to not go within a hundred miles of it. The gypsies told him that there was a legend that said the mountain was cursed and no living thing could touch it and live. I'm not looking forward to what we may find once we break through the top of this thing."

Slane was no longer hungry. He felt hopeless, beaten. Even if they got out, which Peter was sure they would, a world of snow, wind, and avalanches not to mention more Wolves would be waiting for them. He looked at Cassius who was finishing off the last remaining shreds of meat on the fish skeleton and then to Peter.

Peter picked up on Slane's body language. "Quite a story, huh?"

Slane nodded.

"Yes," said Peter. "Cassius tells quite a story. Legends, stories, curses. What are you going to believe, Slane? Those mythical creations or the fact that we're sitting here? Old man's tales versus the facts? The facts are we are here. The facts are we are continuing to survive. The facts are we are going to break out of the top of his mountain and we'll figure the rest out later."

Peter stood and walked over to Slane. "We could have eked out a living in the Dead Lands. We could have stayed and probably survived another ten to fifteen years. But we decided to rightfully restore you to the land of your fathers and to take up this quest knowing there was a good chance we wouldn't live to see it through. We have risked everything and we will give our last breaths. So, whatever is waiting for us outside this cave, we will deal with it, right?"

Peter looked at Cassius who was still picking at the fish bones.

"Right, Cassius?"

"Oh yes, right! Yes, yes, we are forever committed. Don't worry Slane. You know, sometimes you worry too much."

"Well, can you blame me?" Slane cried. "I mean all the legend-death-avalanche-Wolves stuff makes me kind of nervous. Plus, we haven't seen natural light in months. I think I'm going a bit crazy from these Spirals."

"I was just testing you, Slane," Cassius replied. "You're going to hear a lot of legends and stories which may or may not be true and you're going to have to stick to your deep confidence in yourself and your abilities."

"So you lied to me?"

"No, I really did have that conversation with that old man. My point is that whether those legends are true or not, it shouldn't sway you from your mission."

"Cassius is right, Slane," Peter added. "As we return to the real world you are going to encounter various enemies, some of them you can see and some that you can't. Some will be swirling stories that will make you doubt yourself. Learn to sift truth from fiction but never veer from what you know to be truth and your quest."

Slane nodded. He felt foolish. Once again, he realized how young and inexperienced he was compared to his comrades. He laid his head back and soon was fast asleep.

....

He awoke to Cassius shaking him.

"Slane, wake up! Wake up!"

Slane pulled himself to a sitting position and rubbed his eyes.

"What is it?" Slane asked groggily.

"Great news! Peter thinks he may have found a break in the rocks! Get the pack ready. Here are a few fish that I caught this morning."

Slane slowly got up.

"Where...where is Peter?" Slane felt a jolt of energy as the news registered.

"He's up ahead. We decided that after yesterday we should probably make camp for an extra day to give you rest and we were right. You've slept a long time. While I caught more fish, Peter decided to follow the river. He returned not long after and said that the Spirals were thinning and he saw beams of light. The air is much cooler up ahead too."

Slane shivered. "It does feel cooler now that you mention it. Cassius, if there is snow, what am I going to do? I don't have any other coverings than these."

"Don't worry, Slane. We'll think of something when the time comes. The important thing is that we get out of this mountain. One step at a time."

"Right." Slane readied the pack and picked up a fish and took a bite. He wolfed down the two fish, tossing the bones over his shoulder. He scooped up some water from the river and gulped it as fast as he could, then picked up the pack and his bow and slung them over his shoulder.

"Let's go!"

He followed Cassius up a makeshift path littered with boulders and rocks. Cassius hopped and fluttered from rock to rock while Slane scrambled along behind him. They journeyed for nearly thirty minutes without saying a word, concentrating on finding Peter. Slane kept an eye on the Spirals attached to the ceiling. They were diminishing. A large boulder hid the river for a brief moment and he saw Cassius disappear over the top of it. Slane hugged the side of the boulder and slid around it keeping his eyes on the ground so as to not lose his footing. He noticed a gleam on the stones and water at his feet and he looked up. There before him was a shaft of light shining through the darkness about two hundred yards ahead. It had been so long since he had seen light that it looked like fire. Instantly he felt the temperature drop about thirty degrees.

"There it is!" Cassius called.

Slane felt his pulse quicken, and as he neared the shaft he had to shield his eyes.

"Where is Peter?" he asked Cassius.

"I'm not sure. I'm going to fly up and take a look."

Slane tried to watch Cassius fly up but the light burned his eyes. He looked around and noticed they were in an opening a little larger than their cave back at the Dead Lands. The river continued onward, which must be where Peter was. After a few minutes Cassius landed next to him.

"What did you see?" Slane asked eagerly.

"Snow. But the good news is that we're not as high as I thought."

"Does the descent look treacherous?"

"It's hard to tell. Parts of the mountain are craggy but there are some smooth parts. I think taking some rocks with us to throw at the snow drifts to release loose snow will be wise."

Slane opened the pack and wrapped the Wolf skin around him. His eyes adjusted to the light and he walked closer to the crack through which the light was pouring. He glimpsed the first sight of blue sky he had seen in months. He felt a sense of hope and adventure surge through him. The crack was about ten feet above them and only the size of his body. Every now and then a breath of bitingly cold air stung his face. After having lived his whole life in blistering heat, the cold air was a strange sensation.

Peter soon rejoined them and told them what lay ahead.

"In about five hundred yards there is a bit of a difficult climb and the path narrows considerably. Right beyond that lies our opening. Slane you'll need to use caution as it is very slippery. I believe we have enough resources here to give us a good start to get down the mountain. Cassius, you will catch as many fish as you can. In this weather the meat should keep."

Cassius nodded.

"Slane, I want you to gather enough mushrooms to fill the sack inside the pack."

Slane made a face.

"I don't like them either but they are a good source of energy and keep hunger at bay. Understand?"

Slane and Cassius nodded. Slane grabbed the sack and backtracked the way they had come, reaching under the rocks to pick the small brown mushrooms. He hated the taste of them but they provided energy and one mushroom could kill the sensation of hunger for hours. As he picked up the rocks he wondered if any human being had ever stood in this place. He wondered how old these rocks were and how many thousands of years it took for this mountain to form. Suddenly Slane felt very small and insignificant. After filling his sack with mushrooms, he rejoined Peter and Cassius. Cassius happily presented a pile of fish and Slane used another sack to wrap them. After gathering their belongings, they made their way to the opening.

The path Peter led them on was very steep and Slane lost his footing several times. It didn't help that his worn leather moccasins offered him hardly any grip on the large wet rocks. The narrow sections were barely big enough for Peter to squeeze through much less Slane with the enlarged pack, bow, and quiver. Slane shoved the pack, bow, and quiver through the small opening and used all his strength to pull himself through while Peter and Cassius waited on the other side. Suddenly, the cave was filled with light. Slane shielded his eyes for a few minutes while they adjusted to the cascade of light pouring through the opening. Once his eyes adjusted, he walked towards the opening where Cassius and Peter were standing. He felt his breath leave his body and he felt dizzy. Slane reached for Peter for support.

For the first twelve years of Slane's life, he had only known the red hot, burnt landscape of the Dead Lands. The putrid air which consisted of smoldering ash was all he had to breathe, so it was not at all offensive to him. Not until entering the underground cave with the river had he ever experienced anything different. Looking out on this new landscape, he witnessed his first glimpse of the outside world and what he saw both overwhelmed and amazed him. The first thing that hit him was the air. Cool, crisp, and clean, the air created a longing within him and he felt he couldn't get enough as he gulped breath after breath. His eyes opened wide as the burning cold ripped through his windpipe to his lungs. Yet he wanted more. A second lightning bolt to his senses was the dazzling array of sparkling white snow accented by the deep blue shadows created by the peaks and valleys of the surrounding mountains. Next, the bluish-black cloudless sky provided the sensation of unlimited galaxies of space and time along with the impression of being infinitesimal. He turned to speak to his comrades but nothing came out. All three stood awestruck by the beauty and horror of what lay before them. *How are we going to navigate this beautiful but treacherous terrain?*

Peter broke the silence.

"These are the words of the Ancient, which were spoken to me in the days of my youth.

A bruised reed he will not break and a smoldering wick he will not snuff out. Though the fig tree does not bud and there are no grapes on the vines, though the olive crop fails and the fields produce no food, though there are no sheep in the pen and no cattle in the stalls. The Ancient is my strength; he makes my feet like the feet of a deer, he enables me to go on the heights."

"Let it be said so," whispered Cassius.

"And it is thus spoken and so it is true," Peter and Cassius said in unison.

Slane felt a surge of courage and determination.

A ledge jutted out from where they were standing and Slane stepped out and was met by a gust of cold wind. He wrapped the Wolf skin tighter around his neck and looked around, noticing a slope close to the ledge that led downward. It appeared to be a path. He picked up a rock and tossed it about ten feet. He could still see the top of the rock after it landed.

"There's our path," he remarked.

"Lead the way, chief," Peter said from behind.

"Show us the way, Slane," said Cassius.

Slane turned and grabbed the pack, bow, and quiver. He looked briefly at Peter and Cassius and took his first step off the ledge onto the snowy path. Peter and Cassius looked at each other and smiled. They had just seen the Warrior King in Slane's eyes.

· ·

"It's time to stop, Pierce."

"Okay." Pierce stood trancelike staring at the mountain.

Cade put the figures in a special chest high on a shelf. He turned to see Pierce watching him. *He's thinking something.*

"You ready?" Cade asked.

"I'm going to be a writer," Pierce said affirmatively.

Cade pulled up a chair next to where Pierce was standing. "That is great, Pierce. I believe you have a gift for writing. Are you still working on the story?"

"Every day whenever I get the chance."

"I noticed you don't bring me scripts anymore."

"That's because you understand what is going on and how Cassius acts. If the story changes or if something happens to Cassius, I'll let you know."

"Okay. I miss reading it, but it's like I get to see what is happening through our play sessions."

"I'm keeping it top secret, like a real writer," Pierce said as he looked down at his shoes. "You haven't told anybody about it, have you?"

"Just Dr. Cap, my mentor."

"He's the one that taught you, right?"

"He's the one," said Cade.

"Well, he's okay," Pierce said.

"Yeah, he's safe," Cade reassured him.

Cade stood and motioned Pierce towards the door. "Time to go, my man."

"Okay."

Cade and Pierce walked down the hall and went outside. It was a bright sunny afternoon and very warm. Summer was just around the corner. A blue jay landed about ten feet from them. It hopped once and looked at them.

"Hi, Mr. Blue Jay," Cade said. They both stopped walking.

"What's he saying?" Pierce asked eagerly. It was a game he loved to play where Cade did one of his voices whenever they saw a squirrel or a bird.

"Whatcha ya'll think ya'll doin?" Cade said in a southern drawl.

"Well Mr. Blue Jay, me and Pierce here are walking," Cade responded to himself in his normal voice.

The blue jay hopped again.

"Well, I think walkin' is about the dumbest thing I ever did see," Mr. Blue Jay said, hopping again.

Pierce burst out laughing. "Keep going!" Pierce said, trying to stay as quiet as he could so not to scare the bird.

"Well, we can't fly like you so we have to walk. But we like it."

"Well, ya'll jus' look ridiculous, jus' so ya'll know. And I might even poop on your head!"

Pierce doubled over and nearly fell. He held his sides as wheezes of laughter poured out of him.

"Well, that wouldn't be very nice at all, Mr. Blue Jay!"

The bird hopped again.

"Ya'll cut our trees and take away our land – we gotta fight back!"

"But can't we get along?"

"Well, I'm supposin' ya'll look okay. What's that boy's name anyway?"

Cade looked at Pierce. "Tell him," he whispered.

"Pierce."

"Pierce? Oh, that's a fine name, fine name, I say! I can tell you gonna be an amazin' man when you grow up, Mr. Pierce, and I'm happy to meet ya!"

"Okay," Pierce replied, giggling sheepishly.

"Mr. Blue Jay, we enjoyed talking with you but we must keep walking. Pierce has to get back to his cottage."

"Alright, alright, alright," Mr. Blue Jay drawled. "Ya'll take care and I'll see ya 'round this here place."

As they walked forward the blue jay took one hop and flew away. Pierce, still giggling, looked up at Cade.

"How do you do that?" Pierce asked.

"Do what?"

"All those voices you do!"

"Oh, those. Well, I've done voices since I was a kid. Spent a lot of time alone, I guess. I just use my imagination and out comes the voice. You should try it."

Pierce shook his head. "I don't think so."

"Maybe one day we'll practice. You'll be surprised."

Pierce became his usual withdrawn self as they neared the cottage.

"See you tomorrow, Pierce," Cade said as he opened the door for him.

"Bye," Pierce said softly.

17
DESCENT

Slane, Peter, and Cassius slowly descended the Guardian. They followed the path that Slane found. Slane was irritated by the slow going.

"Why can't we go faster?" his face crinkled in annoyance. "I'm sick of going so slow."

"Those who rush are those who die in these situations, Slane," Peter responded.

Cassius flew ahead and pointed out where loose snow was gathered. Slane tossed rocks to loosen it which sent it barreling down the mountain at terrific speed. Sometimes Cassius dropped a rock or two. The trio soon realized that the mountain was an optical illusion. They could see forests and even green vegetation below them, and it seemed as if all they need do was simply march down a few hundred yards or even slide to reach it. But in reality, the tree tops were miles away and the drop below them revealed deep crevasses flanked by sharp crags and peaks.

"Wickedly deceitful is the Guardian," remarked Cassius.

Still, Slane was relieved to be out of the cave. The sunlight felt good and despite the snow, it was not as cold as he thought it would be. Peter said that the heat of the Dead Lands kept the air warmer and he believed that if they got around to the other side of the mountain there would be less snow which would make their descent easier.

"Once we're down to the tree line, we can make our way back to the side of the mountain that will take us to the Border of the Dead Lands."

"And we can finally make a fire!" Slane exclaimed. He imagined the heat and the sizzle of roasted potatoes and cooked meat. He swallowed hard to stop his mouth from watering.

They continued slowly down the slope checking each step to make sure it was safe. Since morning, they had made little progress. The sun was beginning to drop and so did the temperature.

"We better make camp," Peter said, sniffing the snow packed on the side of the mountain.

"And how do you suppose we do that?" Slane asked, snorting as he looked at the wall of snow.

"Right here, dig here," Peter said placing his paw on the snow, level with Slane's waist.

"What?" Slane looked at Cassius.

"Do it," Cassius replied, and nodded towards the pawmark.

Slane took his bow and struck the snow with the end of it, putting all his might into the blow. He felt it give way and he fell forward into soft packed snow. He looked up to see a small cave with a five foot opening of ice that he had just burst through. Peter poked his head through.

"There we are," he said, "Now let's get this snow cleared out and we'll settle in for the night."

Slane shook his head. "How did you...Oh, never mind," he said and began scooping up snow.

"You're getting quite an education on this trip, Slane," Cassius snickered. The Warrior King still had a lot to learn.

Once the snow was cleared, Peter showed Slane how to pack the remaining snow up along the ice to create a makeshift door. Soon, there was only a small opening at the top of the wall where Slane had initially broken through. They were protected from the biting cold wind that began to swirl as the sun went down. Slane opened the pack and passed out fish and mushrooms to his comrades. They ate in silence. After dinner Slane looked up at the hole and watched the sky go from red to black. He arose and peered out. It was a sight he would never forget. The stars looked so close that he felt he could reach out and pick them out of the sky. Slane turned and looked at Cassius and Peter with his mouth agape.

"Even in the most awful of places and circumstances you will always find beauty if you look for it," said Cassius.

"Remember that, Slane," Peter echoed as he stood up on his hind legs to look out of the small opening. "You never know where you'll find yourself in life."

Slane looked at his comrades and thought of all they had gone through. Losing their status in society, their homeland and its comforts, and cursed to take on animal forms. Finally, banished to a land where nothing was meant to live. Yet here they were. Loving him, teaching him, and willing to die to take him back to the land of his fathers.

When it came time to go to sleep, Peter and Cassius formed a tight wall around Slane. Slane pressed his back to the back of Peter. Cassius huddled tightly to the front of Slane and he could feel the heat pouring from the great bird. The wind whistled outside their little cave but the three comrades slept a peaceful and healing sleep, huddled together without worries or cares, comforted in the presence of each other.

⋯⋯⋯⋯⋯⋯⋯⋯⋯⋯⋯⋯⋯⋯

When morning came, Slane and his comrades set out again. Once again the sun shone brilliantly, creating dancing prisms of light on each flake of snow and dazzled Slane's eyes. They made good progress, stopping now and then to rest and wait for Cassius to tell them what was ahead. Before they set off that morning, Peter showed Slane how to wrap his feet with the animal hide that they brought with them when they began their journey. Slane laced his leather shoes with an extra piece of leather and tied it with twine. His feet were cold but not unbearably so despite the snow. The extra Wolf skin in the pack proved to be invaluable. Slane sewed it to his outer garment, which made him look like a wild animal. He liked the feeling of the extra weight and it made him feel powerful. Cassius said he looked like a king in his robe.

The greatest challenge they faced so far, in addition to the snow drifts and wind gusts, was navigating a series of cascading ledges. Some of the drops were only a few feet, but some were over ten feet down from one to the next. The piles of snow cushioned the fall, but Slane was afraid that one of them would not be strong enough to hold them. Cassius reassured him by landing on the ledge first.

"Jump, Slane! Nothing to worry about! Very solid!" he would yell, hopping up and down on the snow.

"You're not the one jumping!" Slane yelled as he held his breath and smashed into the pile of snow, rolling forward. Peter followed behind him, grunting from the impact.

Cassius assured them that the ledges continued all the way down to a clump of trees where they could make camp.

"Are the distances between the ledges any greater than what we've already covered?" Peter asked as they took a break to eat some mushrooms.

"There is one that looks pretty long," Cassius replied. "But I think there's enough snow on the ledge below that will cushion your fall. It's the best way down."

"I wish we had wings," Slane said, looking at Peter.

"Trust me, I've said that a thousand times in the past," Peter said, spitting out the stem of a mushroom. "We'd all be home in a week."

Cassius laughed. "It's the journey that builds character, right?"

"Yeah, something like that," Slane said.

They continued down the mountain, jumping from ledge to ledge, like fleas moving down a giant dog while Cassius cheered them on.

They reached the ledge with the large drop below it. Slane looked over the edge and gasped. It looked to be at least 30 feet down.

Peter lit into Cassius. "What do you mean bringing us this way? Do you want us to die right here?" Anger flashed in his eyes. It was one of the few times Slane saw Peter angry and not his usual calm, Zen-like self. "How do you expect us to make this jump?"

Slane looked at Cassius. Cassius was calm, unfazed by Peter's tirade. Peter stepped towards him. "Well?" he roared.

"I have a plan," Cassius said calmly.

"Well, what is it?" Peter said, stomping his foot impatiently.

"There is something you can't see," Cassius replied.

"All I can see is that Slane and I are about to die!" Peter said as he gestured towards the edge with this head.

Slane said nothing but felt every bit of Peter's anger. It would be dark in less than an hour and he and Peter were exhausted. The temperature was dropping. Suddenly the wind began to whip up from the bottom of the ledge. It sounded like a tornado. The Guardian was waking up and appeared hungry to devour the hapless travelers who dare trespass upon her. Slane looked down from the ledge. The proposed campsite at the tree line was visible but a few more ledges stood between them and the trees.

"Just below this ledge are a series of strange gnarly trees jutting from the side of the mountain. There are vines that hang from them and I believe they are strong enough to hold Slane with you holding on to him. They don't go all the way down but you'll be able to drop from a safe distance. I yanked on them as hard as I could and I believe they are strong. Time is of the essence." After speaking, Cassius stepped towards the ledge and gestured with this wing to the vines hanging just below the lip of the ledge.

Peter and Slane looked at each other. Slane looked over the ledge, felt the wind, and noticed that snow was beginning to fall. "We have no choice, Peter. Let's get in position. I can hold us."

Cassius disappeared as he flew under the ledge and returned with the vine in his beak.

"Leave the quiver and bow, I can carry those," Cassius commanded.

Slane set the bow and quiver down and strapped the pack to his back. He reached and took the vine from Cassius's beak. It was hard and knobby as if stricken with some dread disease. Slane gave it a yank and was pleased to feel its strength. He wrapped the vine around his right hand, looped it around his left leg and bent down and motioned Peter to climb on his lap. It occurred to Slane as Peter climbed up and Slane wrapped his left around him that he had never done this before, yet he knew exactly what to do as if something was guiding his every move. Peter latched his teeth around the leather strap of the pack that wrapped around Slane's chest.

"I've got you," Slane said to reassure him.

"I trust you completely," Peter replied.

Slane approached the ledge. He could see the slope of the mountain hundreds of feet below, their menacing sharp tips surrounded by wads of snow. He and Peter would have to swing out over this fatal abyss in order to descend to the ledge below. Slane felt the blood rush from his legs and his head felt light. Peter sensed his fear.

"Don't look down there: Focus on your target. Let your mind see what you need to do and block out everything else."

Slane didn't respond but instead closed his eyes and visualized their descent. He gripped the vine as tight as he could and opened his eyes again, then stepped towards the ledge, bent his legs and gradually slid his feet over the edge of the ledge. He released his hand slowly and used his right foot to squeeze against the vine wrapped around his left leg. They descended. Five feet, ten feet, the ledge below got closer and closer.

"That's the way, good job, Slane! Almost there!" Cassius called as he landed below them.

"You're going to have to swing a bit to get momentum to get over to the ledge before you drop down," said Cassius. "But don't worry, I can help with that."

Slane and Peter were finally about three feet from the ledge. Cassius flew and grasped the bottom of the vine below Slane's feet and pulled with a mighty tug as far as he could and then released. Slane and Peter felt themselves swing like a pendulum out over the desolate landscape and then back towards the ledge.

"Now!" Slane yelled, and Peter jumped from his arms onto the ledge. Peter grabbed the vine with his teeth and Cassius with his feet, creating a tether to the middle of the ledge. Slane slid down slowly and finally felt the ground below his feet. The three comrades looked at each other with relief in their eyes. Night was quickly approaching and there was no time to celebrate. They quickly descended the final ledges and reached the scrub of trees and snowless ground. Protected from the wind by the trees, Slane began gathering wood for something he had dreamed about for months. A fire; blazing and hot. He piled some sticks for kindling and found a few dead logs that were partially dry. He grabbed the flint from the pack and began to work on getting something to catch. After about ten minutes of trying, a small piece of bark began to smolder and then smoke. A tiny flame burst up and Slane packed sticks around it. Once those began to burn he placed two of the larger logs across it. Looking at the flame and feeling its warmth he felt hot tears of gratitude and relief form in the corners of his eyes. They had faced a nearly impossible task of descending the mountain, facing death many times. The firelight was like a tiny oasis of protection and hope.

Cassius left to scout the area to make sure there were no Wolves. Peter gathered logs and sticks and brought them to Slane. By the time Cassius returned, the fire was roaring.

"What a sight for sore eyes!" he exclaimed, ruffling his feathers to gather in the heat.

232

"And freezing bodies," Slane added as he cupped his hands and held them close to the fire.

"Any food left in the sack?" Peter asked.

"Just a few mushrooms and three potatoes," Slane answered.

"Let's divide it up and pray we find something around here," said Cassius, hopping back from the fire as a twig popped, sending embers skyward. "We should find more and more food now that we are finally off the mountain."

Slane roasted his potato on a stick while Peter and Cassius simply ate theirs. The food only fueled the hunger pangs that ripped through their stomachs. But each member was thankful for the fire. They talked into the night and wondered what the rest of their journey would bring. Soon, they were fast asleep.

••••••••••••••••••••••••••••••••••••••

It was a dreary stormy day at Boyd. The rain pelted the large windows and the big oak swayed with gusts of wind. But the mood in the playroom was exultant as the beautiful dance of play went on, making the participants completely unaware of time or space that existed outside this magnificent realm.

"Here is the vine!" Cade shouted as he held Cassius with a piece of string around his beak and flew him on the ledge by the mountain.

"Is it strong enough?" Pierce asked as he moved Slane towards the edge of the ledge and took the string and put it in Slane's hand.

"Pull it, you'll see it is!" Cade yelled as he moved Cassius forward.

"Hurry, the wind is getting really strong!" Pierce said urgently as he moved Peter on the ledge. Pierce tied the string to Slane's hand and used a rubber band to strap Peter to the toy soldier. Pierce's face was set in earnestness. He patiently connected the string to the makeshift ledge on the mountain with two pieces of clear tape and then tested it by tapping the soldier and the attached fox with his finger and smiled as the duo swung back and forth. He did it again and again.

"The vine is strong," Cade said.

"Yeah, it's really strong and they don't need to worry. They are going to be okay."

Pierce watched his two heroes swing back and forth for at least two minutes. He often did this during play, especially at a moment when Slane or one of the animals was facing great peril and found a way of escape. When the trio fought the Wolves that nearly killed Slane, he lay next to the battle scene for over an hour. Cade waited. He didn't know how long Pierce would suspend play and didn't care. Early on, Pierce had laid in the sand watching Slane, Peter, and Cassius around a pretend fire for nearly forty-five minutes. Sometimes Cade wondered if he might stay there all day. Cade was prepared for anything when working with kids who had survived neglect, abandonment, or abuse. *Patience and silence,* Dr. Cap had emphasized.

"The brain is literally rewiring itself," Dr. Cap began. "The trauma that is experienced by the child creates a cascading effect in the different parts of the brain. Ongoing, repeated events such as neglect or abuse send messages through the brain's wiring that eventually bypass the alarm center."

"So after a while, the chaos of abuse or the experience of neglect becomes a 'normal' for the child?"

"Correct. If something happens long enough, the brain accepts it as normal. This causes a whole realm of destructive thinking and behavior, not to mention an inability to successfully bond to healthy human beings. Eventually, as the child grows, events that resemble the chaotic situation will trigger emotional, cognitive, and behavioral reactions that send the child, now an adolescent or adult, right back to that primal survival mode."

"PTSD."

"That's right," Dr. Cap sighed. "And seventy to eighty percent of the kids who come to Boyd have suffered some form of neglect, abandonment, or abuse."

"That's why play is so important," Cade concluded.

"Yep," Dr. Cap replied as he removed his glasses to clean them. "Because play helps the brain heal, pure and simple. The more time that a child spends in free, uninterrupted play in the presence of an affirming, compassionate adult, the more that child's brain shifts to a new 'normal,' where safety and love dominate."

"So when the person's brain stays out of 'fight-or-flight' mode, or survival mode, they begin to act, think, and feel differently."

"Precisely. Virginia Axline, someone you've heard me talk a lot about, demonstrated the healing power of play and believed that the therapist should never bring his or her agenda to the process. She believed that play in it's purest form along with the affirming presence of the therapist was all that was necessary for the child to grow and heal."

"Let's go! We don't have much time!"

Pierce startled Cade out of his thoughts. He grabbed Cassius. "You can do it, Slane! Slide down a little at a time!" Cade shouted as he moved Cassius up and down, making the bird's wings flap.

Pierce let out the string lowering Slane and Peter to the ledge below.

"I knew you could do it!" Cade shouted as he landed Cassius on the ledge, making sure he didn't knock it down. Cade and Pierce spent nearly thirty minutes fashioning outcroppings made of duct tape strapped around crumpled balls of construction paper. Once Slane and Peter reached the ledge Pierce untied the string from their hands and stood them up.

"Whew, we made it," Pierce said, taking deep breaths to simulate Peter and Slane's voices. "Let's hurry down, guys! Night is approaching fast." Pierce bounced Slane and Peter down the rest of the ledges and huddled them at the base of the toy mountain. Cade flew Cassius down.

"This is where we'll stay tonight. I'm going to make a fire. Peter, help me get some wood."

"I'm going to fly around the area and check for enemies. I want to make sure we're alone."

"Affirmative. Good thinking, Cassius. We'll get camp set up and look forward to your good report." Pierce went to the shelves and took some brown felt and LEGO pine trees. There was a plastic camp fire from some forgotten camping set from the 1950's. *Thanks Dr. Cap for never throwing anything away.* Pierce arranged the campfire and trees on the brown felt and lay down with his face on the floor as he moved Slane around the campfire. Cade circled the room several times and landed Cassius on the brown felt.

"What did you find?" Pierce said as he moved Peter towards Cassius.

"Nothing to report," Cade replied. "I canvassed a five mile radius and saw nothing."

"We're almost out of food but there's a few potatoes and mushrooms," Pierce said, putting Slane in a sitting position around the fire.

"Tomorrow we should be able to find more food now that we're down to the tree line," Cade said in the voice of Cassius.

"I think with Slane's shooting skills with his bow and my ability to flush out game we are going to be okay. Might be a little hungry for a few days, but we've been hungry before," Pierce moved Peter closer to the fire.

Pierce lay very still watching the three figures. Cade sat cross legged near him and waited. He watched Pierce watching the figures. *I would love to know what he's thinking.* Pierce had a look of pure contentment on his face.

Later, when Cade walked Pierce back to his cottage, Pierce surprised Cade with a question.

"Why do you do this?"

"Do what?"

"You know, play with kids like me, spend time with us."

Cade paused and slowed his walk. A thousand thoughts hit his brain.

Why is he asking this? Does he doubt my genuineness? Does this mean he's realizing I am genuine? What if I say the wrong thing? What would be the wrong thing? Cade thought of the many different theoretical approaches to therapy and how each one would handle a question like this differently. Some would say to never answer a personal question. Some would say hand the question back to the client. Some would say be aloof and unavailable; keep the personal shrouded in mystery. *I hated it when I was a kid and adults didn't give me a straight answer. I felt put off and disrespected. I'm going to be real with him like I am with all the kids I work with.* His work with children with autism had taught him to forget about typical boundaries and be grateful that communication was occurring. He thought of what Dr. Cap said in an internship class when this topic arose.

"I can't give a blanket answer for all situations," Dr. Cap began. "But I can say that you should judge a personal question and the potential answer by the length and depth of the relationship, and whether or not the answer would disrupt the child's progress. Remember that children, especially the abused and abandoned, don't have any idea about boundaries or the intricacies of relationship. They will ask questions, and we must show them the respect to either answer the question or tell them that you can't answer and gently with compassion direct the child back to the therapy."

Cade took a deep breath. "There are many reasons, but perhaps the most important one is that I want to know my time here on Earth was spent bringing hope and light into young people's lives to help them on their journey to adulthood."

"When did you decide that?"

"When I was young. Someone was good to me and I never forgot it."

"Were you in a place like Boyd, too?"

"No, I had parents. But they died. I lived with my aunt and uncle who raised me."

Pierce stopped walking and stared at Cade. "How old were you when they died?"

"About eight. Car crash. They died instantly." Cade looked down at Pierce. He motioned to a bench under another sprawling oak. Cade wiped the bench with his hand to clear away dust and leaves and they sat. "They were coming home from a weekend away and a drunk driver ran a red light. Boom."

"What did you do? I mean, when you found out?"

"Well, my older brother and I were awakened by our aunt whom we were staying with. The instant she shook me awake, I knew something was wrong. Really wrong." Cade's voice drifted off. A mockingbird landed close to them and picked at a worm next to the sidewalk. They watched the bird pick up the worm and followed his path up into the tree.

"My aunt held us and we cried. I remember feeling so empty, it was like there was a hole that stretched all the way from one end of the universe to the other inside of me. Then came the funeral; then the family grieving, all that stuff. It was decided that Jonathan and I, he's my older brother, would live with my mom's sister and her husband."

Pierce sat hunched over. His troubled face appeared dark and Cade wondered if he might cry. Neither said a word for more than five minutes.

"So you know," Pierce finally said in a soft voice.

"Know what?"

"What it's like."

"Yeah, I know," Cade said as he leaned forward to look into Pierce's eyes. "But I'll never know what it was like exactly for you, Pierce. You have suffered in a way that only you know and it is your path that you have walked."

"Were your aunt and uncle kind?"

"My aunt was. My uncle was very strict and I felt as though he resented my brother and I being there. My brother left as soon as he was eighteen and graduated from high school."

"Did your uncle hit you?"

"He spanked us a lot, and for the smallest things. But he wasn't abusive in the sense of knocking us around for nothing. He was hard on me but it proved useful when I got out in the real world. Toughened me up, you know?"

"Did you want to kill him?"

"I don't remember that. Maybe once I felt that way. It just made me miss my parents a lot more when I felt abused."

"I wanted to kill my mom's boyfriends. I thought about it, plotted how I would destroy them and torture them."

"I bet it was hard to sit there and feel like you could do nothing."

Pierce nodded. "Yeah, it was."

The late afternoon sun was lengthening the shadows. Pierce would be late to supper but Cade didn't care. He had free reign when it came to the young people with whom he worked. Dinners, school work, and bed times could be rearranged; a doorway to emotional growth and connection didn't open very often and usually didn't stay open very long.

"Can I tell you a secret?" Pierce asked. There was hesitation in his voice.

"Sure."

"I feel love for my mom but I feel like I hate her too."

"Tell me what you mean, Pierce."

"Well, it's a lot like Slane and his dad. He feels a longing to know him and be close to him, you know, all that stuff a kid wants. But he hates the man his father became and all that he threw away. Because of his father's selfishness, Slane didn't have a father and was banished from normal society to a desolate and lonely place."

"And he has to overcome immense obstacles in attempting to rejoin society," Cade added.

Pierce nodded. "I hate who my mother became and what she did. Her selfishness and destructive actions made it impossible for her to love me and I suffered because of it. But I loved her. And I do love her.

I would do anything to see her again. I want my mom." Pierce let out a guttural sob that took Cade by surprise. He looked over and saw Pierce with his head in his hands, his back heaving with deep breaths of grief. Cade leaned down and put his arm across Pierce's back.

"Let it out, Pierce, it is okay to cry. I'm here with you," he said softly.

The sobs continued for a few minutes. Cade heard the dinner bell and watched as hungry children left their cottages and hurried to the hall. He wanted to make sure they would not be disturbed and thought about walking Pierce back to the playroom, but their bench was nearer to the school area which had been vacated for an hour. It was best to let Pierce cry.

Cade was no longer threatened by children crying. Early on in his work, it bothered him. Children should be happy. Children shouldn't cry. There was too much to be happy about. Now he saw things in a different light. He had enough experience to know that it was indeed a sacred thing for a child to release emotions in his presence, especially a young man like Pierce. He welcomed the tears as a sign of growth and healing. He was comfortable in a person's grief, and had no problem digging through their walls of impenetrable sadness.

Pierce's sobs lessened, then stopped. He wiped his eyes and nose several time with his sleeves, the snot leaving a shiny snail trail across his shirt. Cade stayed quiet. Pierce said nothing. The only sound was the faint chirping of the birds getting ready to settle in for the night. Finally Pierce spoke.

"I knew. I can't tell you how I knew, but I knew."

"Knew what?" Cade asked, wanting to be sure of what Pierce was talking about.

"That you had a parent die. I can always tell. I didn't know that both died, but I knew at least one."

Cade nodded. "That's remarkable. You have a gift."

"Not much of a gift," Pierce retorted. "Seems more like a curse."

240

"Or maybe you're meant to use that gift somehow."

"Like do what you do?"

"Perhaps," Cade responded.

"Doctor Cade I need to ask you something." Pierce wiped his nose one more time on his sleeve.

"Sure, anything," Cade said, picking up a twig on the ground between his feet. He snapped it in two and held one half between his thumb and forefinger and flicked it. It flew end over end and landed in the grass out of sight.

"Can we go places?"

"Like where?"

"Well, like can you take me around town? I mean, I still want to have our sessions, but I wondered if sometimes we can leave Boyd."

Cade paused. "Well, I will have to get special permission but I think it will be okay. Where do you want to go?"

"I want to go back to where my mom died. I want to see the trailer and go back to that place. I can't explain why. I just need to that's all. And if you don't take me, I'll go anyway."

Cade stifled a laugh. He had never heard Pierce sound so determined. It was almost comical to hear him sound so earnest.

"Let me talk to the right people and I'll make it happen," Cade said, smiling. He looked down at Pierce. "Are you ready for dinner?"

Pierce nodded. "I'm actually hungry tonight," he said as he stood up. They walked towards the dining hall as the last bit of daylight faded into darkness.

18
UNCHARTED TERRITORY

"Have you ever taken a kid off campus?"

Cade and Dr. Capstone were sitting on the sprawling front porch that wrapped around the professor's home. Dr. Cap sometimes joked that there was more porch than house. It was one of Cade's favorite places. He had spent many a Friday evening on this porch, reviewing the week and savoring the summer evening breeze while sipping on Dr. Cap's famous homemade lemonade.

"I have," Dr. Cap replied as he placed his feet up on the railing of the porch. "Why do you ask?"

Cade told his mentor about Pierce's request.

Dr. Cap stroked his chin and looked out at the lawn. "There was a young man about twelve or thirteen that I worked with whose parents had been killed in a car accident. His name was William but everyone called him Billy. He had gone to live with family members, maybe an aunt or uncle, but it didn't go well. Something about their kids – they didn't get along with him or didn't like him. Anyway, when Billy came to Boyd he had a lot of anger and pushed everyone away. It took me a long to build a connection with him because he didn't trust anyone. It was evident that he felt abandoned and had not dealt with his parents' death at all."

"What did you do?"

"Well, Billy pulled all the tricks to try and get himself kicked out of Boyd. Of course, back in those days there wasn't anywhere else for him to go. He broke stuff in the playroom and when that didn't work he attacked me."

"What?" Cade asked, nearly choking on his gum.

Dr. Cap held up his hand. "I'm being totally honest. Came at me with a broom once and then tried to whack me with a Tonka dump truck."

"Did you call the staff?"

"Absolutely not. For what? So they could put him in restraints for twenty-four hours? That would just make him more mad and cause even more damage. I had to show him I was in for the long haul and that I would not, under any circumstances, reject him. I did emphasize that there were rules, and if he followed them there would be no reporting to the staff. He didn't try to hurt me again."

"How did you get him to stop?"

"I called him William."

"What?" Cade asked incredulously. "It was that simple?"

"Pretty much. I was up against a wall and he had the dump truck over his head and wasn't backing down. I knew that thing could do some real damage and I just blurted out 'William! Put that thing down!' and he did. He hated the name Billy but never told anyone. Instead of saying anything he just got more and more mad about it."

"How did you find that out?"

"Eventually in our therapy he told me he had an Uncle Billy who was a drunk and a scoundrel. When people called him Billy it made him think he was going to end up like Uncle Billy. His mom never called him Billy; she always called him William. When I called him William something clicked. He put the truck down and collapsed on the floor. It was the turning point in our relationship."

"Where did you take him?"

"He eventually told me that the family members with whom he was placed were awful people. They used him like a slave and his cousins purposefully did things to injure him or get him into trouble. In fact, William's anger was only partially tied to his parent's death. It was more about being placed into a literal hell for nearly two and a half years that drove the anger. He told me that he had not visited his parents' grave since the funeral and he wanted to go there. So, I made the arrangements and we went."

"What was it like?"

"I didn't really want to go. I don't think any of us look forward to sitting with people while they are grieving. But once we do, we find it can be a miraculous and sacred experience, and that's what this was. It was like watching a transformation in William." Dr. Cap paused and took a sip of his drink and set it back on the table. He put his feet down on the floor and stretched his arms before placing them behind his head. "He literally changed from an emotionally stunted, angry kid into a mature young man," Dr. Cap continued. "I've never seen a change that dramatic in such a short amount of time. It was incredible."

"What do you think happened?" Cade asked, watching moths swarm around the streetlight that had popped on a few minutes ago and was now burning brightly with an energized buzz.

"Closure. People forget that kids often don't get to say a proper goodbye to their loved ones. Especially for kids like William who lost both parents on the same day. Adults instinctively want to shield children from death so the child is whisked away from the hospital bed, the casket, or gravesite as quickly as possible and usually never to return. William needed to say goodbye but was never given the chance. He couldn't articulate what he was thinking and feeling because of the grief and he wasn't in a nurturing environment that allowed him to work through the grief."

"I think that happened to Pierce, too," Cade said. "He watched his mom burn to death and then was in the foster care system and then he came to Boyd. I think that's why the story of Slane means so much to him. It's the first time in his life he's able to be in control of something. It just dawned on me that I don't know if he even got to attend his mother's funeral. I'm going to check on that."

"It's important for the child," Dr. Cap interjected. "I'm guessing there wasn't a funeral since he so strongly desires to return to the site of his mother's death."

"Wow, I never thought to find out about the funeral," Cade said, scratching his head. "I guess we assume everyone we love gets a nice funeral. I remember my parents' service vividly. It was nice. My aunt took me to their graves all the time. You're right – it's a big deal to have that picture and experience of a resting place for the rest of your life."

Dr. Cap looked over at Cade. "When I heard your story you shared in our class about your experience of losing both parents in a car crash I immediately thought of William."

Neither man spoke for a while. Cade broke the silence.

"So how will I know if Pierce has worked through his grief?"

"He'll play it out. It will come out in the story. You'll know." Dr. Cap stood and stretched.

"What do you think it will look like?" Cade asked, feeling afraid to hear the answer.

"If I had to bet, I'd say a major player in the story is going to die soon."

•••

"Let's move out!" Peter said, nudging Slane who sat up sleepily. "First light, we need to get moving. Cassius, time to scout."

Cassius nodded and lifted his great wings, pausing a moment to scan the sky, which had a tinge of light creeping over the blackness. With two great flaps he lifted, and with one more he was gone. Slane rubbed his eyes. Cold air swirled around him as he got up and stretched. His growling stomach reminded him that there would be no breakfast. He grudgingly expressed this point to Peter, but as usual, received a logical answer minus emotional comfort.

"Hope, Slane, and a positive mindset is what is needed now. Leave the complaining for those who are ready to die. Besides, now that we are below the tree line, we should be seeing a lot more animals. Look on the bright side: You'll get a lot of bow practice."

Slane said nothing. They finished packing and had just finished when a large object landed right next to Slane. It was a huge fish. They heard a victory cry and looked up to see Cassius circling above them.

"There's more where that came from!" he cried as he zoomed out of sight.

"The Ancient provides!" Peter cried, ripping into the fish while Slane remained riveted to the spot, both stunned and speechless.

Cassius soon joined them with another large fish. Slane dug his hand into a chunk of the red meat that coated the inside of the silver skin. It was the best meat he had ever tasted. His eyes widened and Peter read his mind.

"As we move out of the Dead Lands you're going to realize how good food really is," Peter remarked.

"And how much you've been missing," Cassius added, a slab of skin and meat dangled from his beak.

"It's incredible!" Slane said, feeling a rush of energy surge through his body and brain. He felt like he could kill ten Wolves. "Why didn't you guys tell me how good things taste outside the Dead Lands?"

"And make you even more miserable?" Peter asked. "Better to not know and then be surprised."

"Yep," Cassius replied. "Those who yearn for that which they cannot have will have only misery and self-loathing."

Peter and Slane looked at each other and burst into laughter.

"What?"

"Mister Philosopher! Leave the heavy stuff to Peter, okay?" Slane replied, chuckling.

"I have wisdom, you know!" Cassius said indignantly. "I am an Eagle! Master of the skies!" He fluffed up his feathers and shook them.

"Calm down, Cassius," Peter said soothingly. "We're just having a bit of fun. Besides no one said you didn't have wisdom; it just sounded funny the way you said it."

"Hmmmph," Cassius retorted. He ripped another large section of flesh from the fish and turned from both of them. "No more fish for you guys, I guess."

"Hey Cassius, can I ask you a question?" Peter asked, winking at Slane.

"Okay," he said hopefully as he turned back to Peter and Slane.

"What happens when a bird gets offended?"

Cassius thought for a moment. "I don't know," he said cautiously.

"He ends up in a fowl mood! Get it? Fowl? Bird, fowl!" Peter shouted while Slane rolled backwards and howled with laughter.

Cassius stared at the two of them. "Very funny. You two could be the clown princes of the Dead Lands." He turned away again. "I'm going to scout now, and maybe you two will realize how valuable I am."

"Cassius, wait. We were just kidding," Slane called.

Cassius took a hop and soared into the air. He did not look back. Slane watched his friend lift into the sky into the morning sun and thought he had never looked so graceful.

"Let him go, Slane," Peter said, chuckling. "He's very sensitive at times."

"Has he always been that way?"

"Ever since we were little. I remember one time I made a comment about his blue pants he was wearing, which looked ridiculous by the way, and he blew up and didn't speak to me for a week."

Slane giggled. "And people probably perceived you as the serious one."

"Probably. But remember, the ones who like to dish out the jokes are often the ones who can't handle them in return."

"And that's Cassius," sighed Slane.

"Yep, that's Cassius. C'mon, let's start moving. We've got daylight."

Slane grabbed the pack, quiver, and his bow. Peter led the way along the edge of the trees.

"We'll stay along the tree line so Cassius can easily spot us."

Slane nodded. The path was easy and Peter was an excellent guide. Compared to their descent of the Guardian over the past few days, it felt like a simple hike in the woods. After about thirty minutes they reached a clearing and Peter decided to stop and wait for Cassius.

"There's some heavy woods up ahead and I don't want him to lose us," Peter told Slane.

"What if he's really mad and wants to make us wait a long time?" Slane asked.

"I wouldn't worry about that. The good thing is that, unlike when we were kids, Cassius gets over things quickly now."

Peter's intuition proved to be correct as they heard the screech of their friend a few minutes later.

"Well, you didn't get far without me did you?" Cassius said with a vicious stare.

"Okay, Cassius, Slane and I have talked it over and we're sorry," Peter said. "Please tell us what you found."

"Hmmmph," Cassius replied. He took a deep breath. "Okay, here's what I saw. The good news is that we are very close to the river that makes the border. The bad news is that it is swift and swollen because of the thawing of the snow, but I believe I've found a good crossing point that isn't too far out of our way. I think we can reach it by nightfall."

"Any enemies?" Slane asked.

"None that I saw, but there was evidence of some Wolf camps near the river."

"There's a thick forest up ahead," Peter remarked. "Should we go through it or around it?"

"Thick is right," Cassius responded. "In many places I couldn't see the ground, so I can't say for sure what may be lurking in there. The best bet is to go around, but that makes it unlikely that we'll reach the crossing point of the river."

Slane looked at Peter. "What do you think?"

"It's a risk for sure because we don't know what we may face in there. But on the other hand, we would get out of this forsaken land quicker. We still don't know what dangers await us as we near the river. Taking the risk of going through the forest may save us in the long run. What do you think, Slane?"

Slane looked at the forest. It was thick as Cassius had said. He could see the detail of the outermost trees but a velvet darkness seem to shift like a mist behind them. He shivered. He imagined them crossing the river and stepping onto the land that lay beyond the Dead Lands. It would be the first time his feet touched any soil other than the decayed, burnt, landscape that he had called home since his first year. He wanted to be out of the Dead Lands so badly he could taste it. But now was the time for caution. He was sure. They would go around the forest even though it would mean making camp and reaching the river crossing tomorrow.

He was just about to tell his comrades his thoughts when a piercing and horrifying noise reached his ears. His eyes met Peter's and in an instant they knew from where it came.

"Wolves!" Peter exclaimed. "Into the forest! Now!"

"I'll distract them as much as I can!" Cassius yelled as he lifted into the air with one mighty flap of his wings. Tiny swirls of sand spiraled across the ground. "Stay on a westerly course and you'll meet the river!"

Slane turned and saw the tip of Peter's tail disappear into the darkness. He tore into a run and felt his feet flying over the earth. If it wasn't under such awful circumstances, he would have been overjoyed at how fast he could run. Instead, the sickening black fluid of dread spread through him and coated every part of his insides.

"Peter!" he yelled.

"Over here, Slane!" Slane turned and saw the reddish orange of his dear friend.

It took a few seconds for Slane's eyes to adjust to the darkness. The heavy canopy of leaves blocked out nearly all the early morning light of dawn. A mist clung to the tree trunks like a giant spider web.

"Stick to my backside, Slane!"

"Cassius said to keep heading west!" Slane yelled.

"Affirmative!" Peter yelled back. And he was off.

Slane fixed his eyes on the tip of Peter's tail and tried to follow every step and dodge every trunk and branch. The tips of branches cut into his face and he tripped and nearly fell several times on the large roots that protruded from the forest floor. At times he lost sight of the tail, and then it would appear as suddenly as it had disappeared. He abandoned all thought except to follow the tail of Peter. They ran for what felt like an hour; then Peter finally stopped.

Slane collapsed on the ground. His chest heaved and he was unable to speak for several minutes. Peter stood with ears erect, listening for the sounds of their pursuers.

"I think we've lost them," Peter finally said. "I can't hear anything."

"That's the best news I've heard in a long time," Slane whispered.

"That doesn't mean they're not following us," Peter said as he lay down next to Slane. "But I think we've put enough distance between us and them to buy us some time to get out of here."

"How did they find us?" Slane asked.

"The fish." Peter spat out the words as he scanned the dark woods. "We've gotten lazy and careless. We travelled so long in the cave without the threat of the Wolves that we forgot to cover our tracks and leave no carcasses. It's my fault. I should have remembered."

"I should have too. Don't blame yourself, Peter. The good thing is that we got away from them." Slane felt his heartbeat returning to normal.

Peter looked at Slane. "We must be diligent, Slane. We must remember that we are forever to be strangers in strange lands until we claim the land that is rightfully yours. Everyone we meet is going to think about killing us, and there are many dangers once we leave these borders. The Wolves will be the least of our worries, I'm afraid."

Slane nodded in agreement. There was nothing to say. Peter was right.

"C'mon, let's get moving," Peter said as he lifted himself up.

Slane followed. Their pace was swift but not a full out run.

After about two miles, Peter stopped. "Look, the trees are beginning to thin!" he said. "I think we're almost out of the forest. I think I can hear the river."

"Good," Slane said. "Because I need a drink!"

Peter and Slane pressed on and finally reached a small clearing. Slane could finally hear what Peter's finely tuned ears had heard. *The river!* Slane imagined its blue tumbling waters and dipping his head right into the water. From up above they heard the piercing cry of Cassius, and looked up to see him circling above them. They ran a few hundred yards to the edge of the forest where Cassius was waiting.

"Cassius!" Peter cried, running towards his friend. "Tell me, what happened to the Wolves?"

"We must hurry, comrades! I did my best to hold them off and took them on a wild goose chase, but they picked up your scent and eventually followed you into the forest and I lost sight of them."

"Do you think they are following us?" Slane asked. "We didn't hear their howls."

"It's not worth taking the chance," Peter said. "The quicker we get to the river the better. Slane, get an arrow ready."

Slane whipped an arrow from his quiver into his bow and turned to face the woods behind him. He saw nothing. Perhaps the Wolves were watching them, waiting for the right moment.

"There are some caves above the rise where the river breaks into two parts," said Cassius. "It's close to the crossing point and I think we can camp there for the night. Follow me!"

Cassius flew low to the ground and headed straight for the cliffs in front of them. Peter and Slane ran and followed him. Slane periodically turned to look behind them, but saw nothing. He was just about to tell Peter that so far there was no sign of the Wolves when they heard a howl off to their right. They turned to see a pack coming out of the woods near the spot where they met Cassius.

"Wolves!" Slane yelled. He and Peter were almost to the rise of cliffs that led up to the caves Cassius had found.

Slane saw a pile of rocks that led up to the cliffs. He sprinted to them while Peter tore off after Cassius. In a few bounds, without taking his right hand off the end of the arrow that remained drawn in his left, Slane reached the top of the rocks and turned. He zeroed in on the lead Wolf and released the arrow. It slammed into the skull of the great beast and it dropped instantly, its head hitting the dirt while the body scrunched up behind it before rolling several times. The Wolves behind it looked bewildered and turned to look up at Slane, who had already reloaded and shot another through the eye socket. It dropped instantly. Two more fell in less than ten seconds as Slane's hands worked their magic in precise, repetitive movements. The remaining Wolves were watching Peter scramble up towards the caves along with Cassius, but stopped in their tracks to focus on Slane. For a brief second Slane panicked, knowing he didn't have enough arrows or time to take all of them. He instinctively stepped up on the rocks behind him while keeping an arrow ready. He could only go about five more feet before he reached the wall of the cliff. He counted eight Wolves. There were six arrows in the quiver and the one in the bow made seven. The Wolves realized that Slane was alone and vulnerable and closed in. Slane saw their red eyes pulsing with lust for his flesh.

Slane shoved the fear from his mind and released another arrow into the skull of the Wolf closest to him. It fell in a hairy black heap, its teeth flashing a paralyzed snarl. The other Wolves jumped back while Slane felled two more in a flash. The remaining Wolves circled each other in confusion and two bolted back to the woods. Their reaction told Slane he had killed a dominant male. Three Wolves left to deal with. Two appeared undecided as to whether pursuing Slane was worth the risk. But the other showed no fear at all. It was clear this was the new alpha male and he was ready to destroy and devour the threat before him. Slane could see this male was not as large as other Wolves he had killed, but it was fast and strong. Anything other than a head shot would only make this Wolf more of a killer. He looked down to check his footing and suddenly the Wolf lunged. Slane stumbled and released the arrow which struck the Wolf just above the shoulder. It screamed in pain and took two bounds up the rocks to where Slane, on one knee, struggled to get another arrow out of his quiver. He saw the Wolf lunge and Slane gave up on the arrow; instead he hit the Wolf across the face as hard as he could with his bow. The Wolf yelped and stepped back, stunned for a few seconds. Slane wasted no time and slid his knife from his belt and in one undercut motion jammed it with all his might into the throat of the beast, who released a bellow that pierced Slane's eardrums. The beast leaned forward trying to clamp its jaws around Slane's neck and dug razor sharp claws into Slane's leg, which sent a lightning bolt of pain radiating through his thigh. Slane shifted his weight and pulled the Wolf's claws from his leg while removing the knife from the Wolf's throat and in a flash shoved it into the chest of the beast, hoping that it would find the heart. The two remaining Wolves instinctively bounded up the rocks to join their comrade. Slane saw them coming and felt a flash of panic rip through him. At that instant he felt the Wolf attacking him go limp. The blade had found the heart.

He shoved the dead Wolf off him and without hesitation the other two were upon him. He slashed with the knife wildly and caught one across the nose and it screamed in pain. He jumped and flailed his arms and the Wolves backed up; the one that was cut dabbed its nose with its paw. Slane kept the Wolves at bay with the knife pointed at them in his outstretched hand. He slowly reached down without taking his eyes off the Wolves and picked up his bow with his other hand. He glanced down and saw his quiver about a foot away. He stretched his foot to try to hook the strap with his toe. The Wolves, sensing his divided attention lunged and all Slane saw as he looked up was barred teeth and terrible outstretched razor-like claws. He put up his arms to cover his face and rolled away, thinking that at least one of them would gouge his backside but he felt nothing. As he finished his roll and sat up to break into a run he heard a ferocious growl followed by a gurgling sound and a whoosh of wind followed by a high pitched scream of a Wolf in severe pain. Slane turned to see Peter at the throat of the Wolf that was about to devour Slane and Cassius's talons were bone deep in the neck of the second one. Slane grabbed his bow and quickly loaded an arrow. He aimed at the Wolf that Peter had by the throat.

"Peter! Release!" he shouted. Peter immediately let go and when the Wolf turned to face him, Slane's arrow entered the skull between the eye and ear of the Wolf's left side. It dropped instantly. Slane slid another arrow into position and pointed it at the Wolf that Cassius had maimed by tearing most of its skin from the skull and neck.

"Cassius! Release!" Slane called, releasing the arrow into the skull of the bewildered beast as soon as Cassius let go and lifted up into the air.

All three stood speechless as the last Wolf twitched on the ground attempting to hang on to the last shred of life it could muster.

Slane collapsed on the ground exhausted from his ordeal.

"Slane!" Peter exclaimed, rushing to Slane's side. "Are you alright?"

"He's bleeding from his leg," Cassius exclaimed. "Here, let's have a look."

"I think it's fine, really," Slane said, still trying to catch his breath. He felt very tired and his throat felt like it was on fire.

"It looks okay," Cassius said. "But we need to get to the river to wash it out. Come on, help him up Peter."

Peter shoved his nose under Slane's arm and lifted. Slane stood and wobbled for a moment, then got his footing. They headed toward the river and found a creek that broke off from the main waterway. Slane fell headlong into it and took long drinks. Peter told him to be on the lookout for Wolves, but Slane didn't care. *Let them come.* The water felt so good he didn't want to leave it. Eventually Slane succumbed to his comrades pleas. The sun was setting and they needed to make camp. They found a ledge that jutted out over the river that served as a lookout station from attacks. By the time Cassius announced he was going to scout one last time for potential enemies, Slane was fast asleep.

The next day Cassius brought breakfast in the form of succulent fish that the trio ripped into without saying a word.

"How is your leg?" Peter asked Slane.

"It's sore, but I think it is mostly just a surface wound," Slane replied.

"That's a good thing," Cassius added. "We've got a few miles left before we cross the river."

"I'm not worried about that," Slane said, frowning.

"What are you worried about?" Peter asked.

"I only have one arrow left," Slane said, kicking his quiver, sending it sliding away from him.

"There are some good reeds along the river bank," Cassius replied. "And you know where to get the best feathers in all the land," he said as he bowed in front of Slane, laying his wings out straight before him.

Slane laughed. He had perfected the art of making arrows in a short amount of time, but he hated to be without them. They had become a part of him since he was old enough to walk.

They made their way along the river to the place where Cassius thought they could cross. The river and the vegetation on the other side was a beautiful sight and one that Slane had never seen. He found himself transfixed by the color green. Peter kept nudging him in the back to keep him from staring.

"I can't help it!" Slane exclaimed. "Don't you see that?"

"We see it, we see it," Cassius grumbled. "But if we don't cross soon that's about all we're going to see as the Wolves feast on our carcasses."

"Now, Cassius," Peter said as he laughed. "Let Slane take a moment to soak it in."

"Hmmmph," Cassius said as he lifted off to scout.

Peter and Slane looked at each other and smiled.

They reached the crossing point by mid-morning and both Peter and Slane helped each other swim across by Slane keeping the quiver wrapped around him and Peter holding the strap in his mouth. The crossing went without incident and Slane laughed at how skinny Peter was when he was wet.

"Very funny," Peter said to Slane. "At least I have fur to cover my bony carcass – imagine how tired I get of looking at you all day."

"Oh, is someone a little sensitive all of a sudden?" Cassius joined in the ribbing.

Peter gave himself a mighty shake and was instantly transformed back into his bushy self.

They spent the rest of the day gathering supplies. Slane found over a hundred reeds and busied himself cutting feathers and sharpening Wolf bones that he brought with them from the Dead Lands. Peter sniffed out a patch of potatoes. As the sun set, they sat under a tree with a fire blazing and potatoes roasting on the ends of sticks.

"Praise be to the Ancient," Peter said as the last bit of light left the sky.

"Praise Him for He is good and kind," answered Cassius.

"He has delivered us from danger," said Slane.

"He has kept our feet from falling," Peter added.

"*A thousand may fall at your side,*" Peter went on. "*Ten thousand at your right hand, but it will not come near you.*"

Cassius followed. "The Ancient says *'I will be with him in trouble, I will deliver him and honor him.'*"

"*'With long life will I satisfy him and show him my salvation,'*" Slane said, lifting a stick with a potato on the end as high as he could.

"For His mercy endureth forever!" exclaimed Peter.

"For His mercy endureth forever!" shouted the trio into the night sky.

Before he fell asleep, Slane looked across the river at the Dead Lands and saw a thunderstorm in the distance. The lightning lit up the craggy mountains and scorched landscape. He reached out and touched the green soft grass and breathed a sigh of relief. It was finally over. They were out of the Dead Lands. Never to return.

••••••••••••••••••••••••••••••••••••••

We are driving to where my mom died. I asked Dr. Cade if he could take me and he said that he would. I have learned that most adults say "I'll try," or "We'll see," but that usually means no. Dr. Cade said he would and here we are. I asked if I could put my window down and he said okay. I like riding with the window down no matter how hot it is outside. Today is warm but not too hot. The day my mom died it was really hot. This is the first car ride I've had in a long time. I like riding in the car. I think they should take kids who live at Boyd out for car rides on a regular basis. It would help keep them from going crazy.

I am seeing a lot of other cars. Now that I'm older I'm noticing the different shapes and types of cars. I want a car someday. It would be cool to be able to leave whenever you wanted to and go anywhere. I want to go all over the United States. I want to go to Arizona and Alaska. I want to see the ice and the desert. I wonder where all these people are going? Dr. Cade drives slow. I want him to go faster but I won't tell him that. He is nice to take me today. I don't recognize any of the streets or buildings that I'm seeing. My mom never had a car of her own. It always belonged to whatever man she was with. I don't remember seeing her drive. I guess she could drive if she had to, but I don't remember seeing her drive. She never had anything of her own, especially a car. She always depended on others for everything. I don't want to depend on anyone for anything. I don't know how she ended up that way. I guess some people just think that they need someone else to take care of them. I will never be that way.

We are listening to the radio. Dr. Cade is listening to a talk program on the radio where they are talking to an author of a book. Dr. Cade says he is famous and very successful. Dr. Cade said he has read almost all of the books and this man is one of his favorite authors. Dr. Cade says he wants to write a book someday. I think he could. He says that I will definitely be a writer if I continue to write and read. I listen to the man on the radio. He said that he lived in an orphanage when he was young and he learned to believe in himself because no one else did. He says that his struggles that came early in his life made him a successful person and a good writer. Dr. Cade says that his books have really tough stuff in them but they are good and make Dr. Cade feel happy about the work that he does. Dr. Cade said that people who go through tough things as kids can take one of two paths: either be a victim and stay stuck in feeling awful, or turn it into positive and become stronger. I think I am the second one. That makes me feel good.

I think I know where we are now. I have seen that red brick building before. I think it used to have a big tree out front but it must have fallen down. I can't really remember. Yes, I do know where we are now. There is a lake with a lot of ducks and birds and people walking around feeding them. My mom took me here when I was really small and a swan or a goose or something chased me and bit me on the butt. I remember screaming and trying to kick it. Mom swooped down and picked me up and we ran. Then she started laughing and I stopped crying and screaming and laughed too. We sat in the grass and giggled.

Then we went back and fed more birds. I didn't want to but she made up some silly song. "Birds can't hurt me, they are just a bunch of bones and feathers," she sang. I laughed again and no more birds bothered us. She wouldn't let me leave there until I conquered my fear. I just realized that now. It was one of our favorite places to go, especially when one of her boyfriends hit her or if she needed to just forget about everything for a while. I might ask Dr. Cade if we can go there sometime.

I remember the railroad tracks we just crossed because we got stopped by a train there for a long time. I remember my mom turning around and going another way. There is the street that we used to live on. It has a big forest behind it and I remember my mom telling me to go play in the forest and not to come home until it was almost dark. Now I think she was doing bad things and that's why she wanted me to go there, but at the time I just thought she wanted me to go and play. I see the trailer park where we lived for a while too. That is where I had Slane and played with him all the time. The trailer we lived in is still there. It had holes in the floor and at night rats would come up through the floor. One day I thought there was a cat in my bedroom but it was a rat. I remember being really scared. I see the junk yard with the big steel fence and curly razor wire on the top. I remember asking mom why it was there. "Because people want to steal stuff," she said. I asked her why in the world people would want to steal old rusted junk and she laughed and said, "Why do they put fences around graveyards?" and we laughed and laughed. She was good at answering my questions with a question which made me think about things a lot I guess.

Now we are getting closer to the park but I can't remember what street it is on. Dr. Cade knows right where to go. I don't know how he knows but he does. I hope I know all the streets when I get older and drive. I wonder if the trailer that blew up is still there. *My throat is so dry. I wish I had some water. I wish my heart wasn't beating so fast and my lungs didn't feel so tight.* Dr. Cade has told me to not be afraid of my emotions. They are just feelings that come and go. He says to think of Slane and how he's scared sometimes but he keeps going. That helps me feel better. *My stomach feels like it's doing flip-flops.* There is the park. We are pulling in. There are weeds everywhere and a big sign that says "Condemned No Trespassing." I ask Dr. Cade if it's okay that we are here and he said yes. "It's just a sign," he said. I see the trailer. It looks like a freaky face with the mouth hanging open where the explosion happened. My mom died here. She died right over there by that trailer. Dr. Cade asked me if I want to get out. I wait for a few minutes and then I tell him I do. Something told me I needed to come here.

••

"Do you want to listen to music?" Cade asked as they pulled out of Boyd Home.

Pierce shook his head.

"You sure?"

Pierce shook his head again.

"Okay, I'm going to listen to a show that comes on around this time. Maybe there will be something good on."

Cade tuned to the local public radio station and heard the familiar host introducing her guest, an author whom Cade admired.

"Hey, Pierce," he exclaimed, "This guy is one of my favorite authors! You can learn some writing tips from one of the best."

Pierce nodded but said nothing.

They drove on and occasionally Cade would tell Pierce something about the author's books and what he knew about him. Pierce seemed interested but didn't say anything. *What in the world can he be feeling? He must be nervous. Who wouldn't be? He's going to the place where he watched his mom die.* Cade weighed the therapeutic impact of the visit for a few days before making the request of the administration at Boyd to take Pierce off campus. While it could create setbacks, he believed that Pierce never would have asked if he didn't feel as though he needed to do this. Cade did not tell the administration the details of the trip, only that it was part of the therapeutic relationship and growth to take Cade off campus for an off-site recreational therapeutic activity. Cade remembered Dr. Cap's instruction regarding ethical dilemmas due to a course of therapy that contained risks: "If your intention is for the overall good of the child, then proceed with the therapeutic approach you have chosen."

They drove through town and headed towards the part that was literally 'on the other side of the tracks.' Cade had been in this area before, conducting follow-up visits with children and their families following reunification. He had never been to the park where Pierce was when his mother tragically died, but he knew where it was. Cade watched as the houses became shabbier and spread apart and other than a few warehouses, no places of business could be seen. They crossed the railroad tracks and Cade looked at Pierce. *I think he knows where we are.*

"Do you recognize some of these places?" Cade asked.

Pierce nodded. "Yeah," he said in a soft voice.

They passed a few sad looking trailer parks and Pierce strained his neck to look at them. *I bet he lived in some of those.* They drove on and came to a small bend in the road and turned onto a bumpy road that had long been abandoned. Weeds sprouted from the asphalt making it look like the road had sprung a leak and the weeds, like green shoots of water, were frozen in time. They came to a clearing and on the left was the park. Next to it was the trailer. Cade took a deep breath. *Wow.* The park had been built as part of a county project to improve the communities on the outskirts of town by putting brand new dwellings complete with landscaping and parks with walking trails in an effort to raise the standard of living in the area. It didn't work. After the trailer exploded, all funding for the project ceased and the other trailers were removed. The park was fenced off and the equipment taken away. The only remnants were the large cement cylinders that children could use as tunnels and the heavy steel framework for the swings. It reminded Cade of a post-apocalyptic landscape. Pierce asked him about the "no trespassing" sign. Cade told him not to worry; it was just a sign.

The trailer was a shell of a structure and still had police tape around it. The gaping hole left the inside of the structure visible and part of the wallpaper on the adjacent wall flapped feebly in the slight breeze. The charred jagged edges looked like black teeth. Cade thought he saw a chair inside. Birds flew in and out. Cade looked at Pierce.

"Do you want to get out?"

"Yes," Pierce replied as he opened the door.

They got out of the car and walked to the fence.

They found a section that was bent upward where people had pushed through despite the order to stay out. *What could be better for the neighborhood kids than an abandoned park?* Cade held the fence up and let Pierce pass under and then he slipped through behind him. Once through the fence they walked about ten steps and stopped. Pierce looked around. The trailer was about thirty yards from where they were standing. Cade said nothing, respecting the sacredness of the moment. Pierce took a few more steps and stopped, staring at the trailer. Cade wondered what was going through his mind. Pierce walked towards one of the concrete tunnels and peered in. Then he disappeared from view. Cade waited to see if he would pop up but he didn't. Five minutes passed. Nothing. He walked to the pipe and looked through it. Pierce was lying in the bottom of the tunnel, his head and left ear pressed against the sandy bottom. He stared at the trailer.

Cade walked around to the end closest to Pierce's head and sat down in the hot sand. A dragonfly buzzed above Cade, dive bombing for some invisible insect and then zoomed away. It was still. A slight breeze moved the tips of the trees. There were no sounds from the trees or surrounding landscape. No birds, no activity, no sounds from the road. Nothing. *It looks like a graveyard.* He looked down at Pierce, who seemed very small. *Should I give him a reassuring touch? Put a hand on his shoulder? Surely I need to say something!* And then like a bolt from the sky Cade remembered the prayer that Dr. Cap read to his classes and kept in a frame in his office.

'Lord, make me an instrument of thy peace…'

'Where there is hatred let me sow love…'

'Where there is injury, pardon…'

'Where there is doubt, faith…'

'…darkness, light…'

'…sadness, joy…'

'…grant that I may not so much seek to be consoled as to console, to be understood as to understand, to be loved as to love.'

The words washed over him. "When we feel the urge to fill the space of silence with words, or to offer reassurance in some way whether physical or verbal, it is often out of our own selfish desire to make ourselves feel better or to hurry the therapeutic process along because we are uncomfortable," Dr. Cap said one day in a lecture. "Let the power of your presence do the work, be a silent witness to the pain and sadness. Never, under any circumstances should you act out of your own selfish desire to make yourself feel better." Cade lay down in the sand, placing his ear down and feeling the gritty pebbles on his skin. He fixed his eyes in the direction where Pierce was looking. He slowed his breathing down and waited. Cade saw the trailer in all its bombed out glory. He could see the gaping hole and the black edges. Suddenly, it dawned on him. This is where Pierce ran and hid. From this vantage point he saw everything. The people pouring from the trailer in an effort to get out. The bodies thrown from the force of the explosion. The fragments. The blood. The burning bodies. The screams. His mother, ripped in two, while half of her clung to the last shreds of life breathing her last. From right here, Pierce watched. Cade shuddered to think of what Pierce saw and the visual images that he carried with him for all these years.

Pierce hummed softly. It reminded Cade of how Pierce hummed early in their work when he was dealing with something overwhelming. Cade lifted his head and looked around. He thought that if someone passed by they might think he was dead. Sweat dripped down his forehead and he could feel his shirt sticking to his back. He wondered how much longer it would be. He glanced at Pierce who continued to hum. His eyes did not leave the trailer. Cade laid his head back down and looked at the trailer and the landscape. He refocused his mind and brought himself to the present moment. Pierce was the most interesting kid that he had ever worked with and if this is what he needed to move forward, then Cade would lay here until it got dark.

Suddenly, Pierce stopped humming. He sat up in the tunnel. It was as if he had been in a trance and awoke. He scooted along the bottom of the tunnel feet first and pulled himself out with his hands. Cade sat up, brushing sand from his shirt and hair. Pierce looked at Cade with an inquisitive look as if he wondered why in the world Cade was lying on the ground. Pierce stood and walked toward the trailer. Cade followed a few steps behind. Pierce reached the fence that separated the park from the trailer and stared at the ground. Cade stood next to him. After a few minutes Pierce pushed the post that the fence was connected to and it easily gave way creating a gap. He slipped through and held it open for Cade who squeezed through.

They stood just a few feet from the trailer. It tilted towards them and appeared as if it would swallow them in one gulp if they weren't careful. The breeze caused the flaps of material hanging from the roof to scrape against the charred tin. The eerie sound made Cade's skin tingle. Pierce stared at the ground for a few minutes and then knelt. He reached out and touched the dirt, placing his hands palms down. Then he began to swirl his fingers around making figure eight patterns. Cade kneeled next to him and watched Pierce's hands. After a few minutes of swirling, Pierce stopped and looked at his hands as if he was inspecting each grain of sand. Cade stood and continued his role as silent witness. Pierce took a few steps and sat on some charred wood that sat in a clump of weeds. Cade found a stump of wood and sat it next to the wood Pierce was sitting on and slowly lowered himself next to Pierce.

"My mom died here. She burned," Pierce said quietly staring at the ground where his hands created the patterns.

"Yes, she did," Cade responded.

"She told me to run to the park and I did. I hid in the tunnel and watched. She tried to get out but the trailer exploded. I saw her burn. I saw her die."

Cade looked at him and nodded. "You saw her die," he affirmed.

Pierce nodded. "I saw her die," he repeated.

"I always knew that my mom wouldn't live long. I didn't know exactly when she was going to die, but I knew you couldn't live like she did and live a long life. I think she stayed alive as long as she could because of me."

Cade nodded.

Pierce leaned up against Cade and Cade put his arm around his shoulders. Cade felt a twitch in Pierce's shoulders and then his body heaved. Cade looked down and saw tears pouring out of Pierce's eyes and felt their warmth through his shirt. Pierce put his head against Cade's chest and Cade pulled him close. Pierce released a low pitched guttural cry and Cade felt his body collapse into his. Pierce's sobs came heavy and continuous. Cade closed his eyes and imagined the doors on his heart and soul being thrown open to give this boy every ounce of comfort and empathy that he could find.

"I'm with you, Pierce," Cade said quietly. "You are safe."

"I miss you so much, Mom," Pierce said when his sobs subsided enough for him to talk. "I had to come back here to say goodbye." His chest continued to heave while he gasped for air between sobs. "I think that I hate you sometimes, but I don't hate you. I've chosen to forgive you but I hate the stuff you did and the people you chose to be with when I needed you. We could be living together right now in a nice little house and have a normal life. Instead, this is the last memory I have of you."

More sobs, more tears. Cade held him close and whispered "It's okay, let it out," repeatedly while gently rocking him.

They sat without saying anything for at least ten minutes. Pierce stopped crying and he wiped his eyes on his shirt sleeve. He stood and walked to the sand in front of the trailer where he made the patterns with his hands. He reached in his pocket and took out a tiny bottle with a cork stopper. He carefully scooped some sand into the bottle, making sure it was full. Then he pushed the cork onto the top of the bottle and pressed it as hard as he could. He held it up in the sunlight and stared at it.

"It's done now," Pierce said. He looked at Cade. Cade squinted as he stared at Pierce, the afternoon sun creating a cascade of light behind him. In the light Pierce looked like he had grown a foot in height. Cade stood.

"Let's go," Pierce said. "I'm ready."

Together they slid through the opening in the fence and got in the car. They drove back to Boyd without saying a word. Cade parked the car and got out. He started to walk towards the cottages and noticed Pierce was still in the car. He turned and walked around the car to the passenger side and peered through the window. Pierce was leaning forward in the seat. He held the bottle of sand and was turning it slowly in the waning sunlight. Cade waited by the car. After a few minutes Pierce opened the door and got out. Cade shut the door for him. They walked from the parking lot towards the cottages. Pierce stopped when they reached the bench between the dorms and the dining hall.

"Want to sit down?" Cade asked.

Pierce nodded.

They sat and watched the sun drop. Cade noticed that it was around the same time of day when they would often sit and talk after their sessions.

"Anything you want to talk about?" Cade asked, his voice cracking from emotional fatigue.

"Yes," Pierce said softly.

Cade waited.

"I want to tell you thanks for taking me today."

"You're welcome, Pierce. I'm glad I could be there with you."

"Seems kinda weird doesn't it?"

"What do you mean?" Cade asked, looking at Pierce.

"That my mom died that way."

"People die all sorts of ways," Cade said. "There's no right way to die. It just happens."

"I had forgotten a lot of what happened," Pierce said.

"What do you mean?" Cade asked.

"When I came here it was really strong in my mind. Like I could see it and I played it over and over. Then over time it went away. I could remember pieces of it, like the explosion and seeing my mom's burning body but I didn't see the trailer anymore in my memory. Today I saw the trailer and just how bad it was. Why do you think they didn't take the trailer away?"

Cade cleared his throat and felt anger rising within him. "Because most people really don't care about poor people. If that happened in a nice part of town, it would have been removed immediately and probably a whole new park would have been erected within the month. Sorry to be such a downer, but you asked."

Pierce nodded. "It's okay, I like honest answers."

They sat for a few more minutes in silence and then Pierce stood up.

"I'm hungry," he announced. "Can you walk me to the dining hall in case they give me grief about being late?"

"Sure thing, my man."

"Hey Dr. Cade?" Pierce asked.

"What?"

"Will you keep my bottle of sand for me? I'm afraid that it might get stolen or broken in my cottage."

"No problem. I will keep it secret and keep it safe."

"And I will ask you, 'Is it secret, is it safe?' just like Gandalf asked Frodo when he put Frodo in charge of keeping the ring," Pierce said with a big smile on his face.

"Just like Gandalf," Cade replied as he took the small bottle of sand and slid it into his pocket. He knew exactly where he would keep it.

19
LAND OF MY FATHERS

Slane, Peter and Cassius spent the next three weeks getting used to the new land. The air was clear. There was color – glorious colors! The rich green of the grass and leaves of the trees magnified the dark browns of bark and limb, which complemented the blue of the sky. Slane poked sticks into the ground to see the black dirt underneath and watched earthworms wriggle deeper into the soil. He rubbed the dark soil on his fingers and examined the different colored grains that stood out in the grooves of his skin. The water was clear. More than once Slane reached in a pool to grab a fish only to realize that it was several feet down. He moved across the land in a stupefied state, his senses drunk from overstimulation of all he experienced. The trio's progress was slow, and purposely so. Slane's leg needed time to heal and he had to make more arrows. Peter and Cassius were overjoyed at being out of the Dead Lands, their prison where they had suffered. They camped by rivers and in lush valleys. They sang and played games. Slane hummed tunes while whittling his arrows and Peter rolled in the grass on his back. Cassius said the fresh air made him even more aerodynamic and he performed high speed maneuvers to the delight of his comrades.

It took a few weeks for Slane to stop looking around for Wolves. Peter and Cassius laughed at his paranoia. While they admired his diligent watchfulness, they reminded him repeatedly that there were no

Wolves in this land. Other dangers, perhaps, but no Wolves.

"Like what?" Slane asked one evening as he sucked the juice out of a roasted onion.

Cassius and Peter looked at each other.

"A dragon," Peter said calmly.

"A what?" Slane asked, tossing the onion aside.

"And a giant snake," Cassius added.

"A dragon and a giant snake?" Slane shouted.

"Oh, and there may or may not be an army of mutant stag beetles as big as that boulder over there," Cassius replied waving his wing.

"Hold everything!" Slane shouted. "You never told me about all this stuff! When were you planning on telling me all this?" He waved his hands as he paced around them.

"What does it matter?" Peter asked him with an amused look on his face.

"Well, it does matter!" Slane replied.

"Why?" Cassius asked. "If you knew all this, would you have stayed in the Dead Lands? Would you not return to the land of your fathers and reclaim what is rightfully yours?"

Slane stopped pacing. He was silent for a moment as he pondered the question. Cassius was right. What did it matter?

"Dragons, snakes, mutant what-evers, those are just names, Slane," said Peter. "The truth is, it doesn't matter what name you give a challenge – it's just another challenge. This quest isn't just your quest; it is ours too. What you face, we will face."

"How do you guys know that those things are out there?" Slane asked looking towards the distant hills. "Have you encountered them?"

"No," Peter said. He stood and gave himself a shake.

"But we know they exist and we know who will send them to stop us," Cassius replied.

"The Evil Queen?" Slane asked. "But it's been years. How do know that she is even still alive much less in power?"

"We passed markers near the river," Peter replied.

"What markers?" Slane asked.

"Two crossed swords within a shield," Cassius replied. "Carved into the trees at the edge of the forests."

"She marks everything as hers to remind all that she is in charge and that they have nothing," said Peter. "She loves to make people beg from her and when she gives, it most certainly will be taken back."

"With a vengeance," added Cassius.

Slane was quiet. The euphoric feeling was gone. He felt darkness settle over him. He had been a fool, dancing in this new land as if it was already his. Peter and Cassius were right. Certainly there was more ahead of them to worry about than just mere Wolves. Dragons, giant snakes, not to mention he needed to assemble an army. Who was going to believe that he was Roland's heir? He was just a kid with a scruffy talking eagle and a fox. He imagined seasoned soldiers laughing in his face and he and Peter and Cassius leaving in shame. Certainly the Evil Queen had a vast army and everyone feared her. Even dragons and giant snakes did her bidding. They had risked everything to leave the Dead Lands and walked right into failure. Slane got up and walked to a large tree and watched the sun dipping low in the sky, sending fire red and orange flares up into the blue sky. Even the sunsets were different outside of the Dead Lands.

Slane felt sheepish for how he was feeling and he certainly wasn't going to tell Peter and Cassius. They could probably tell anyway. *Now wait just a minute Slane. You didn't come through all of this with two friends who would give their lives for you if this didn't mean something. Think of all the Wolf attacks! The Octopus! The hardships and trials of leaving the Dead Lands!* He thought back to the stories around the campfire, how Peter and Cassius told him about the quest to return him to his proper place in his kingdom, and the stories of the prophecy and the Ancient. He remembered his friends telling him about his grandfather and father, and how the Evil Queen spread tyranny over all the lands. *So what if you're a kid? There's been lots of kids who have done amazing things. Kids have slain Giants! Besides, Peter and Cassius know people who are still alive who will remember them and do anything to help them. There is still good in this land.* "And we will find the good," he said to himself.

He looked up at the sky and saw the first stars of the night sky coming into sight. He looked up at the tree he was standing under and reached out and touched the bark. It was thick and beautiful. Then he saw something. Just above his hand was a carving. Two swords crossed with the outline of a shield around them. But there was something underneath it. He leaned in closer. Underneath the Queen's mark was a line and underneath the line was an R sitting on top of a crown. Peter and Cassius didn't tell him about that part of the mark. Maybe they forgot. Slane walked back to the campsite. He felt better after his talk with himself. He gathered a few sticks and tossed them on the dying fire.

"Welcome back, soldier," Peter said, winking at him.

Slane sat by the fire and returned to his arrow making with a renewed focus. He threaded feathers through the shaft and tied them. Then he looked down the shaft with his eye to make sure the arrow was true. The last thing he did was attach the sharpened bone to the other end and made sure the shaft and bone fit snugly. .

"I can't wait to have hands again," said Cassius watching Slane's hands glide over the shaft of the newly created arrow. He sighed deeply.

"Won't be long, my friend," Slane replied. He looked into Cassius's eyes and then over to Peter. "I promise you both I will live to see the day when you both return to your human forms, and you will too."

Slane returned to his arrow making until it became too dark and his eyes got tired. He threw another log on the fire and watched the flames eagerly lick the fresh wood. He thought about the mark he saw on the tree.

"So why is the Queen's mark represented by two swords?"

Peter had been snoozing with his head on his paws. He raised his head and spoke. "The two swords represent the two lands that she controls as one; the one that she stole from Tiberius and the other that she took after the death of your grandfather."

"The swords also represent the fact that she rules by the sword, with military might in order to intimidate her subjects," said Cassius. "The shield represents the one unified kingdom."

"What about the 'R'?" asked Slane, tossing a twig into the fire and watching it glow for a moment before being consumed completely by the white hot coals.

"What 'R'?" asked Peter.

"Underneath the swords and shield I saw an 'R' sitting on top of a crown," Slane responded.

Cassius came to full attention. "You saw no such thing!" he exclaimed.

"This isn't something to joke about, Slane," Peter said, standing up.

Slane looked at his friends incredulously. "I saw it right over there!" he exclaimed, pointing in the direction of the tree.

"Show us!" Cassius cried.

Slane grabbed a partially burned branch from the fire to use as a torch. "Follow me," he said calmly.

He held the burning stick close to the tree so Peter and Cassius could see the mark. It was there. After a moment of silence, Peter and Cassius let out whoops of joy.

"They live!" Peter shouted.

"We are not alone!" Cassius exclaimed.

"What does this mean?" Slane asked as they walked back to their campsite.

"It means that there is still an underground resistant force. People know the truth and have organized, waiting for the right time," Cassius replied.

"But this is the outskirts of civilization," Slane remarked. "No one comes out here."

"That's just it," Peter replied quickly. "The resistance is underground, living in the shadows, the outskirts. There might be someone watching us right now."

Slane looked in the darkness that surrounded them and shivered.

"They know the prophecy, Slane, and they are waiting," said Cassius.

"Waiting for who? Waiting for what?" Slane asked.

"You," Peter said quietly.

Slane was quiet, taking it all in.

"Tomorrow we rise with the dawn," Cassius said as he hopped up on a log where he settled in for the night. "We will scout the forest and follow the markers. Peter and I know what to look for and we will seek out the resistance fighters. Hopefully we can meet up with them soon."

"What do you look for?" asked Slane.

"There is a secret code," Peter said. "More than just the symbol on the tree."

"Like what?"

"Sticks placed in certain patterns, patterns dug in the ground, markings on rocks," Peter paced as he talked. "Each marking spells out a secret language that informs, inspires, and gathers resistance fighters together in secret meeting places."

"How did they come up with this language?" Slane asked, imagining the ingenuity of masked and hooded warriors.

"Oppression often creates a silent strength and intellect that is quite remarkable," said Cassius. "Over the years, this strength became the heartbeat of the people who moved out of the Cities to live in the wilderness areas. Those who believed the prophecy wanted to be ready when the time came to band together."

"This is why we are so excited," said Peter. "Cassius and I were worried all those years in the Dead Lands because we thought the resistance would die. Tomorrow, Cassius will drop messages in certain areas to let them know."

"What will he drop?" asked Slane.

"Two sticks attached together in the form of an X," Cassius replied.

Peter showed Slane how to make the symbol using two sticks five inches in length tied together with a piece of pine straw. Slane quickly made four or five.

"Get your rest tonight, Slane," said Peter. "You can make more at first light."

Slane awoke to Peter nudging him under his arm and the smell of smoldering coals. Morning. He sat up with a feeling of rejuvenation at the thought of finding resistant fighters and creating an army. *My Army.* His mind reeled at the thought. It was strange how he felt ready and unsure at the same time. He got the fire going and then made ten more symbols from sticks that Peter gathered. Cassius had already taken the ones from the previous night and dropped them at strategic points along the edge of the forest. He returned with a beautiful fish that Slane gutted; he put the meat on a spit over the fire. They ate quickly, then put out the fire and gathered their belongings. They headed northwest along the edge of the forest. Slane continued to make the symbols and Cassius flew ahead, dropping a few every mile or so.

"How will they know what to do when they find these?" asked Slane, putting two more on the ground where Cassius picked them up and took to the sky.

"The X represents a meeting place," said Peter. "There is a large underground cave that is accessible only by tunnels. The resistance movement decided it would be there that they would gather when the great king – that's you – returned."

"Where is the cave?"

"It is in the valley of the Craggy Mountains. That's where we are heading. If all goes to plan there will be a large group waiting for us. Having Cassius is a huge advantage for us with his ability to spot settlements from the air and communicate with fighters along the way. Hopefully we'll run into some soon."

Throughout the day the routine continued. Slane became adept at making symbols while he walked and Cassius went on missions to drop them and look for camps of fighters. By midday they had covered several miles and decided to camp under some large oaks at the edge of the forest. Cassius brought Peter and Slane fish and Slane shot a rabbit. While the rabbit meat cooked over the fire, Cassius told them he saw some smoke on the horizon and after they ate he would go investigate the source. He and Peter hoped that it was one of the villages of the resistance perched on the edge of civilization. As soon as they finished eating, Cassius bid them goodbye and told them he would meet them at sunset.

Slane and Peter followed the edge of the forest. Compared to the terrain of the Dead Lands and coming down the Guardian, Slane felt like he was floating on air. The moss that covered the ground was spongy and massaged his feet with every step. He felt strong and confident with a quiver full of arrows and the news about the resistance fighters. He imagined a band of warriors following his lead into battle with swords drawn and armor shining while riding on thundering steeds.

"So Peter," Slane began, jumping over a log. "Tell me about these warriors of the resistance movement?"

"Who?"

"You know, my future warriors. The members of my future army?"

Peter stopped walking. "You really want to know?"

Slane stopped and faced him. "Yes. Why? What's the problem?"

"Slane," Peter began, "I think you should know the truth about your 'warriors.'"

"Yeah? So tell me already!"

"They are farmers," said Peter.

"Farmers?"

"And sheepherders."

"Sheepherders?"

"Yep."

Slane looked at Peter in disbelief. He was speechless.

"Oh, I almost forgot," said Peter.

"About what?" asked Slane.

"The goatherders," Peter responded with a wry smile.

"What!" Slane yelled. "I thought you said these were 'resistant fighters?'"

"Correct."

"What about warriors and skilled killers?"

Peter laughed darkly. "They were killed along time ago by the Evil Queen. All dead."

Slane was silent. His confidence flooded out of him.

"After Cassius and I got away we found out that she found them all and arrested them. Then she tortured and killed them," Peter said quietly, hanging his head. "They were noble, Slane. Mighty men. Loyal. Fierce. All of them refused to bow to her. All these years later I've asked myself if I would have been so brave knowing that I was marching towards my death."

Slane stayed silent, giving respect to his friend and his memories of the great warriors.

Peter turned and faced him. "Your army is going to be composed of farmers and common, every day folk. I hate to disappoint you, but you need to know. They won't be skilled warriors in the sense that you and I think of it, but they all have warrior spirits. They are tired and hungry for sure, and only have the most simple of weapons, but they come with passionate hearts and a desire for freedom. And freedom is the only thing that humans will willingly give their lives for."

"I…I just imagined a polished army, that's all," stammered Slane.

"I know," Peter said, reassuring Slane. "But don't judge these fighters based on what you see. Look into their hearts and you'll find more than capable warriors."

Peter and Slane continued on. Every now and then they would check the trees on the outskirts of the forest for the symbol of the resistance fighters. They found a few and Slane felt a jolt of hope with each one. As the afternoon gave way to evening, Peter and Slane came to a large clearing. Peter listened intently and Slane watched his ears twitch back and forth. Slane thought he heard the sound of voices and was just about to tell Peter when Peter bolted.

"Follow me!" he said and was gone in a flash of red.

Slane took off running behind him, trusting Peter's extraordinary senses of hearing and direction. After a few minutes of running Peter stopped.

"Do you hear something?" Slane gasped, feeling his chest heaving.

"Quiet," Peter whispered.

"This way!" Peter said taking off again.

They tore through a small patch of trees and Slane saw lights flashing ahead. It was a series of camp fires. They stopped at the edge of the trees and Slane saw groups of men around several campfires that glowed brightly in the early evening light.

"Are they friend or foe?" Slane asked.

"Not sure. I'm looking for Cassius," Peter replied.

Slane scanned the groups. They looked like the type of people Peter described. Common, plain, friendly yet determined. This had to be a group of his future soldiers. He was just about to tell Peter to let him go out and greet them when they heard a familiar voice behind them.

"Fancy meeting you here," said Cassius, laughing as they nearly jumped out of their skin.

"Cassius!" Slane said, hitting him with the end of his bow.

"I knew you'd find me, Peter," he said, winking slyly.

Peter ignored him. "So are these friendlies?" he asked, nodding his head towards the camps.

"Oh them," Cassius replied. "Let's go meet some of your new soldiers, Slane."

Pierce placed Slane, Peter, and Cassius in the middle of plastic trees at the edge of the sandbox. He lay down next to them and watched them intently. His lips moved frequently with just the faintest whisper. Cade knew that there was imaginary dialogue going on when Pierce did this, something Pierce had not done in a long time. In the weeks after visiting the scene of his mother's death, Pierce played alone and returned to the patterns of play he exhibited when Cade first began working with him. He barely acknowledged Cade when he arrived at the playroom, avoiding eye contact. He entered and set about the business of play, moving the mountain where he wanted it and gathering various props such as weapons, trees, and soldiers. Cade expected this; Pierce's regression was a normal reaction and one that Cade knew was part of the risk of taking him to the scene of his mother's gruesome death.

Surprisingly, his interaction with peers in the dorms and at school was exemplary according to the reports from teachers and dorm staff. He was more outgoing, talkative, and voluntarily participated in dorm events. One day, Mrs. Simmons, the rec director, caught Cade between sessions and excitedly told him how Pierce had joined in a kickball game and ran in a relay race. Pierce was ecstatic to hear the news, and it was not the only positive report. Mr. Edwards, the language arts teacher told Cade that Pierce read a poem in front of the class after raising his hand when Mr. Edwards asked for volunteers. On one of Cade's trips to the administrative offices, he observed Pierce interacting with a group of boys after lunch. It appeared that he was showing them something on a hand held video game. Cade smiled as he saw them all laugh together at something Pierce said.

Cade was overwhelmed with feelings of pride and gratitude as he saw the signs of Pierce growing into an integrated, whole self. The fragmented pieces that had been shattered by years of neglect, abuse, and abandonment, not to mention the hideous trauma of witnessing his mother's death, had been taken apart, sanded, and put back together through play. The jagged edges were laid out, examined, and smoothed in the shelter of the playroom. The playroom acted as a sort of intensive care unit and for nearly five years had been a safe haven. Cade's affirming presence allowed Pierce to return to the innocence of childhood and fill in the empty spaces that had been passed over during the tumultuous events of his childhood. Pierce had weathered the initial storms of pubescence and was moving into the middle years of adolescence, and showing a confidence and social ease that many of his neurotypical peers did not possess.

Since Cade wasn't included in the play in the last few weeks, he could only surmise what was happening in Pierce's fantasy world of Slane, Peter, and Cassius. Pierce hadn't brought him a manuscript in a long time, and Cade didn't ask. He could tell that the trio had gotten down from the mountain and had one last battle with the Wolves before finally leaving the Dead Lands. It was around this time that Pierce had visited the place of his mother's death and Cade understood that the Dead Lands represented Pierce's past. The new land represented Pierce's new growth and he, like Slane, was stronger and more confident. Cade was disappointed to not be included in the play but knew he must be patient and continue to provide Pierce with an affirming presence. He was aware that his work with Pierce was an extraordinary experience, and Dr. Capstone reminded him that this was no ordinary case. Cade had seen many children healed through the power of play, but the intensity of Pierce's play was unique. No child with whom he had worked had ever written a story while playing it out during the sessions. No child had come up with a story so complex with characters so real. While many of the children with whom Cade worked had horrible pasts, none had the multiple traumas that Pierce had experienced. None had Pierce's high IQ and while Cade was familiar with Asperger's syndrome, Pierce was the first child on the Autism spectrum with whom he had worked directly.

Early in Cade's training, he read a book by Virginia Axline called *Dibs In Search of Self.* In the book, Axline, a child therapist, works with a boy named Dibs who doesn't speak and has severe emotional and social problems. Axline used a type of play known as non-directive play therapy in which she provided a safe and warm environment and allowed Dibs to lead the play. She did not hurry the therapy or manipulate it in any way, and she believed the child deserved utmost respect at all times. Axline reflected Dib's feelings back to him, which increased his confidence and coping skills. Playing freely gave Dibs the ability to express himself. Over time, Dibs showed a gradual and remarkable change resulting in him being able to express himself and rejoin society as a well-adjusted young man. Cade was stunned when he read *Dibs* and it influenced his passion for play therapy. He read parts of it each year.

Each step of his work with Pierce was a real life version of *Dibs.* Cade mentioned this to Dr. Cap.

"Consider yourself blessed," Dr. Cap said, when Cade had stopped by his office after he took Pierce to the site of his mother's death. "Even though it's hard work, it is the case of a lifetime."

"I'll be honest, sometimes I worry about messing it up," said Cade.

"Remember *Dibs*?" Dr. Cap asked.

"Yes, of course."

"Well there you go," Dr. Cap said with a smile.

Trust the process and stay present. It was one of the things he loved about play therapy: He didn't need to force an agenda. But at times this was hard. He had to fight the urge to make the children he worked with grow and change, to tell them what to do to be the person he believed they should be.

Pierce sat up and looked at Cade, brushing sand from the side of his face.

"Dr. Cade?" he asked.

"Will you be Cassius again?"

"Sure," Cade said, getting up and sitting down next to Pierce. "What's going on?"

"Okay," said Pierce, moving Slane, Peter, and Cassius against a row of trees. He quickly positioned plastic army men around the Lincoln Log pieces that represented a campfire. "Slane is about to meet members of his army for the first time," Pierce said excitedly. "As Slane, Peter, and Cassius have traveled into Slane's future kingdom, they have been looking for signs of resistance fighters. They have seen marks on trees and Cassius flew ahead and found this group assembled on the outskirts of the forest."

"Cool," replied Cade. "What do you need Cassius to do?"

"Cassius is going to fly ahead and rally more troops. Once a decent size army is formed, they will march and ultimately face the Evil Queen."

"Got it," Cade said, feeling a surge of joy rising inside him. He picked up Cassius and lifted him into the air.

"Let's go!" Pierce shouted. He moved Slane and Peter out towards the soldiers. "All Hail Slane!" he exclaimed as he moved the Army men around.

20
REVOLUTION

Dr. Cade took me to where my mom died. I got to see the trailer and the park where I went to hide. It was hot and it was exactly like I remembered it. The trailer was still there and had a big black hole in the side of it. I remembered everything that happened once I saw it again. I remembered my mom telling me to go play and how I felt scared when she didn't come out of the trailer. I knew something was wrong and I remember finally feeling brave enough to go to the door of the trailer. Part of me couldn't believe that I was standing inside the park and I felt very strange for a while. I walked to the pipe and got in it where I ran when my mom told me to run away. I laid there for a long time and felt the gritty sand on my face as I stared at the trailer. It looked like a monster with jagged teeth leaning over to devour someone. I saw the door fly open in my mind and my mom screaming for me to run. I remember running like my feet were floating over the ground and I knew that something bad was going to happen. I remember turning around to see the people pouring out of the door and there was my mom. For a moment in time she was frozen and then the explosion happened. I will never forget seeing her hair and body lit up with the white bright light of the explosion in the first nanosecond of the explosion.

I felt weird being at the scene again. I felt paralyzed. Something was drawing me to the trailer; it beckoned like a dark cave with a mesmerizing energy pulling me to it. It was scary. I could almost hear it breathing. I waited until I was ready. Dr. Cade stayed with me and he didn't say anything. Honestly, I kind of forgot he was there until he came over and laid down on the sand with me. He just stayed there and stared at the trailer with me. As I realized he was with me I felt strong. I felt like I did in the playroom when I learned to trust Dr. Cade. If he was with me I knew I would be okay. One of the things I was thinking as I stared at the trailer was all the times that I hoped my mom was going to change and yet she never did. She would leave a guy for a few weeks but then she always found another. I realize it now, but at the time I didn't know I felt so angry at her; I felt like I wasn't enough for my mom. She needed drugs, she needed men. She had a hole somewhere inside her that could not be filled just by being with me. I felt it as a little kid but I couldn't put it into words. I just felt angry and sad. I didn't know why I felt that way, but now I do. Laying in that tunnel and looking at that trailer helped me realize something else too. I don't hate my mom. I felt a peace come over me. As I have played out the story of Slane I have discovered forgiveness, because Slane has forgiven his father and accepts that he isn't a part of his life. Even though Slane has no mother and no father, he has friends who have been like parents. Peter and Cassius are probably better than parents in a lot of ways, now that I think about it. Without the tough times, Slane wouldn't be prepared to be the warrior king that he is.

Even though my mom died and even though I didn't have a lot of time with her, I know now that she loved me in the best way that she could. Some kids at Boyd never even knew their parents. They have no concept of sitting in a parent's lap while eating pizza and watching a movie, cuddled up and laughing. As I stared at the trailer I realized that she just didn't have a whole lot to work with in the parenting department. I also realized that my urge to go there was about putting it behind me. It's over. It's done. It's a chapter and it doesn't need to be revisited. I finally got up and walked to the fence in front of the trailer. I realized that the trailer wasn't a monster waiting to eat me but it was just a trailer. Dr. Cade walked with me and pushed the fence up as if he knew that I needed to walk on the ground where my mom's body burned. He sat a little ways off on a stump and watched me. He just let me be. He's so good at that. How does he know? If I worked with kids, I would want to be just like him. I walked on the dirt and looked at the trailer up close. It looked like a bomb went off inside and there were burned parts everywhere. There was a family of birds living in it and probably a ton of other creatures. I stood about where I stood that day that the door opened and my mom screamed for me to run. I imagined her coming out of the trailer and I looked at the ground where she would have been when the explosion happened and she burned. I looked at the sand for a sign of blood or burned flesh but there was nothing. Just sand. I took the little bottle that I have had with me for a long time and scooped up some sand to put in it. Once it was full I put the cork on very tight. It is my reminder that this happened; I came back to face my fear and sadness; and it is over and behind me.

I sat next to Dr. Cade on the stump. I suddenly felt like I was going to throw up or cry. I cried. Really hard. I remember Dr. Cade comforting me and telling me to keep crying. I cried for a long time. I remember after that I felt like a miracle happened inside me and there was a lot of light inside and warmth. I felt comfort and I guess that's what love feels like. Love for my mom, love for me, love for just being alive. Dr. Cade says love and gratitude go together. I'm grateful to be alive now. Like Slane, I have left the Dead Lands. There are good things for me. Sitting on that stump something told me everything was going to be okay. It was peaceful. I filled a bottle with sand from the exact spot where my mom died. I gave the bottle of sand to Dr. Cade and he told me he would keep it secret and safe, just like Gandalf said to

Frodo. I know he will. He always does what he says.

•••

Over the course of a few months, Slane's army was gathered. They were a rag-tag bunch of sheep herders, goatherds, and farmers from all walks of life. Men, women, and even adolescents lived on the outskirts of the land, driven there by the Evil Queen's treachery. Many had spent time in prison and many had endured slanderous accusations in the courts that resulted in loss of property and everything they owned. They told Slane, Cassius, and Peter stories of those who had been killed by the Queen's soldiers. Slane's soldiers were angry, hungry, and ready to make a change.

"The very things that start a revolution," Peter said to Slane one evening as they sat around the fire.

The army grew and so did Slane's confidence. Peter was right. These people might be simple laborers, but they were brilliant and very brave. Slane continued his transformation that began in the Dead Lands: He was growing from a boy to a man. Peter hardly recognized him now as he strode through the camps, spending time with each loyal soldier. The resistance was well organized and the system of communication was flawless. Cassius flew ahead and scouted for camps while soldiers on foot scampered into the woods and rocky crags, gathering more and more soldiers who seemed to appear right out of thin air. Cassius told Slane that he would soon be meeting with a group of older men, former guards of his grandfather who lived in the high mountains. These old warriors had heard of Slane's arrival and were making their way to the plains to join the army. Slane asked Peter and Cassius about them.

"They are called the Rogues. They are the last of the great warriors who were young men and fought under your grandfather," Peter told him.

"Did you ever meet any of them?" Slane asked.

"Never," Cassius replied. "But we knew about them because their stories were legendary. I thought they all died."

"We all did," Peter added. "But apparently they made everyone think they were dead but they were really living high in the mountains waiting for your return, Slane."

"Why didn't they fight?" Slane asked.

"They knew that the Evil Queen had turned nearly everyone against them. They believed the prophecy and decided to wait for you."

Slane was quiet as he imagined these great warriors, now probably with white beards and creaky limbs. He trusted Peter and Cassius but he wasn't sure how much help these old guys would be.

The next day, the growing army traveled towards a rise in front of a range of mountains. They made camp.

"Where are the Rogues?" Peter asked.

"Be patient," Cassius replied. "They will be here."

Slane used the time to continue to talk to the troops. There were several women in the camp and Slane enjoyed talking to them. He had never seen a woman until now. Peter explained to him that they would be fighting alongside the men. Slane looked confused.

"Why wouldn't they?" Slane asked.

"Well, I thought you'd be surprised, that's all."

"No, I'm happy to have all the soldiers," replied Slane.

The thought suddenly dawned on Peter that Slane was completely unaware that most of the world believed that a woman's role was preparing food and having babies. The time in the Dead Lands had sheltered him, and Peter was glad. Peter knew that these women had lost everything just like the men, including their children at the hands of the Evil Queen. The women would be fierce fighters.

Slane's visiting was interrupted when he heard a commotion from the far side of the camp nearest to the mountain range.

"Here they come!" he heard a few people shout.

He hurried through the crowd and, from a distance, saw the crowd parting and what appeared to be large, slow-moving scraps of gray metal moving through the crowd.

"Where is he?!" shouted the one in front.

Slane walked towards him. The crowd pointed at Slane before he could say a word. The man, large in bulk and with a long red beard strode straight up to Slane and stood in front of him. Slane said nothing. The man took two steps forward until his nose nearly touched Slane's. Slane noticed his eyes were piercing and glowed with an energy that made Slane shiver.

"State your name!" the man shouted.

"I am Slane, grandson of Roland, heir to the throne of this land, and leader of this army," Slane said calmly.

Immediately the man fell to one knee and so did the others, which took Slane by surprise. He didn't know what to do and was thankful when he noticed Peter standing to his right and Cassius stepped up on his left.

"Tell them to rise," Peter whispered as he nudged Slane.

"Rise, my good soldiers, and tell me your names," Slane said reverently, surprised by his ability to say the words in a noble tone.

The leader promptly rose and looked Slane in the eye.

"I am Gilbert, of the Beck clan and I am the leader of this bunch of rowdy renegades," he said with a smile as his eyes twinkled. He looked back at the soldiers behind him. "We are the Rogues!" he cried, motioning to those behind him. "Step forward ya bunch of rusty coots and address your warrior king!"

Each one stepped forward, their ancient armor rattling and clanging against weapons tarnished with age. Each stated his name and clan with pride. There were twenty in all. They were old but Slane was struck by the gleaming light in their eyes that communicated wisdom, strength, and not a hint of fear.

"We served Roland, all of us," Gilbert began, his eyes welling up with tears. "The greatest king this world has ever seen. We served him out of duty and a love that few experience, for him and this dear land." He swept his arm to encompass the beautiful country side. "All this was once ours and there was peace. We have waited a long time for you to come, Slane."

Being in the presence of Gilbert and his men made Slane feel ten feet tall. The fear and doubt he felt at the beginning of the gathering of the soldiers was gone. While they ate dinner that evening, Gilbert and the other men told him of the great battle in which Roland was killed and how terrible it was to lose such a great warrior. They told him of the goodness of Tiberius and how everything fell apart after his death. They told Slane how the Queen took over the land and how many were killed; Gilbert and a few of Roland's mighty men, the men that Slane just met, fled into the mountains where they lived until now. The Cities of Light were no more. Gilbert told Slane of the promise he made to Roland before the battle that took the King's life.

"I told him that I would protect his kingdom and his name. That any descendent of Roland would be mine to protect until my dying day. The prophecy began to circulate and we devised a way for those still loyal to Roland and still alive to communicate and be ready for the day when his heir returned. You are meant to be here, Slane, and you will be crowned King of the Cities of Light."

Slane stared into Gilbert's eyes and felt a fire rise within his belly. He felt his muscles swell with might and his senses sharpened noticeably. Something changed within him in that moment and he was completely aware of it. He bowed to Gilbert.

"As you fight for me, so I will fight for you," Slane said.

"Tomorrow we must make our plans to overthrow the Queen," Slane said, lifting his bow.

Gilbert placed his hand on Slane's arm. "First, we must show you something. It's not far from here and we think you should see it."

Slane looked at the other soldiers who nodded their heads.

"What is it?" Slane asked.

"Best to wait until morning," Gilbert said, giving him a wink.

"I've seen it, Slane," Cassius said. "Trust me, you need to see it too."

The next morning, Slane, Peter, and Cassius set out with the Rogues towards the mountains. In the distance, Slane could see a wall of granite at least a thousand feet high. It appeared as if they were walking into a dead end. It reminded Slane of the Dead Lands because it appeared desolate and forgotten. Nothing grew near this mountain and from the vantage point of the camp that they had just left, it seemed as though it was a place to avoid. Suddenly, the wall was right in front of them. Slane blinked and looked behind him. The camp was still visible, and he could see people moving around. What just happened? He turned back around to see Gilbert in front of him.

"Confused?" Gilbert asked with a grin.

Slane nodded. "I thought we had miles to go, what happened?"

"It's an optical illusion," Cassius said. "The granite wall of the mountain only appears far away and so high because of the way the land slopes down. It makes it look miles away from back there and the desolation of the place gives people the mindset to stay away."

"Now, that's enough to squeeze your brain, but watch this!" Gilbert said excitedly.

Slane watched him gallop towards that granite wall that was about twenty yards away. Suddenly he disappeared. Slane gasped.

"Wizardry!" he cried, stepping forward. The Rogues laughed and hit each other on the back.

"Hello!" Gilbert said, his head appearing to float above the ground and then disappeared again.

"What's going on?" asked Slane, not knowing whether to laugh or be perturbed.

"Step forward, sir, and try it yourself," said Aaron, one of the other Rogues as he held his arm outstretched towards the place where Gilbert disappeared. Slane walked towards the wall and felt apprehensive. Was it magic? Sorcery? What in world could it be? He was about to walk right into the granite wall that towered above him when he noticed two walls. When Gilbert disappeared he had actually stepped between the two walls that were close together. The one closest to where Slane had stood was actually a small rise of granite. The seemingly massive wall of granite visible to the camp, which seemed miles away, was actually a taller wall from another mountain set behind the first one. The patterns on the granite made the two structures look like one impenetrable wall. Slane saw Gilbert standing on the other side and when Slane passed through he burst into laughter.

"If only I could capture the look on your face!" Gilbert said doubling over.

Slane was too dumbstruck to talk. He had never seen anything like it. The others walked through behind him. He heard Peter and Cassius gasp collectively and turned.

"It's Roland's hidden castle!" Peter said.

"What?" Slane asked, and then he saw it.

The ground sloped into a lush valley that was surrounded by mountain peaks. There was a river that flowed into a large lake and in the middle of the Lake was an island. There, on the island stood a large stately castle complete with ramparts and turrets. It was the most beautiful thing Slane had ever seen.

"That's what we've been doing since we left the kingdom," Aaron said proudly. "We've rebuilt one of the castles of your great-great grandfather, your namesake. It is yours now."

Slane swelled with pride. While they walked to the castle, Gilbert explained how they found this place when they fled as fast and as far as they could once the Queen went on her rampage.

"We thought we were cornered for sure," Gilbert said. "We backed up against the wall of granite and decided to fight to the death."

"We were sure we were done for," said Rupert, another Rogue with a streak of white through his red beard.

"We saw them coming off in the distance. We were tired and out of resources. Suddenly, as we backed away from our imminent deaths, one of us noticed the opening and disappeared. We followed and realized our enemies couldn't see us. We watched them turn around and keep going. Then we stumbled upon this lush valley with naturally growing wheat and vegetables, and took up residence in the castle. We've been here ever since, rebuilding the castle and storing up supplies."

They neared the castle which was accessible only by a drawbridge. The Rogues bragged about how they constructed it just as it had stood in Slane's great-grandfather's day. Peter explained to Slane that this land was long forgotten and over time people thought that the castle had been destroyed. Soon, nobody even bothered to look for it.

"As children we were told that it sank into the ground and disappeared, but it was here all along," Peter chuckled.

They crossed the drawbridge and entered the main gate. The Rogues had replaced many of the crumbling stone blocks and cut new wood for the floors. The large great room was what the Rogues were most proud of.

"Roland built this castle as a hideaway where he and his men would be protected," said Aaron. "It was designed to be big enough to hold his army and supplies. This great room was used for entertainment and important strategy meetings."

"Imagine the banquets that your ancestors held here, Slane," Gilbert bellowed, his voice echoing off the huge walls.

"And will one day have again," Aaron said as he bowed to Slane.

They took Slane up to the second floor which held many bedrooms and chamber rooms for smaller meetings or banquets. This opened up to the third floor that led to the top of the ramparts. Along the ramparts was a wide walkway that allowed for many soldiers to gather and defend the castle. Slane imagined his great-great-grandfather leading his armies from battle back to the castle and enjoying feasts and dancing in the great hall. He imagined soldiers keeping watch on these very walkways, calling out the night watches. He imagined the castle bustling with activity during the day: Documents being written up and signed with the king's seal, court proceedings deciding disputes between clans, and throngs of people bringing in harvested crops and livestock. This was Slane's castle, from whose throne he would reign. But first, they had to defeat the Evil Queen. Yes, there was that. Slane felt his feet return to the ground.

He could see remnants of a city that once surrounded the castle. The Rogues told him that at the time of his great-grandfather, this was the central part of the kingdom. It was well protected and had all the natural resources it needed to provide for a large city. They told Slane that it would once again be restored, and they showed him where many of the resistance fighters had begun building new dwellings and shops. The Cities of Light would be relocated here, and he would reign over the cities, just like his ancestors.

"Now for the good part," Gilbert said, taking Slane's arm. "Wait til you see this!"

They descended down a tower on the north part of the outer wall, walking down a narrow winding staircase that led to a large stock room filled with weapons and tools. Gilbert walked to a large rug that was spread on the floor and picked it up. He pointed at the floor. Slane moved closer and looked. He didn't notice anything at first, and then he saw a slight discoloration in the floor that was hardly distinguishable. Gilbert removed his sword and hit the floor with the hilt and a trapdoor swung open, startling Slane. He peered down into the darkness and saw cobblestone steps winding down. One of the Rogues handed him a torch.

"Go ahead, sir, and we will follow," Gilbert said, allowing Peter to follow Slane, who descended with Cassius on his outstretched arm.

The winding cobblestone steps led down to a room. Gilbert took Slane's torch and lit torches placed on the walls. Slane saw a tunnel in front of them.

"Was this some sort of dungeon?" asked Slane.

"We're not sure," Gilbert replied.

"What does that tunnel lead?" asked Peter.

"Oh, that," Gilbert replied. "You're going to like this," he said pointing his torch down the tunnel. "It leads all the way to the Queen's castle."

Slane, Peter, and Cassius looked at Gilbert in astonishment. Gilbert explained how they found the tunnel and that it stretched over twenty miles. They spent the last several years researching the length of the tunnel and found that the end of it surfaced in an old stockroom in a forgotten part of the Queen's castle. The Rogues blockaded that end of the tunnel in case the Queen's minions found it. They stockpiled food supplies and weapons at stations throughout the tunnel in preparation for the assault of the resistance.

"It's solid and in great shape all the way through," Gilbert said. "This tunnel will allow us to infiltrate the Queen's castle from the inside, while forces attack from the outside. We figure we could send hundreds through the tunnel fairly easily."

The group returned to the surface, exited the castle and went back to the camp. Two more groups of resistance fighters had joined since then. Peter estimated the ranks had grown to about one thousand or more. Gilbert projected another four thousand would join on the way to the Queen's castle. Slane, Peter, and the rest of the Rogues spent the rest of that week planning strategies for the battle. They appointed leaders to gather weapons and build weapons and to be in charge of regiments. Cassius continued his flying missions to round up resistance fighters and to help spread the word that Slane had returned. He flew all the way to the Queen's castle and the resistance forces were ready to join as Slane and the current army advanced. Cassius' reconnaissance determined they had enough soldiers and weapons to defeat the Queen and her forces. Gilbert surmised that many of Queen's soldiers would turn once they saw Slane had returned. Peter didn't want to bet on that, but at least acknowledged that it was a possibility.

The army was divided into two groups: Those who would attack the Queen's castle and gather soldiers on the way, and those that would stay at the camp and begin the march through the tunnel in order to attack the castle from the inside. Gilbert and Aaron would accompany Peter, Slane, and Cassius, while the rest of the Rogues would lead the charge from the tunnel since they knew its secrets. Divisions of archers and foot soldiers were formed. A second division of foot soldiers who were battle trained were given horses to ride. Slane had never seen a horse, much less ridden one, so he spent a few hours each day learning to master the art of riding. By the end of the week he had mastered holding the reigns in his teeth and shooting his arrows while the horse ran at full speed. Right before they departed on their mission, Gilbert and Aaron orchestrated a banquet to formally recognize Slane as the Warrior King and to give the army the plans for the upcoming battle.

The banquet was held in the great hall. The castle was alive with light from the many torches and candles. There was a festive spirit in the air. The old kitchen burst into life as the ovens roared and delivered delicious delights to the makeshift soldiers. Meats of all kinds were provided, along with fruits, vegetables, and sweet cakes. There was a great deal of singing and telling of tall tales. Slane had never felt so good. He sat between Peter and Cassius. One of the Rogues had made a large perch for Cassius to sit on. The hope of a new life was stirring in everyone who was present. As the meal came to a close, Gilbert stood and called everyone to attention.

"My friends and countrymen, I am honored to bring you all to this place of our forefathers, who defended this land and created equality for all."

"Here! Here!" everyone cheered.

He told the history of the land, and how darkness had taken over. He spoke of the hope that sprang up in each resistance fighter, those who were both present and those who would join them on the way.

"I am old, but I have seen the prophecy fulfilled. I remember the words of the Ancient, told to us by our fathers.

'I am with you and will watch over you wherever you go, and I will bring you back to this land. I will not leave you until I have done what I have promised you.'"

"And here we are," Gilbert said with tears forming in his eyes. "All of us here are witnesses to this promise fulfilled, and I am convinced that nothing will stand in our way as we continue on to defeat the Queen!"

A loud cheer went up from the hall, complete with rattling of swords and banging cups on the tables.

"Now," said Gilbert reverently, "I ask my fellow Rogues to join me up here."

All of the Rogues joined him and Gilbert nodded to two of them who picked up a large wooden chest that was in the corner of the room and brought it to the front of the hall. Gilbert looked at Slane, and motioned him to come forward.

"Master Slane, please join us."

Slane got up and stood in front of Gilbert. The two Rogues who brought the chest over opened it.

"Master Slane, please kneel."

Slane kneeled in front of Gilbert, facing him and waiting.

"Hand it to me," Gilbert said to the two Rogues who opened the chest.

"I hold in my hand," Gilbert said, raising his arms, "The crown of Slane the Great, great-great-grandfather of our Slane who kneels before me."

A collective gasp went up from the crowd and it surged forward.

"Master Slane, by the power vested in me as your grandfather's sworn protector and advisor, I place this crown of your fathers upon your head as the symbol of power and sovereignty over this land. As I vowed to your grandfather, I give my life to serve you and protect you as long as I have life in this body. Please rise."

Slane felt the heavy crown upon his head and with it came a surge of adrenaline. He stood and faced Gilbert, who turned him around to face the crowd.

"Behold your Warrior King!" Gilbert bellowed.

Every person in the room kneeled with their heads bowed towards Slane. He looked at Peter who was also kneeling. Cassius had dropped from his perch and lay prostrate with both wings spread out before him. Suddenly as he looked at Peter and Cassius, he noticed a bright light growing around them. At first Slane thought he was just light-headed from the rush of the excitement of the moment, but he realized that something was happening. Before he could say anything else, Peter and Cassius were hidden by a light so bright that Slane had to shield his eyes. People began to stand up to see what was going on and murmuring filled the room. The light seemed as though it would split the castle in half, and then as sudden as it began, it was gone. In the place of the fox and the eagle were two men, who stood stunned, staring at their bodies and new clothes.

"Peter? Cassius?" Slane said, rubbing his eyes as he stepped towards them.

Peter and Cassius, finally back to their human form, hugged each other and laughed as they jumped up and down.

"Slane! It's us!" Peter cried, holding his arms open for Slane.

"Oh, it's you, it's really you!" Slane exclaimed as tears ran down his face. He pulled back and stared at them, seeing their human faces for the first time in his life. All the Rogues were amazed and the people in the hall pressed forward to see the transformed beings.

"It's us!" said Cassius. "We're back! We're back!"

The rest of the evening Slane did not leave the presence of Peter or

Cassius. The men who had given their all to protect him were no longer in animal form. The quest was complete. Slane truly was the Warrior King.

••

Cade watched the scene with awe. *I can't believe this! The quest is complete!* Pierce was fully verbal in his play, narrating the action as he went along. He even mimicked several different voices of the various characters that had been added in recent months. After Slane was crowned by Gilbert, Pierce took two medieval soldiers and put them in place of the stuffed animals. Pierce flung them behind him and they slid across the floor under a table. The transformation of Peter and Cassius marked a significant portion of the story and was a picture of Pierce's continued growth. In the year since they had visited the scene of the death of Pierce's mother, Pierce had made many friends: he sang in the choir and was the leader of the chess team. He appeared like any fifteen-going-on-sixteen year old. He was social and outgoing, and he told jokes now. His outward personality was that of a grounded, contented young man who, although still a bit awkward in many ways, was not afraid to share his thoughts and feelings. He continued to write and put short stories in the Boyd monthly newsletter, for which he had become editor. The residents tore through the pages to find the next story by Pierce, and the English teacher created a writer's workshop where Pierce mentored young people who were inspired to write after reading Pierce's story. Cade worked with him on being compassionate to the younger children, and to curb his sarcasm, brought on by his difficulty to see things from another's perspective at times.

Cade wondered if he would still be involved in the play now that Peter and Cassius had been transformed. Pierce reassured him.

"You're still gonna be Cassius," Pierce told him like a director might coach an actor. "But of course he can't fly anymore. Good thing he did all that flying already to gather the resistance fighters," Pierce said. He looked completely satisfied. "Don't worry, I'll tell you what to do and how the battle's going to go."

"I'm honored to be part of your story. I'll do whatever you tell me to do," Cade said.

A blue jay landed in the big oak and Cade and Pierce watched him for a while.

"When this is over, I may not play here anymore," Pierce said shyly.

"You are free to play here anytime you want and in any form you choose," Cade responded.

Pierce looked around the room and at the castle in the sandbox with the characters all around. "It really is a good story, isn't it?" he whispered. Pierce answered his own question. "Yes, I think it is."

21
THE FINAL BATTLE

"Perhaps it is easier to understand that even though we do not have the wisdom to enumerate the reasons for the behavior of another person, we can grant that each individual does have their private world of meaning, conceived out of the integrity and dignity of their personality."

—Virginia Axline

I have been coming to this playroom for a long time. It is a place that I will never forget. I like the big windows and the big tree. I have finished my story and I think it is good. I know something has really changed in me but I don't know what that is. I am talking to people and I can say what I think and feel, and I can tell jokes. People like my jokes. They say I am sarcastic. I like that. The other day when I was in choir I made the teacher laugh so hard she couldn't lead us for about five minutes. She kept cracking up! It made me feel appreciated and noticed. My chess team is the same way. They always want me to say something funny. I like this part of myself. I like who I am now. I have found that I am funny and I like that. I know that I am smart and I like that. I can sing and I understand music and I like that. The thing I like the most about myself is that I am a writer. I may be leaving Boyd soon. I have been selected to begin college classes in the fall since I have all my high school credits. They told me that I can go live at the university with other kids my age who have finished high school early.

I told Dr. Cade that I probably wouldn't come back to the playroom anymore after my story is done. He said that was okay. Now that I'm sixteen I feel like I don't need it anymore. I told him that I wouldn't mind seeing him to talk now and then. He said whatever I wanted was fine. I told him about leaving Boyd and going to the university. He said that my future is full of possibilities. It's funny that he never tells me what to do. Even when I was young and in all that trouble he never talked about it. He just let me be myself and play. I want to be like him someday. I don't want to do what he does but I want to be calm like he is. He is wise and kind. I want to be like that. I may put him in one of my stories someday. He is my Peter and Cassius. He is a mixture of wisdom, strength, kindness, and faithfulness. The playroom is his kingdom and he is the Warrior King of helping kids like me, how I used to be. He said he may be leaving Boyd also to teach at the university and start his own counseling practice. I know that he will be good at whatever he does.

....

The day of the attack had finally arrived. Slane and Cassius led the largest section of the army under the cover of night onto a ridge overlooking the valley where the Queen's castle and surrounding city was located. Peter, Gilbert, and Aaron led another section to the surrounding hills and waited for the signal to attack from the south. The Rogues led a thousand soldiers through the tunnel and were ready to attack from within. They would set the castle on fire and burn it from the inside out, destroying anyone they found along the way. The smoke rising from the castle would signal the other groups to begin the attack. Slane felt slight apprehension, but overall he was confident they would defeat the Queen. While she had a more formally trained army, his army had the element of surprise. And his fighters were tired of living like animals and were ready to own property and live in freedom.

It was the one thing that people would die for, Peter told him on more than one occasion.

The first light of dawn traced across the sky. The dew was cool, and patches of fog leftover from the night hung in clumps across the valley. Slane checked his bow. One of the soldiers had restrung it for him and it was perfect. His quiver was full thanks to the many helping hands who made arrow making much quicker. He thought about his new role as Warrior King. *Leader of the army yet ruler of the people.* It would be no small task. But then again, leaving the Dead Lands was no small task. Staying alive against all odds was no small task. Peter and Cassius helped him then, and they would help him now. He knew that a ruler was nothing without wise advisors, and he had the best.

"Should be anytime now," Cassius said as he sat down next to Slane.

Slane nodded. "I haven't seen anything yet. Are the soldiers ready?"

"More than ready. They've waited for this for a long time. You know, there is something I want to tell you before we go into battle."

Slane looked at Cassius. "What is it?"

Cassius took a deep breath. "I need to tell you, now that you are my king, I am no longer your caretaker. For so long I was there to help you and protect you, almost like a parent. So if I seem a bit distant, it's because I'm adjusting to this new role."

"It sounds funny when you say 'You are my king,'" Slane said feeling himself blush. "I mean, I'm still who I was. I'm just taking on new responsibility."

"I know, Slane, but you have to understand that the others expect you to be in that role."

"Yeah, but you've been like a father to me, Cassius." He wiped a tear. "There are times when I just want it to be us again which I know sounds weird but that's how I feel. Just us around the fire being silly and listening to your stories."

"I know, we all yearn for what seems like simpler times. But this is what destiny has brought us and it is the path the Ancient has chosen."

"Sometimes I feel like I'm ready to be the Warrior King, like something just takes over and I'm natural at it. But them sometimes I'm not sure if I can do it or I look into the eyes of the people and I realize that they see me as some kind of savior. That's when I get a little freaked out."

They scanned the horizon but there was nothing.

"Cassius, please promise me that there will be times when I can come to you when it's just us and I can be myself – you know, the Slane you know. I need that and I will always need your guidance, and if you lose your sense of humor I'll have you turned into a chicken instead of an eagle!"

Cassius laughed. "Of course. Our little secret, okay? I will always be here for you, until my dying day."

"That means a lot to me," Slane said as he wiped his eyes with his sleeve. "By the way, I need to tell you something."

"What's that?"

"I know that there really isn't a Dragon or Giant Snake," Slane said, jabbing Cassius in the ribs with his elbow.

"How'd you find out?" asked Cassius, grinning ear to ear.

"Gilbert and Aaron. I mentioned it to them when we were in the castle talking about battle plans. I thought they were going to fall down from laughing."

Cassius laughed. "We just wanted to keep you on your toes. You know, keep you humble."

Slane laughed. "I get it now, but I wasn't too happy at the time."

Cassius sighed. "Boy, it feels good to be human again," he said as he stretched. "I do miss the flying…but I'm ready to meet a special girl and have a family of my own. Maybe a small farm, something like that."

"You'll get all that dream, I'm sure of that. Plus," Slane winked and nudged him, "I know some pretty powerful people that can make those things happen for you."

Cassius laughed. "Don't forget us little people."

"Smoke on the horizon! Smoke on the horizon!" A voice bellowed behind them, jerking them back to reality.

Slane and Cassius jumped to their feet and got on their horses. Cassius sped down the line of soldiers to spread the word.

"Formation ready!" Slane yelled, pulling his horse around to face the soldiers.

"Move ahead!" Cassius yelled, thundering towards Slane.

The soldiers let out a cry and followed their king as Slane and Cassius thundered down the hill. Slane felt adrenaline coursing through him. The lead soldiers caught up to Slane and their horses matched Slane's stride for stride. Hooves pounded, armor clanked, and men yelled. They swept down into the valley towards the castle. Smoke was billowing from the middle of the castle. Slane saw something out of the corner of his eye and thought it was an avalanche. He realized it was the other army led by Peter, Gilbert and Aaron cascading down the hills in a mixture of men, horses, and weapons that glistened in the morning sun just coming over the rise.

As they neared the castle, Slane saw peasants pouring from the village. Men, women, and children, many still in nightclothes were running haphazardly along with dogs, cows, and chickens. Slane had given strict orders that no civilians were to be harmed and if any wanted to join their cause, they were more than welcome. The Queen's soldiers were visible among the villagers, working hard to secure the outer walls of the castle. A battalion of soldiers had mounted horses and were coming towards Slane's group. They had good armor, which the Rogues had warned Slane about. They wore coats of mail armor on their arms and legs. Breastplates, leggings, and helmets all made of polished iron made them appear menacing. Slane put the reigns of his horse in his mouth and gripped the sides of his thundering steed with his knees. He drew his bow and loaded an arrow. He picked the lead soldier and aimed at one of the eye slits in the glistening armor. He lost sight of it after he let it go but saw the soldier lean forward on his horse and bounced twice in the air as his horse continued to run at full tilt. He fell with a thud onto the ground. Slane loaded another arrow and felled two more before the groups slammed into each other. Suddenly he was in the middle of chaos. Horses overturned, men on the ground as they ran and crawled towards each other. The clanking and ringing of swords hitting each other and the grunts of those who had been wounded. Slane saw an opening to his left and tore through it skirting around the back of the group. He was relieved to see it was not a large group. He killed four more soldiers in a matter of minutes and wounded at least five. He saw Cassius slashing through the air with his sword while still on his horse and barking commands to those around him.

Slane's group quickly destroyed the soldiers with only a few casualties. They regrouped and were within fifty yards of the castle when a rain of arrows descended upon them. Slane saw a few of his soldiers fall immediately, and the others stopped in their tracks.

"Keep moving!" Slane shouted. "Shields up!" he ordered as he lifted his shield over his head and felt two arrows slam into the leathery shell. He could now smell the smoke from the burning castle. His men reached an outer gate which was guarded by a few dazed soldiers. Slane's foot soldiers quickly eliminated them while others cut the ropes that lifted the gate. A swarm of Queen's men awaited them and rushed towards them. Slane was happy to see they either purposely left their helmets off or in the rush of things couldn't find them but either way his arrows found their mark and he dropped at least twenty while his men engaged the rest in hand to hand combat. He tied his horse and kept his bow ready as he entered the gate. He took down several more guards and was careful to avoid being seen from the walkway above. He could see the flames shooting from the main tower of the castle. His soldiers rushed past him;

he followed and found himself next to Cassius.

"The Rogues are purging the inside of the castle!" Cassius yelled above the din. "Peter's group has taken the south wall. They are going to join us but there is a large garrison ahead. Hopefully the Rogues will meet us in the middle and we'll join together. It's the last big challenge we have to face! Victory is nearly ours!"

Slane knew that his arrows were getting low. Used arrows were usually defective, particularly those yanked from a body but he found a few lying on the ground. These were probably dropped from the soldiers on the top wall who left in haste to tend to the fire and the attack on the south wall. While he was fairly good with a sword and very good with a dagger, the bow was his weapon of choice. But the bow was cumbersome in close combat situations. He pushed the thought from his mind and loaded an arrow. The soldiers continued their advance. Occasionally Slane would feel a body underneath him as he walked forward. If it was soft he knew it was one of his army; if it was hard it was one of the Queen's men still wearing heavy armor. They reached a large courtyard area. It was the last stand of the Queen's soldiers and they were fighting to the death. As they went down, more poured out of the burning castle. Slane used his remaining arrows and each found a victim. He slung his bow behind him and drew his sword and dagger and entered the fray.

The Queen's soldiers were expert swordsman and their armor gave them the advantage in close quartered combat. Slane's soldiers were severely lacking in training and combat skills, but their surprise attack had given the resistance fighters an immense advantage. Gilbert told Slane about the advanced armor and Slane asked for solutions. The Rogues suggested a unique strategy for this problem. The armor, while effective in protecting its wearer, made the person a bit clumsy. The Rogues chose several of the large men and women who were strong enough to wear armor and wield large battering ram-like clubs to strike the armored soldiers, thus throwing them off balance and knocking them down. Once on the ground Slane's soldiers could easily take their weapons and eliminate them. Slane witnessed the plan working beautifully. He watched a large woman with a huge club hit two soldiers from behind, sending them flying.

Slane battled a soldier and easily disarmed him and ran him through with the soldier's own sword. Another came from behind a wall to attack one of Slane's soldiers and Slane caught him in midair, running him through the front with his sword and stabbing him in the back with his dagger. Many of the soldiers discarded their weapons and armor and attempted to surrender but Slane had given strict orders to kill all of the Queen's soldiers until she appeared and surrendered. He knew that while the battle raged there could be no compromise and no mercy. She was too evil to trust. He hoped that she had been found during the destruction of the castle. At this point in the battle, there were only a few of the Queen's soldiers left and some had fled. Slane ordered a large number of his army to chase them down and, if they agreed to surrender, to take them captive. Cassius stood and saw Slane coming. He held up his arms as a sign of victory and then Slane saw a look of terror cross his face. Immediately Slane felt something hit him from the side and he slammed into the ground. His sword was knocked from his hand but he had his dagger. He looked up to see one of the Queen's soldiers straddling him. The soldier held his sword high in the air ready to plunge it into Slane's neck. Just as the blade was coming down Slane saw a blur and the soldier was off him in a second.

"Cassius!" Slane yelled. Slane rolled and got up and saw Cassius run his sword through the back of the soldier and then hit him in the head with the hilt. The man was dead.

"My brother, you have saved me!" Slane called and rushed to hug Cassius.

"Are you hurt?" Cassius asked.

"No, just a blow. I'm fine!" Slane replied.

They looked around and saw that there were no more of the Queen's soldiers in the courtyard. Slane's soldiers came to congratulate Cassius and a cheer went up. Slane saw a few arrows on the ground and he put them in his quiver.

"We have won, Slane! We have won!" Cassius cried. "We need to find Peter and Gilbert," he said, just as a huge section of the castle wall tumbled to the ground in a pile of burning rubble.

"Halt! Hold it right there! Nobody move a muscle!" A voice called from up on the remaining part of the wall behind them.

Slane and Cassius and the few remaining soldiers turned to look. The last living archer of the Queen's army had his bow drawn and an arrow pointed right at Slane and Cassius. Cassius shoved Slane behind him and stood in front of him.

"Do not move out from behind me," Cassius hissed.

Slane did not say a word.

One of Slane's soldiers stepped forward and shouted "Come down from there! You're surrounded and…" Slane heard a sickening *thwick* as an arrow stuck the man right in the throat. He was dead before he hit the ground.

Slane turned back and the soldier had another arrow pointing at them. He drew it nearly in the time it took for the other arrow to kill Slane's soldier.

"I don't know who you two are, but I know you're somebody important," the soldier said with an evil sneer. "You're protecting him, and that means he's somebody really important. Word has spread that Slane the grandson of Roland has returned to claim the throne. So, if I kill him, I'll be a hero and this whole thing will be over."

"You're wrong, soldier!" Cassius called out. "He's my son and I'm willing to die for him. He is young and has much life in front of him."

Slane slid his bow from his shoulder. He knew that he could kill the man in an even draw, but with the soldier being an expert archer and already having an arrow drawn, he knew there was no possible way. He felt a sense of panic rise up his spine. Cassius stood firmly in front of Slane.

"Keep talking, we can distract him," Slane whispered to Cassius.

"What a noble father you are," the soldier said. "But I don't believe you. I believe that the man you are shielding is indeed Slane, from the prophecy."

"What prophecy?" Cassius asked.

"Don't toy with me, soldier! You know the prophecy of which I speak. The prophecy that says…"

Just then Slane heard a commotion behind him and saw the soldier shift his aim to whatever was happening behind him. A rock whizzed through the air at the archer, narrowly missing his head. As soon as the archer saw what was happening he released his arrow which struck the interfering soldier in the skull, killing him instantly. In a flash Slane loaded an arrow, drew his bow and stepped from behind Cassius to his right. The soldier loaded another arrow as soon as he killed the soldier behind Slane and took aim at Slane, releasing the arrow in one smooth motion as Slane released his. Suddenly everything went dark and Slane felt himself hit the ground. He was sure that he was hit and closed his eyes and waited for the pain. It didn't come but he noticed it was hard to breathe. He opened his eyes and saw the face of Cassius staring at him.

"Cassius?" Slane asked.

"He's hit!" one of Slane's soldiers yelled. Three of them lifted Cassius off Slane and Slane sat up, reloaded his bow and pointed it up towards where the archer had been standing.

"No worries, My Lord," one of the soldiers said. "You killed him."

Slane looked down and horror filled his heart. An arrow was sticking out of Cassius' back.

"Cassius!" Slane cried as he dropped to the ground.

Blood trickled from the side of his friend's mouth.

"Quick! We need to do something!" Slane looked around at the soldiers.

"Slane," Cassius whispered.

"Yes, Cassius?" Slane laid his head next to him.

"Don't move me, the arrow is through my heart and I only have a few moments left." He turned his head to look at Slane and laid his head on the ground. His eyes were distant and clouding over. He heaved a sigh and Slane could hear blood gurgle in his lungs.

"Don't talk, Cassius," Slane said as he laid his hand on Cassius' face.

"I must," Cassius began. "I want you to know that I am so proud of you, Slane. You are destined to be the Warrior King and your name will be known for generations. You are kind but fair, brave but wise. Keep Peter close: He will advise you well." He coughed up some blood and closed his eyes.

Slane's eyes filled with tears. He thought Cassius was dead but noticed he was still breathing.

"There is one more thing," Cassius said weakly. "I love you."

"I love you too, Cassius!" Slane cried. "I will never forget you," he said, his chest heaving with sobs and his eyes pouring out tears.

Cassius looked into Slane's eyes for a brief moment, and then took a deep sigh. Slane watched the last flicker of light and life leave his dear friend. Slane lifted to his knees and raised a cry that reached the heavens in a roar of pain and sadness. He pounded the ground with both hands and gritted his teeth. *Why? Why did Cassius have to die!* There was no relief from the emotional pain that he was feeling. For the first time in his life, Slane was experiencing the death of a loved one. Cassius had been a parent to him, caring for him from the first year of his life. He raised Slane, teaching him to hunt, protect himself, and make decisions. With the instincts of an eagle, he taught Slane to see beyond what was in front of him. He taught Slane to look through problems. He taught him to see solutions that did not readily appear. He taught with a sense of humor. Most of all, he guarded Slane with his life, more than once risking his life to save Slane's. And in the end, he made the ultimate sacrifice for Slane.

His fellow soldiers came and put their hands on his shoulders but he shrugged them away. He wanted to be alone. Alone in his own world. Alone on his own planet, his own universe. Away from everyone. This felt so awful. He looked at Cassius lying there dead. Noble, handsome, self-sacrificing. Suddenly the world came spinning back to him. He heard the crackling of the burning castle and smelled the singed stone and wood. In the distance he could hear the shouts of soldiers. His soldiers. He raised himself up and grabbed his bow, quiver, and sword. He would finish this battle. He would claim this land as Cassius said he would. Slane told the remaining soldiers to wrap the body of Cassius along with their dead and take them away from the castle in case the fire spread to the courtyard. He sprinted to his horse, which was still tied where he left it, and jumped on, tearing away towards the north end of the castle where he could see Peter's battalion and the Rogues putting the finishing touches on the Queen's remaining soldiers.

....

Cade felt the tears sting his eyes. He held the figure that represented Cassius next to the Slane figure that Pierce held. *I'm going with my heart here; Pierce will tell me if I do something wrong. I'm so honored to be included in his play, he has entrusted me with everything.* Cade had never felt such an honor in being in such a sacred place. Cassius had been hit and now he and Slane would say goodbye forever.

"Keep Peter close. He will advise you well," Cade said, lifting Cassius up so he could whisper the words. He then laid the figure's head back down on the sand.

Cade felt the moment and something stirred within him. He pondered what would be right, what would be proper. Pierce trusted him. It was coming from Cade's heart and was part of the play. There were no mistakes in the space of trust and unconditional regard. He felt the words rising within him. He could not stop them.

"There is one more thing," Cade said lifting Cassius slightly for the last time. "I love you."

Cade held his breath. What would happen next? He waited.

Without hesitation, Pierce pushed Slane closer towards the figure of Cassius.

"I love you too, Cassius!" The pitch of Pierce's voice went up and his breaths were shallow and quick. He looked up at Cade. "I will never forget you."

Pierce released a wail of anguish as he played out the grief of Slane. Cade honored him with silence and affirmation of this holy act. Suddenly, Pierce sat up and shouted, "I will finish this battle and claim my land!"

••

The battle ended. Slane and his army were victorious. The castle was destroyed and the Evil Queen was tried and put to death. Slane ordered it done quickly and without fanfare. She had caused enough pain and ruin. Over the next several months all the remaining villagers traveled to the land of Slane's reclaimed castle. It became known as the Castle of Redemption. One by one the Cities of Light were restored. The land produced fine fruit and vegetables and peace reigned once more. The people lived and prospered and Slane was revered as the Warrior King. He reigned along with Peter his trusted advisor for many years and he was forever remembered for his wisdom, kindness, justice, and strength.

••

Ten Years Later

"Cade, honey, let's go! We're going to be late!" Erin called to Cade.

"In a minute!" Cade called. He typed a few more words and closed the computer.

"Your mom's okay with the kids, right?" He asked.

"Yep, I talked to her about thirty minutes ago. They are doing fine. Today they are going swimming. My dad will pick us up at the airport tomorrow evening."

"Great," said Cade, grabbing the key card to the hotel. The door shut behind them.

He looked at his wife and pulled her close and kissed her on the cheek. "You look stunning," he said smiling.

"Thank you," said Erin. "This is a big night for you."

He pulled the invitation out of his coat pocket. "A national book award. I can't believe it," he said, shaking his head.

The car was waiting for them. As they wove through the New York City traffic, he reflected on the last few months. It had been a whirlwind with all the phone calls and letters. He was glad tonight was finally here.

The car stopped at the large hotel where the book awards were to be given.

"We're supposed to be done around nine," he told the driver. "We'll have two more with us afterwards and we'll be going to dinner."

"No problem, sir," the driver replied. "I'll be here."

They walked through the palatial hotel lobby. Hotel staff directed them to the banquet hall which was full of tables and well-dressed people. A staff member checked their invitation and directed them to their table. He and Erin found their seats. A large screen in the front of the room read:

Welcome to the Annual National Book Award
New York City, New York

Tonight's Award Winners:
Non-Fiction: The Destiny of the Masters by Helen K. Rumsley
Fiction: Slane the Warrior-King Series Book One: The Dead Lands by

Pierce Emerson
Poetry: Sands of the Nether by Windfall James
Young People's Literature: The Rain Never Stopped by Rachela C.
Mitzovanich

Cade looked at Pierce's name with indescribable pride. He and Erin sat down and Cade felt a tap on his shoulder. He turned around to see Pierce and a girl standing behind him.

"Hey!" Cade exclaimed as he stood to hug Pierce and meet his guest.

Pierce introduced his guest as Lillian, his girlfriend of a year.

"Where do they have you guys sitting?" Cade asked as he hugged Lillian.

"Right up front," Pierce said, pointing. He looked uncomfortable in his tux.

Lillian and Erin excused themselves to go to the restroom.

"So, New York City, huh?" Cade exclaimed.

"Yeah," Pierce said, looking down. "It's a pretty cool place, and since the series has taken off it's been easier to live here because it cuts down on the travel."

Cade nodded. "You said you don't like to travel very much," he said, smiling.

Pierce grinned. "I like the places I go, I just don't like getting there."

Cade put his hand on Pierce's arm. "Pierce, I am so proud of you. This is an honor to be here with you. I can't believe it."

Pierce smiled. "Quite a journey we've had, you and me. Only you know just how far I've come. Hey, I wanted to show you something," he said reaching inside his coat.

"What is it?" asked Cade.

"You might remember him," Pierce said as he pulled out Slane. The battered, weather-beaten toy had not lost the grim and determined look on the scruffy face.

Cade felt a surge of joy. He took Slane from Pierce. "Slane," he said, turning it over and over.

"He's been with me ever since the last day in the playroom when you gave him to me. He's why all this has happened. Well, that, and you."

Cade looked at Pierce. "You allowed me to be present, Pierce. And it truly was an honor."

• •

A few weeks later a package arrived at Boyd. The receptionist called Cade in the playroom to tell him. At lunchtime, he went to the office and saw a large box waiting for him. Cade borrowed some scissors and cut the tape on the box. There was a sealed tube and a square package covered in brown wrapping paper. He sliced the tape at the top of the tube and pulled out a large poster. Two office staff helped him lay it out on a table in the conference room. It was a movie poster. *The Warrior-King: The Dead Lands* splashed across the top of the shiny poster. Depicted on the rest of the poster was Slane as a teenage boy with his bow drawn while a huge black wolf with teeth like a buzz-saw and evil red eyes stretched out in a full leap ready to devour the young warrior with razor sharp claws extended. Peter the Fox and Cassius the Eagle were in the background coming to Slane's defense. He could see the dead, ravaged landscape of the Dead Lands as a backdrop to the action. The poster was signed with Pierce's distinctive signature.

He went to the box and took out the object wrapped in brown paper and carefully cut it open. Inside was a beautifully bound set of the three books in the *Warrior King* series. A handwritten note was inserted into the first book. Cade pulled it from the pages of the book.

Dear Dr. C.,

Here are the latest hardcover editions and a poster for the movie, which comes out in a few months. I signed each of the books on the inside pages. Book Three is dedicated to you. I told you on our last day that I would never forget you and I never have. This story has been inside me since the day I met you and watching it unfold was a tremendous experience. You helped

315

me become a writer and didn't even know you were doing it. You helped me heal in ways that I can't explain and you were the only person that let me be me and allowed me the freedom to explore my pain, sadness, and fear through play. I shudder to think what the traditional mental health system would have done to me if they got their hands on me. God had other plans and put you in my path.

Lillian and I will be married next year and I am paying for you and Erin to come up. I'll take care of all your expenses. My publisher will take care of all the expenses, that is. I insist. They insist. I can't thank you enough. You will always be in my heart and a part of all I do.

Yours Truly,

Pierce

CPSIA information can be obtained at www.ICGtesting.com
Printed in the USA
BVOW08s2251170216

437033BV00002B/131/P